*Shirley Davie*

PATHS UNKNOWN

Very Best Wishes
To My Dear
Friend, Lou's
Sister, Carrie

*Shirley Davie Owen*

Available in print and ebook editions

Book design: JenniferToughDesign.com

Published by Pixelita Press
An imprint of Baxter & Preston, LLC
PixelitaPress.com
BaxterandPreston.com

ISBN 978-0-9851871-6-3

My special thanks to Pamela Moore Dionne and Sharon Maureen Carter for their unwavering support and for giving me the motivation to keep on going. I thank Jennifer Tough Hemsley for her support and enthusiasm about this novel and her agreement to publish the work under the Pixelita Press imprint. I thank my family for their belief in my endeavors. And last, but certainly not least, I thank the authors who took time out of their busy schedules to provide jacket reviews.

THIS ONE IS FOR MY FANS — WALTER, KIM AND GRAHAM.

# *Part One*

## CHAPTER ONE
### *July 1887*
### *The Rectory, Beechmere, West Cumbria, England*

I was not given to dark moods, but the morning of that last Saturday in July I awoke feeling unaccountably morose.

I ran a hand through my dank hair then gingerly swung out of bed and stood for a moment, stretching the kinks out of my spine. Wiping the perspiration from my forehead with my night dress sleeve, I plodded to the open window, certain that a few breaths of fresh, salty air would cure the doldrums.

No sooner had the thought struck, however, than I remembered that this summer of Her Majesty's Jubilee we were in the throes of a drought. The air was thick and heavy, the sky over Beechmere's gray-tiled rooftops enamel blue. And Lord it was hot. Calcutta hot; too hot for dogs to summon the energy to bark or children to shriek or rooks to caw.

Here on the West Cumbrian coast, a mere two miles from the capricious Irish Sea, we were more habituated to storms than fine weather. Or should I say, too fine weather, for everywhere was desert dry, the earth cracked as the skin of a scurvied sailor. And throughout the length and breadth of Britain the pleasant pastures of Mister Blake's oft-sung hymn, *Jerusalem,* were scorched, as was our once lush lawn at the rear of the rectory.

But this turned out to matter not one jot to my siblings -- eleven-year-old Annabel and seven-year-old Edwin. When I accompanied them outside soon after two o'clock that afternoon—thankfully, by then all traces of my dejection had evaporated—their dear faces bloomed with delight.

"Take your books and blankets and sit over there under the sycamore where there is an abundance of shade," I said, indicating the ancient tree whose leafy canopy spread out over the lawn.

"*Must* we have quiet time, Liddy?" Edwin had never once called me Lydia.

Before I had a chance to respond, Annabel—ever the authority—rushed in with, "You know what will happen if ---?"

"Yes." Edwin exhaled a long-suffering sigh. "I do. Excess activity after a meal---"

"Results in poisoning of the digestive system," Annabel said, taking his hand and urging him along with her, whilst I settled myself on a nearby garden bench.

As I opened my parasol its incongruity struck me afresh. Odd enough that the silk and lace confection had been a gift from Papa on my twentieth birthday a fortnight ago. But even odder was his actual acknowledgment of the occasion, when one considered that for the past seven years the birthdays of all three of his children had gone by unheralded. Oddest of all, though, had been his announcement as we were finishing lunch today.

The way the children's jaws had dropped and my own eyes bulged, you would have thought he had given us leave to dance naked through the village. But his actual words as he rose from the dining table were, "You may amuse yourselves in the grounds this afternoon, children. And you, dear Lydia, may also take your leisure in the garden. You have been working far too hard these days."

*Dear* Lydia? I curled my mouth in derision. When, pray tell, had I become dear? "These days?" I spoke out loud, punctuating the two words with a harrumph. What about these years ... seven to be exact? Ye gods, while most of the girls with whom I had grown up were married or at the very least betrothed, all that appeared to loom on my horizon, I thought as I retrieved a slim, dog-eared volume from my skirt pocket, was spinsterhood.

I ran a hand over the book's cover. For certain, the only place I would find romance was in this *penny dreadful* novel and the half-dozen others I possessed. I snorted a soft laugh. It never ceased to amuse me no end that they had been Mama's. Imagine ... a parson's wife, and now a parson's daughter, reading such trash ... and relishing it.

With a twinge of guilt, I moved my focus to the children. What quiet paragons of industry they were, their books set aside for now, their busy fingers splitting stems and threading daisies—astonishing, given the lack of rain, that the flowers had managed to grow there—then adorning each other with a myriad of chains.

As if he had felt my eyes upon him, Edwin glanced up and called out, "Is it time yet, Liddy?"

"Soon poppet. Count to"—I pulled the figure from the air—"five hundred, and then it will be."

Returning my attention to the *penny dreadful*, I gave a little shiver of anticipation. A minute or two of searching, and I found my place: the rose arbour where the hero and heroine were gazing with burning passion into each other's eyes. My pulse quickened as strong, masterful Victor drew his adored Albertina hard against him, bent his head, brought his lips down on hers and murmured ...

"Great God in Heaven." The words flew from my mouth of their own volition while I shot back to earth, my heart drumming in my chest. Something had struck me with enough force to almost unseat me.

"Sorry Liddy, it was my wing." Edwin streaked by, arms flapping. "I am flying."

"And doing a dreadful job of it." I took a couple of steadying breaths. "Did you count to five hundred as I instructed?"

"Five hundred-and-two actually," he shouted over his shoulder as Annabel forged ahead of him. "*I* am doing a splendid job," she said, winging her way around the garden's perimeter.

"Bully for you," I said through clenched teeth.

I squirmed in my seat, conscious all at once of the bones of my corset— beastly contraption that it was—digging into my ribcage. Thank the Lord a bustle—although required attire for church and church-related functions—was not de rigueur for an afternoon in the garden. Stifling heat or not, though, petticoats, stockings and drawers were. Deuced things; I felt like a trussed fowl in them ... a sweating fowl, at that.

Fanning myself with one hand, I undid my gown's top buttons with the other and pulled the muslin away from my throat. Eyes closed, I inhaled the scents of lavender and sage, then slowly released my breath.

Hardly had the air left my lungs, however, than Edwin's ear-splitting, "Save me, Liddy, the monster is going to eat me up," made me snap open my eyes. "What in creation ...?" I trailed off—amusement replacing irritation as the scene registered—and roared with laughter.

Lord, how I envied the *monster.* Ever the tomboy, she had tucked her skirt in her drawers and rolled her stockings down around her ankles. And now, with a howl that would have done a demon proud, she was in hot pursuit of her brother across the grass, a cloud of dust rising behind her.

"I should not worry, dear heart," I managed between laughs. "Your sister devoured far too much lunch to have any room left for you."

That Annabel ate with the gusto of a farm-worker showed in her tall, buxom figure and round, rosy face. With her gray eyes and wavy hair in the darkest of browns, she took after our father, while I—at barely five feet—and Edwin, had inherited our mother's diminutive frame and blue eyes.

Edwin's curls were of the same chestnut hue as mine and we shared the same pink-and-white and smooth complexion. In truth, my brother was pretty enough to pass for a girl. But he was no namby-pamby; I had seen to that. "Stature is no indicator of strength," I had drilled into him … into myself as well. "Think of yourself as strong, and you will be strong."

As if to prove the adage, he had at this very moment, leapt onto Annabel's back and she was capering about screeching, "Get off me, you little horror." Eventually he did, and off they shot again, rowdy as ever.

Not bothering to raise my voice, I said, sighing, "Do try and be civilized with each other. And do modulate your voices." I glanced towards St. John's Parish Church graveyard next door. "I swear, you are making enough noise to wake the dead."

Not only had the children no lessons to contend with until the return of their governess, Miss Bamford, in September, now they had this freedom which was so unaccustomed they hardly knew what to do with it. Oh but how gloriously unfettered they were, and what a joy to see them larking about for a change.

Hopefully, they had not disturbed Papa, though. I glanced up at the study window and gave a start when I saw his tall figure framed there. Heart thudding, I cast my eyes down and swiftly secreted my book beneath the folds of my skirts. Any moment now and he would throw the window open and rail at the children. My stomach churning, I braced myself for the onslaught. But none came. And when I finally stole another look, my father was thankfully nowhere to be seen.

Reverend Thetis Fullerton. Distant, cantankerous, morose, best described the man. For the past seven years—following Mama's death and Edwin's birth —he had occupied a world circumscribed by sermons, church services and ministrations to his flock -- a flock that clearly excluded his three children.

"Your father is a good and devout man, strong in his beliefs, but not nearly as strong in matters of everyday living," Mama had said days before her demise. "I am afraid he will be of no earthly use after I am gone. So you must promise me, my dearest girl, that you will take the helm, care for your Papa and the children and hold the family together."

The prospect of shouldering such responsibilities had terrified me. But there had been nothing else for it, of course; I had had to agree.

After all, there were no grandparents waiting in the wings. Papa had been ten—and away at boarding school—when his mother, two younger brothers and his only sister had fallen victim to the cholera epidemic of 1849. Grandfather Fullerton had survived and never remarried. He had died suddenly the year before I was born. And if there were any other relations on that side of the family, no mention had ever been made of them.

As for Mama, she had been an only child, as had both her parents. Her soldier father had died in India at the hands of mutineers when she was ten. And Grandmother Rutledge had dropped dead at fifty, eleven years ago.

Immediately following Mama's death Papa had at least had the good sense to arrange a wet nurse for Edwin, and he had called upon various women in the parish to assist me with the rudiments of housekeeping. And with cook, the governess and a scullery maid on hand, I had managed to perform adequately.

I felt the sudden welling of tears in my eyes, a heaviness in my heart. Mama ... sweet Mama ... my dearest friend and ally. Would I ever stop missing her ... her joy in life ... her boundless love for us all ... her mischievous ways? How she would have applauded this afternoon's activities, I thought, staring off for a time, then reaching once more for the solace of my book.

But this was the moment the children chose to come barreling over. Plainly done in, they sat, one each side of me. The sound of their laboured breathing overlaid the buzzing of bees in the nearby lavender bushes, and the cheep-cheep of sparrows from the rectory's eaves.

After a time, I said, "I take it monster and prey have had enough jollity for one day then?"

"Rather." Edwin used his shirt sleeve to swipe at the curls plastered to his forehead. "I swear she has absolutely worn me out."

"It was you who wore me out, you silly goose," said Annabel, engaged in a struggle to free her frock from the confines of her drawers.

I welcomed their banter; it left no room for me to descend into the doldrums again. "Worn out or not," I said, rolling up my parasol, "you certainly had a jolly time of it."

Edwin yanked on my sleeve. "Shall we be allowed to do this every day, Liddy?"

"I rather doubt it."

"What do you suppose came over Papa?" Annabel asked.

"I have not the slightest notion, dear."

"Could you ask him if we may play again?" Edwin leaned forward for a better view of me, his face solemn.

Several seconds passed before the question registered and I answered, "Of course, poppet," mussing his hair. "Although I must warn you that I cannot guaran ..."

The sudden onset of a strident ringing of the bells from the tower of St. John's next-door made my heart lurch. "Great God"—I clapped a hand to my chest—"practice is not allowed at this hour." Unless a funeral required it, Papa strictly forbade bell-ringing on Thursday, Friday and Saturday afternoons; in his opinion the creative juices required for the production of his two Sunday sermons could not possibly flow without peace and quiet.

I ground my teeth at the frenzied quality the ringing had now taken on, shouting to Annabel, "Are you aware of any funeral today?"

"No," she mouthed, covering her ears with her hands.

Rising, I urged the children to their feet. Ye gods and little fishes, it sounded as if Victor Hugo's Hunchback had been let loose. What the deuce had possessed the bell-ringers? Papa would be positively livid, and as usual, it would fall to me to smooth things over.

"No use all of us being made deaf; we may as well go inside." I gave Annabel a nudge. "Make yourself respectable, first, dear. You, too, Edwin. Tuck in your shirt and pull up your stockings. I swear, Papa would have a fit if he saw the state of you both."

Once the pair had complied, I said, "Come along, then. If I am not mistaken, Mrs. Dixon said she had made a fresh batch of ginger beer, and that jam tarts were on her baking agenda this afternoon."

Swiftly, we headed for the cobbled courtyard alongside the rectory. We were halfway across it when the clanging ceased as abruptly as it had begun, so startling us that we stumbled into each other, wide-eyed, and stood stock still in the heavy silence. Despite the heat of the sun, I shivered and chafed my arms.

Annabel frowned. "Why did the bells suddenly stop like that?"

"I have no idea."

"Is something wrong?"

"I rather doubt it. In fact, I would say the cessation of that abominable racket makes everything right. Do you not agree?"

Annabel shrugged uncertainly.

"May we still go to the kitchen for ginger beer?" asked Edwin.

"And tarts?" said Annabel, her appetite for sweets clearly overriding her worries, now.

I nodded in the affirmative, and once we were inside the rectory and the children heading for the kitchen, I hurried upstairs to my father's study.

I tapped on the door. Receiving no response, I followed up with a louder, more-insistent knock. Nothing. Had he done the unthinkable and fallen asleep over his sermon-writing? Steeling myself against a possible tirade, I eased open the door and stood on the threshold.

Papa was nowhere to be seen. Since he would not allow the once-weekly cleaning woman access to his study, the pervasive odour of dust and mildew and stale cigar smoke was no surprise. The sun poured in through the casement, spotlighting his desk. Normally piled with books and strewn with papers, it was disquietingly clear of everything but inkstand, blotter, and two pens arranged next to each other in perfect symmetry. Glancing about the room, I felt an odd sense of relief; at least, here, the customary chaos held sway.

A tall fern stand, bearing a copper pot which contained soil but no plant, served as an ash tray; in it were three malodorous cigar stubs. Stacks of papers and leather-bound tomes teetered on open shelves, in glass-doored cupboards and on tabletops. Old copies of the Parish Magazine, more books and screwed-up bits of paper lay scattered about the floor.

Cautiously maneuvering from one open space to another, I reached the desk and scanned its top. Nothing ... other than what I had observed from the doorway, and—not surprisingly—a good deal of dust in which I idly drew noughts and crosses while considering the fact that if any parishioners had been in dire need of Papa, they would have sought him out at the rectory and I would have heard the comings and goings.

Perhaps he had not had time to order his sermon-writing thoughts before the racket next-door had begun, and he had been so incensed by it he had stormed over to the church to investigate. A moment or two of mulling and I decided that had to be it.

Wiping my dusty fingertips on my skirt, I made for the door. At this very minute I'd wager those bell-ringing miscreants were receiving a drubbing they would not soon forget.

———

I was about to pass through the lychgate onto the wide graveled path which cleaved the graveyard and led to the church entrance, when I heard a commotion. I halted, head cocked. The church door was ajar, and as I set off again and approached the steps leading up to it, I heard several voices. Was one of them Papa's?

The sudden emergence into view of a quartet of men—none my father—severed the thought. At the sight of me, they froze. I recognized Geoffrey Emmins, the curate, Wilf Bradbury, the verger, Mr. Hampton, one of the gardeners, and a grave-digger whose name I did not know.

"Have any of you seen the rector?" I asked, drawing nearer.

No one responded. Instead, the fellows bent forward, foreheads touching, forming a knot reminiscent of a rugby-players' scrummage, and began a low, agitated-sounding conversation whose content was impossible for me to discern.

After what seemed an age, the group dispersed, and the curate hurried down the steps towards me, his surplice flapping like raven wings over his long, black cassock, an expression of consternation on his face.

"Oh my dear Miss Fullerton"—he halted within inches of me—"we were just about to ---"

"I asked if anyone had seen my father."

"Perhaps we should return to the rectory ... where you will be ... er ... more comfortable."

"I am perfectly fine right here, thank you." My heart all at once took on an uneven rhythm which made me a little breathless. "You have yet to answer me. Papa? Is he in the church?" I made as if to side-step Geoffrey Emmins and mount the steps.

But the verger quickly barred my way. "'tis best you not go in there, miss." The grave-digger nodded his agreement.

I felt my dander rising. "For pity's sake, tell me what is going on?"

In a tentative movement, the curate advanced on me, then in a swift motion captured my hands in his. "I am afraid there has been a terrible accident."

"Oh lord." I wrenched free. "Is it one of the bell-ringers?"

"No ... not the bell-ringers. In the tower ... he must have been inspecting ... perhaps testing the ropes ... the bells ... we are not certain." The curate's face contorted. "It is your father, Miss Fullerton. I am so very, very sorry to have to tell you this, but he is ... dead."

## CHAPTER TWO
### *August 1887*
### *The Curate's House, Beechmere, West Cumbria, England*

Fortunately, Charlotte Emmins and I were of the same height and petite stature, and of the three gowns the curate's wife had offered me in place of my own worn, black bombazine, I had selected a light-weight crepe—sans bustle —for this scorching afternoon the third week in August.

I crossed to the bedroom window and looked out onto the park-like front garden. There, a graceful weeping willow overhung a lily pond, and crazy-paved paths dissected expansive lawns then meandered among flowerbeds filled with scarlet, yellow and white roses, blue delphiniums, pink carnations, purple irises.

The house—a gift to the couple from Charlotte's wealthy parents, and as impressive as the grounds—was a place one could easily become used to. The children already had and in fact, just the other day Annabel said, "I hope we can stay here forever, I positively adore it." "I do, too," said Edwin, and I had not had the heart to disabuse them of this notion of permanence.

How oddly unaffected they seemed by their father's death, and how fortuitous for me; at least I had no histrionics to deal with. I had given them the news within an hour of receiving it myself. "That means we are orphans," Annabel had said matter-of-factly and then gone about her business, while Edwin's only concern had appeared to be whether or not the horses in the cortege would sport black plumes.

If I thought the children's response odd, what about my own? All I had felt—and without the shedding of a single tear, mind you—had been the kind of regret one experienced at the passing of an acquaintance. I shook my head sadly. What sort of a person did that make me? As cold and impassive as my father? My mind quickly rejected the idea. How could I be cold when my love for Edwin and Annabel was so fierce?

Thank the Lord we three had each other. Thank the Lord, too, for the Emmins, with whom our lives had been inextricably entwined this past month. Poor Geoffrey. He had clearly felt dreadful having to tell me that the rectory was no longer our home. "I am afraid the wheels have already been set in motion for a new rector to take over the position next week," he had said.

The news that we would be turfed out had come as no surprise, of course. That our eviction was to occur so soon, however, had shocked me and—in all honesty—thrown me into a panic. I had thought we would be allowed to stay on at least until Papa's will was settled and the funds disbursed to me, thus enabling me to set up house in Beechmere or some neighbouring village.

Salvation—albeit temporary—had come from Charlotte. "You must stay with us for as long as it takes to thoroughly sort out your affairs," she had said. "I shall send over a couple of my staff with the carriage and they will help you pack and load your belongings."

I perched on a bench before the dressing table, now, aimlessly repositioning the various silver-topped bottles and jars. How quickly the decampment had been accomplished. Within two hours of Charlotte's announcement, we three Fullertons were comfortably settled in here, Edwin sharing a room with seven-year-old James and four-year-old Henry; Annabel and I in this spacious bedroom across from the nursery, which housed the twin baby girls and their nursemaid.

The funeral arrangements had been attended to, also. "You are not to concern yourself," Geoffrey Emmins had said. "Charlotte and I will be glad to see to all the details."

"Including the laying out," Charlotte had added. "There are women in the parish—and very discreet ones, I might add—who are experienced in these matters."

Thank God for small mercies, I had thought, wishing with all my heart that I could share the children's dispensation and escape the ordeal of viewing my father's dead body.

The rectory's windows were draped in black, that day, the front door hung with a black wreath. At the sight of me standing on the step—flanked by the curate and his wife—cook burst into tears and drew me into a fierce embrace, calling me a poor, dear soul. The Eccliastical Committee had apparently requested she stay on until the viewing and funeral were over. After that, she planned to go to her sister's in Dorset, she said.

"'e's in the drawing room," she whispered, indicating its door as if I were a stranger to the place.

A black cloth covered the mirror over the mantel. The Viennese regulator clock on the wall beside the fireplace had been stopped. For as far back as I could remember, Papa had wound the timepiece every eight days, and it seemed odd not to hear the steady ticking and see the cherub-decorated brass pendulum swinging back and forth.

In the centre of the silent, darkened room, bracketed by flickering candles and banks of white gladioli and lilies, which seemed to give off an overwhelmingly sickly-sweet odour, stood a wake table bearing the black-satin-lined coffin in which Papa rested.

What had struck me most about him was not the marble-white deadness of his face—made more macabre with the play of candlelight and shadow—but his attire. Instead of the clerical vestments in which I had expected to see him, he wore black trousers and frockcoat over a white shirt, with a black cravat wound about his neck and knotted at the throat.

Clearly, the intent was to hide the marks left by the rope, I had concluded, pressing my fingertips to my mouth lest I forget myself and divulge my thoughts. Even though Papa was to be laid to rest in the churchyard's hallowed ground next to Mama, it was no secret that dissension existed about the manner of his death. And maybe it was thought this burial in layman's garb would—in some way—placate the dissenters.

It had not placated me. Nothing would. I pushed away from the dressing table, now, and got up. No matter that Geoffrey Emmins had called it a dreadful accident. Papa had taken the coward's way out; of that I had no doubt. And—God forgive me for my cold-heartedness—my contempt for his action knew no bounds.

My gaze moved to the clock on the mantel and my stomach began to churn. In less than a quarter of an hour the solicitor would be here. I began pacing, hugging myself about the middle, in an attempt to quell my nervousness.

I was silly to worry. Say what you would about him, my father was sure to have provided for his family, I told myself. Mama had brought an income to her marriage, which would have passed to him on her death. So there was bound to be a respectable-enough legacy; at least sufficient to cover the annual lease on a small place, continue to pay for the children's governess and a small household staff, and support all of us until Edwin came of age and Annabel married.

I halted before a watercolour on the wall; it depicted a cottage of the story-book variety with a thatched roof, hollyhocks flanking the gate and roses clambering over the masonry. I chewed on my lower lip. Old maid or not, I still would be able to create the kind of home I had always dreamed about: windows hung with chintz curtains; walls painted sunny yellow; friends gathering around us. And maybe in years to come, after my myriad responsibilities were met, I would meet someone and find companionship … even love.

Perhaps—I clicked my tongue against my teeth, scoffing at myself—the Queen would invite me for tea. "Perhaps," I said out loud, "you should do the sensible thing and wait and see what Mr. Haycox has to say."

"The children and I will go for a long walk," Charlotte had told me after lunch. "That way, you will have the privacy you need."

Now, everywhere seemed abnormally quiet, the atmosphere funereal. And no wonder, I thought, halting before the wardrobe's full-length mirror and regarding my reflection.

Following current fashion, I wore my hair Princess-Alexandra style, with a curly fringe, the rest upswept into a cluster of curls at the crown, secured with a pair of black, gutta percha combs. Imagine eleven more months of this dreary mourning attire. I leaned into the mirror and made a face. Just look at the way the garb seemed to give my skin a yellowish cast and scoop out hollows in my cheeks where none had previously existed.

I straightened, fiddling with my white lawn collar; at least it provided a little visual relief, as did the white weepers at my wrists. Lauded for their handiness during crying fits, the detachable cuffs were of absolutely no use to me, of course, except as ornamentation.

My eyes were as clear, as blue as today's sky, I noted, leaning into the glass again. Perhaps I should give them a rub and redden them a little; at least then, there would be the appearance of grief.

A knock on the bedroom door put paid to my inner debate.

Mary, Charlotte's maid, stood on the threshold. "Mr. Haycox is in the study, Ma'am," she said. "Give 'im a cup of tea, I did, an' told 'im you'd be down shortly."

Moments later I entered the study, and a shrunken little fellow with a halo of white hair rose from behind the mahogany partners' desk. In a voice bordering on the falsetto, he introduced himself and indicated the seat opposite. Once I had settled myself, he followed suit.

Over the tops of his spectacles, he regarded me with humid eyes and said, "I shall not prevaricate, Miss Fullerton. Suffice to say that your father retained me some time ago to act on his behalf." He withdrew a sheet of paper from the stack in front of him on the desktop. "I have here your Papa's last will and testament … in which he bequeaths to you …"

I held my breath while he brought the document to within a couple of inches of his nose and squinted at it, as if he were an entomologist viewing a rare specimen. I felt an insane desire to scream, "How much … how much?" But instead, I said through clenched teeth, "The sum of?"

The solicitor shot me a befuddled look.

"My father's will? You were about to tell me …?"

"Ah yes. So sorry. Here we are. The sum of … one hundred guineas which---"

"Per quarter?" I said sharply, manners forgotten.

"Dear me, no. I am afraid you misunderstand, Miss Fullerton. Your father's assets amount to a total of one hundred guineas, which—as I was attempting to say—I am instructed to give you immediately."

I watched in stunned silence as he produced an envelope from his attaché case and slid it across the desktop. "A draft drawn on your father's bank."

Dumbly, I reached for the missive and dropped it in my lap. One hundred paltry guineas? Great God in Heaven—my blood beat at my temples—there had to be a mistake. I leaned forward, gripping the desk's edge. "But Mr. Haycox"—I stopped for breath—"there has to be considerably more than this. My mother left quite a sum, and Papa surely would have---"

"You are perfectly correct, Miss Fullerton. Were it not for a string of rather unfortunate investments and the economic recession with which we have been plagued for some time, now, your father would have been quite comfortably off. He had high hopes of recouping his losses, but sadly …" The solicitor hitched his shoulders and turned up his palms in an attitude of regret.

My stomach heaved. I lowered my head and focused on the envelope in my lap. Rage surged through me, making my scalp tingle, my hands shake. Any second now and I would scream, I was certain.

"There is some good news, however."

I collected myself, willed the hot blood away from my face, made my expression bland.

"You and your siblings will be provided a home."

"You mean the church has ---?"

"No … nothing of that nature."

I ran a puzzled hand across my mouth. "Of what nature, then?"

"You are to live with a relation."

"But we have no relations."

"Your Papa had an aunt."

I felt my eyes widen. "An aunt?"

"Sister to your grandfather."

"As far as I know my grandfather did not have a sister."

"I am led to believe that he did. I gather there was some kind of a scandal. I am not privy to the details, nor do they concern me."

"Where is this aunt?

"In the south-east, in Sussex. Close to a village called Burgess Hill, which I understand is about forty miles from Brighton."

"The seaside resort?"

"Indeed. The most salubrious of places, from all accounts, its seawater possessing the most astonishing properties."

I thought, Who gives a fig? Then I asked, "What is this woman's name?"

"Ernestine Hadfield." Again, Barnaby Haycox delved into his attaché case. Brandishing a couple of sheets of paper, he said, "Your father's letter of instruction."

Curious, I scooted forward.

The solicitor noisily cleared his throat. "Dear Barnaby, following my demise, I ask that you write to my aunt, sister to my late father, and inform her of the sad straits in which my children are left." Mr. Haycox stopped reading long enough to pull a large handkerchief from his breast pocket and mop his brow.

"As previously explained, a familial rift caused severance of all contact with this dear lady, but I feel bound to appeal to her now, as my children's last surviving relation and beg that she take on their care for the foreseeable future."

"For many years, an acquaintance has kept me apprised of my aunt's circumstances. Childless, and widowed a decade ago, she is from all accounts, a woman of ample means, and despite her three-score-and-ten years, in tolerably good health."

"It is my fervent prayer that Aunt Ernestine will welcome my dear children with open arms. For what better gift to ease the loneliness of widowhood, childlessness and old age than that of the company of her own flesh and blood?"

Mr. Haycox stopped reading, removed his spectacles and polished them on his jacket lapel before repositioning them on his nose.

"Is there more?" I asked. "Did he not, for instance, include any fatherly words for his dear children?" I could not keep the bitterness from my voice. "No apologies? No great wisdom? No ---?"

"Nothing along those lines, Miss Fullerton. Merely thanks in advance for my adherence to his instructions … which resulted in receipt of this reply from your great-aunt." He had set aside the letter and proceeded to wave another sheet of paper. "If I may?"

I dipped my chin in response.

"Dear Mister Haycox, of course I shall take the poor, dear creatures in. To this end, I enclose herewith twenty pounds which should be more than sufficient for your purposes. Kindly muster my great-nieces and –nephew post-haste and dispatch them by rail as soon as possible, informing me by telegram of their arrival time at Burgess Hill, the closest station to Hadfield Hall. My man will be there to meet them."

With that, the solicitor lapsed into silence, subsiding into his seat, as if physically spent.

"Nothing else?" I shook my head in disbelief.

"A railway time-table with the routes and times noted." The old gentleman gathered his papers together, slipped them into his attaché case, then rose stiffly and came around the desk to my side. Patting me on the shoulder, he said, "I am so very sorry, Miss Fullerton, for your misfortune."

"As am I, sir. So"—I got to my feet—"when do you propose we *poor creatures* be mustered, then?"

"The sooner the better, I should think. I know these are extremely trying times for you, but an opportunity has been offered you, now, to make a new life for yourself and your siblings."

"How right you are, Mr. Haycox." I pasted a smile on my face. "Thanks to my father's foresight, our futures seem positively assured."

Something akin to relief showed in the solicitor's eyes. "Now, about the arrangements. I shall need your decision as to a departure date, of course, in order that I may purchase the tickets and telegraph your great-aunt."

"That will not be necessary." I thrust out a hand. "If you will turn everything over to me, I shall be happy to relieve you of all responsibility."

After a long pause, and with obvious hesitation, the solicitor handed me the money and timetable. "Are you quite certain you will be able to manage, Miss Fullerton?"

I felt my jaw tighten. "I most assuredly am, sir." Summoning the maid with a tug of the bell-pull on the nearby wall, I added, "I have been managing —and quite nicely, I might add—for the past seven years."

How I would fare from now on, though, I thought with a sinking heart, might prove to be a vastly different story.

## CHAPTER THREE
### *September 1887*
### *Hadfield Hall, Sussex, England*

On the evening of Thursday, the fifteenth of September—a mere fortnight after my meeting with the solicitor—an elderly, gaunt-faced woman identifying herself as Mrs. Boot, housekeeper to our Great-Aunt Ernestine, ushered the three of us into the expansive gaselier-lit foyer of Hadfield Hall.

Like immigrants fresh off the boat, we huddled together on the black-and-white chessboard of a marble floor watching Mrs. Boot struggle to close behind us—and bolt—a front door massive enough to hold back a marauding army. "Lord o'mercy"—the housekeeper drew in a long, rasp of a breath—"we was beginnin' to think yer'd got lost. 'ave y'any idea of the ti---?"

A sudden, cacophonous chorus of gongs and rings and chimes cut her off. Over the din I shouted, "I most certainly do, Mrs. Boot. Unless I am very much mistaken, it is eight o'clock."

"S'right," she said. "Eight-o-bloomin' clock. Dratted things," she went on as the last note died away. "By the time they're finished with their dingin' an' dongin', yer cannot 'ear yerself think."

I could not contain myself. "Four," I said, having glanced about and discovered the source of the racket. "You have four grandfather clocks?" They were positioned one on each of the dark-panelled walls, along with a Jacobean oak hallstand, an assortment of side chairs and small occasional tables, several potted palms and a shudder-inducing bronze, depicting a wolf attacking a stag.

"Never mind four; there's thirty-odd more scattered about the place," said Mrs. Boot.

Annabel's and Edwin's shocked eyes met mine.

"Rather partial to clocks is the mistress," the old woman continued. "Likes the tickin' an' the tockin' an' all them bells goin' off. Winding 'em's a full-time job, I'll tell yer. Never mind all the oilin' an' cleanin' an' whatnot. Though 'tis not me what 'as to do it; 'tis Thomas ... Mr. Mason ... 'im what brought you from the sta ---"

"Speaking of your mistress ... my great-aunt," I cut in, anxious to forestall the woman's ramblings, "will we be ---?"

"Yer will not be seein' 'er right away. Asleep she is."

I could not believe my ears. "You mean she has already retired for the night?"

"Lord, no. She nodded off by the fire in the drawin' room. Tired 'erself out waitin' for you lot, she did."

I bristled at the thinly-veiled accusation in the woman's tone. As if it were our fault the railway timetable had been a work of fiction, and the train had been delayed two hours.

"An' all the time pesterin' me somethin' chronic," Mrs. Boot went on, "askin' if yer'd arrived yet. 'ad 'erself a sherry or two, she did, 'bout six, an' been noddin' off … wakin' up … noddin' off … ever since."

Annabel gave a loud yawn and lolled against me, and Edwin whispered, "I am hungry, Liddy."

"Lord love us"—Mrs. Boot clapped her hands to her cheeks —"just listen to me natterin' on. Off with those coats and bonnets, now; the cap, too, young master."

Once the housekeeper had hung the garments on the nearby hallstand I asked, "What about our cases?"

"Mister Mason will 'ave taken 'em up to your rooms, dear. So yer've no need t'worry on that score. Come along, now." She made for a passageway which gave off to the right, gesturing for us to follow.

After passing several closed doors, we reached an open one from which a delectable aroma wafted. Here, Mrs. Boot stopped and poked her head in. "Brought yer some visitors, Agnes," she said in a loud voice, then to me, "In yer go. Cook'll give yer some vittles, an' I shall come back later on."

In the kitchen, a beaming, plump-faced woman with a prow of a bosom, bustled across the red-tiled floor to meet us. "Well I never," she said, drying her hands on her apron.

"How do you do," I said, introducing myself and the children.

"I am Mrs. Catterly, dears. But you must call me cook. Lord love us, we thought we had the wrong day."

"I am afraid the train was delayed."

"Don't surprise me none. You wouldn't get me on one o' them contraptions. Belchin' their steam and puffin' their smoke an' makin' enough din to wake the dead."

Like a Jack-In-a-Box, Edwin popped out in front of me and blithely said, "I am rather partial to trains."

Suppressing a smile, Mrs. Catterly said. "Even so, young sir, you an' your sisters must 'ave 'ad quite a day. Purely done in by the looks of you. An' famished, too, I'll warrant."

Annabel and Edwin nodded with mute enthusiasm, while I said, "We are a little peckish."

"Then wash up over there at the sink and sit yourselves down." The woman indicated a long, deal table set with Blue Willow china and bearing a platter laden with doorsteps of golden crusted bread. As soon as we were seated and I passed the plate to my poor starving mites, they fell upon it like a pair of street Arabs. And when moments later, Mrs. Catterly set down a tureenful of steaming soup she identified as beef and barley, and said, "Tuck in while it is good an' hot," neither the children nor I needed encouragement.

We had just finished second helpings when the housekeeper reappeared. "Mistress is awake," she said, "an' askin' for yer."

The woman shepherded us through the house and brought us to a halt outside a pair of double doors. "I'll leave you to it, dearie," she said. "I shall be in the kitchen with cook. Come an' fetch me when the mistress is finished with yer an' I' shall show yer to yer rooms. Give a knock, so she knows yer 'ere."

I was about to do so—gently, so as not to startle our great-aunt—but Edwin beat me to it and pounded on the door like a constable after a criminal.

"Ye gods and little fishes." I grabbed my brother's arm, then dropped it at the sound of a sonorous, "Come in."

Wide-eyed, I opened the door, and we hesitantly entered a gas-lit room so cavernous, so filled with antique furniture, paintings, busts, beaded works and bric-a-brac, it might well have been the basement storage of a museum.

I watched, dumbstruck, as a tall, silver-haired woman rose from an armchair next to a fire banked high enough to heat a castle. The shimmering folds of her emerald green gown—which must have been silk or satin—caught the firelight, as did the jewelry at her throat and ears. She raised a lorgnette to her eyes and peered through it. "And who among you was the overly-enthusiastic knocker?" she asked, her voice rich and theatrical-sounding and with a slight slur to it.

Clearly intimidated, Edwin lifted a hand and made a noise like the squeak of a mouse.

"Hmmm." She gestured impatiently. "Come in, come in, closer now, do not dilly-dally."

Stepping forward in unison, we halted within a couple of feet of our new-found relation. The thick, sweet odour emanating from her made my nose wrinkle of its own accord.

I searched the patrician face for a family resemblance, but saw none. My great-aunt had startlingly-few wrinkles for one as old as she was purported to be. Her forehead was wide, her nose long and narrow and her mouth thin-lipped and turned down as though in permanent disapproval.

"Better … much better." With more deliberation than appeared necessary, the woman lowered herself into the chair she had so recently vacated. A decanter containing what must have been sherry, and an empty glass stood on the table next to her. She filled the glass, tossed back its contents and then refilled it and noisily slurped from it.

I gave each of the children a surreptitious nudge and sent them a telepathic warning. Not a smirk ... not a word ... not a giggle. To my surprise and relief, they obeyed.

The old woman tipped the last drop of sherry into her mouth and leaned sidelong in order to set down the glass. "Now," she said, straightening, "let me get a good look at you." She raised the lorgnette again, and I felt skewered by her dark, curious eyes.

"I take it your journey—although clearly much delayed—was a comfortable one." She was overly precise and slow in her speech. "And I trust you find the accommo ...dations here to your liking?"

How odd, I thought—still caught up in my examination of this long-lost relation—that her hair was so silver, yet her eyebrows were black.

"You may speak."

I started at the imperious tone. Lord, what was it she had just asked me?

"Assuming you are able and that I have not been bamboozled into taking on a trio of mutes."

Able ... able to do what? I tried to catch Annabel's eye, hoping she would come to my rescue. But she was too caught up in her study of the room's contents. Edwin, also, was oblivious, his astonished gaze resting on a stuffed fox in a glass case set against the nearby wall.

A few more anxious seconds passed and then suddenly, thankfully, the clocks—I saw only one, but there were perhaps three or four judging from the ringing and chiming sounds coming from the dim confines of the room— provided me with a temporary reprieve. And as the Roman centurion-flanked bronze and marble monstrosity on the mantelpiece struck its final note, my faculties miraculously returned to me.

"Oh no ... so sorry," I stammered. "We are ... you have not. We are not. To be sure our journey was a protracted one, it being quite some distance from the northwest to the southeast coast, and admittedly, the train was not the most comfortable conveyance in the world and as you, of course, pointed out, it was much delayed. And thank you, but we have yet to see our accommo ..." I broke off, aware all at once that I was rattling on like a runaway brougham on a rutted road, and that my great-aunt was regarding me with a mixture of puzzlement and alarm.

"For an eleven-year-old, you have a great deal to say for yourself, child."

I felt my eyes widen. Great God in Heaven, was the woman's brain addled? "Madam, I am afraid you are confusing me with---"

"Me." Annabel came to life with the most unladylike guffaw. "You have it all wrong," she sputtered.

"I beg your pardon?" A crimson flush traveled from the old lady's chest to her throat.

"Apologize," I muttered to Annabel out of the side of my mouth. "I am Lydia, Great-Aunt, the twenty-year-old."

"I am so sorry," Annabel said. "I did not mean to be impolite."

"Well, child, impolite or not … eleven years old or not, I declare one could make three of your sister out of you. You are plump as a Christmas goose, while she is a puny enough little chit to have come from the work house."

Annabel bit down on her lower lip, clearly determined not to say anything she might regret, while I stood, poker-faced, thinking, *And you, you scrawny, mean-spirited, inebriated, over-perfumed old bat, are certainly no masterpiece, yourself.*

That Edwin chose this moment to barge in saved the day. "How do you do, ma'am, delighted to meet you?" he said, with a low bow and one hand extended. "I am Edwin Fullerton and I am seven."

Arching an eyebrow, Ernestine Hadfield gingerly took Edwin's hand and gave it a half-hearted shake. "Hmmm." She pursed her lips. "And what a dainty little thing you are. Had you not been wearing trousers, I should have taken you for Annabel. Do you sing prettily, child? Or dance?"

I gritted my teeth and clenched my fists at my sides. I detested sarcasm, especially when directed at a child.

Clearly unaware, Edwin answered brightly, "I do sing, but not very well, I am afraid. And Papa did not allow dancing."

"Does any one of you play an in..stru … an in …stru …ment?" Her speech had become slower, more precise, her mouth shaping the words in such an exaggerated fashion that it struck me as comical.

"No," I said biting back the laughter that threatened to burst from me.

"No," chorused Edwin and Annabel.

"Hmmm. What do you do, then?"

"In what way, ma'am," I asked.

"What skills … what talents do you have?" She took another slurp from the glass she had once again refilled. "I had thought to be enter …tained. Do you recite poetry? Have you a solilo.. so..lilo… quy or two in your re.. pertoire? Do you paint?" Not waiting for an answer, she waved a dismissive hand. "No matter. I am sure I shall find a use for all of you before too long. That is quite enough for now. You may go. But first"—she patted herself on the cheek—"you may kiss me good …night."

The children looked at me askance. *Must we?* was the unspoken question in their eyes.

I gave an imperceptible nod. *Oh yes, dear hearts, from now on—like it or not—we must do anything and everything this woman tells us to do.*

## CHAPTER FOUR
### *September 1887*
### *Hadfield Hall, Sussex, England*

The next morning I awoke to what sounded like the clatter of pots and pans. Exhausted after a fitful night, I wearily hitched myself up to a sitting position and once I had rubbed the sleep from my eyes, squinted the room into focus.

The curtains had been drawn back and the sun poured in through the windows, illuminating a girl about Annabel's age, clad in a black-and-white maid's uniform. With a look of fierce concentration, she was emptying hot water from a bucket into the bowl on the wash-stand which stood against the wall to my right.

Not wishing to startle the maid, I waited until she had completed her task. Then I said, "Good morning."

"mornin' Miss," she answered, bobbing a quick curtsy.

"And you are …?"

"Daisy, Miss. Sorry for the racket, but Mrs. B said I was to rouse you an' tell you breakfast is ready in the dinin' room, and that the mistress is waitin' for you to join 'er there."

"You will have to give me directions, Daisy, since I am unfamiliar with the layout of the house," I said, swinging my legs over the side of the bed and standing.

"Turn right at the bottom of the stairs, miss, then it's the second door on the left."

"And what about my sister and brother?" I asked, reaching for the dressing gown draped over the back of a nearby chair.

"Already downstairs, miss. Mrs. B sent me up earlier on to 'elp 'em with their ablutions. 'cordin to 'er, Mistress said they was to 'ave their breakfasts in the kitchen with cook."

"I see." I was not sure that I did. Was this segregation at mealtimes to be a regular thing?

Whilst I attended to my toilette, I revisited the worries that had kept me awake a good part of the night. I was still fretting several minutes later when I silently stood on the dining room's threshold.

I took in the long rosewood table and my great-aunt, seated at its head, stern and—thank the Lord—seemingly sober. When she noticed me, she gestured for me to sit in close proximity to her, and I complied.

At the forefront of my mind was one particular worry, and unable to contain it a moment longer, I said, "The children have had a governess for several years, Great-Aunt, and I wonder what plans there might be for their continued education."

"Whilst I wonder, Miss, why you do not have the courtesy to at least wish me good morning before you start your"—she extended her bejeweled hands, palms-up—"interrogation."

"Oh, so sorry, Great-Aunt. Good morning."

She smiled behind thin lips. "I should think so. Good morning."

Her enunciation was perfect today, her voice rich and liquid, and she looked composed and elegant in a high-necked, dove gray day gown. "Food, Lydia," she said, gesturing to an assortment of silver-domed dishes on the sideboard. "One cannot engage in intelligent conversation without benefit of sustenance."

I helped myself to a couple of rashers of bacon, one sausage and an egg. I was ravenous and could have consumed far more. But having already been deemed a "poor dear creature", I had no wish to come across as a "poor starving creature" also. I did, however, take two slices of toast from the silver rack and slather them with butter and marmalade, although I ate everything with restrained little bites whilst Ernestine Hadfield held forth.

"Now, as to your concerns about your siblings' education"—she dabbed her mouth with her serviette—"you will be pleased to hear that I have engaged a tutor for the children."

"A tutor?" I halted in mid-swallow.

"A Mister Obediah Callenforth, an old and trusted family friend who is currently staying here at Hadfield Hall."

Did she mean old in years, I wondered, or old in friendship.

"An exceedingly fine man, an equally fine teacher. He will begin tomorrow, promptly at eight." She waited for me to finish chewing and swallowing. "And I shall expect you to prepare the children for their lessons."

"Prepare them? In what way, Great-Aunt?"

"Make sure they are dressed appropriately, that they are clean and, of course, wide awake. I caught a glimpse of them this morning as they were making their way to the kitchen, and I must say they looked like a pair of ..." She hesitated, gauging my expression. Perhaps the angle of my chin challenged her, or she saw the flash of anger in my eyes ... I do not know. In any event, the woman's voice softened as she continued with, "They appeared to be somewhat disheveled."

I bit down hard on my toast and took an inordinate amount of time crunching and swallowing. I followed with a gulp of tea and a deliberately-clumsy replacement of my cup on its saucer. Finally, I said with no attempt to disguise my annoyance, "I was not aware that they were being roused from their beds, Great-Aunt. Had I been given the opportunity, I would have supervised their toilette, as I always do."

The old lady raised one dark eyebrow and looked down her nose at me. "You would do well to watch your tongue and your manners, young woman, and pay heed to your ... *situation*."

I felt myself flush at the none-too-subtle warning. Nothing else for it but to kowtow, of course. "My apologies, Great-Aunt," I said, stiffly.

She dipped her head in acknowledgement. "There will be weekly tests for the children and they—Edwin especially, if he is to make his way in this world —will be expected to treat their studies with the utmost seriousness."

"They have always been attentive, Great-Aunt, and anxious to learn." I made sure my tone was deferential. "And I should tell you that Annabel is an extremely intelligent girl. In fact, her mathematical abilities would put most of us to shame."

The old lady took up the folding spectacles which hung from a chain at her bosom. Not bothering to open them up, she used them as a monocle and regarded me through the single lense with disconcerting intensity. "That is as may be, Lydia, but as we all know, mathematical abilities are of absolutely no consequence where a girl is concerned."

Inwardly seething, I took a breath deep enough to fuel a rebuttal, but Great-Aunt Ernestine forestalled me with a raised hand and said, "I take it you, yourself, are properly educated?"

*Not that it matters one jot to you, madam.* "Indeed I am. I had a governess from age six to sixteen. And subsequently, although Papa concluded I needed no further education since he had no aspirations for me other than as his housekeeper and the caretaker of his children, I did continue to study."

"I see. And were those studies related to domestic affairs?" The question held a note of ennui which galled me no end.

"No, Great-Aunt, decidedly not. History, geography, languages, philosophy, literature—*especially penny dreadfuls*—have always been of great interest to me."

"My late husband was quite the scholar. The library shelves are filled with his books on every subject under the sun." She took up her spectacles again, unfolded them, polished them with her serviette and returned them to her bosom. Then she sipped her tea for a time. Finally she deigned to speak again. "The library is where the children's lessons will take place. It seems the logical place."

I did not think she expected a comment and so I remained silent.

"Every morning from eight until noon," she continued. "One half-hour for luncheon in the kitchen with cook and the other staff. Then jobs for all of you from half-past-twelve until five."

"Jobs?" I sat forward.

"Yes. You will assist Mrs. Boot in the running of the house; from what I understand of your experience, you are certainly well-equipped for the task. Annabel will be a maid-of-all-work, helping me from time to time with dressing and undressing and caring for my wardrobe etcetera; assisting cook in the kitchen, and helping Daisy and Prue, our two housemaids, with sewing and mending."

Annabel … cooking, sewing and mending, not to mention attending to the personal needs of Ernestine Hadfield? I mentally threw up my hands at its inconceivability. "But Great-Aunt ---"

"She will learn." Ye gods, the old lady must have read my mind. "Does the child know how to sew her own frocks?"

"No. I …" We had always used a seamstress in the village.

"Well, I would say it is high time she learned." She looked me up and down. "You, of course, will be in mourning for several more months, so clearly there is no great rush for concern about your wardrobe."

"As for Edwin's responsibilities … he will help Mason with the winding and maintenance of the clocks. The boy will also assist in the garden. I am afraid things have become rather overgrown and a little tidying up is required."

I was dumbstruck. I did not know what I had expected, but it was certainly not this.

"Do I make myself clear, Lydia?"

I took a quick drink of tea, replaced my cup in its saucer and found all I could say was, "Er … well … I ---"

"To clarify then … you will present yourself and the children in the library at eight o'clock tomorrow morning. Meanwhile, you will meet with Mrs. Boot, cook, Daisy and Prue, Mason, and Ledward, our head gardener, in order to discuss the children's—and your—various responsibilities. Your job, of course, will be a full-time one, eight until five daily."

This was nothing new; I had been used to a full day's work for as long as I could remember.

Great-Aunt Ernestine rose and rearranged her skirts about herself. "From now on you and the children will take all your meals with cook. I shall send word when I wish to meet with you again. Understood, Lydia?"

I nodded and watched her as she made for the door.

Reaching the threshold, she turned and smiled broadly. "Assuming we all pull our weight," she said, "we shall get along famously."

And if our weight is not pulled to your liking, I thought, listening to her swish off along the hall. Then what?

I waited a few minutes before heading to the kitchen in search of Annabel and Edwin. They were nowhere to be seen. But I found cook washing the breakfast dishes.

"You just missed them," she said, drying her hands on her apron. "They've gone off gallivantin' in the grounds." She patted me on the arm, as if to reassure me. "A bit of larkin' about will do 'em good … put some color in their cheeks. They'll 'ave their noses to the grindstone soon enough, from what I hear."

I thanked the woman and turned to leave. "If you want to p'raps see where they are," she said, "go into the library—next-door-but-one to the dinin' room —an' out through the French doors onto the terrace; you'll 'ave a grand view from there."

Cook was right. The view was splendid. About a hundred yards away was a white-painted summer house built in the round, with latticework walls, a miniature cupola on the rooftop and steps leading up to the interior. Beyond lay acres of grassland, burned gold by the long, hot summer and dotted with oaks and elms. On a hillock in the distance was a copse of what looked like silver birches. And off to my right, ancient, over-arching sycamores—in full leaf now—made a shady-looking tunnel of the long, curving drive which dissected the property.

Directly below the terrace—accessed by a flight of steps and surrounded by a crumbling, low stone wall—was a garden. I exhaled a cynical breath. A little tidying-up was needed? A wild profusion of pink, red and yellow roses bloomed on overgrown and crowded bushes which had clearly not seen a pair of secateurs in years. I carefully descended the steps which were as uneven and lichen-encrusted as the terrace's flagstones, then meandered the weed-ridden graveled paths, relishing the sweet, heavy aroma and the feel of the sun on my back.

At the center of the rose garden, a trio of ornate, iron benches encircled a sundial. I sat, lulled by the warmth, my mission temporarily forgotten, closed my eyes and let my thoughts drift.

How grand Hadfield Hall must have once been. Carriages full of laughing visitors must have trundled up the drive. Battledore and shuttlecock, croquet, maybe cricket, would have been played on lawns as green and smooth as a billiards table. There would have been garden parties, too, with red-and-white striped marquees and long tables laden with all sorts of scrumptious dishes, as well as champagne and cold lemonade. I felt my mouth break into a smile. I could almost hear the whoops and shouts of children … Almost hear? My eyes flew open. I could hear …

I got to my feet and shaded my eyes with my hand.

There they were, emerging from the summer house. Annabel saw me first and waved; Edwin followed suit. Then they started racing towards me, shouting unintelligibly, and I set off to meet them.

Annabel careened into me, almost bowling me over, then threw her arms around me. "Oh, Lydia," she said breathless, red-faced, "we absolutely adore it here … far, far more than the Emmins."

"We do … we do," said Edwin, who looked as unkempt as one of Fagan's urchins. "We have been to the woods and we found a brook, then a pond with frogs. See." He thrust a hand in my face, opened it long enough for me to glimpse a tiny green creature, and continued with, "His name is Cuthbert and I am going to ask cook for a jam jar ---"

"And the summer house has window seats," Annabel cut in, raking back her unruly mop with one hand, attempting to fasten the top two buttons on her bodice with the other. "We could have tea out there and … oh yes, there is a dovecote, too, Lydia , the other side of the woods and a barn. We could play all day long out there. It truly is divine, with so much space to run about in and trees to climb and …" She paused and shook her head dazedly, seemingly overwhelmed by the myriad possibilities.

Edwin took the opportunity to leap back in with his thoughts. "We could leave right after breakfast," he said, "and gallivant—that is what cook said we were going to be doing this morning—all day, every day." Maybe cook would make us picnics."

"Capital idea," Annabel said.

I raised a staying hand. "Hold on," I said, cringing inwardly, hating myself for having to be the bearer of bad tidings. "I am afraid you are going to have to change your plans."

## CHAPTER FIVE
### September 1887
### Hadfield Hall, Sussex, England

Obediah Callenforth turned out to be not at all as I had imagined him. For some untold reason, I had formed a picture in my mind of a distinguished middle-aged man, strong-featured and graying at the temples.

But in reality, the fellow to whom the children and I were introduced at eight o'clock the next morning was old—at least as old as my great-aunt—and round: round of face and bald pink head; round of belly; round of eyes—which were watery blue and bulging—even round of voice, with his pronunciation of each syllable, each word in a peculiar, full-mouthed manner.

He was obsequious to a fault, also. Wet-lipped hand-kissing accompanied his, "Charmed I am sure." And after that came, "Rest assured, my dear young woman, the little miss and the little master will flourish under my tutelage."

The *little miss* shot me a look of indignation, and since she was not always above voicing her displeasure, I frowned a warning, which she thankfully heeded. Then I said, "I am certain they will, Mr. Callenforth," although, in truth, I very much doubted it.

For certain, Ernestine Hadfield held the fellow in great esteem. In his presence, she became almost flirtatious, resting her hand on his arm and laughing like a girl at his remarks, which were not the slightest bit clever and in my estimation did not merit amusement. Who was he, to her? I idly wondered, immediately discounting the question in favor of the more pressing one: How would he be with the children?

Behind a Davenport desk and a chair, he had set up a blackboard on an easel at the head of the vast, book-lined library. Whilst he and Ernestine Hadfield stood alongside it now, deep in conversation, I conducted Annabel and Edwin to the table which was to be their desk. "Sit down quietly," I said.

Seeing two slates—together with sharpened slate pencils for writing and sponges for erasing—Annabel frowned and muttered, "Where is our paper and ink, Lydia?"

None was evident. Clearly, Ernestine Hadfield deemed such things too expensive. "You will just have to make do with what you are given," I said in a low voice, noting the two Bibles, two reading books of a moralistic nature, one Latin text book and two abacuses on the table.

I felt a tug on my sleeve and looked down to see Edwin staring up at me with wide, tear-filled eyes. "Will he beat us?" he whispered.

I followed his gaze, and saw the object of his fear: A cane, in full view on top of the tutor's desk. I gave an inward shudder. He had better not, I thought, gently patting my brother on the back. "Of course not, dear," I said. "That is only for children who misbehave, not good boys such as you."

I noticed the tutor bending low over my great-aunt's hand, kissing it, and wishing her a good day. She, in turn, called out to me, "It is high time the children began their lessons, Lydia, and well past time for you to see to your duties."

*And who, pray tell, was responsible for the delay? I dare say you and your gentleman-friend had a good deal to do with it.* "Yes, of course, Great-Aunt," I sang out.

Then hastily kissing the top of each of the children's heads and reminding them of the importance of attentiveness, studiousness and general good behavior, I made my exit.

The problem—as I later discovered—was that in the first place I had not had Edwin turn out his trouser pockets for my inspection, and in the second, I had omitted to remind the boy that not everyone was as passionately fond of frogs as he. Therefore, Cuthbert's sudden appearance on Obediah Callenforth's desk during the *amo ... amas ... amats* of his Latin verb conjugation—according to Annabel's gleeful lunchtime rendition of the events—sent the fellow into purple-faced, apoplexy. "He tried to kill him," she said.

"Kill who? Edwin?" I clutched my throat in fake horror.

Glancing up from the pastry she was rolling, cook had a good chuckle.

"No ... Cuthbert. Mr. Callenforth chased him all over the library. But he proved to be an excellent jumper."

"Mr. Callenforth? He looks rather stout for that type of activity."

At this, cook laughed out loud and Annabel quickly caught on and joined in.

I suddenly realized Edwin had not yet put in an appearance. "Where is your brother?"

"Mr. Callenforth kept him back, said they needed to have a serious talk."

"Oh Lord." I clapped my hand to my chest, in genuine alarm this time, and started for the door.

At that very moment, Edwin appeared.

"Are you alright?" I leaned down, sizing him up from head to toe, then gently took him by the shoulders. "You are not hurt, are you?"

"Yes, I am."

My heart lurched. "What did he do to you?"

Edwin aimed the toe of his boot at an uneven tile on the floor and said tearfully, "He is a beastly man, Liddy. He made Cuthbert jump out of the window."

"Did he hit you?"

"No, but he told me I was a very wicked boy and if anything like that happened again the consequences would be DIRE." Edwin raised his voice and drew out the word for emphasis.

I exhaled in relief.

"He said I was wicked, too," Annabel said, wiping her soupy mouth with a serviette. "For laughing, and egging my brother on."

"And did you? I asked.

Annabel shrugged. "I might have."

All I said was, "I see." Had I been present, I might well have done the same thing.

I turned back to Edwin, drew him close and hugged him. "I am so sorry about your little friend, but I am certain by now he will have found his way home."

He pulled away and looked up at me. "Do you really think so, Liddy?"

"Of course I do. I dare say Cuthbert has a great many brothers and sisters ---"

"And cousins," Annabel interjected.

"Yes … cousins, too … all kinds of relations, in fact. And next time you go on a frog hunt—it will have to be on a Saturday, of course, because of your various duties—you are bound to discover one of them and I am certain he—or she—will be delighted to take up residence here with you. But not"—I put on my stern face—"to accompany you to your lessons."

"Sit down and eat your soup, there's a good lad," cook said.

And he did, with the happiest of smiles on his dear face.

Frog hunts, indeed. The very last activity I would wish to engage in. All I wanted, now, was for Edwin—Mr. Callenforth, too, of course—to forget about Cuthbert.

But I had an uneasy feeling that as far as that gentleman was concerned, our woes were just beginning.

## CHAPTER SIX
### *October 1887*
### *Hadfield Hall, Sussex, England*

The afternoon of the first Monday in October, several days into my new regimen, Mrs. Boot handed me a leather-bound ledger and signaled me to follow her along yet another of the myriad passageways Hadfield Hall possessed. "'tis time to check on the spirits," she said.

I felt my eyes widen. Ye Gods, was the place haunted? "Do you see them often, Mrs. Boot?" I asked. But she appeared not to have heard, shuffling on ahead of me and eventually halting at a door on the left. From within the folds of her skirts she retrieved a large iron ring from which she selected a key and unlocked the door; it groaned open, seemingly of its own accord. And I felt the hairs on the back of my neck rise.

More rummaging in her pocket, and the housekeeper produced a silver vesta case. She took out of it a couple of matches and said, "You wait 'ere while I go on in an' light the lamps." And with a surefootedness clearly born of familiarity she disappeared into the room's dark recesses. After what seemed an eternity—but doubtless amounted to a matter of seconds—the doorway was suffused with golden light and Mrs. Boot called out, "Yer can come on in now, dearie."

Taking a couple of tentative steps across the threshold, I glanced about. It took only seconds for the scene to register and for a great gust of laughter to burst from me. "Oh Mrs. Boot," I sputtered, arms spread to indicate the bottle-laden shelves lining all four walls, "these are the spirits you were talking about. And I thought you were ---"

"What?" The housekeeper had seated herself at a deal table to my right and the light from one of the two oil lamps on its top illuminated her puzzled and annoyed face. I felt another paroxysm of laughter about to overtake me, but managed to contain it. "Nothing," I said. "I am sorry ... I was being silly."

She shook her head as if she thought I were balmy and with a loud and protracted sigh said, "Yer'll be a sight sorrier, dearie, if the mistress asks for the still room inventry and yer do not 'ave it."

"Oh, now I see. We are to count the room's contents. So where do we start, Mrs. Boot?"

"First things first," she said. "See them bottles on the shelf beside yer?"

I nodded that I did.

"Pass one over will yer? Do not matter which one, they're all much of a muchness."

A corkscrew lay on the tabletop; she reached for it and within a few turns had the bottle of gin I had handed her open. "A little bit o' libation never did no one no 'arm," she said, with a gap-toothed grin. Then she took an astonishingly-long guzzle which she followed with a breathless, "Start countin' wherever yer like, dearie. They're all marked with what's in 'em. Then yer can check yer numbers against them in the ledger."

"Very well." I opened the book and searched it for the appropriate entries.

Meanwhile, the housekeeper took another gulp of the spirits, wiped her mouth on her sleeve and said, "We 'ave t'order whatever's been drunk."

"Replenish the supplies," I said.

"Keep the mistress 'appy. Likes 'er still room stock kept up, she does."

I attempted to begin the count, but Mrs. Boot interrupted and I lost my train of thought. "See all that sherry an' claret," she said, her arm waving perilously close to the shelf in question.

"Yes ... I see it here on the ledger page, too. One dozen of each at last count."

"An' ooo-ooo-ooo"—the housekeeper made the word sound like an owl call—"d'yer s'ppose they're for?"

"My great-aunt?"

She pointed an accusatory forefinger at me. "Wrong," she said, swaying in her seat. "For 'is bleedin' lordship, that is oooo."

"His lordship?"

"Obediah. Adorable Oh—beeee—diiiii—ah. 'im what's teachin' yer young 'uns. 'ave they said anythin' about 'im lately?"

"No, not a word. They have been unusually quiet on the subject, actually. Which would seem to indicate that everything is proceeding smoothly." As I spoke the words, I felt a flutter of something close to unease.

"Maybe so. But remind me later on, 'an I'll show yer 'ow yer can be certain about the state of affairs, as yer might say."

"How do you mean, Mrs. Boot?"

She ignored the question, too intent on the gin bottle, now, and staring in obvious disbelief at the small amount left in it. "Not much point in leavin' that paltry bit," she said, opening her mouth and tossing the liquor back, then noisily setting the bottle on the tabletop. Her watery gaze fell on me again. "Yer needs to keep an eye on that one," she said.

"Mr. Callenforth? What did you mean about the state of ---?"

"'e's a right so-an'-so, I can tell yer. Cook cannot stomach 'im," she carried on. "Daisy an' Prue cannot abide 'im. An' my mister thinks 'e's a … well … enough said on that score."

No use attempting to make sense of Mrs. Boot's earlier, mystifying comment at present. The old woman was in her cups. "Sounds as if the fellow is a touch unpopular," I said. But my dry tone was lost on her.

"Tell yer what, though," she continued, "the mistresss is proper smit, an' no denyin'."

Emboldened by the housekeeper's state of inebriation, I set down the ledger on the table and sat. "Who exactly is he, Mrs. Boot? I mean, how does my great-aunt know him? I gather he has quarters here, but has he lived at Hadfield Hall for very long?"

The housekeeper scratched her bird's nest of snowy hair for a long moment, as if to release her thoughts. "Come for a visit a few weeks 'afore the three o' you. Next thing we know, 'is trunks an' what not is delivered an' the mistress announces that '*er dear old friend* will be stayin' for"—she licked her lips as though lubrication were required—"an in—deee—term—in-ate period."

"I see."

"From what I 'ear, 'e was 'er sweet'eart years ago, 'fore she met Mr. Hadfield."

I did not ask how she heard. I was well aware that servants had an uncanny aptitude for digging up information about their employers.

My curiosity thoroughly aroused, now, I scooted my chair forward and rested my elbows on the table. "What happened?"

"Seems as though, Ooooobediaaah, didn't 'ave no means. Just a poor schoolmaster 'e was. They was all set to elope, the pair of 'em … she 'ad 'er bags packed an' everythin'. I dunno all the details … such as where they was s'pposed ter meet 'an where they was goin' ter go, but the brother got wind o' things from all accounts, an' that was that."

"The brother?"

"'s'right. 'er only relation, 'er guardian, the one with all the money. A lot older than 'er, from what I 'ear, an' with nary a kind bone in 'is bod."

I unfolded my arms and sat up straight. "He intercepted them, then?"

"Dunno about that, but 'e put a stop to their gallop, an' no denyin'."

The housekeeper took up the empty gin bottle and regarded it with bleary-eyed disgust. "Somebody must o' been at this 'afore I got to it. For certain I 'ad no more'n a couple o' swigs. Be a dear an' stick it on the top shelf—at the back—and count it in with the rest. We shouldn't want to get no one in trouble, should we?"

"Of course not, Mrs. Boot." Making use of a nearby footstool, I hid the evidence, as instructed.

"Good girl," the old woman said, yawning loudly. "Think I am goin' ter 'ave ter leave yer to it, now. Will yer be alright, with the countin' an' whatnot?"

"Of course."

With difficulty, the housekeeper got to her feet and stood, swaying slightly. "I'll be off, then."

"Before you go, Mrs. Boot, you said earlier that I was to remind you to show me something … something to do with Mr. Callenforth."

"'s'right, I did. But it will 'ave to wait, dearie, till another time. Purely done in, I am."

And with that, she made her unsteady exit, leaving me to wonder and worry.

## CHAPTER SEVEN
### *October 1887*
### *Hadfield Hall, Sussex, England*

At a couple of minutes before nine o'clock the next morning Mrs. Boot and I were at the linen press on the upstairs landing, folding freshly-laundered tablecloths, when she suddenly said, "Right. Told yer I'd show yer what's what, didn't I? Come on, then."

Today the housekeeper was sober and purposeful, as she urged me to follow her downstairs. Our destination turned out to be the study, and once we were in it, she said, "Sssssshhhhhhh," her finger to her lips. I was tempted to laugh out loud as the last notes of the clock cacophony died away. I could have bellowed like a bull pursued by a toreador and not have been heard.

"Over 'ere," she said in a barely discernible voice, directing me to the paneled wall which separated the room from the adjacent library. She held up a staying hand and I watched in surprise as she slid back a small, square, heavily-carved section in the paneling. Turning, finger to her lips again, she beckoned me close. I leaned in and was amazed to see a peep-hole about three-quarters of an inch across. It must've been there for centuries, I thought, the reason for its existence lost to history. I slanted a look up at Mrs. Boot and she nodded encouragement.

I looked through the opening and forgetting the housekeeper's warnings, let out a horrified gasp. There were my two dear ones, each wearing an enormous dunce's cap, each standing in a corner at the head of the room, faces to the wall, while behind them their cane-wielding tutor strutted and postured, every snap of his cane causing the children to flinch.

I turned away from the spy-hole, fists clenched against my breasts, tears of rage and frustration stinging my eyes. "That beastly man," I said in a half-whisper, "is terrorizing the children. I have to do something to stop him."

Mrs. Boot gently shoved me aside and with the utmost care, slid the panel back in place. "There's nowt yer can do, dearie, 'cept keep an eye on things an' make sure the young'uns 'eed Mr. Callenforth an' watch their p's an' q's an' learn all their lessons proper."

"I shall go to my great-aunt," I told the housekeeper as we mounted the stairs minutes later. "Tell her what is happening."

"Yer don't know nothin'. Me neither. I 'aven't seen no canin's, neither 'ave you. Besides, if young'uns doesn't be'ave theirselves they 'as ter take their punishment."

"But they do not misbehave, Mrs. Boot, you know that? The incident with the frog was merely a misunderstanding."

"Reckon yer right, dearie, them young'uns o' yours is good as gold, far as I can tell. But be that as it may, will not do yer no good to complain about 'is lordship. Told yer the mistress was smit." She halted, sucked in a couple of deep breaths, then continued. "Sure as eggs is eggs she will not 'ear a word against 'im. Besides, 'ow could yer know about the goin's-on? Not like yer in that library, yerself, with 'is lordship,' learning' yer letters an' such."

"But I saw it, Mrs. Boot, saw it with my own eyes. The way that dreadful man was ---"

"Spyin' eyes they was though, wasn't they?"

Irritated, I asked, "Why on earth did you tell me about the peep-hole in the first place?"

We reached the top of the stairs and Mrs. Boot fought for breath for several seconds before answering. "Thought yer should be made privy to it all, I reckon. Don't mean I knows what is to be done about it, though." She jerked her head in the direction of the linen press. "Best put it all from yer mind for now. There is a sight more cloths to fold an' the silver needs gettin' out for Daisy and Prue to polish."

I trudged along beside the housekeeper, my head in a whirl.

"An' there's your young Annabel's sewin' jobs to be sorted for this afternoon."

"Yes, I know." I shook my head and sighed heavily. Mrs. Boot was absolutely right; nothing could be done about the Callenforth situation at present. All I could do was watch and wait and endeavour to figure out the best course of action.

---

In truth, I often wished I had never been made aware of the existence of that blessed peep-hole. I did my best not to look through it, but every day it lured me and made of me a reluctant witness to the suppression of my siblings' spirits.

I wanted them to rebel, to be naughty, to scream at that dreadful tutor, who was forever telling them what dullards they were. But, of course, I could not, would not do such a thing.

What I could do, however, was encourage Edwin and Annabel in every other way possible.

I began to make a great fuss of Annabel's sewing efforts, which were at first clumsy—she had never held a needle and thread in her life—but after a few weeks, she had become surprisingly skilful. "I swear, I need a magnifier to see your hem stitches," I told her one afternoon in late October. "They are so beautifully small. And as for your herringbone, satin and feather stitches—not to mention your French knots—they are as finely-executed as any I have ever seen."

"Great-Aunt Ernestine examined my work the other day. She said it was quite good and asked me to make and embroider a bed jacket for her," Annabel said.

"There, you see. She recognizes your skill with a needle, too."

Annabel looked pensive for a moment, then her face fell. "But Mr. Callenforth thinks that I am ---"

"You are clever, Annabel dear, in many, many ways." I cupped her chin with my hand and looked into her eyes. "Never believe anyone who says otherwise. Alright?"

She nodded her agreement.

"Speaking of your cleverness, I understand from cook that you are becoming quite the pastry-maker."

Annabel giggled. "The first batch I made was horrid. Lord knows how I managed it, but it was a positively-vile-looking grey, and hard enough to knock somebody out, according to cook. She threw it out for the birds, and they turned up their beaks at it. But now, I do believe I have mastered the art." She puffed herself up and strutted. "My apple pie is the talk of the kitchen."

"And the dining room," I said. "I heard that just last night Great-Aunt Ernestine remarked on the tenderness of the pastry."

Annabel grinned from ear-to-ear, and I felt my heart sing at the sight of her happiness.

"Your brother's fine works are causing quite a stir, too," I said.

A shadow passed over Annabel's face. "I know. But he is driving me mad, Lydia. I cannot have a regular talk with him anymore and when we do have time off from our studies and our work, he does not want to play with me. I declare, he is a frightfully dreary brother these days."

I squeezed my sister's shoulder. "I will have a chat with him," I said.

The thing was that although Edwin was not at all enamored of his gardening duties and subjected me to a daily dose of complaints about his scraped knees, broken fingernails and blisters, as well as an assortment of aches and pains more befitting a Chelsea Pensioner than a seven-year-old, he did adore—in truth, was fanatical about—his clock-related duties.

Winding the clocks was just a small part of his job. He was being taught all about the mechanics of the inner workings, too. We in turn—Annabel and I —were receiving so much instruction about pinions and pivots and pendulums and bushings and escapements and numerous other bits and pieces, we were fast being driven to distraction.

I chose teatime a few days hence to have a word with Edwin. The very first sentence out of his mouth as we settled at the kitchen table was, "Mr. Mason and I cleaned a marvelous movement in a carriage clock this afternoon, Liddy." I promptly placed a finger to his lips and was about to begin my talk when all at once Great-Aunt Ernestine appeared in the doorway. The sight of her face wreathed in smiles so astonished me that I forgot what I had been about to say.

"Edwin, dear boy," she said, sweeping into the kitchen. "I understand from Mason that you are applying yourself most admirably to your clock duties."

My brother seemed lost for words. So I nudged him and muttered, "Manners," and he scrambled to his feet. "Thank you Great-Aunt."

"As a mark of my appreciation for your efforts, I should like to give you this." She reached into her reticule and extracted a magnificent-looking gold pocket watch on a chain; she held it out to Edwin.

Cautiously, he took it from her. "For me?" he asked, wide-eyed.

"For you, child. It belonged to my late husband … your great-uncle."

Edwin explored the watch-face with reverent fingertips. "It must be very, very old, then. Positively ancient, I should think, rather like yoursel--"

"And very precious," I barged in, fearing Edwin's progression towards a full-blown faux pas. "You must be certain to take excellent care of it."

"Oh, I will, Liddy, I will."

And he did. In fact, he became positively obsessed with the watch.

I did not know it, but he took it with him to the schoolroom one morning in mid-November.

I had steeled myself that morning and was determined not to look through the peep-hole. When I did, it always upset me. And so my intention was to merely check the study—Prue and Daisy were supposed to have dusted, but sometimes their efforts left a lot to be desired.

The first thing I heard when I entered the room were loud noises coming from the library next door … what sounded like raised voices … thuds … screams, even. I clapped my hand to my mouth. "Oh, my Lord, the children."

I lurched across the room, scrabbled at the panel, fumbled with the concealing door and slid it back. Then, my heart thumping so high in my chest I could hardly breathe, I put my eye to the spy-hole.

## CHAPTER EIGHT
### *October 1887*
### *Hadfield Hall, Sussex, England*

Rooted to the spot, I did not know whether to laugh or howl with outrage at what I saw.

Edwin must have launched himself at Obediah Callenforth and managed to clamber up on his back. Arms wrapped around the fellow's neck, legs clamped about his corpulent middle, my delicate little brother was hanging on for all he was worth while the tutor violently thrashed about and bellowed like a speared rhinoceros, "Get off me you beastly boy, get off me, I say."

Meanwhile, Annabel—in crimson-cheeked fury—was dancing about like a prize-fighter, pelting the tutor with a dunce's cap and shouting, "Give it back to my brother, you thief … you rotter … it is not yours."

The watch, of course. Edwin's prized new possession. Callenforth had it clutched in his fist, the dangling gold chain flashing in the light as he flailed back and forth. Annabel made an unsuccessful lunge for it and Callenforth lashed out, barely missing her.

I hardly had time to gasp, when I caught a glimpse of my brother's determined face and heard his infuriated, "It is mine … mine, you hear," along with the repeated slap of his small hand as it came down on the tutor's bald pate.

This clearly was too much for the old reprobate. Turning puce, he roared an inhuman sound and once more struck out in Annabel's direction, this time sending her sprawling. Then with the agility of a much younger man, he suddenly rose up on his toes and performed an astonishing pirouette, which caused Edwin to fly off his back and land with a horrible thud on the wooden boards.

The scene so stunned me that several paralytic seconds passed before I snapped to my senses and slammed shut the spyhole, stumbling from the room and into the hall. Tripping over my skirts in my haste, I navigated the few steps to the library door and flung it open.

There stood Obediah Callenforth—his face a vicious mask—his cane poised and clearly ready to strike Edwin's still-prostrate form.

Vaguely aware that Annabel had risen to her feet, I turned into a woman possessed, charged across the room and threw myself at the tutor. "Leave him be, you despicable old goat," I shrieked, pummeling him with my fists until he finally dropped the cane.

He tottered backwards and said in a high, querulous voice, "You are mad, quite mad."

"Indeed I am." I held up a fist as though ready to strike him, forcing him to further retreat until his back was against the wall, advancing on him close enough, now, to see beads of perspiration trickling down his fat, veined cheeks. "Mad as Mr. Carroll's Mad Hatter, in fact. Mad as The March Hare. While you, you great sniveling lout, are an utter dullard."

I caught the sound of giggles and a sidelong glance at Annabel and Edwin revealed their grinning faces. Edwin had his precious watch clutched to his chest and was rocking on his heels in excitement.

"A dullard, do you hear me, Mr. Callenforth?" I said.

For certain his round eyes could not have grown any rounder. But they appeared to be about to pop out of their sockets and his mouth fell into a large "O", revealing uneven, yellowish teeth.

"And we are well aware what happens to dullards, are we not, Mr. Callenforth?"

He frowned and gave an uncertain shrug, then cleared his throat as if preparing to answer.

But I did not give him a chance. "The dunce's cap, if you please," I said to

Annabel.

I took it from her and waved it before the tutor's frightened eyes.

"Tell Mr. Callenforth what dullards must wear, children," I said.

They both chortled and sang out in unison, "A dunce's cap."

"Correct. Edwin, dear, come here and help me keep guard. Annabel, bring the stool over, please. The cane, also, just in case we need it."

"Sit," I told the tutor in my most authoritative tone, "and do not dare move." With a firm hand applied to his shoulder, I helped him obey.

To be sure the cap was a difficult fit, being clearly too small for the man's overly-large orb of a head, but I persevered until I had it tugged well down over his eyes and mouth, in effect rendering him blind.

"There we are." I stood back, surveying my handiwork. "That will do very nicely, thank you," I said, with barely suppressed laughter.

A muffled sound came from beneath the cap, and I leant in close to his ear and said, "What was that, Mr. Callenforth?"

"You will pay dearly for this ignominious act," came the mumbled response.

Ignominious? I shook my head, straightened, shrugged. He was perfectly right, of course. We would pay. But for the present, I did not care one jot.

"Come along, children." I bracketed each of them with an arm and we headed for the door. "Let us leave Mr. Callenforth to ruminate on the error of his ways."

I heard a strange, strangled sound—something along the lines of an apoplectic gargle—as we hurried from the library. I think I heard something crash, too, moments later. Foolish man had undoubtedly tried to come after us, with his cap still in place. Who, pray tell, was the dunce, now? I thought idly, greeting cook with a smile as we entered her comforting domain.

"You all look mightily pleased with yourselves," she said, wiping a floury hand on her apron. "What've you been up to?"

"Oh nothing much," I said, pre-empting the children's responses. "Just righting a few wrongs is all."

"Hmmm. Sounds serious. Are you 'ungry?"

Two newly-baked, crusty loaves on a rack alongside the stove, gave up their wonderfully-yeasty aroma and I said, "We most certainly are, cook. We have expended rather more than our fair share of energy this morning."

Eat, drink and be merry, I thought, as I sat at the table next to the children. For tomorrow you may … not die, certainly. What then? Be locked up? Forced to drink bread and water? Scrub floors or scare crows or sweep chimneys for the rest of our days?

Retribution was, of course, inevitable.

Oh but whatever the cost—I smiled to myself, mussing Edwin's curls, tracing the curve of Annabel's cheek—today's activities had been more than worth the effort.

## CHAPTER NINE
### *October-November 1887*
### *Hadfield Hall, Sussex, England*

Word came from on high late that night.

I was about to get into bed when there came a tentative-sounding knock at the door. I opened it with caution, unsure who my visitor might be.

Prue stood there, looking as nervous as I felt. "Sorry, miss, but Mrs. Boot sent me," the girl said in a rush. "Said I was to tell yer the mistress says there's not to be no school till further notice."

"Hmmm," I said, raising an eyebrow.

"There's more," Prue said. "The mistress will no longer require—she drew the word out to give it emphasis—"Miss Annabel's ... presence in 'er chambers."

"I see."

"There's more, miss."

"Carry on," I said evenly, growing more impatient by the second and wanting to say, For pity's sake, just spit it all out, Prue.

"You is to ... contin...ue yer duties ... all three of yer, that is, miss. Mornin' till night. I mean, I think Mrs. Boot said yer was to work like us— Daisy an' me ... from ..." She trailed off, frowning. "Sorry, I think there's more, but I forget the rest, Miss Lydia."

I had had all the more I could take. "Fine, Prue. You get off to bed, now. I shall check with Mrs. Boot tomorrow and sort everything out with her."

—

"Things is ter stay same as always fer you, dearie," Mrs. Boot told me after breakfast the next morning. "'cept yer to start at six an' finish at nine."

"'struth," I said, setting the household account book down on the table we were sharing. "I certainly would not consider the addition of six hours to my workday same as always."

"That's as may be, dearie. But tis what the mistress says is to 'appen an' that's that." She leaned forward, her rheumy old eyes gleaming. "Reckon yer'd want to stay clear of 'is Lordship, on account of 'is bein' a mite out o' sorts." She gave me a knowing wink and a nod. "'ear tell 'e's took to 'is bed, poorly-like, an' the mistress 'as been backin' an' forthin' an' moppin' 'is fevered brow, so ter speak."

At this juncture I had no desire to hear about Obediah Callenforth's state of health or lack thereof. "What about the children?" I asked. "Exactly what are they to do?"

"They's to be up at 'alf-past five—same as Daisy and Prue an' the rest of 'em. Twenty minutes off fer their breakfasts, twenty minutes for their dinners at noon, twenty minutes for their teas at four o'clock, then work till bed at nine."

"That is inhuman," I said.

"In'uman or not, tis what all o' them below-stairs 'as 'ad ter put up with fer as long as I can remember, an' long afore that, I should think."

"Of course." I said, all at once realizing the insensitivity of my remark. "I imagine, like everyone else, we shall all get used to it."

"Reckon yer will, at that." Mrs. Boot nodded at the oak clock on the mantelpiece. "An' reckon yer'd best rouse them young'uns smart like, it bein' after eight already." She gave a regretful shake of her head. "'fraid, I'm obliged to let the mistress know if the new rules is broke ... so ter speak"

And so began our slavery ... so to speak, as Mrs. Boot would have said, along with Great-Aunt Ernestine's continued and unnerving silence, which was clearly designed to punish us further. She was still in residence, of course, but from all accounts keeping to her quarters and enjoying regular visits from the detestable tutor.

There were other visitors, too, the last week in November, according to Daisy and Prue, one a solicitor from London, the other a chartered accountant from Brighton.

Puzzled about the extent of the girls' knowledge, I said, "I realize these gentlemen would have given you their calling cards, but how on earth were you able to ascertain their occupations etcetera, when neither of you is able to read nor write?"

"We both nipped in to Mrs. Boot and 'ad 'er read the cards to us 'afore we took 'em up to the mistress," Prue said.

Ah, Mrs. Boot, fount of information, ruler of the below-stairs roost, and luckily my good, and unlikely friend.

"Nothin' ter say yer cannot give the two young'uns a lesson or two yerself," she said to me over brass-polishing one morning. If you was to take a couple of slates and slate pencils from the library, an' one or two o' them readin' books, I wouldn't say nowt ter nobody."

"Oh Mrs. Boot, you are very kind to think of that," I said, "but to be honest, by the time my day is over the children and I are ---"

"Plum tuckered out. Reckon yer right, yer would be, not bein' used ter workin' dawn till dusk an' all."

Never mind plum tuckered out, we were exhausted by the end of each day. And never mind lessons. We had hardly any time for conversation, even less for recreation.

But at least Edwin was content with his clocks, although much less enamored of his outdoor responsibilities. And Annabel grew more and more adept with her needle, and became quite the dab hand at cooking. With only a few weeks until Christmas, there were fruit cakes, plum puddings, mince pies and the like to be made, and she was in her element. She was also privy to a great deal of below-stairs gossip and every night when I tucked her in, she had a tidbit or two to share with me.

"Great-Aunt Ernestine is having money troubles," she said importantly, on a Saturday in late November.

"Good Lord." I sat on the edge of her bed. "Where on earth did you hear that?"

"Cook and Mrs. Boot were talking and I think they forgot I was there. Cook said Great-Aunt Ernestine had told her she was to economise—I think that was the word she used—in the kitchen. She was to buy cheaper cuts of meat, serve more spuds and swedes and less of the fancier veges to the servants. Then Mrs. Boot said she reckoned the mistress was having money troubles."

"Really?" I frowned, thinking how grand Hadfield Hall was, and what an unlikely state of affairs this sounded.

"Are we servants, Lydia?"

I smoothed back an errant strand of her dark hair. "No, we are not." *Even though we are being treated as if we are.*

"After that, Mrs. Boot said something about having to account for every penny she spends these days. And how she is fed up … to here." Annabel raised a hand over her head.

"Is that so?"

"Cook said, too, that Prue had overheard Great-Aunt Ernestine and Mr. Callenforth"—she wrinkled her nose in distaste as she said the man's name—"talking about the sorry state of her … affairs … or was it shares … I am not certain." Annabel traced the pattern on her counterpane with her fingertip. "What does that mean, Lydia?"

"Whatever it means, I am sure it is nothing for us to worry about, dear."

Annabel snuggled down under the covers and yawned. "Oh there was one more thing cook said Daisy heard. Something about Great-Aunt Ernestine telling Mr. Callenforth how grateful she was that she had him to help her manage her money and her …affairs."

Annabel yawned again and closed her eyes. "Mrs. Boot said, never mind manage her money, before he was done, he would have it all. Sorry."—her voice drifted into a whisper— "that is all I can think of right now."

I planted a soft kiss on Annabel's forehead and left her to her dreams while I headed for my room, weighed down by a niggling apprehension.

## CHAPTER TEN
### December 1887
### Hadfield Hall, Sussex, England

A vague unease continued to plague me as damp, gray November gave way to cold, crisp December.

Both Great-Aunt Ernestine and the tutor remained incommunicado. An occasional snippet of inconsequential information about one or both of them came to me from time to time via the below-stairs telegraph.

Meanwhile, the children and I slaved on.

Then, suddenly, one afternoon towards the end of the first week in December, when I was arranging freshly-laundered table linens in the dining room sideboard drawer, Great-Aunt Ernestine appeared.

"Good afternoon, Lydia," she said, with a bland smile.

In my astonishment, I dropped a cloth on the floor. I bent to retrieve it, making a clumsy attempt to refold it as I straightened.

"Take your time," my great aunt said, seating herself at the table, "I am in no great hurry and can certainly wait while you put the tablecloth away."

Once I had accomplished the task, she directed me to sit across from her.

"While you and your siblings have been provided ample time to reflect on your actions of several weeks ago," she said without preamble, "I have been giving a great deal of thought to your futures." She brushed an imaginary spot from her bodice front and rearranged her blue silk skirts, then fixed me with a long, unreadable look.

I glanced away, a nervous flutter in the pit of my stomach. The guillotine was finally about to drop. Lord knew what she had in mind for the three of us. Permanent servitude, I should not doubt.

"As you know, I did not ask to have you here." For some untold reason, the statement took me aback, and I gave her my full attention, now.

"I merely indicated to your father's solicitor," she went on, "that I would take the three of you in for an indeterminate period, with the thought that … well, never mind what I was thinking. Suffice to say, I never once anticipated that I would be providing a home for a trio of out-and-out ruffians." She closed her eyes momentarily and gave a little shudder. "Needless to say your behavior shocked me to the core. And the fact that none of you has come forward with an apology is truly beyond the pale."

I drew in a sharp breath, indignation turning my cheeks hot. "But you have been unavailable to us and besides, we were not at fault. We were attempting to defend ---"

"Mr. Callenforth still has not recovered from your attack on him. You were acting like a pack of wild beasts. And there can be no possible excuse for such conduct."

I leaned forward, opening my mouth to protest at the injustice of her words, but my great-aunt held up a staying hand and I subsided into my seat, fists clenched in frustration. Short of clapping my hands over my ears, I could do absolutely nothing but listen to her sermon.

"At my stage of life, I will not ... cannot ... tolerate upsets of this nature. And aside from the issue of your dreadful carryings-on"—her tone seemed to soften slightly as she continued—"there are my newly-straitened circumstances to be considered."

She must have noticed my puzzled expression and, surprisingly, felt the need to explain herself.

"An unfortunate downturn in the financial markets has led to a fairly significant decrease in my investment income."

Lord save me, I thought, gritting my teeth in annoyance. Papa all over again.

She cleared her throat and fiddled with the tiny buttons on her bodice, then avoiding my eyes and moistening her lips, said, "I am afraid there is nothing else for it. I am going to have to make alternative arrangements for the three of you."

"Alternative arrangements?" I said. "I do not understand."

"I am looking into other ... accommodations for you."

I reared up in my seat, my heart suddenly in my throat. "What sort of accommodations? Where? With whom?"

My great-aunt made a show of clearing her throat, then said in a rush, "For the children, a fine establishment in Yorkshire, with an excellent reputation. And for you, a position with one of the better families in the county."

"Yorkshire?" Her meaning struck me like a physical blow and I drew in a loud breath. *God in Heaven, she means an orphanage for Annabel and Edwin. And for me, the life of servitude I thought about earlier.* "But you cannot do this, Great-Aunt ... send the children away to Yorkshire and keep me here in Sussex. You absolutely cannot separate us."

She raised a sardonic eyebrow. "I absolutely can, and I will."

I sat up, my spine rigid. "But I am all they have. I am like a mother to them."

"Be that as it may, child, this is the best possible solution for everyone."

"No ... no, Great-Aunt." I got to my feet, almost toppling my chair in my haste to rise. "It is the worst possible solution. You do not understand," I said fiercely. "I promised Mama I would always take care of the children ... that I would keep the family together."

The old lady shrugged. "I am afraid life is fraught with disappointment, child, and sad to say, broken promises." She slowly rose, looking directly into my eyes, and flinching imperceptibly at the devastation she must have seen there. "I am sorry things did not turn out as I had hoped."

Bitterness rose like bile in my mouth. *Liar. You cannot wait to be rid of us.*

"Just as soon as everything is finalized, you and I will confer again, Lydia. Meanwhile, you will all carry on as usual."

With that, she turned on her heel and made for the door, while I stood, weak-kneed, supporting myself on the table-edge, making no attempt to staunch the flow of my tears.

Ernestine Hadfield's footsteps died away. My sobs faded into soft hiccups before finally petering out. I sank into my seat and buried my head in my hands. *Oh Mama, I have failed you and I have no idea what to do, now.*

*I am afraid life is fraught with disappointment, child.*

I straightened, wiped away a residue of tears with the back of my hand, and glowered. A Great-Aunt Ernestine homily was the very last thing I expected—or wanted—to invade my mind.

There she went again, I thought angrily; calling me child. And it was not as if it were one slip of the tongue; it had happened several times during the weeks we had been here. Never mind that I had set her straight the day of our arrival. And never mind that I was a woman, doing a woman's work.

I made a disgusted sound at the back of my throat. I had not been a child for eons.

*But you could be one now.*

The idea came unbidden, taking me aback, causing me to shake my head in puzzlement.

Then, right on the heels of the thought flashed the realization. No ... it was more than that. My eyes widened, my pulse quickened.

This was a revelation ...

One that could change everything.

## CHAPTER ELEVEN
### December 1887
### Hadfield Hall, Sussex, England

After our meeting in the dining room, my great-aunt had gone directly to her study, according to Mrs. Boot. And in my eagerness to speak with her again, I had felt no compunction whatsoever about disturbing her.

Her annoyance was transparent but it did not faze me. I slipped uninvited into the seat across the desk from her and said, "What I have to discuss will take only a few minutes."

"It had better be a few," she said, indicating the stack of papers in front of her. "I have a multitude of tasks awaiting my attention."

Without further ado, I said, "I wish to be sent to Yorkshire, too."

She raised her lorgnette to her eyes and stared at me in disbelief. "You wish what?"

"To go with Annabel and Edwin to the or ---"

"But that is impossible. You are far too old for an or ... for the home I have in mind."

"Do you remember, Great-Aunt, when you first met me, you mistook me for Annabel?"

She passed a reflective hand across her mouth. "Perhaps I do, I am not certain. You were very late in arriving that night, and I recollect that I was extremely tired."

*Inebriated, actually.*

"I suppose it is possible that I may have made that assumption."

"Oh you did, Great-Aunt, you really did. And you also used the word puny, to describe me."

My great-aunt shifted uncomfortably in her chair. "Assuming I did use such a word—and I certainly have no memory of it—what I must have meant to say about you is that you are extremely slight."

"Exactly." I jumped up out of my chair, spread my arms and pirouetted. "Look at me. I am puny, there is no doubt about it. And Annabel would make three of me, as you also said that first night."

Great-Aunt Ernestine sighed long-sufferingly. "I am fast losing patience. If you are attempting to make a point, child, then please do make it."

"Ah-hah." I raised my hands, palms up. "You said it again."

The old lady startled me with a slap of her hand on the desktop. "Enough. You will waste no more of my valuable time with your theatrics. And I will not allow this ridiculous interrogation to continue." She pointed to the door. "Go, see to your duties and be done with this nonsense."

But desperation emboldened me and I would not be silenced. "You called me child, Great-Aunt; you are always calling me child. And my point is that I can very easily *be* a child. I can be thirteen … a year older than Annabel, who incidentally will be twelve on the twelfth. Then all you have to do is secure a place for me with Annabel and Edwin. Tell them you have three children who need a home instead of two. I am sure it would be far less complicated than having to find a separate domestic position for me."

Without another word, I slipped into my chair and waited, motionless, my gaze glued to my great-aunt's now-unreadable face.

She had taken up her pen and pressed the end reflectively against her lower lip. She closed her eyes and I could see their back and forth movement beneath the lids. Her forehead creased in a frown, smoothed out then creased again.

I could contain myself no longer and blurted, "I can alter one of Annabel's frocks, do my hair differently, act differently. I have always had a knack for that sort of thing. Mama used to say I was a regular Sarah Bernhardt."

A lift of one of her dark eyebrows was the only indication my great-aunt had heard me.

On ticked the minutes, the study's quartet of clocks marking their passing with nerve-wracking loudness, while I rolled one thumb around the other, crossed and uncrossed my legs and counted backwards from one hundred.

Finally, Great-Aunt Ernestine opened her eyes, blinked, owl-like, several times, returned her pen to the inkstand and refocused on me. "Well, she said, with a decisive dip of her chin. "I have given your proposition a good deal of thought."

I edged forward on my seat and gripped the edge of the desk so hard my knuckles turned white.

"It really is quite an ingenious plan you have come up with."

I held my breath while she selected a piece of what appeared to be stationery from the stack she had at hand. I exhaled. Further agonizing seconds passed as she retrieved her pen and dipped it in the inkpot.

At last—pen poised—she looked at me again.

And Ye gods and little fishes, I almost fell off my chair; she was actually smiling.

"So," she said, smoothing out the sheet of stationery, "we have Edwin, aged seven, Annabel, aged …?" She glanced up at me and tilted her head inquiringly.

"Twelve," I said, "at least she will be in a very few days."

"Then you, Lydia, must be thirteen? Agreed?"

My great-aunt's acquiescence so surprised me that it rendered me stupid.

A long moment passed before I was able to gather my wits and stammer, "Er … yes … agreed, absolutely."

"And how old are you, then, child? The ghost of a smile accompanied the question.

I pulled myself together. "Thirteen," I said decisively. "I am Lydia Fullerton aged thirteen."

## CHAPTER TWELVE
### *December 1887*
### *Hadfield Hall, Sussex, England*

Not wishing to worry the children, I kept the news of our January departure to myself. Great-Aunt Ernestine had already assured me that she would not breathe a word to anyone until everything was finalized.

I still clung to the faint hope that there would be a different outcome. After all, the season of goodwill would soon be upon us. Perhaps all would be forgiven; Obediah Callenforth would go on his way and I could take over as the children's teacher. Perhaps Great-Aunt Ernestine's coffers would miraculously refill themselves and life could go on—not that it was the best of lives—as it had before.

But nothing was going to change, I realized, when my great-aunt summoned me to her study a fortnight before Christmas and told me that she had received a response from the Home.

"May I ask what its name is, Great-Aunt. You have yet to tell me."

"Brackford House," she said. "Now, where was I?"

"You said you had heard from them."

"Oh, yes, so I did. The news is good. They informed me that they have places for the three of you," she said, looking pleased with herself. "The only thing I did not foresee is that they require you be examined by a doctor prior to your admission."

"A doctor?" I sat without being invited.

"Yes, they have their own physician on staff. And I am to advise them of a day and date suitable for his visit here."

"Here? He is coming here? But why do we have to be seen by a doctor, Great-Aunt? I do not understand."

"To insure that they are not taking on any pigs in pokes."

"Such as this pig?" I said, patting my chest, worry making my voice shrill. The last thing I needed was to come under a doctor's scrutiny.

"No … no, child." She waved a dismissive hand. "Sick persons. Consumptives and the like."

"And what will this doctor do?"

"Examine the three of you, of course."

"What sort of an examination?" My heart had fallen to my boots. The game would surely be up before it had started.

"A cursory one, I imagine. Eyes, nose, ears, mouth. A check of your lungs with a stethoscope to your chest."

I glanced down at myself. Thank the Lord my breasts were small and could easily pass for those of a thirteen-year-old.

You do know what a stethoscope is, child?"

"Yes. I remember seeing it used on Mama."

"Do not look so glum, Lydia. I am certain you have no need to worry. Your ruse will not be discovered, as long as you act and dress the part. Incidentally"—she rummaged among her papers and extracted a document —"I have your new birth certificate." She scrutinized it through her lorgnette. "You were born on the fifteenth of July, eighteen-seventy-four. You have the same birthdate; only the year has been changed."

She reached across the desk and handed me the paper. "Put it in a safe place, Lydia. There may come a time when you have need of it. The Home has not requested birth certificates; I merely gave them dates of birth for the three of you and that has seemed to suffice."

I carefully folded the document and slipped it in my skirt pocket. "Have you decided when the doctor is to come here, Great-Aunt?"

"Yes, I have settled on Thursday, the fifth of January. All the seasonal festivities will be behind us by then."

"And when do you think we will leave Hadfield Hall."

"If all goes according to plan, the date agreed upon is the nineteenth … also a Thursday."

"Meanwhile"—my great-aunt rose and came to stand beside me—"we will make the best of your remaining time here. I will see to it that you have a grand Christmas, an unforgettable one, in fact. And Annabel needs a birthday party – a trifle belated if my memory serves me correctly. Twelve on the twelfth, I believe you said." She touched my shoulder and it took all my self-control not to shrink from her. "I do so want you to remember your stay here as a happy time."

I could not believe my ears. A happy time? I closed my eyes against the dull throb that had begun at my temples. Great god in heaven, how much better off we would have been not to have come here in the first place, only to have our hopes raised then dashed. Interlacing my fingers, I pressed my thumbs to my mouth, so as to contain the accusatory words I dare not say.

"Are you all right, Lydia?"

I snapped open my eyes. Great-Aunt Ernestine's face loomed, an expression of concern softening its hard planes. Counterfeit concern, for certain, I thought cynically.

"Of course I am," I lied. "I could not be better."

## CHAPTER THIRTEEN
### *December 1887*
### *Hadfield Hall, Sussex, England*

"Oh my Lord," I said to the children as we followed Prue into the dining room on Boxing Day afternoon.

"Mistress says yer to sit an' wait. She'll be 'ere shortly," the girl said, leaving the children to gape and squirm with excitement at the banquet laid out before us.

Great-Aunt Ernestine had kept her word as regards Annabel's belated birthday party a fortnight earlier. Although she had not attended it herself, she had instructed cook to prepare a special tea, complete with birthday cake and whatever else Annabel fancied. She had also sent a gift for her great-niece -- a delicate little seed pearl brooch which Annabel now wore at every opportunity. All I had been able to come up with from Edwin and me had been a lace handkerchief and a length of velvet ribbon.

We had had a memorable Christmas, too … with the servants, that is, not with Great-Aunt Ernestine and her paramour. A Christmas tree had been delivered to Mrs. Boot's quarters and lit with candles, and we were all invited to gather around it on Christmas Eve, drink cider (a sip or two only for the children), and sing carols. Christmas morning, we sat at the deal table in the kitchen with cook, Prue, Daisy, Thomas Mason and Mr. and Mrs. Boot, laughing and joking with each other as we opened our stockings, which were filled with sweetmeats and nuts and apples and a shiny new shilling for each of us.

I had the coins in a pouch secured with a cord around my waist, the same pouch in which I kept my precious portrait miniature of Mama. I felt the comforting convexity of it now, beneath my fingertips.

I surveyed the table, resplendent in its pristine white linen and lace cloth, and laid with the gilded, blue-and-white Worcester service usually reserved for special occasions. Sparkling cut glass goblets and the sterling silver cutlery I had watched Daisy polish last week, graced each place. I nodded to myself. All this bounty, I thought with irony. And surely a last good meal for the condemned.

At one end of the long table, Cook's famous ham and chicken pie took centre stage. Next to it, sausage rolls basked in glorious puffs of pastry. Alongside them was an assortment of watercress, cucumber, meat- and fish-paste sandwiches -- dainty crustless triangles which could be devoured in two bites if one forgot one's manners. At the other end of the table a trifle mounded with thick Devonshire cream reigned supreme; surrounding it were cake stands bearing jam tarts, scones, a chocolate cake, and my favourite—a pink-and-yellow-checked Battenburg cake wrapped in marzipan.

"I did the marzipan," Annabel said, breaking the awestruck silence, "and the puff pastry for the sausage rolls, but I have never ever tasted anything I have made. That is not allowed, cook says."

"No surprise," I muttered.

"Today," the one sonorous word stopped the three of us in our tracks, "the rules are changed. You may partake of everything you see laid out before you."

Great-Aunt Ernestine swept in, as Prue hurried to pull out a chair at the head of the table. The old lady sank into it, her ecru taffeta skirts rustling about her. She dipped her silver head in acknowledgment of each of us and smiled.

"Eat, drink and be merry. Prue, pour the tea if you please, then leave us."

For the next several minutes the only sounds at the table were the sighs of pleasure from the children as they tucked in with gusto, and the occasional chink of cutlery on porcelain. *Lambs to the slaughter.* The thought came unbidden and my stomach clenched so, I could hardly eat another bite.

Finally, the old lady filled the protracted conversational void with a pleasant-sounding, "Well now, has everyone had elegant sufficiency?"

"Oh yes, thank you," said Annabel. "It was positively delicious"

"Indeed it was, Great-Aunt," Edwin said, wiping his mouth with his serviette.

"Very well, you may leave the table, now, and go to your rooms and amuse yourselves while your sister and I converse. First, however"—she looked benignly from one to the other—"is there anything you wish to say to me?"

After chewing on her lower lip for a time and glancing at me as if for inspiration, Annabel said in a rush, "Happy Boxing Day, Great-Aunt Ernestine. And thank you for tea. Oh … and I know I thanked you before"—she patted her chest in the spot where the brooch was pinned—"but I wanted to tell you again how very much I like my birthday present."

A barely perceptible dip of Great-Aunt Ernestine's head followed Annabel's breathless outpouring.

"And I am pleased to be able to tell you," Edwin added importantly, fishing his watch from his pocket and squinting at its dial, "that I have been eating and standing here for exactly thirty-two minutes."

"Oh do run along, children," the old lady said with an overly-loud sigh, and a dramatic—almost tragic—swipe of her hand across her brow. "I am disappointed, to say the least. I had high hopes that you would have thought about your transgressions and had something meaningful to say to me."

That the remarks sailed over the children's ingenuous heads and the two skipped out of the room looking more carefree than they had in weeks, gave me a perverse kind of pleasure. And I could not resist saying, with barely concealed glee, "I am afraid, an apology is the very last thing on their minds, and on mine, too, if I am included in your high hopes."

She opened her mouth to speak, but I cut her off. My days of deference were over. "I have been trying to say this for some time, but have not been allowed to. Whatever your friend, Mr. Callenforth, may have told you, he was the perpetrator and the children the victims of his violence." I reached for my glass and took a quick gulp of water.

My great-aunt sat ramrod straight, gripping the arms of her chair. "You are a fool, Lydia, if you think for one moment that I would take your word over that of a dear and trusted friend."

"But he st ---"

"Enough." She brought the flat of her hand down on the table and I almost jumped out of my skin. "I will hear no more on the subject. You would do well to remember that you have sought and obtained my cooperation in your upcoming plans. And I believe I have proved to be your ally, not your enemy. Is that not a fact, Lydia?"

"Yes," I said, realizing I was balancing on a threadbare tightrope and must exercise the utmost caution with every step I took.

## CHAPTER FOURTEEN
### *January 1888*
### *Hadfield Hall, Sussex, England*

I waited until the second of January to tell the children the news of our impending banishment from Hadfield Hall.

I had had Daisy light the fire in my bedroom before breakfast, and by the time Annabel and Edwin and I convened there, mid-morning, the frost on the window had melted and the room was warm and inviting.

"Sit here," I said, patting the eiderdown on my double bed and directing them to make themselves comfortable against the bolster and pillows at the head, while I perched sidesaddle at the foot.

"We are to have another adventure," I said cheerfully.

Annabel wriggled in anticipation. "What sort of an adventure?"

"A frog hunt?" Edwin asked, his face lighting up. "Are we going to find Cuthbert's brothers and sisters?"

"No, dear. No frog hunts, I am afraid."

His face dropped, and I carried on with great enthusiasm. "We are going to travel on the train again. Remember how you enjoyed our last journey?"

Before he had a chance to respond, Annabel said, "I did not enjoy it one bit. The seat was so hard it made my posterior numb. I was deathly cold and starving, too, by the time we reached the station here."

"We all were, dear. As you recall, the journey took far longer than anticipated. Hopefully, this time it will be different." In truth I doubted it, if the current freezing weather was any indication and if our accommodations proved to be in the open carriages reserved for second-class passengers.

"Where are we going?" Annabel asked, frowning.

"To a rather special place, actually, where there will be dozens of others just like you ... children who have no parents ... no regular home."

"You mean an orphanage?"

"Well, yes, I do," I said. "How do you know about orphanages?"

"Remember how Papa used to tell us we must be thankful for the food on our plates and think about all the poor children who had none?"

"I certainly do."

"Well, one day I asked him who the children were and where they lived, and he said they were called orphans and they lived together in very large house called an orphanage, with many rooms, and people there to take care of the children."

"I see," I said, surprised that my father would have been that forthcoming, considering his speak-when-spoken-to rule and general taciturnity.

"Where is the *awfulage*, Liddy?" asked Edwin. "Is it in Africa?"

Annabel rolled her eyes and tutted. "Silly, it is the heathens who are ---"

"No, Edwin, dear," I said, cutting off Annabel before she had an opportunity to further correct her brother. "The orphanage—which incidentally is known as Brackford House—is here in England, in Yorkshire, which is several counties northwest of us. And according to Great-Aunt-Ernestine, it sits in a lovely spot on the moors, where there is a great deal of open space and an abundance of good, fresh air."

"I rather like fresh air," Edwin said. "Cook says it brings roses to my cheeks."

"You do not want roses, you are a boy," Annabel said with disdain, as she stretched out her legs and rotated her slippered feet, first one way then the other.

"Yes I do." Edwin rubbed his fingertips over his cheeks and tipped his chin in defiance of his sister. "I want them."

Annabel shrugged, exhaled a loud breath and returned her attention to me. "Why do we have to leave here?" she asked

"Our great-aunt's health is somewhat compromised and her financial situation has become untenable."

The children looked at me with blank expressions.

I simplified things for them. "She has become rather poorly and has too little money with which to care for us."

Edwin looked thoughtful, then said in a matter-of-fact tone, "She does not want us anymore."

Annabel nodded in mute agreement.

"It is not a case of her not wanting us," I said, frustrated. "When you are grown you will understand that circumstances beyond our control often dictate our decisions, and certain ramifications ensue." I mentally shook my head. What sort of long-winded nonsense had I just spouted?

One moment Annabel appeared bemused by my rhetoric, the next she looked panicked. "But you are a grownup person, Lydia," she said, in a high, tight voice, "which means you cannot come with us to the orphanage? What is going to happen to you? Where will you go?"

Her tone was clearly upsetting Edwin. His worried eyes skittered back and forth between me and Annabel. "I do not want to go to an awfulage … an orphanage … Liddy. I want to stay with you," he said.

I reached for my little brother and drew him close. "You will stay with me, my darling. I will be coming with you." I stretched out a hand to Annabel; she grabbed it and held on tight. "Do you think for one minute I would leave you two to fend for yourselves? I will always take care of you."

Edwin pulled away and looked up into my face, as if to check the veracity of my words. "Will there be clocks for me to wind, Liddy? And will I be able to take my watch with me?" He withdrew it from his pocket and ran a loving hand over its face."

"There are bound to be clocks, dear. And I am certain the powers-that-be at Brackford House will be happy to have your help. And as for your watch … of course you may take it."

Annabel had continued to hold onto my hand throughout this exchange. Now, she released it and swiped a couple of tears from her cheeks.

I rubbed her foot, remembering how this soothed her. She visibly relaxed and I said, "Now, I want you to sit back again and make yourselves comfortable. I have a great deal more to tell you. And I will need you to attend to my every word."

Their eyes never left my face for the next few minutes as I explained the situation and the need for all of us to maintain the utmost secrecy regarding my plan. I finished by saying, "So, in a nutshell, three days from now, on Thursday—the day the doctor comes to examine us—I will become your thirteen-year-old sister."

Hardly had I placed a full stop at the end of my last sentence, than Edwin said, "It is a secret, a really big secret." He got to his knees and bounced up and down with excitement.

"It most certainly is," I said, calming him with a firm hand on his shoulder.

Unusually sombre, Annabel said, "I will absolutely, positively never tell a single, solitary soul. Even if I am tortured, I will never tell."

I swallowed a smile and said, "Thank you, dear," signaling the pair to get down off the bed

"So," I said. "How old is your sister, Lydia?"

"Thirteen," they chorused. And then they danced around me singing, "Our sister is thirteen," over and over and over until I had to laughingly tell them to stop.

"I shall need one of your frocks," I told Annabel. "One you have outgrown will be perfect. And perhaps a couple of your hair ribbons. And on Wednesday night I should like you to put ringlets in my hair."

"But I do not know how."

"You have seen me do it often enough with your own hair. Now it is your turn. I will gather together sufficient rags for the task and between the two of us I am sure we will manage."

"May I help, Liddy?" Edwin asked.

"I see no reason why not."

Annabel was clearly about to express her displeasure at the idea, but all at once she appeared to have a change of heart. "I suppose you will do well enough," she said to her brother.

"We will all do well enough," I said, conjuring a cheek-aching smile which quickly infected the children.

Anyone looking at us would have thought we were an inordinately happy trio.

But in truth, I was frightened to death.

## CHAPTER FIFTEEN
### *January 1888*
### *Hadfield Hall, Sussex, England*

According to Great-Aunt Ernestine, the name of the doctor from Brackford House was Phillip Latham. He would doubtless be old and dour—I had yet to meet a doctor who was not—and would have a scraggly gray beard and sour breath, I concluded. His scheduled arrival time was four on this Thursday afternoon, and I was instructed to present myself in the drawing room at half-past-two for what Great-Aunt Ernestine called, a dress rehearsal.

With the various dingings and dongings of the myriad clocks as my accompaniment, I entered stage right. My great-aunt was asleep in an armchair by the fire, illuminated by an Argand lamp on the small, round table next to her. When I closed the door, she suddenly snuffled awake.

Hitching herself upright and taking a moment to orientate herself to her surroundings, she said, "Close the curtains, child. I have no desire to look out on a day as cold and dreary as this one. I should not be a bit surprised if it snows."

I went to the first of the three windows and gazed out on the cheerless scene. The sky was a dull and foreboding slate colour. Silhouetted against it were sinister-looking skeletons of trees, moving sluggishly in the icy wind. And the once-green velvet lawns were now reminiscent of faded, threadbare carpets.

In the distance, beyond the summerhouse, I saw two small figures— Annabel's and Edwin's—chasing after each other, and when I cocked my head I fancied I heard their shrieks and shouts to each other. My great-aunt had given them dispensation to play outdoors—I had made certain they were well bundled-up, of course—and inclement weather or not, they were clearly enjoying themselves.

I felt an enormous wave of sadness engulf me. This might well be the last time the children enjoyed such freedom. Our lives were once more in a state of flux. And we three were helpless to change things.

"I did not ask you to stand there daydreaming, Lydia."

I returned to earth with a start, quickly drew the curtains and wheeled about. "A snowfall would please Annabel and Edwin no end," I said. "That is all well and good, Lydia. But it will please me not one jot." My great-aunt reached alongside for her half-empty sherry glass, downed the contents and returned it to its place on the table. Then, using the long handle of her tortoiseshell lorgnette to direct me, she said, "Come over here in the light."

Once she had finished her head-to-toe examination of me, a sherry-fueled smile blossomed on her face. "My oh my … quite a transformation, I must say. Turn around and let me have a good look at you."

Feeling awkward and ridiculous, I complied. I had found the green-and-blue plaid wool frock languishing in the bottom of the trunk Annabel and I shared; she had outgrown it two years ago and eventually it would have been altered to fit her again. As it was, it suited my needs perfectly, with its high, demure-looking neck, lace-trimmed yolk and a hem that reached mid-calf. I felt discomfited by the thought that my lower legs—although encased, of course, in woolen stockings—were revealed to one and all.

"Excellent," the old lady said, sherry glass in hand again. "And your coiffure is certainly a sight to behold."

Whether or not she meant it as a compliment, I do not know; but I took it as one and smiled. I patted the clusters of ringlets framing my face. "For the most part, Annabel's and Edwin's handiwork," I said.

"Your attire and your hair are acceptable. But your voice ..." She tapered off and left me hanging while she refilled her glass from the decanter and took a generous gulp.

"What about my voice, great-aunt?" She had gestured for me to sit opposite while she put down her glass and dabbed at her mouth with a lace handkerchief .

"It is too ... mell ... mellif ... luous ... too low. You must raise it a note or two. Add a little breathiness ... perhaps a stammer of uncertainty here and there. Listen to your siblings. Take your cue from them."

I chewed on my bottom lip for a time. My siblings did not exhibit breathiness or uncertainty in their speech; they were decidedly forthright. Nevertheless, I recognized the importance of humouring the old lady, so I said in a voice much higher and faster than normal, "That is a very, very clever idea, Great-Aunt."

"Excellent. You are a quick study, child. Now"—she fingered the cameo on the velvet ribbon at her crepe-paper throat and leaned forward with an air of confidentiality —"let me tell you about another of my very clever ideas. I called a meeting of the entire staff earlier today and apprised them of your ... what shall we call it? Ruse? Disguise?"

Great God, what if one of them were to say something to the doctor?

"Do not look so worried, child. I made it abundantly clear that if anyone breathes a word of this they will immediately be given the sack."

"But what about Mr. Callen...?"

"Obediah?" A hint of a smile played across her mouth. "Oh you need have no fear of any involvement on the part of Mr. Callenforth. He is away for a fortnight or so and will not be returning until well after your departure."

I subsided with relief into my chair.

"I know you have had your differences with the dear man. But I must tell you he is an absolute boon to me and I should not be able to manage without his help."

I did not respond. But I thought, You are a fool, a silly old woman, whose head has been turned.

"Now, what about Annabel and Edwin? Have you sworn them to secrecy? And have you schooled them well as to how they must conduct themselves where you are concerned?"

"Yes to both questions, Great-Aunt. They will not give me away." *Oh, but you, our only living relation, you will give us all away like rags to the rag-and-bone man.*

"Quarter to three," the old woman said loudly, as the clocks launched into their strident chorus. "You had better call the children in now, and have them tidy themselves up. It is important that you all look your best."

Like livestock on market day, I thought, heading for the door.

"Be sure to return by half-past three."

---

"Great-Aunt Ernestine will no doubt be asleep," I whispered to the children as we approached the drawing room three-quarters of an hour later.

I was right. Her mouth gaped open and her chest rose and fell like a pair of bellows, while her rhythmic snores created a peculiar harmony with the hiss and sputter of the fire and the ticking of the clocks.

"Sit still and do not say a word," I told the children, pointing to the settee at right-angles to our great-aunt's chair and the fireplace.

I occupied the seat I had vacated earlier and studied the old lady. Had things turned out differently, I might have felt empathy for her decrepitude, for the general pitifulness of her advanced years. As things were, though, all I felt was a curious sense of detachment … the same detachment I had felt with Papa's demise. Like Papa, this woman did not care one whit for us. I folded my arms and cupped my chin in one hand, expelling a long breath. On second thoughts, perhaps she held us in minute affection. After all, she had given each of us the Christmas shilling, saying she wished it could have been more. And she had agreed to my proposition.

My great-aunt suddenly flopped to one side and hung over the arm of her chair; if she slipped any further she would be in danger of falling in the fire. I shot out of my seat and had just about managed to heave her upright when she came to. "'Struth, child"—she swatted at me as if I were a gnat—"what are you trying to do to me?"

"Stop you from going up in smoke. Another minute and you would have been in ---"

"Nonsense. Do stop dithering about, and sit down." Her dark eyes swept the room and finally settled on Annabel and Edwin. She blinked like a startled bird, then collected herself. "Good, everyone is present and accounted for. Except the doctor, of course." She glanced at the Roman centurion monstrosity on the mantelpiece. "Five past four. I hope he is not going to be one of those dreadfully tardy types."

Apparently the fellow was not. He arrived only fifteen minutes past the scheduled time – a miracle, given the unreliability of the railways.

Quarter past the four-oclock hour had just sounded when a knock came at the drawing room door and Prue entered.

Handing Great-Aunt Ernestine a visiting card and turning away from her to fix me with a round-eyed, slack-jawed gaze, she said, "Oh Miss Lydia, just look at you. I 'ardly would've known you."

"Prue." Great-Aunt Ernestine rose and rapped her smartly on the shoulder with her lorgnette. "Not another word to my great-niece, do you hear me? Keep your mouth closed if you value your job. Now, what about this?" She waved the card under the girl's nose. "Do I take it this gentleman is waiting?"

"Sorry, ma'am. Er … yes … 'e is. Daisy's 'elpin' 'im with 'is 'at an' coat an' galoshes. Shall I show 'im in?"

"Of course you should, you stupid girl." She followed Prue across the room. "Right away. And be ready to serve tea later, when I ring for you."

My heartbeat quickened. What if the old codger of a doctor found one or all of us had some obscure condition which made us unacceptable? What if there appeared to be something about me that gave the game away? What if …?

"Mrs. Ernestine Hadfield?"

I heard his surprisingly musical voice first. Then I saw him. And, ye gods and little fishes, he was young, thirtyish, perhaps. My first glimpse of him was in profile—strong beardless jaw, largish high-bridged nose—as he bent over my great-aunt and kissed her hand. A swatch of his blue-black hair fell forward and he swept it back as he came upright.

He had a black leather portmanteau in one hand; with the other he guided Great-Aunt Ernestine back to her seat. He stood by while she settled herself, then turned to face us and smiling a slightly lopsided smile said, "Good afternoon, children."

Annabel and Edwin responded, but all I could do was bite back a gasp. A swift train of heat traveled up my body and settled in my cheeks. Had I been standing, my knees would most certainly have buckled.

Lord save me. The face I was looking into was that of Victor, hero of my favourite *penny dreadful* novel.

## CHAPTER SIXTEEN
### *January 1888*
### *Hadfield Hall, Sussex, England*

"Lydia."

Great-Aunt Ernestine's voice returned me to my senses.

"Have you forgotten your manners, child?"

Willing the fiery tingling in my cheeks to recede, I managed to untie my tongue enough to mumble, "Good afternoon, doctor."

He tipped his head in acknowledgement. "All right then," he said, extracting a sheet of paper from his portmanteau and perusing it. "We have Edwin aged seven, Annabel aged twelve and Lydia, thirteen." He placed his case on the settee beside the children and came around behind the armchair I occupied, resting his arms on its wingback. "Has your great-aunt told you what to expect, children?" he asked.

The old lady leaned forward in her chair clearly about to speak, but Annabel forestalled her with, "No, but our sister has."

"Really?"

I felt the doctor's eyes upon me and squirmed in my seat. I should have remembered to tell the children on no account to defer to me.

"She said you will 'zamine our eyes, ears, mouth and nose," Edwin piped up. "And cook told me we should have our legs looked at, too, to make sure we do not have crickets."

A chuckle came from behind me. "I believe you mean, rickets, young man."

Rickets. Great God. What on earth was cook thinking about putting such notions in Edwin's head? I drew my knees together. I certainly was not going to allow this fellow to inspect my legs.

"What are they?" Annabel asked, with a worried frown.

No longer able to contain myself, I blurted, "It is a disease common to poor children who do not get enough fresh air or sufficient good food to eat." Oh Lord … I forgot to change my voice..

"Very good." The doctor patted my shoulder in approval.

"She is an intelligent girl," said Great-Aunt Ernestine. "Exceedingly well-read for one so young."

"Indeed she is," Doctor Latham said, suddenly leaning in on me and so startling me that I shrank back and uttered the silliest, most mortifying little squeak. In the next breath, however, my chagrin turned to satisfaction with the thought that my behavior was perfect for a thirteen-year-old girl with ridiculously-bobbing ringlets.

He unfurled and looked down at me, snaring me with his laughing hazel eyes. "And does the young lady consider an inspection for rickets a necessary component of this afternoon's examinations?"

"No she does not," I said in a high, breathless voice. "Despite our constrained circumstances, my sister and brother and I come from good stock and have not been at all malnourished." Oh Lord save me. What was I thinking? Constrained circumstances? Malnourished?

Doctor Latham raised one eyebrow. "I see," he said, retrieving his bag and extracting a stethoscope. "In that case, we will think no more about it. If you will all come over here behind the settee and stand side-by-side, I will attend to your ears, eyes, noses and mouths, as you said, Edwin, and I will also listen to your lungs and hearts."

Lungs and hearts. Oh my Lord. I could feel my face flushing again and my heartbeat speeding up as I positioned myself next to Annabel.

"Let us begin with you, my boy," the doctor said.

"But Edwin always ---"

I stopped Annabel's whining with a nudge. And when she glowered at me, I slanted a murderous look at her. Despite the role in which I had been forced to cast myself, I was still queen of this court.

"I hope you will not object, if I do a little rearranging, Mrs. Hadfield," the doctor said. "In order to ensure the best possible lighting I will need to remove the plant from the stand here and replace it with one of your oil lamps."

"Do whatever you deem necessary," my great-aunt said.

Doctor Latham worked silently, his handsome face serious. I forgot my nervousness and watched in fascination as he inserted an odd-looking instrument into my brother's ears and then used a combination of a small mirror and lit candle to view his throat and look into his eyes. When the doctor mentioned pulse-taking and reached into his inside jacket pocket for his watch, Edwin beat him to the punch and with amazing sleight of hand produced his own timepiece. "May we please use mine instead of yours?" he asked excitedly.

"By all means." The doctor placed a couple of fingers on Edwin's wrist and said, "What about a stethoscope, old chap? You would not happen to have one of those hidden away, would you?"

My brother exploded with laughter. "No, of course not. You are being silly."

"Edwin," I said sharply, forgetting myself. "You ---"

"--- are being very rude," Great-Aunt Ernestine said with deliberation. "Apologize to the doctor."

I thanked her for the rescue with a slant of my eyes, while my brother muttered a deflated, "Sorry."

Doctor Latham patted Edwin's shoulder. "Quite all right, old chap. Now"—he took up his stethoscope and applied the bell to Edwin's chest—"I want you to breathe deeply, in and out."

A minute or two more, and the examination was over. "Well, my dear fellow, you are as fit as a prize-fighter," the doctor said.

"May I listen to your heart?" Edwin asked, indicating the stethoscope hanging around the doctor's neck.

"Of course." Doctor Latham grabbed a nearby footstool and sat on it, making himself easily accessible.

Round-eyed, Edwin said, "It sounds just like one of my clocks. Tick-tock … tick-tock … tick-tock."

"Your clocks?" Doctor Latham said, having to raise his voice over the half-hour din the four in the drawing room were now making.

"He has been assisting my man with their maintenance," Great-Aunt Ernestine said as the last notes died away, "and become quite the expert in the process."

"I see." The doctor held out a hand for his stethoscope and directed Edwin to sit down on the settee again while he turned his attention to Annabel. "And what have you been busying yourself with, young lady?" He employed the same methods of examination of ears, mouth and eyes he had used with Edwin.

Annabel launched into an animated description of her daily activities, stopping only when the doctor signaled her to do so as he palpated her neck, then listened to her heart and lungs. Once he had finished, he gave her a reassuring pat on her shoulder and said, "Well, my dear girl, your work must agree with; you are in excellent health."

My sister pointed to his stethoscope. "May I listen, as Edwin did?"

"Of course," he said good-naturedly, perching on the footstool again and allowing himself to be subjected to a good five minutes of inspection.

Finally, Annabel said in a serious tone, "Good steady heart beat, Doctor Latham," and he laughed heartily while Great-Aunt Ernestine looked on with a befuddled expression.

"Now, Annabel," the doctor said, "if you will sit down next to your brother, I will see to your sister."

I sucked in a long breath and exhaled slowly, willing my heart to return to its normal beat. I looked everywhere but at the doctor as he inspected me, and I castigated myself for my earlier foolishness. This man was not Victor and this was no *penny dreadful* novel. This was cold, harsh reality. Our fate was being determined right here … right now.

"Hmmm. Pulse a little rapid," Doctor Latham said, his long, finely-boned fingers resting on my wrist. I focused on his nails; they were clean and neatly cut. Then my gaze moved to his eyelashes. Lord, they were thicker and longer than my own.

His hands were all at once on my neck, probing, caressing. *Lord ...not caressing. Exploring. Examining. He is a doctor, for pity's sake.*

Now the bell of the stethoscope pressed against my breast. My heart thrummed against my ribcage. I was breathing so fast I felt dizzy.

"Hmmm. You seem rather perturbed, Lydia." The doctor's voice purled in my ear. "None of this is frightening you, is it?"

I nodded a vehement no. *Breathe in and out, in and out, in and out.*

He pressed the back of his hand against my forehead. "You are uncommonly hot, child. Are you feeling ill?"

I pulled back and flashed him a contemptuous look, mortified that he saw me as a child, not as a woman. No sooner had the thought formed, however, than I realized the insanity of it ... the danger even, and I rushed to reassure him.

"No, doctor, I am fine, fit as a fiddle in fact, have never felt better in my life." I thought of snow and ice and frost and Arctic blasts, willed my skin to cool, my pulse to slow. A moment later, I touched my forehead and felt my eyes widen. Ye gods, I must use the power of my mind more often. "Feel for yourself," I said. "No fever whatsoever."

"By Jove, you are right." The doctor removed his hand from my forehead. "Feels perfectly normal. Must have been one of those anomalies, I suppose."

"An anomaly, most definitely," I said.

"Well, Mrs. Hadfield," Doctor Latham said, packing his instruments away in his portmanteau, "that is that, then. The three children appear to be in excellent health. All that remains, now, is for you and I to iron out the final details."

"We will do it over tea," my great-aunt told the doctor, rising and reaching for the bell pull by the mantelpiece.

"Off you pop," she said to us, with a dismissive sweep of her arm. "Go to the kitchen and tell cook I said she is to feed you well ... give you as much as you want of anything you want."

Edwin and Annabel—poor, dear innocents that they were—made a mad scramble for the door.

"You make it sound as if we are the condemned, Great-Aunt," I said without forethought, and the old lady was clearly so lost for words she did not even chastise the children for their bad manners.

I was not interested in a response. I turned on my heel and trying to maintain an aloof dignity, crossed the room stiff-backed, my shoulders squared. I took my time. I was in no hurry to rush headlong into the next chapter of my life.

I felt Doctor Latham's eyes upon me as I reached the door. I glanced over my shoulder and saw in his gaze compassion, admiration, and something else … something unidentifiable. "Do not worry, child, I will make certain you and your siblings are treated well," he said.

For some untold reason, I believed him. But I did not respond, having no idea what to say. I turned face-forward, opened the door and exited into the hall. As I quietly closed the door after myself, I heard the doctor say, "Interesting girl … something rather curious about her … something I cannot quite put my finger on."

Interesting man, I said to myself, smiling. Far more interesting than Victor.

### CHAPTER SEVENTEEN
### *January 1888*
### *Hadfield Hall, Sussex, England*

Once the wheels were set in motion, they spun with the speed of a runaway brougham.

On Monday morning, four days after Doctor Latham's visit, Great-Aunt Ernestine summoned me to the dining room. "Sit down, Lydia," she said, "and pour yourself a cup of tea."

When I had finished sugaring, milking and stirring, she said crisply, "You will be departing early tomorrow morning, so you and the children will need to pack your bags today."

*Hooray. Hooray. I can hardly wait.*

"Mason will take you to the station directly after breakfast in time for you to catch the nine o'clock train to London. Arriving there, you will change trains for the journey north to York." She unfolded—then consulted—a sheet of paper which lay on the table beside her plate. "After that you will carry on by carriage, traveling seven miles to the village of Grassington, then a further three to Brackford House."

I felt myself flush with a mixture of worry and annoyance. I took a drink of tea and clumsily replaced my cup on its saucer. This was all so ridiculous, so overwhelming. I was a novice traveler. How would I know which platform to go to, which train to take? Which ---?

"You will be quite alright, child." Great-Aunt Ernestine had clearly seen the worry on my face. She reached across the table and patted my arm.

"Someone from Brackford House will be there to meet you."

"At the station in London, you mean?"

"Yes."

"But how will he —?"

"She, actually." Lorgnette in hand, my great-aunt looked at the paper once more. "A Miss Amelia Dunn. Some sort of an assistant, I believe."

"But how will we know who she is and how will she recognize us?"

"You will take my cartes de visite and use the blank back of each to identify yourselves. Lydia, Annabel, Edwin will suffice. Your surname will not be necessary."

I took the proffered visiting cards; they were of the larger variety and well-suited to the purpose she had in mind for them.

"India ink and a nice bold hand," the old woman said.

"A string around our necks?" I asked with sarcasm.

"No, child. Safety-pinned to your front," she said earnestly.

I finished my tea, and had hardly put down my cup before Great-Aunt Ernestine was urging me up and out of my seat. "Off you pop then, Lydia," she said with a false smile. "You have a great deal to do, and the clocks are ticking away."

And dinging and donging and clanging and chirping and chiming and ringing and driving me positively insane. My pulse pounded at my temples. I covered my ears against the eleven o'clock cacophony as I made my way along the hall. Hadfield Hall was a madhouse, I thought, with bitterness. The sooner we were away from it, the better.

————

After an early breakfast the next morning, the children said their goodbyes to the staff. I had visited cook the night before and asked her to spread the word that a happy front needed to be maintained. To all intents and purposes, I told her, Edwin, Annabel and I were embarking on a thrilling excursion and I wished to maintain that illusion for as long as possible.

The plan worked admirably. By the time everyone had said his or her enthusiastic piece, the children were beside themselves with excitement and could hardly wait to be off.

Making sure they were well bundled up against the cold, I sent them outside. "You will be cooped up on the train for a great many hours," I said, "so you may as well have a jolly good play until it is time for us to depart. Keep an eye on your watch," I told Edwin, "and make sure you are at the front door on the dot of eight and ready to board the carriage."

As soon as the children were out of earshot, cook said angrily, "Damned if

I understand it. Fancy turfin' the three of you out and sendin' you to an orphanage, when there is all this room 'ere."

"It ain't fair," Daisy said.

"No, it ain't, an' no denyin'," said Prue, sniffing back little sobs. "But you are ever so clever, miss, dressin' up like that an 'all, so as you can stay with 'em."

"Thank you," I said.

Mrs. Boot must have taken to the bottle early and was already in her cups. "The mistress'll be sorry, you mark my words," she said, grasping my hands. "Yer a luv, that's what y'are, a bloomin' bleedin' luv, an' don't never let nobody tell yer no different."

"I shan't," I said, throwing my arms around the old woman and hugging her close. She had been like a grandmother to me. A friend, too, old as she was.

"'tis 'im, she said. "That coviv … conviv … connivin ol' bugger."

"King Callenforth," said cook, picking up the bread dough she had been kneading and slamming it down on the table with enough force to kill it.

"Things was all right 'fore 'e come along," Mrs. Boot said. "'tis 'im what said you was to go, yer know?"

I sank down in a nearby chair, waiting for her to continue.

"I 'eard 'em talkin' one night an' 'e says, yer mus' be strong, Ernestine, me dear. Reco'nize that yer took on too much of a burden. They'll be better off at the orphanage, I can assure yer, 'e says. an' you'll be better off with 'em out o' yer life."

I gave a rueful nod and said, "I am not a bit surprised."

"'e wants her an' 'er money all to 'imself," said cook.

"But she contends she is in difficult financial straits," I said.

"Not so difficult, I'll warrant, that she needs to throw 'er near an' dear out." Cook attacked the bread dough with renewed ferocity.

"'tis all tommyrot, if y'ask me," said Mrs. Boot.

"Well, there is nothing to be done about it, now." I rose and made the rounds, kissing first Prue, then Daisy on the cheek, hugging cook, shaking Tom Mason's hand as well as Mr. Boot's, and once again enfolding Mrs. Boot in my arms. Standing back and looking from one dear face to another, I said, "You have all been so kind. You have been like a family to us, and I thank you with all my heart." A lump rose in my throat and, afraid that I might burst into tears, I made a show of coughing behind my hand.

"Y'alright, dearie?" Mrs. Boot asked, producing a small silver flask from her apron folds. "Need a little nip?"

I sighed. "I probably do. But no, thank you. No nips for me." My voice was husky with emotion and hardly recognizable to me as my own. "I will miss you all terribly. And if it is within my power to return some day and visit you, I promise you, I will."

"You do that, me love," cook said, pausing in her kneading to draw one arm across her tear-streaked face.

"God be with yer, dearie." Mrs. Boot said, all at once seeming perfectly sober.

Unable to say another word, I nodded, raised my hand in a gesture of farewell and stumbled from the room.

By the time I entered the drawing room in search of my great-aunt, moments later, I had found my voice again. And I needed no invitation to use it.

"Another quarter of an hour and we will be out of your life for good," I said in a strident voice, so startling the old lady—who was dozing in front of the fire—that she clapped her hands to her breast and gasped for air. "Great God, child, is it your intent to have me dead and in my grave before you depart?"

I did not bother to answer, but thrust at her the identification cards I had completed the night before. "Do these meet with your approval?" I knew I was shouting, but did not care.

The old woman blinked and waved me away. "They are fine, child, just fine. Must you raise your voice so? Especially this early in the morning."

"Indeed I must, Great-Aunt, in order to make my point."

"Point ... what point?" She fumbled for her lorgnette, then peered through it as if to assess my mood.

I stood over her, hands on my hips, chin tipped at a defiant angle. "That you are a foolish old woman. And that you will live to regret what you have done."

"How dare you take that tone with me?"

"How dare you cast out your own family members?"

I felt my eyes blaze, and I leaned in on my great-aunt, glorying in my ability to intimidate her.

She shrank back. "I thought you understood," she said in a querulous voice, "I am too frail, too impecunious ... too ---"

"Piffle," I said with a toss of my head which made my annoying ringlets bounce. I straightened and stood over her. "We worked like slaves for you. We did the very best we could. You should have respected us as valued members of your family. You should have kept your own counsel, and not listened to ..." I stopped myself, realizing the futility of my outburst.

"I did what I thought was best," Great-Aunt Ernestine said in a small voice.

"Best for you, certainly not for us." I said, feeling suddenly deflated.

She reached out and put a tentative hand on my arm. "I am sorry, Lydia. Perhaps I was a little hasty. But I am afraid it is too late, now. The die is cast. And I am far too old and tired to retrace my steps."

I bit down on my bottom lip to stop it from quivering.

"You will be well treated at Brackford House. It has the finest reputation and the most genteel of orphans, from what I understand. Besides, that charming Doctor Latham assured me he would keep an eye on you."

"And do what?" I said with cynicism.

Great-Aunt Ernestine shrugged. "I thought perhaps you would derive comfort from the knowledge," she said.

I responded with a derisive sound at the back of my throat, which the old lady chose to ignore. "You must call the children in now," she said, rising laboriously. "Mason will be waiting for you."

"I am well aware of that, Great-Aunt, as are the children. Rest assured they have their instructions and will not be late."

"I will have Prue bring me my coat and bonnet, and I will see you off."

"I would much rather you did not, Great-Aunt. Let us just say goodbye here and now, and be done with it."

Without demurral she presented me with her cheek; I touched my lips to the papery skin and said, "Goodbye."

"Have faith in the Almighty," the old lady called after me as I made for the door.

"I might as well have faith in the Man in the Moon," I said under my breath.

Then, as I strode through the house, I heard in my head Mama's dear, lilting voice. *Have faith in yourself my brave, strong girl. Have faith in yourself.*

I hugged the words to myself, drawing comfort from them as I descended the front steps into that bitter winter day.

Mr. Mason was pacing alongside the carriage, slapping himself on his upper arms to keep warm. "The young'uns is already settled in," he said, stopping to hand me up into the vehicle, then clambering into his seat.

Budging Annabel over so that I could sit between her and Edwin, I glanced at their expectant, trusting faces. "So, my darlings," I said, "are you ready?"

They nodded in enthusiastic unison.

"Well, then let us get on with it." I leaned forward and rapped on the small rectangle of a window behind the driver's seat. "Tally-ho, Mr. Mason," I called out, much to the children's delight.

As the carriage creaked into motion and the wheels began to churn over the gravel drive, I gazed beyond the window at the leaden sky. I slipped one hand into Annabel's, the other into Edwin's and held on for dear life.

Lord knew what the future held for us. But at least for now I had kept my promise to Mama.

I had held our family together.

# Part Two

## CHAPTER EIGHTEEN
### January 1888
### Brackford House, Yorkshire, England

"We have arrived." The disembodied announcement startled me awake. Gradually, I became aware of the dim interior of the slow-moving carriage and the crunch of gravel under its wheels.

The voice, I realized, was that of Amelia Dunn, the pleasant-but-taciturn young woman with the pale, round face, who had accompanied us on the London to Yorkshire leg of our journey.

It had been a frustrating time, for I had been itching to ask her all sorts of questions, especially about Doctor Latham. Was he married, for instance? Did he live at Brackford House? Was he as congenial a fellow as he had seemed? But I had to remind myself of my new role and remember the adage that children were to be seen and not heard.

I did ask her, however, if she were an official at Brackford House. She laughed and said, "No child, not an official. More of a lackey."

I feigned ignorance. "What on earth is that, Miss?" I asked.

"An errand-runner. A fetcher of children, such as you three. A Jack—or should I say, a Jill—of all trades. I help Mrs. Bell—Matron, as she prefers to be called—in a multitude of ways."

I liked the young woman's voice. It had the same sing-songy cadence as that of the Cornish couple who had been members of Papa's congregation.

"The house is directly ahead," Miss Dunn said, now, and I eased my stiff, aching body upright in my seat, careful not to disturb Annabel and Edwin, who were lolling against me. They had fallen asleep shortly after we had left the village of Grassington, while I must have followed suit sometime later.

"I cannot see a thing," I said, craning my neck.

"You will, in a minute."

As if she had directed it, the watery moon slipped from behind a cloud, and hung above the skeleton of what appeared to be a sycamore, affording me my first view of Brackford House. Like the rectory, but at least three times its size, the gray stone house was the ubiquitous Georgian style -- a two storey box with multi-paned rectangular windows; above—within the high-pitched roof space—were attic rooms with dormers. In the centre of the roof was a tall chimney from which a plume of smoke rose. There were two more chimneys, one at each end of the edifice.

Puzzled, I said, "The house is very dark. Except for a flicker of what looks like firelight in the third window to the right of the front door, there does not appear to be a single light showing."

"Doubtless everyone is in the dining hall, which is at the back an' in a separate building. The main meal is served at the end of the day. After that, there are evening prayers, then bed."

Lord, how dreary, I thought. No reading, no dominoes or ludo, no charades or cards. Despite our heavy workload at Hadfield Hall, the children and I had always found time for games or books before bed.

"Every single night?" I asked.

"Except Saturday. Dinner is served at noon, then there is tea at four an' no prayers that night."

I could not muster any enthusiasm. I merely grunted a response.

The carriage continued on past the front door and the wide flight of steps leading up to it, rounded the corner and in a moment, reached a cobbled yard at the rear.

"You had best rouse your brother an' sister, now," Miss Dunn said.

By the time we had chattered across the cobbles and come to a stop outside a well-lit, detached single-storey building directly across from the back of the main house, I had managed to wake both the children.

Annabel yawned, stretched and asked, "Where are we?"

"At Brackford House," Amelia Dunn answered.

"I am hungry, Liddy," Edwin said.

"Me, too," said Annabel.

After a tick, I said—as a thirteen-year-old would—"Me, too."

Edwin held up his watch to the meagre light. "It is is two hours past our tea time."

"Six o'clock? Good Lor ... Goodness," I said. "No wonder we are starving, Miss."

"Well," Amelia Dunn said, "you see this building here?"

We all nodded that we did.

"It contains the kitchen an' the dining hall. So, if you will follow me"—she was already out of her seat and opening the carriage door—"after I have had a word about your luggage with Baxter, the driver, I will see what Mrs. Jessop, our cook, can come up with for the three of you, an' for me. You are not the only ones who are ravenous."

With her monumental bosom and plump red face, Mrs. Jessop was cut from the same cloth as Hadfield Hall's Mrs. Catterly. Her demeanour, however, was entirely different. She had about her a slovenly air, was hard-eyed and tight-lipped, and I could have sworn she smelled of ale.

Clearly having dealt with the cook before, Miss Dunn smiled and nodded through the woman's diatribe about rules and mealtimes and all the extra work involved in serving food after regular hours. "You are absolutely right, Mrs. Jessop, to be upset," she said with an unctuousness I found sickening, but at once realized was calculated. "Our delay was unavoidable due to our day-long journey. An' we would be most grateful—would we not, children?—if you would be good enough to make an exception an' provide us with a little sustenance."

*For God's sake feed us, you great lump.* "Most grateful," I said, giving Annabel a nudge which she passed on to Edwin. Then the two parroted the two words.

"Alright then, just this once," the cook said with a sour expression.

Just this once? The woman was an absolute numbskull. As if we would be charging about the country again, when we were going to be inmates here for Lord knew how long.

Turning away from us and trudging across the stone floor to a large black-leaded range, she called over her shoulder. "Sit yerselves down over there at the table."

We did as we were told, then waited as she noisily dished out food from a couple of copper saucepans, then forked slices of some kind of meat from a large oval platter.

"Lucky for you all them other little 'eathens didn' eat the lot," she said, standing over us, arms akimbo, after she had set down a plate in front of each of us.

The food was not a patch on Mrs. Catterly's, the bill of fare consisting of cold roast beef, boiled potatoes—eyes included—and cabbage.

Nevertheless, we all wolfed it down.

When Edwin had finished cleaning his plate, he piped up, "Is there any pudding, cook?"

"Lord love us." Mrs. Jessop let out a great guffaw. "Is there any puddin', cook? says 'e." She slapped the tabletop with her ham of a hand, making us jump out of our skins and causing Miss Dunn to drop her fork on her plate and her knife on the floor. Once she had retrieved the utensil, she said in a quiet, even voice,"There is no pudding served at Brackford House, Edwin."

Clearly bent on having the last word, my brother said under his breath, "Mrs. Catterly always gave us pudding," and I tried to kick him under the table, but missed.

"Thank you, Mrs. Jessop." Amelia Dunn quickly got to her feet and indicated with a dip of her head that we should follow suit.

"Yes, we all thank you, too," I said, slanting a look at my sister and brother, "do we not?"

"Yes," they said.

"Hmmm." The cook mopped her sweaty brow with her apron. "Yer will not be gettin' no more special meals like this, yer know. An' yer sure as eggs is eggs"—she thrust her whiskered chin forward to emphasize her point—"will not be gettin' no puddin'."

*If I had pudding I would empty it over your fat head, then stuff it down your throat.* "Of course, Mrs. Jessop." I smiled sweetly. "We understand."

"Come along then, children," Miss Dunn said, clearly having no desire to linger. "We have a great deal to do before this day is over."

—

"Now, you girls need to change into these nightdresses." Amelia Dunn thrust the linen garments at us. "They are all the same size, so it makes no difference which one you choose."

"What about Edwin, Miss?" I asked.

"Edwin is no concern of yours." She had grabbed his hand and was holding onto it.

"Through that door behind you, you will find a bathing an' changing room. So give yourselves a wash while you are at it. Meanwhile, I will take Edwin over to the boys' wing,"

"Boys' wing, what boys' wing? Edwin must stay with me, Miss … with us," I said.

"Yes. Otherwise he will be ever so frightened," Annabel said.

Looking anxiously from Annabel to me, then to Amelia Dunn, Edwin did his best to free his hand from hers. But she hung on to him. "Frightened or not —an' he has no need to be—he cannot stay here with you. Boys an' girls are housed in different wings. But you have no cause to fret, you will be able to see your brother."

"When?" I asked.

"Soon. Tomorrow I should think. This is not a prison, Lydia. But there are rules that must be followed."

"But who will take care of him?"

"Mr. Hazelhurst is in charge of the boys."

"But we have never been separated before," Annabel said.

"Liddy"—Edwin tugged and twisted his hand, but all to no avail—"I want to stay with you and Annabel."

Amelia Dunn gritted her teeth in determination, released Edwin's hand momentarily and grabbed him by his upper arm. "Come along, young man. You do not want to get your sisters into trouble do you? You most certainly will if you disobey me."

The lie did the trick. With one last imploring glance over his shoulder, Edwin allowed himself to be led away. "Get into your nightdresses, girls," Miss Dunn called out. "I have a little more business to attend to after I deliver Edwin, but I should be back in quarter of an hour."

She was true to her word. I had Edwin's watch to prove it. During dinner I had surreptitiously persuaded him to give it to me for safekeeping. I would guard it with my life, I had told him.

"Is Edwin alright," I asked.

"Of course he is," Miss Dunn said. "He and Mr. Hazelhurst are getting on famously. As I told you, you have no need to worry about him, Lydia."

*Of course I do, you silly woman. He is a small, vulnerable boy with nobody but me to protect him.*

"I hope you are right, Miss," I said.

"You have other things than your brother to think about, now. First of all, there are your uniforms." Miss Dunn went to a tall cupboard on a nearby wall, and unlocked it with the key she retrieved from her pocket. She reached in, then handed each of us a frock in a faded moss green wool, along with one pair of drawers and a cotton petticoat each."

"Everyone wears the same," Miss Dunn said. "Yours is for an eleven-year-old," she told Annabel. "Yours for a thirteen-year-old," she said to me.

Simultaneously, we examined the frocks and underwear. It took only an instant for us to reach the same conclusion. "You take these," I said. "And I will take yours," said Annabel.

"There is a darn in this frock," she said, frowning over a spot on the bodice.

"The sleeve seam on this one has been mended," I said.

"They will be darned an' mended a sight more before they are done with," Miss Dunn said.

"What about our own clothes?" I asked. "And what happened to our suitcases?"

"You will have a trunk under your bed in which to store the clothes you have on. An' as for your cases, they are on the bottom shelf in the cupboard here."

I bent down to take a look.

"When you grow out of the clothes you have been given, we will see about providing you with a larger size."

Of course, no danger of that existed as far as I was concerned. And as for Annabel and Edwin, it did not bear thinking about. To do so, would beg the question I had no desire to ponder: What would happen after Brackford House?

I felt my shoulders slump. Things were looking worse by the minute. But at least, thank the Lord, I still had my own petticoat. Sewn into the waist was the special pocket I had made; in it was the portrait miniature of Mama, our shillings from Great-Aunt Ernestine, Annabel's seed pearl brooch and now, Edwin's precious watch.

Amelia Dunn closed and locked the cupboard and then gestured for us to follow her. "I will take you across to the house, now, then upstairs to your dormitory. It must be close to half-past seven. Everyone is allowed thirty minutes of leisure before bedtime at eight o'clock, so you will have a chance to acquaint yourselves with the other children."

———

The chatter from a clutch of girls gathered around a glowing fire at the far end of the dormitory stopped dead when I closed the door behind us.

The room was illuminated by two oil lamps positioned one each end of the mantelpiece, as well as candles burning beside each of the forty or so beds, some of which were occupied.

I spoke in a low voice. "Beds fifteen and sixteen are ours; the numbers are hanging on the wall at the head of each, according to Miss Dunn. I see number one here, on the right, so ours must be ... Come on." Clutching my uniform under one arm, I took Annabel's hand and urged her along with me.

"Here we are," I said, stopping several beds down the row, "Fifteen and sixteen."

The occupants of seventeen and eighteen craned for a good look at us, then smiled and murmured low, "Hellos".

Looking over her shoulder, Annabel whispered, "Why are they all staring at us?"

"You mean the ones by the fireplace?"

She nodded.

"Because we are the new girls, I imagine. No doubt they were subjected to the same scrutiny when they first arrived at Brackwood House. The best thing to do is ignore them."

Annabel sat on the edge of her bed while I followed my own advice and looked around with studied nonchalance. The high-arched ceiling and lofty semi-circular-headed windows reminded me of of St. John's. The dormitory looked about as long as the rectory's back garden, but was a great deal narrower, with a bare, scrubbed pine floor and a central aisle, a few feet wide, separating the rows of identical iron bedsteads. Under each bed was a shallow-looking trunk about the size of a child's coffin, and next to each, a simple one-drawer, wooden stand bearing a candle in a copper holder.

Whoever had been charged with the room's decoration must have had the same penchant for green as did the maker of our frocks; the walls were painted a light-but-sickly shade and the blankets on the beds were bottle green.

I undid the top button on my nightdress now, and rolled my shoulders. The room felt oppressive and the heavy linen made me itch. But at least the garment was clean and roomy ... a regular marquee, if the truth were known, and heaven-sent after that scratchy woolen frock of Annabel's.

"Well, I suppose we'd best see to the business at hand and put away our clothes." I bent down and pulled out the trunk from beneath my bed. Annabel did the same, and as she lifted the lid, said under her breath, "They are still staring."

My nerves jangled. I dabbed at my sweat-beaded upper lip. Ye gods and little fishes, being stared at was the very least of my troubles. Aside from not knowing what in creation was in store for us here, I had Edwin to fret about.

"I said they are still ---"

"I heard you," I said, fighting for composure. Poor Annabel's anxieties were beginning to get the better of her. "And as I said," I continued, softly, reassuringly, "we need to put away our clothes. Then, we shall see about perhaps befriending the gawpers."

Moments later, my task completed, I pushed the trunk back under my bed and then did the same for Annabel." Straightening, I turned to face the silent onlookers who—like us—were clad in long-sleeved, high-necked nightdresses.

"Good evening," I said. "I am Lydia Fullerton and this is my sister, Annabel."

A general shuffling of feet and fidgeting followed and then someone—a female I thought, although the voice was gruff—said, "Well la-di-da. So what do yer fink yer doin'?"

Annabel and I exchanged a puzzled look. In the dim light, determining which girl had spoken was an impossibility.

"Yer cannot just take any bed yer pleases." The knot of watchers unravelled and the owner of the disembodied voice—a girl head-and-shoulders above everyone else, and with a peculiar rolling gait—advanced down the aisle towards us, a motley entourage of about a dozen or so girls in tow.

My heartbeat quickened as she drew near. I put my arm around Annabel's waist and pulled her close. So much for Great-Aunt Ernestine's assurances about the refinement of Brackwood's orphans. This beastly-looking girl with dull, close-set eyes and a mouth as wide and slack as a toad's, had bully scrawled all over her face. She stopped at the foot of my bed and, like a malevolent genie, planted herself, arms folded across her chest.

I swallowed hard. She was three times my size. Size had nothing to do with anything, I reminded myself. Remember what you always told Edwin. I stretched myself to my full height, arched one sardonic eyebrow and said in as bored a tone as I could muster, "I beg your pardon, but I fear you are vastly mistaken."

The girl's eyes flared. "Well, la-di-da." She turned to her cronies. "'er ladyship fears I am vastly mistaken."

"Indeed she does," I said, my dander rising. "We were assigned these beds by Miss Dunn." I removed my arm from Annabel's waist. "Sit on yours," I said, nudging her towards it as I sat on mine. "And we have absolutely no intention of moving from them."

"Well, la-di-da again." The girl leaned over me and brought her face so close to mine I could smell her sour breath. "I'm the boss 'ere. Agatha Neeves is me name. What I says goes. An' what I says is get yer bleedin' bods off the bleedin' beds. Ain't that right, girls?"

"Yes," chorused her minions.

I turned away, for a moment, to escape the foul odour, and caught Annabel's distraught eye. Mercy, she looked as if she were about to go into hysterics. Exactly the sort of reaction bullies loved. What to do … what to say? Nothing? Of course not. I must do something. Stand up to this dreadful individual … call her bluff. But what if she became violent? What if …?

"Eh, you, Miss beggin'-yer-pardon. Lost yer tongue, 'ave yer?"

Before I had a chance to think of a response, her big hand snaked out and yanked open the neck of my nightdress. "Got any tits in there?" she said.

I jerked away, my face burning with embarrassment and rage. "How ... how dare you?" I sputtered.

"Oh, laaaa-di-da. 'Ow dare I, is it? Same way I dare this." She gave me a shove and I fell back. "Get yer arses off the bed like I told yer or ..."

"Lydia, can we not just do what ---?"

"No." I struggled to a sitting position. "Absolutely not. My sister and I will not move and you cannot make us." Oh, horrors ... just look at the creature, she was turning six shades of purple. That deuced hasty tongue again. Mama had always said it would get me into trouble. But I could not ... would not retreat now. "This is my bed. And that is my sister's, so I suggest you remove that ungainly bod of yours, and continue on about your business leaving us to see to ours."

"That's it. Yer've gone an' done it good an' proper, now." Agatha Neeves rocked from side to side, fists clenched, and I inched back, reaching a protective arm out towards Annabel.

"Made me purely mad, yer 'ave." The beastly thing raised her fists like a fighter about to take on an opponent. "Been ever so naughty yer 'ave. An' I've got just the thing for them what's naughty ... 'aven't I, ladies?"

Ladies? They were sheep. I should not have been a bit surprised if instead of "Yes" they had said, "Ba-aa—aaaaa."

"Know what it is?" The girl left the question hanging for a moment, then turned to her cronies. "Tell 'em," she said, "tell this pair what it is."

"The cane," they said as one.

"The cane," came a startling echo from a single female voice, "which will shortly descend upon the posterior of Miss Agatha Neeves—wait by the door girl—and on the posterior of anyone else of similar persuasion."

Agatha Neeves hestitated only long enough to fix me with a murderous look, then she slunk away and the gaggle of girls scattered. From their midst emerged a tall, black-clad woman with shoulders as broad as a man's. She strode across the pine boards, stopping within a couple of feet of us, her bespectacled eyes gleaming in the lamplight. "Do I make myself clear?" she called over her shoulder.

A unanimous, "Yes, Matron," followed.

"Tomorrow, each of you will go without breakfast," she continued, "and proceed directly to your assigned work. Meanwhile, there will be no more leisure time for you tonight. You will get into your beds, now."

The Agatha Neeves contingent scurried to do the woman's bidding. Annabel and I followed suit, unsure whether or not we were included in the directive.

"And the instant I depart the dormitory," Matron continued, "you"—she indicated the red-headed girl in bed eighteen—" will turn down the oil lamps and then all of you will extinguish your candles."

Pointing first at Annabel and then at me," she added, "And there will be no further interference with these newcomers. Do I make myself clear?"

The sheep bleated, "Yes, Matron," and while the woman's attention was focused on the flock, I sent Annabel a triumphant look.

The woman turned back to us. "As for the two of you … I will expect you upstairs in my study at eight a.m. You will proceed there directly after breakfast."

"May we know what time breakfast is served and where?" I asked.

"7:00 a.m. in the dining hall. Just follow the crowd."

"Thank you for rescuing us, ma'am," Annabel said, her usual exuberance returning.

The hint of a smile touched the woman's lips. "Not ma'am, child. Matron, as you surely must have heard." She brushed something off her sleeve, then looked up. "And you are …?"

"Annabel Fullerton."

The woman turned to me and raised a questioning eyebrow.

"Lydia Fullerton," I said.

"Do not be alarmed by what happened here this evening." Her thin lips parted in a smile. "I can assure you, children, there will be no repetition of this nasty business. You will be perfectly safe here at Brackford House."

But all the smiles … all the reassurances in the world could not convince me. And I knew with absolute certainty more nasty business loomed ahead.

## CHAPTER NINETEEN
### *January 1888*
### *Brackford House, Yorkshire, England*

After breakfast the next morning, at a few minutes before eight, Miss Dunn intercepted us on our way up the broad, curving staircase. "Follow me," she said, "an' I will show you where Matron's study is."

"Will our brother be there?" I asked as we climbed.

"I have no idea, child. Matron is the one you will have to talk to about that, not me. I must warn you though, she is in a bit of a tizzy today on account o' the Bishop's visit, so she may not be in the best of humours."

Miss Dunn hustled us along until we reached the end of a wide, carpeted hall. Opening the door there, she directed us to two chairs positioned on one side of a mahogany partners' desk, across from a single, swivel chair of imposing proportions which I assumed was Matron's.

"I will leave you to it, then," the young woman said. "She should not be long."

I vacated my seat long enough to go and stand on tiptoe before the large oval mirror above the mantelpiece. Thanks to hour upon hour of traveling and a night spent tossing and turning, my ridiculous ringlets had died a natural death. Having initially thought them a necessary part of my disguise, I now realized I was better off without them. I needed to blend in with the rest of the girls and draw as little attention as possible to myself. To that end, on rising this morning, I had simply drawn my hair back off my forehead and twisted it into a loose coil at my nape, securing it there with several hairpins. I tucked a few wayward curls behind my ears, now, but they refused to be tamed and in the end, I let them have their way.

"You look older with your hair like that," said Annabel.

Returning to my seat, I said. "It does not matter as long as we continue to keep up the pretense."

"Oh we will … on pain of death."

I smiled. "I certainly hope we do not have to go that far."

An onyx clock on the mantelpiece struck eight and I clapped my hands over my ears, steeling myself for the racket that was bound to follow.

"You have no need to do that, Lydia." Annabel shouted to make herself heard. "There is only one clock. See." She made a broad sweep of the room with her arm. I glanced about, confirming the truth of her statement, then uncovered my ears. Of course, this was a normal house, not the domain of a looney old lady.

It was, however, the domain of *toad face*, as Annabel had christened the bully. Fortunately, she had not returned to the dormitory last night. "If yer worried about Agatha, do not waste yer time," the girl in bed eighteen had whispered after lights-out. "'T'will be The Punishment Room for 'er ternight."

I would have inquired as to the nature of this room, but exhaustion overrode curiosity and the only words I managed to say were, "Thank you," before I fell into a fitful sleep.

I yawned and stretched, now, aware of myriad little aches and pains in various parts of my body. The lumpy straw mattress I had slept on might just as well have been a bed of nails for all the ease it had provided.

For the time being at least—if I put aside my worries about Edwin—these pleasant surroundings afforded me a measure of comfort. A coal fire burned in the grate and the gleaming hearth brasses—fender and fireplace tools and trivets—reflected its glow and made the room feel cosy, as did the rich, burgundy-hued Axminster carpet beneath my feet.

Outside the day was clear and bright and the sun poured in through velvet-curtained French doors a few feet behind the desk, gilding the room's oak-paneled walls. As in Papa's study, there were books everywhere whose old leather smell mingled with the lavender scent of furniture polish.

I made a face. No doubt Annabel and I would be among those doing the polishing and dusting from now on … and Lord knew what else. This was no finishing school, after all, where one whiled away the hours studying the classics or painting china or perfecting one's French in preparation for *The Grand Tour.*

Lulled by the warmth and the sun's benevolent light, I closed my eyes, slouched down in my chair and started to drift off. The concurrent rattle of the doorknob and Annabel's, "She is here," brought me back to earth.

Matron made for her swivel chair and took a moment to settle into it before leaning forward, elbows on the desktop, and studying us. "Well rested, I hope?"

I was tempted to harrumph, but thought better of it. Annabel saved me from the need to respond by saying, "I slept like a top, Matron."

"Good. And breakfast was to your liking I trust?"

*Oh but of course. The thick-as-glue porridge and the weak-as-dishwater tea were indescribably delicious.* "Certainly," I said.

Matron dipped her chin and regarded Annabel over the tops of her spectacles. "And to your liking, child?"

Annabel had had a fit earlier, saying loud enough to turn several heads in the dining hall that if this was the kind of food they were going to be expected to eat, then she would rather starve.

I watched her, now, out of the corner of my eye. That she was nibbling on her lower lip, clearly pondering her response did not bode well. No, no, no, you must not express your opinions about the cuisine, I thought, stretching my leg out to the side and giving her a kick on the shin with my boot toe. I responded to her sidelong glare with one of my pointed looks and said sweetly, "We were both very happy with breakfast, were we not?"

After a nerve-wracking few seconds, Annabel said, "Yes".

"Good," Matron said. "Proper sustenance is most important. Now, let us get down to business, shall we?"

I raised a hesitant hand and she arched an eyebrow at me. "Yes?"

"Our brother, Edwin, was separated from us when we arrived last night? Are we going to be able to see him this morning, Matron?"

"We will discuss your brother later. Meanwhile, you will listen attentively, remembering the rule to speak only when spoken to, and I will tell you about our very special mission here at Brackford."

For some untold reason, the words very special mission made me nervous and I edged forward in my chair and grasped its arms.

"We pride ourselves, here, on our ability to provide the very finest training," the woman said.

Training in what? I thought.

And, like a mind-reader, the woman answered, "Where you two girls are concerned—along with your regular schooling in reading, writing and arithmetic—you will be instructed in the rudiments of housekeeping. Cleaning, cooking, provisioning, sewing, etcetera. That is to say, all the proper womanly skills."

"But miss …" Annabel raised a hesitant hand.

Matron frowned. "What is it, girl?"

"We can already read and write and do arithmetic and I can cook and sew, too."

"As I said before, you are to speak only when spoken to. Is that understood, child?"

Annabel's cheeks flushed and she shook her head in mute agreement.

I stretched my foot to the side and reassured her with a gentle rub of my boot toe up and down the side of her calf.

"And as for the brother you were so anxious to discuss earlier, you will be pleased to know that he will be trained in male pursuits. He will help maintain the grounds and the buildings, grow vegetables, care for the farm animals, and so on and so forth. In this way, we leave not so much as a pebble unturned in preparing all of you children—female and male alike—for your …" Here, she hesitated, creaked back in her chair, threw her arms wide and, as if unfurling a banner, said, slowly, dramatically, "GREAT ADVENTURE."

My favourite phrase, I thought, sardonically. Designed to deceive, for certain. Worry made me forget myself and I asked with ill-disguised belligerence, "So what great adventure might that be, Matron?"

No sooner had I uttered the words, than I realized my gaffe. Never mind that I had used such an insolent tone and had disobeyed the not speaking-until-spoken-to rule, thirteen-year-old children positively did not quiz adults.

But surprisingly—and fortunately—Matron appeared unfazed. "Why your voyage across the Atlantic, child, on a steamship, to the great new world of the Dominion of Canada. You are to be pioneers—and capable pioneers, at that—exceedingly well-versed in all the skills I have mentioned."

Pioneers? Canada? I glanced sidelong at Annabel. She looked as dazed as I felt. "We were told we were to live here in Yorkshire," I said. Let her chastise me for speaking up. I did not care. "Now you say we are to be sent away … overseas." Incredulous, I shook my head. "For how long, and to where, exactly?"

"Five years will be the term of your … apprenticeship. After you have met that commitment, you will be free to do as you wish, stay on or return to England."

"Are we to be sent to the gold fields, then? And will we come back here millionaires," I asked with sarcasm.

"Are we going to be rich, Lydia?" Annabel piped up, clearly also forgetting the rules.

"Quiet." Matron rapped on the desktop with her letter-opener. "That is quite enough from both of you. You will hold your tongues, and attend to what I have to say."

I studied my lap and rolled one thumb around the other. This was all too much to absorb. My head was spinning, my thoughts whirring about like angry bluebottles.

Matron started up again. "There is a dire need for your services with families in the District of Saskatchewan and Provinces such as Manitoba, British Columbia and Ontario. After twelve months of training here at Brackford, and as soon thereafter the date of its completion as passage on a steamship can be arranged, you will travel by sea and land to our Distribution Centre in Ontario. From there you will each proceed to your assigned family."

Horrified, I reared up out of my seat. "What do you mean by you will each," I asked. "Are you saying that once we are transported to that godforsaken place, we will be separated?"

Matron opened her mouth to speak, but I cut her off. "We cannot be. We will not be. We ---"

"Lydia." Annabel's anxious cry returned me to my senses. I glanced from her to Matron, noting the black-as-thunder expression on the woman's face, and I realized at once the foolhardiness of my behavior.

"I am sorry, so sorry," I said to Matron. "Please forgive me." Remembering my counterfeit age, I conjured a tear or two and a catch in my voice. "I am a thoughtless, rude, and ungrateful girl. A frightened girl, too, who has only recently been torn from the bosom of her family. And I will understand if you feel the need to punish me." I would have continued on with more drivel, but my rhetoric had done the trick, I noted, and on Matron's face something resembling empathy appeared to have replaced anger.

"Normally," she said, appearing to collect herself, "an outburst such as yours would result in immediate confinement in The Punishment Room."

That room again. A cell? A torture chamber? What exactly was it, I wondered.

"However," Matron continued, "since it is your first day, I shall make allowances." She examined the blade of her letter opener, then fixed me with a direct look. "And in answer to your earlier question, I shall tell you, now, that it has never been the policy here at Brackford House to separate siblings."

I let out a long, audible breath. Thank God. Whatever befell us, it did not matter as long as we were able to stay together.

"As I was about to explain before our little … interruption, you will be billeted with a farm family who will give you a roof over your heads, food, and of course, work. You will be well ---"

A sharp rap on the door interrupted Matron's continued discourse.

"Come in," she said, frowning in obvious annoyance.

Miss Dunn poked her head in. "So sorry to interrupt, Matron," she said, "but a situation has arisen and your presence is required."

The woman tutted and got up. At the door she conferred in a low voice with Miss Dunn. Then she turned to us and said, "Since you both are able to read, you may each select a book from the shelves and sit quietly in an armchair by the fire until I return. I should not be more than a quarter of an hour."

Neither of us was in the mood for reading, so we did not take Matron up on her offer of books. We did however opt for the armchairs. Annabel promptly nodded off in hers while I sat and stewed.

Ye gods and little fishes ... Canada. Red Indians and tomahawks and—my hand went to my crown—scalpings. And what about Edwin? Where in creation was he? And assuming he was brought here, what then? Would we have daily contact with him ... at meal times and during leisure hours, assuming such hours existed? Would it be here in the girls' wing? If not, where, for mercy's sake?

I aimed a disconsolate kick at the brass fireplace fender, and the scrape of my boot toe against the metal awoke Annabel. "Is Edwin here yet?" she said sleepily. "Did Matron go and fetch him?"

"No," I answered more sharply than I had intended.

"Do you suppose he ran away?" Annabel sat forward, anxious fists to her mouth.

"Of course not." Mercy, off Annabel went on one of her flights of fancy. "The situation Matron is attending to may have something to do with him. She may well bring him back here with her."

Annabel grinned. "You really think so?"

Ye gods, I had no idea. Better distract her, or she would drive me insane with her questions. I bent over the hearth, grabbed the brass poker and came up with it brandished like a sword. "If she does, then we three cavaliers will …" I stopped for effect, my weapon poised, and Annabel broke into a delighted cackle.

I thrust and parried, staying well back from Annabel so as not to risk injuring her and her laughter egged me on. "As I said, we three cavaliers will ready ourselves for Matron's stupendously great ad ... ven..." I raised the poker, preparing for my dramatic finale, and then sang out "ture" in a long, throaty contralto.

"If I were you, I should definitely watch my back."

I froze, listening to the sound of the door closing. Great God, had Matron returned already? No, silly, this was a man's voice, deep and musical. Something vaguely familiar about it. How could that be? I did not know any men here, except for the driver and he was elderly with a gruff voice.

Oh, ye gods, Miss Dunn had mentioned something about the bishop coming today. I stood rooted. *Annabel, do stop grinning like a lunatic.* What to say .. what to do? *Turn around, nincompoop.*

It seemed to take forever for that pirouette. And when I came to a halt, my mind registered a tall man whose shoulders seemed to fill the doorway, before my eyes settled dazedly on his throat. No dog collar, but a cravat in shades of russet and black. My gaze crept up as he advanced. Above the cravat, a clean-shaven chin, with a little vertical crease in the middle; a slightly lopsided mouth over even, white teeth; a mouth that was smiling, now, and speaking. Great god. A familiar mouth. My own went dry. Doctor Latham's.

"The enemy can be a deuce of a problem if you do not face him," he said. "He can creep up on you and have you disarmed before you can say Brackford House."

"Huh? Oh … I … er." My tongue seemed to have swollen, making speech difficult, and I felt a fiery tingling in my cheeks.

He stepped forward to the chair I had vacated and leaned over, resting his elbows on its wingback. His eyes sparkled with laughter, at my expense, I thought with chagrin. "Lydia, right?"

I nodded.

"I should put that away, child, if I were you. I have seen some rather nasty things happen with pokers."

I glanced down and was mortified not only to see the dratted poker still in my hand, but to realize he had called me child, and I flashed him a withering look, tempted to set him straight. But by the time I had returned the poker to its stand and taken a couple of calming breaths, I had composed myself enough to say in a small, meek voice, "Thank you, doctor, for the advice."

"Glad to be of assistance," he said to me, holding my gaze for what seemed an interminably long moment, then to my sister who was looking up at him with adoring eyes, "And how are you settling in, young lady? Annabel … if I remember correctly."

"I do not know," she said. "I know I hated the porridge this morning."

Phillip Latham threw back his head and laughed. "And you, Lydia, did you hate it also?"

"I … er … I …" I did not get a chance to finish. For at that instant, through the door burst Matron with Amelia Dunn in tow.

"Oh thank the Lord, doctor," Matron said, striding across the room and leaving Miss Dunn to hover in the background. "I have been searching everywhere for you."

"Whatever is it?" Doctor Latham asked.

"It is one of today's new arrivals -- the Fullerton boy. He turned into a positive fiend when they went to cut his hair. The scissors slipped and ---"

"What in God's name have you done to Edwin?" I felt the floor pitch under my feet, I heard my own voice as if from far off. "You have killed him. You have killed my brother."

## CHAPTER TWENTY
### *January 1888*
### *Brackford House, Yorkshire, England*

I gasped for breath. Something had exploded in my nose and sizzled behind my eyes and everything rushed in on me, now. Fear ... horror ... fury. My heart climbed into my throat. Oh dear God ... Edwin ... my sweet brother. Had they ...? Was he ...? I struggled to get up, scrubbing at my eyes and sniffing. "What on earth have you done to me?" I asked.

"Smelling salts," came the response, as two pairs of hands assisted me to my feet. Miss Dunn's face loomed into view, and alongside it Annabel's.

"I am afraid you fainted," the woman said, "and Matron charged me with the task of reviving you." Handing me a handkerchief and gesturing for my sister to get out of the way, she sat me down in the nearest armchair and stood over me.

"My brother?" I dabbed at my eyes with the handkerchief then quickly blew my nose. "Please tell me, is he dea---?"

"Absolutely not. When Matron rushed into the staff room and enlisted my help, she said your brother was hurt. If it had been anything worse, she most certainly would have told me."

"Badly hurt?"

"Afraid I have no idea. I was not made privy to any further information."

At least Edwin was alive, praise be. Weak with relief, I slumped in my chair. "How long ago did she and the doctor leave?"

"Two or three minutes at most."

"You almost hit your head on the fender when you fell," Annabel told me, her eyes brimming with tears.

"But you are none the worse for your fall and there is no cause for alarm," Miss Dunn said.

"Where is my brother?" I asked.

"In the infirmary."

"I suppose it could be hours before we are able to see him."

"You may well be right, child. All I know is, my instructions are to wait here with you until Matron returns. Do please for mercy's sake stop hovering, Annabel. Sit down across from your sister."

No sooner had Annabel settled in her chair than I rose. I could not possibly sit still. I was still pacing one hour later when Matron finally reappeared. I stopped in my tracks and hugged myself around my ribcage, afraid any bad news might cause me to fall apart.

Annabel edged forward on her chair, pressed her fingertips to her mouth and let out a tiny whimper.

"Come along then," Matron said briskly, standing at the door and to my amazement, gesturing for us to precede her through it. "If you wish to see your brother, then you had better get a move on."

"How is he?" I asked, hurrying to keep up with her.

"A little battle-worn."

I grimaced at her choice of words, imagining my brother embroiled in a David versus Goliath battle.

"But a day's bed rest and the boy will be fit as ninepence."

Bed rest sounded rather innocuous. I reached for Annabel's hand and squeezed it. Perhaps things were not as dire as I had thought.

"Here we are." Matron had brought us to a stop outside a door marked, INFIRMARY. "Nurse Jamieson is expecting you," she said. "I shall return for you—Annabel—in half an hour, at which time you"-—she tipped her head at me—"are to present yourself in Doctor Latham's office. He has expressed a desire to have a few words with you."

My heart flipped. "Really?" Ye gods, had he cottoned on to me? No, of course, not. Why would he? I had been careful to appear pathetically deferential and childlike?

"Once your meeting with the doctor is over you will find your way back to my study, where your sister and I will be waiting." She dipped her chin and looked at me over the tops of her spectacles, clearly expecting a response.

At my, "Very well," she turned on her heel and strode off, saying over her shoulder, "No need to knock. Just go on in."

The first thing I noticed as I pushed open the double doors and stopped on the threshold was the strong smell of disinfectant; the next was the wave of heat enveloping us. It came from the mountain of a coal fire blazing in the marble fireplace centered on the wall to our right. With its Grecian columns and an abundance of molded flowers, swags and urns, it looked more suited to an aristocrat's drawing room than a hospital.

"Cozy is it not?" A short, wide woman clad in a black frock with starched white collar and cuffs and a white apron, suddenly materialized alongside us.

We nodded in surprised unison.

"Och I am Nurse Jamieson," she said. "An' you must be the Fullerton lasses lookin' for yer wee brother." So strong was her Scottish burr that she pronounced the word *brither.*

Again, Annabel and I nodded, and I said, "Indeed we are nurse … and most anxiously."

"This way then." She indicated for us to follow her along a row of about a dozen iron beds set against the wall opposite the fireplace. Sickroom or not, daylight streamed in through several large, rectangular windows whose curtains were drawn back.

A girl with rivulets of perspiration running down her fiery cheeks tossed and turned in the first bed; in the next, a white-faced tot lay still as an effigy. Two beds were occupied by boys with shorn heads, coughing consumptively, another by a moaning child who had covered his or her head with a counterpane.

At the sixth bed, the nurse stopped and said, "Here 'e is then, the wee lad. He'll no be wakin' fer a while, though, since Doctor Latham gave 'im a spot o' laudanum."

I gripped Annabel's hand and we both gasped. Things were as dire as I had imagined. Our brother's curly head had been shaved down to the scalp and a wide bandage—with a bloodstain beginning to seep through it at his right temple—was wrapped around his forehead. *Oh my poor darling.* "What in God's name have they done to him?" I said.

"Doctor said 'twas a nasty cut. But the lad's young an' healthy and 'twill heal in no time at all, yer'll see."

"His beautiful chestnut curls are gone," I said with a catch in my throat.

"Is that what they will do to us, Lydia?" Annabel asked, touching her own hair.

"No, of course not." None of the other girls had shorn heads, so we were safe in our assumption that we would not suffer the same fate as Edwin.

"They dinna like long hair on the lads," Nurse Jamieson said. "Wi' lasses it can be pinned up or plaited. Not so for the lads."

She patted us each on the back. "Och your brother will be fine," she said, standing back and making room for us. "'tis not like other infirmaries here, yer know. Although the bairns may come to us with a fever, they dinna die of it."

I frowned. Edwin's having a fever was the last thing on my mind.

"Doctor Latham is a great admirer of Miss Florence Nightingale."

I raised a questioning eyebrow. What on earth did *The Lady with the Lamp*—as the soldiers in the Crimean War had christened her—have to do with the situation here?

"And like her," the nurse went on, "he is a stickler for cleanliness."

Come to think of it, everything—everybody—did look spotless. Except for the bloodstain on Edwin's bandage. I leaned over and traced his jaw with a tentative finger. He was pale as the marble fireplace, but his flesh was warm and his breathing steady. With great caution, Annabel reached over, too, and touched the stubble on her brother's scalp.

"Just so yer know and willna be surprised when yer see 'em, yer brother has a few bruises," the nurse said.

"Bruises," I said. "Where?"

Nurse Jamieson pulled back the counterpane, eased out Edwin's limp arm and gently pushed up his nightshirt sleeve.

I drew in a horrified breath and Annabel started to sob. Our poor, dear brother was black and blue from wrist to elbow.

The nurse eased down Edwin's sleeve and tucked his arm beneath the counterpane. "I willna show yer the other arm. 'tis the same," she said. "The wee bairn put up quite a fight from what I hear. There were two of the big lads tryin' ter hold 'im down so Mr. Hazelhurst could get at 'im."

"Brutes," I said, shaking my fists, biting back my tears.

"But they couldna do it for all 'is twistin' an' kickin' an' carryin' on. Grabbed the scissors, 'e did, and would have stabbed those lads if 'e'd had the chance."

"Criminals ... cowards," I said. "He is just a little boy. He has never been away from home before, nor been separated from his sisters."

"Yer no such a big lass yerself, dear," the nurse said. "An' even if yer were, yer couldna change a thing. Anyhow, the wee lad's safe here. Doctor Latham'll take good care of him and see no further harm comes to 'im, I know, so yer mustna fret."

Annabel stopped crying. "I am much bigger than Lydia," she said, with a belligerent thrust of her chin, "and strong, too. I could box their ears and kick their shins and ---"

"I can see yer a brave lass", Nurse Jamieson said, "but yer'd only get yerself in trouble. An' it'd be off ter The Punishment Room with yer. An' yer dinna want that now, do yer?"

Annabel gave a defeated shrug and sat on the edge of Edwin's bed.

"What exactly is this Punishment Room?" I asked.

"It used to be the wine cellar years ago when this place was a regular *hoose*."

Annabel turned towards me and frowned in obvious puzzlement.

"Nurse Jamieson means house," I said.

The woman laughed. "Och aye, so I do. Anyhow, 'tis no a place yer'd want to be visitin'. 'tis as close to a dungeon as yer could get, it bein' a cellar, wi' one wee window lookin' out onto nought but the soil o' the flower beds. An' dark as a grave. Damp an' moldy, too, wi' all manner o' creatures lurkin' about."

"What sort of creatures?" Annabel asked.

"Spiders, a rat or two I shouldna doubt, an' plenty o' mice."

Annabel shuddered. "Maybe I shall not take on the bullies, after all."

"Wise of yer, lassie."

"Do you think they will send our brother there?" I asked.

"No, I dinna. I'll tell yer fer why. I overheard the doctor sayin' to Matron, I should go easy on the little chap. He has had quite an ordeal. On the sisters, too; they have no doubt been beside themselves."

I closed my eyes for an instant and exhaled a long breath. At least he was sympathetic towards us. "I understand from Matron that the doctor wishes to see me," I said.

"Aye, that 'e does." The nurse glanced up at the large, round school clock on the wall. "Yer've twenty minutes left ter spend wi' yer wee brother."

We took up our watch each side of Edwin's bed and retreated into our own thoughts.

At least Edwin was safe for now. But what about tomorrow, the next day? Was he destined for that dreadful-sounding dungeon? Could he be in for the birch rod? Despite the doctor's recommendation, the boy's behavior would surely not go unpunished.

"Poor shorn little lamb." I said out loud.

Annabel had been contemplating her lap. She looked up and said, "Everything is going to be alright, isn't it, Lydia?"

"Of course it is." I spoke with a conviction I did not feel. "Edwin is in good hands and from all accounts will soon be recovered. So I think we can safely say the worst is over."

Wait and see, the voice in my head said. *You still have your meeting with the doctor.*

Hunched over his desk and writing at a furious pace, Phillip Latham waved me into a leather armchair across from him without so much as an upward glance.

The half-past-ten chiming of a regulator clock on the nearby wall filled the ensuing silence. And as the sound died away the doctor looked up, pen poised, and tilted his head. "It is Lydia, is it not?"

Ye gods and little fishes. *No ... it is Queen Victoria.* Was he going to ask me to confirm my name every time we met? "Yes it is."

He took a pen wipe out of the desk drawer, cleaned off his nib, then set the pen back on the inkstand. "If I recall correctly, you are the eldest."

"I am. My sister Annabel has recently had her twelfth birthday and I am thirteen."

"Hmmm."

"And for your information, we have never been separated from our brother before and I have always been the one to take care of him."

*Fool. Why did you say all that? Now, he will start asking questions.*

But "I see," was all he said.

"Lately," I felt compelled to add. "I mean I have taken care of Edwin lately, since our father became ---"

"Unwell?"

"Yes."

The doctor creaked back in his chair. "As the eldest, Lydia, would you say you have some control over your brother's behavior?"

"Well ... yes ... er, I suppose I do. But ---"

"You must teach him to curb his temper, then; otherwise, I am afraid he will find himself ---"

"Edwin does not have ..." My tongue tied itself in a knot and something strange and breath-catching overcame me when my eyes met Phillip Latham's; I had thought them hazel, but now they appeared green or was it ...?"

"You were saying?"

I came to my senses and made a show of coughing behind my hand while I collected myself. Lord, what had I been saying? Oh yes ... Edwin. "My brother does not possess a temper; he is the gentlest of fellows, I assure you."

"Really?" Phillip Latham raised a sardonic eyebrow.

"Yes. He is the dearest, sweetest ---"

"I understand he bit one of the barbers and kicked the other in the ... er ..." He caught himself and winced. "Suffice to say the chap was hobbling about and out of commission for quite some time."

"Well, if Edwin did as you say"—I drew myself up in my seat and glared —"and I am certainly not convinced of it, he was only defending himself against those louts." I inhaled a deep breath, preparing to continue in a similar vein, but all at once realized with dismay that I had abandoned my role. *Act your age, you fool, your counterfeit age.* I shrank into the chair and, slanting a look at the doctor from beneath my lashes, said in a soft, respectful tone, "You saw what they did to his head, sir, and I saw what they did to his arms; he is positively black and blue."

"Nevertheless, he must learn to live within the system and obey the rules,

Lydia." He rested his elbows on the desktop and leaned forward, his eyes holding mine for a long moment. "I know it is a harsh system and I have high hopes that some day we can alter it, but in the mean ---"

"Harsh?" I could not help myself. "It is downright criminal." I grasped the arms of my chair. "I do not mind for myself, I can endure it. But Edwin and Annabel are just children."

"As are you, Lydia," Doctor Latham said kindly. "And you must not … cannot take on the burdens of the world."

I frowned. "But I am not a ch …" I caught myself, bringing my hand to my mouth, realizing what a blunder I had been about to make.

But Phillip Latham appeared not to have noticed. "You must be exhausted," he said. "And no wonder. You have only just arrived here and have had to deal with a situation that would challenge an adult, never mind a child."

I seethed. He had done it again … called me a child. *I am not a child, I am a woman. I am not a child, I am a woman.* Again and again the words yammered in my head and I squeezed my eyes shut, pressing my fingertips to my temples in an attempt to silence the clamor.

The gentleness of his tone finally stopped it. "Are you alright, Lydia?" he asked.

I looked over at him and when I saw the expression of genuine concern on his face, my rage evaporated and I said, "I am perfectly fine, thank you, doctor."

He tilted his head appraisingly. "You are a little flushed, I think. But ---"

"Are you finished with me, sir?"

"Not quite. I wanted to let you know that my plan is to keep your brother in the infirmary for another day or two."

"Then what will happen to him?"

"He will be returned to Mr. Hazelhurst in the boys' wing."

Dumbfounded, I said, "But, doctor, he is the man responsible for my brother being injured."

"No, that is not true, Lydia," Phillip Latham said with irritating patience. "Two older lads were instructed to cut your brother's hair. He became thoroughly unmanageable, needed controlling and consequently sustained injuries. In short, as I said at the beginning of this interview, what got your brother into such a pickle was his temper, Lydia."

I slumped in my seat and shook my head in defeat. As a helpless—and hapless—child I could not win this battle.

"He will be fine, Lydia."

I looked up.

"I will have a chat with the little chap and explain the way the land lies. And I will keep an eye on him and make sure no harm comes to him."

"Thank you, sir."

"And if it will make you feel better, I will have word sent to you when Edwin is out of the infirmary and back in the boys' wing."

"That is kind of you, sir." I felt the prick of tears in my eyes. I blinked and swallowed hard. "Will there be anything else?"

Angling his head, he leaned back in his seat and studied me. "No, nothing more for now. You go on about your business, child."

That deuced word child again. How I had begun to detest it … at least from his lips. I would have made my exit nicely, included a smile and a subservient bob of my head, but the fellow so disconcerted me that I lurched out of my seat—hot and red from his scrutiny—and almost tripped over my feet in my haste to reach the door.

I was still flustered when I reached Matron's study five minutes later. And I had hardly settled in my seat alongside Annabel, before the woman delivered her bombshell.

"You should know," she said, "that henceforth, visits between the two of you and your brother will be limited to every other Sunday each month, between the hours of two and four. This regimen will start on the twenty-second."

Eleven more days until we were allowed to see Edwin again. And only every other week from then on. Great God in heaven. I fought to keep hysteria from my voice. "Can he not be punished in some other way, Matron?" I asked. "Assigned extra tasks or …? I mean, he really is a good boy. The reason for his outburst was that he was so dreadfully fright ---"

Matron slapped the arm of her chair causing Annabel to almost jump out of her skin. "Hold your tongue, child," she told me. "I said nothing of punishment … that is a matter to be decided later. And your brother's purported goodness or lack thereof has nothing whatsoever to do with the matter. It is our rule that visiting hours between male and female siblings are as I have stated. It is also our rule—something you seem to have great difficulty comprehending—that children speak when spoken to and not before."

My heart sank to the soles of my boots. I felt as helpless, as frustrated as the child I was pretending to be. Look at the woman, glaring at us, reproaching us.

"Rules must be complied with," Matron nauseatingly carried on. "Do I make myself perfectly clear?"

"Yes, Matron," we chorused.

"Good." She rose and signalled us to do likewise. "The two of you will go to the dining hall, now, and have your mid-day meal. Afterwards, you will work in the kitchen for the rest of the day. Tomorrow morning after breakfast, Miss Dunn will apprise you both of your daily duties."

Annabel and I had little opportunity for conversation that afternoon. I was too busy with my dishwashing and drying and table-setting, she with her bread-kneading and cake-making.

By the time we were free to talk it was past seven, and dark enough that we needed a candle to light our way to the dormitory.

"It is criminal," I said to Annabel as we mounted the stairs.

"What is?"

"That we are allowed to see Edwin only four hours each month. That means in one year a grand total of ---"

"Forty-eight hours," Annabel piped up, proud of her arithmetical abilities, and missing the serious implications of my statement. "Two whole days," she added smugly.

"Exactly." I moved ahead of her. "Two miserable days out of one miserable year." I exhaled a weary breath. "It does not bear thinking about."

"Will that girl—the horrible one—be in the dormitory?" Annabel asked out of the blue.

By now I had reached the landing and Annabel was on the step below. I stopped, exasperated. My focus was on Edwin. I had absolutely no desire to give any thought to that dreadful bully-girl. Without turning around, I asked, "Do you understand what I have just been saying?"

"Yes." Annabel caught up with me and came alongside. "You said it does not bear thinking about, so I thought we should think about something else … like that beastly girl."

"Annabel Fullerton"—I could not help chuckling—"you really are a caution, you know."

"'An' you, yer bleedin' ladyship …"

I froze, holding my candle aloft. Ye gods and little fishes—my heart gave a sickening thud—our nemesis, Agatha Neeves, looming out of the shadows ahead.

"You an' yer sister are in fer it good an' proper." She spoke in a loud, ominous whisper. "An' there'll not be nobody ter come to yer rescue neiver, cos Matron never comes up 'ere after seven o'clock." She advanced, candle in hand, stopping several feet from us. None of her cohorts seemed to be with her this time. "Yer wanta know somefink? My bleedin' arse is so sore I can't sit down. An' 'tis your faults, the pair o' you."

Exhaustion … worry … I do not know. But whatever the trigger, I snapped. A geyser of white-hot rage surged up in me and I shrieked, "Our faults?" Great god in heaven, I had heard so much rubbish lately from all quarters, but this—vulgar language and all—was positively beyond the pale. "You … you great lump, are without a doubt, the stupidest, coarsest, vilest girl it has ever been my misfortune to meet."

"Bravo," Annabel said, grinning like a lunatic.

The light from the candle in the Neeves girl's hand illuminated her face. With each adjective I uttered, it had grown redder, her eyes had bulged wider, her breathing had become more laboured, which only served to spur me on.

"The soreness of your *posterior* is your responsibility and yours alone. Not mine. Not my sister's. Your own loutish behavior brought you exactly what you deserved. And I am delighted"—I dipped my chin in emphasis —"yes, delighted." I folded my arms and jutted my jaw. "So, put that in your pipe and smoke it, you … you ---"

"Toad face!" Annabel's vitriolic whisper filled the void. And she caught my eye with her own triumphant one.

Ah, well, I thought, observing Agatha Neeves' slack-jawed fury and her pounding of one big fist against the other, in for a penny, in for a thousand guineas, never mind a pound. Lord, but the girl was like some great, snorting, ground-pawing beast, and surely—I studied her afresh and almost laughed out loud—what we were observing here was unadulterated bluff.

"Will she leave us alone, now?" Annabel spoke in a soft, querulous voice next to my ear, her bravado having apparently evaporated.

I handed her the candle. "Hold this, please." I felt calm, all at once, and purposeful. Linking Annabel's free arm in mine, I squeezed it and said under my breath, "Onward and upward. Time for a little bluff of our own. Time to press our point home and rout the enemy for good." I gave another squeeze. "And whatever I say, do not dare contradict me."

Urging Annabel along with me, I halted within a couple of feet of the Neeves girl, who had regained her speech enough to sputter, "You two can't go talkin' to me like that. You … you ---"

"We most certainly can, especially if you insist on being such a thoroughly unpleasant creature. You are to leave us alone, you great lump, do you hear me?" I wagged my forefinger in emphasis. "Leave us in peace. Otherwise"—I drew myself up to my full height, which was still a good foot less than my adversary's—"my sister and I will be forced to take drastic measures."

"Whadayer mean?"

"Magic," I said, exceedingly black magic."

Agatha Neeves' eyes slid back and forth. Her candle flickered from the tremor in her hand. "Whadayer mean?" she asked again.

"Our grandfather—rest his soul—a famous explorer who led many expeditions to the Dark Continent, schooled the two of us in the ancient art of"—I paused both for effect and additional inspiration.

The latter came from Annabel. "Spell-casting," she said, looking mightily pleased with herself.

"Huh?" Agatha Neeves shivered and looked nervously about.

"Spell-casting. Exactly," I said, enjoying myself immensely. "We have the power, my sister and I, to eliminate those who oppose us. We have only to say a few secret words—that is to cast a spell—and we are able to dispatch our enemies."

"Whadayer mean, dispatch?"

"Make them disappear." I made a casual palms-up gesture. "Poof ... just like that ... they are gone."

"Gone ... gone where?"

"Either they disappear into thin air." I slanted a look at Annabel. "Is that not right?"

"Oh absolutely." Annabel nodded enthusiastically, her cheeks reddening from the effort of containing herself.

"Or"—I raised nonchalant palms up again—"they simply die. Anyway, be that as it may, we have been forced to use our spell-casting on only one or two occasions so far. Or was it three? I cannot quite remember?"

"Three," Annabel said with obvious glee.

"So you see," I continued, "you are not dealing with two ordinary girls. You are actually dealing with two extremely powerful magicians."

Agatha Neeves paled and she repeatedly licked her lips. "Oh I do see. Honest I do." Her eyes filled with tears. "An' I'm sorry, proper sorry. I will not ... er ... I will not ..." Her words petered out and she scratched the top of her head and chewed on her thumbnail, apparently so nervous that she had lost her train of thought.

"You will never bother us again," I said, slowly, emphatically.

"Naw. I will not. Not never ever. Cross me 'eart and hope ter ... I mean ... can I go now? I'm bein' punished for what I done earlier in the dormitory an' I'm s'pposed to be sleepin' by meself in the attic an' I ---"

"Go, by all means." I pointed a commanding finger. "And before you go to sleep tonight, think long and hard about what I have said."

The Neeves girl did not answer. All her energy was directed towards escape. And when her last frantic footfall had faded away, I said, "Somehow I do not think we shall have any more trouble with *Toadface,* do you?"

"I should say not. Oh I loved it, Lydia, I positively adored what you said."

"Likewise, I am sure." I tucked her arm through mine. "Spell-casters, indeed. How positively brilliant of you."

Annabel exploded with laughter. "You really think so?"

"I do. Come on. We had better get to bed before lights out."

I sighed. What a joy to see Annabel happy. What sport these past minutes had been, and how grand it had felt to emerge the victor.

Tonight, I would hold onto these images.

Tonight, I would let myself hope. Edwin would recover. The three of us would weather whatever came along.

One day at a time, I told myself.

One day at a time.

## CHAPTER TWENTY-ONE
### *January 1888*
### *Brackford House, Yorkshire, England*

On the Friday two days later, after breakfast and dishwashing, Miss Dunn pulled me aside as Annabel and I were about to enter the schoolroom for our three hours of lessons. "I have a message from Doctor Latham," she said. "He wishes you to know that your brother is fully recovered an' has been returned to the boys' wing."

"I do hope he will not be set upon again," I said.

"I am certain he will not be," said Miss Dunn. "The doctor hinted that he plans on taking a personal interest in Edwin. So it seems you have no need to worry." She glanced beyond us into the schoolroom. "I see all your classmates are seated an' your teacher, Miss Hubbard, is about to begin, so you had best hasten to take your places."

There were only two vacant desks. Annabel opted for the one in the second row and I, the one in the back row, whose anonymity suited me no end.

The teacher was a mild-mannered, mousy young woman who—when she was not clearing her throat and running her fingers through her straggly hair— fiddled incessantly with first one earlobe, then the other.

With my education long since completed, I had no need to attend to this woman and be driven to distraction by her nervous tics. In the unlikely event that she were to call on me for answers, I would have no difficulty providing them. And so I made myself as comfortable as possible on the hard wooden stool, and let my thoughts take wing.

Was my dear Edwin really well again and would the doctor see no harm came to him? And what about our visits with my brother? Would they really commence eleven days hence on the twenty-second, or would Matron make us wait a further fortnight before we were permitted to see him?

Would I be able to keep up this pretense ... this watching of my p's and q's ... my mannerisms ... my voice? And what would happen if I were unmasked? I buried my face in my hands, overwhelmed suddenly by the uncertainty of it all.

"Are you alright?"

I turned in the direction of the low voice and saw it belonged to a dark-haired girl with whom I had exchanged a few words in the bathing room that morning. "I am fine, thank you," I said. "Just a little tired."

"You'll get used to it," she whispered, clearly attempting to cheer me up.

Get used to it? I clenched my fists, fighting the urge to pound the desktop. I did not want to get used to all this. I wanted a normal life. *But you cannot have a normal life. You are to be shipped off to Canada, remember, for five years servitude? You will be an old maid by the time you are finished.*

"Shut up." The words exploded from my mouth of their own volition and I shot to my feet.

All around me girls gawped in astonishment and muttered amongst themselves, while Miss Hubbard—clearly the most flabbergasted member of my audience—rapped on her desktop and said with surprising authority. "Eyes front", then a moment later, "Silence."

Once a hush had descended on the room, the teacher said, "You at the back, identify yourself."

I did as I was instructed.

Astonishingly ticless now, the teacher said, "Did you tell me to shut up?"

"Oh no, miss"—I made my voice catch—"ab--solute--ly not." I clutched my midriff and winced. "What I said was get up, as in I have to get up. You see ... oh ... ouch ... I am feeling rather unwell and fear I may embarrass myself if I do not immediately get to the pri---"

"Well, do not just stand there child. GO."

———

"You was powerful good this mornin'."

I put down my beaker of tea and tilted my head inquiringly at the red-headed girl seated across the table from us. With her pinched little freckled face and bright, dark eyes, she reminded me of a sparrow. "I beg your pardon?" I raised my voice to make myself heard over the din of the forty-odd girls chattering and slurping down their mid-day soup.

"The act yer put on for Miss 'ubbard. Did the same thing meself a few weeks back when I was workin' in the laundry, only I didn't say to Mrs Gallup I was feelin' *rather unwell*. I said I 'ad a bellyache and an' I thought I was goin' to shit all over the sheets."

"Hmmm," I said, masking my distaste for the girl's crude language with an indifferent shrug, while Annabel almost choked on her soup.

"So whadidya do all mornin'?" the girl asked.

I had actually spent an hour in the library, and the other two hours dozing on my bed. But I was not certain I wanted to disclose this information to the girl.

She saved me the necessity, however, by continuing on with her own tale. "I jus' went back to bed an' 'ad meself a jolly good sleep. Does wonders for the collywobbles does that." She chortled. "Even when yer doesn't really 'ave 'em."

"I imagine it would," I said.

"Name's Posy, by the way. Posy Paxton." She leaned forward, resting on her elbows. "Yer probly thinkin' it is a right queer name. Lotta people do."

"Actually, I think Posy is rather a nice name," I said, taking a liking to this chatty girl.

"Lord love us, if that ain't a first. S'ppose it is a sight better than Araminta or Eugenia or Theodosia." She smirked. "Or Agatha, eh?" Popping a crust of bread into her mouth, she chewed vigorously and then said, "Seen yer give 'er a run fer 'er money the other night."

"You mean Agatha Neeves?"

"Yeah … 'er. Always picked on the new ones, she did. But she 'as 'opped it now, yer know, 'er an' the other *yearers*."

*"Yearers?"* I said, frowning.

"'sright. You an' yer sister are weekers … been 'ere a week, 'aven't yer?"

"Less than half a week," Annabel said.

Unfazed by the correction, Posy continued. "Agatha was a yearer. Me, I am a *three-monther.* Any 'ow, as I said, they've all 'opped it. Went ter Liverpool yesterday. About another hour I reckon, an' it'll be—'ow do they say it?—full steam a'ead."

"You mean they left for Canada?" I said, surprised.

"'sright. So yer doesn't need ter worry, there bein' no more like Agatha around. Leastways, not now."

I could have told Posy I felt I had no cause for worry anyway since I had already solved the problem of Agatha Neeves, but I thought better of it. After all, the girl was pleasant and clearly making an effort to be friendly. I smiled. "Thank you for telling us." I nudged Annabel, adding, "That is splendid news, is it not?"

Annabel spooned the last of her soup into her mouth and then gave an enthusiastic wag of her head.

The end-of-dinner bell sounded and we all rose. I was to spend the afternoon ironing; Annabel, darning and mending. We made our way to the door and Posy kept pace with us.

"'ow old are you two?"

Annabel told her, hesitating only minutely over my age.

"I'm thirteen meself," she said to me. "Sisters, right?"

I nodded.

"Yer don't look much alike."

"I take after my father," Annabel said.

"And I after our mother," I added.

"'ear your brother 'ad a bit o' bother. Is 'e all right?"

"Yes, praise be. He spent last night in the infirmary, but I was told this morning he was sufficiently recovered to be returned to the boys' wing. And the doctor assured me he would keep an eye on Edwin."

Posy's face lit up. "Oh 'e's lovely is Dr. Latham."

Lovely? Not exactly the adjective I would have used to describe the fellow. Disturbing might be more appropriate.

"I 'elp 'im sometimes." Posy stopped outside the dining hall door and pulled us aside to allow the gaggle of other girls to pass. "We've got a few minutes 'fore we 'ave ter be at our jobs. "Where was I? Oh yes. Yer see, once you're a three-monther yer allowed to assist the doctor." The girl seemed to puff up with importance as she carried on. "Went with 'im to 'is 'ouse once to pick apples in 'is orchard, 'cause 'e 'ad a sight too many and reckoned we could use 'em 'ere."

"I thought he lived at Brackford House," I said, actually having no notion where he lived.

"Oh 'e does part of the time. I mean, 'e 'as a room 'ere an' 'e often stays. But three days a week 'e 'as a surgery at 'is 'ouse where 'e sees private patients. Toffs some of 'em. Yer know? Wi' more than a few bob."

I fiddled with a sliver of loose wood in the doorframe and casually asked, "Does his wife assist him in his surgery?" .

"Lord, no, 'e don't 'ave no wife. 'is sister, Miss Delphine, 'elps 'im. Ever so nice, she is. Nurse Jamieson goes over there, too, and does for 'im once in a while."

I stopped picking at the wood, my interest growing.

"Anyway, workin' for Doctor Latham makes a change I can tell yer. There is lots of fetchin' an' carryin' … rollin' bandages … countin' out tablets, measurin' tinctures and such like. Easy stuff. Even gives yer a cuppa tea, the doctor does. And"—she licked her lips in an anticipatory manner—"jus' wait till I tell you what else 'e gives yer."

"What?" Annabel and I spoke as one.

Posy crossed her arms over her breasts, tilted her chin and half-closed her eyes, an expression of ecstasy on her face. "Mint 'umbugs," she said. "Lovely big 'uns wiv soft centres."

"Sweets? He actually gives you sweets?" Annabel's eyes filled with longing. "We haven't had sweets in ---"

"Eons," I said, taking Annabel's hand and stroking the back of it. "I know, dear. But we will …we honestly will." *The Lord only knows when, though.*

"It is all on the sly, mind yer," Posy went on. Y'ave ter keep mum about it, or Matron'd give yer what for. I s'ppose yer brother'll be given what for. When yer don't toe the mark around 'ere, it usually means the cane. Or The Punishment Room. Did Matron say anythin' to yer?"

Annabel clutched my arm, suddenly. "Will they cane Edwin?" she asked.

"What? No …not after what he has been through."

Posy nodded balefully. "Dunno about that. Usually nobody around 'ere gets away with nothin'. An' speakin' o' that, we'd best get a move on or we'll be in fer it good an' proper ourselves."

And soon—eleven days from now if all went according to plan—I would discover for myself just how good a protector the *lovely* Doctor Phillip Latham proved to be.

## CHAPTER TWENTY-TWO
### *January 1888*
### *Brackford House, Yorkshire, England*

All did go according to plan and on the afternoon of Sunday, the twenty-second of January, Amelia Dunn—following Matron's instructions—conducted us to the boys' wing. Once there she led us upstairs to a room on the first floor whose furnishings included a pair of shabby armchairs, a small, green-baize-topped game table and four chairs, along with a glass-doored bookshelf. "They want you to have a pleasant time during visiting hours. So you will find playing cards, dominoes and ludo over there on the shelves along with one or two books, I believe, an' maybe a jigsaw puzzle or two."

Annabel and I exchanged a surprised look. Speaking for myself, cards, games and books were the very last things on my mind.

"Will we have the room all to ourselves, Miss Dunn?" I asked. "Are we the only ones?"

"If you mean the only sisters visiting brothers … yes, you are. We did have another couple—a boy an' a girl from the same family—last month, but they have left us now."

"They are not dead, are they?" Annabel asked with an expression of alarm on her face.

"'struth, no. They left for Canada a fortnight ago. At least they were sent to Liverpool an' will be held there until the weather permits their voyage. Now, enough chit-chat. If I am to collect your brother from Mr. Hazelhurst's office at the appointed hour, I must be off." Miss Dunn hurried to the door. "Warm yourselves by the fire, an' I shall be back shortly."

Annabel flopped down in one of the two armchairs and held out her hands towards the blaze while I paced, far too anxious to sit, my mind churning with unsettling thoughts about Edwin … our lives … our futures.

"I wonder if his curls will have grown back," Annabel suddenly said, so surprising me with the question that I stopped in my tracks. I could not help smiling. Here I had been fretting and fuming on a grand scale, when all that appeared to be on Annabel's mind was the state of her brother's hair.

I sat in the chair opposite her. "Not yet, dear," I said. "Remember, it has been less than a fortnight since they shaved his head."

Annabel sighed as if disappointed. "Stubble then."

"Yes, stubble. And you must be certain not to tease him about it. He has been through quite an ordeal and requires our tenderest attention."

Annabel contemplated her lap for a time then stared into the fire. "Everything has changed," she said in a sad, faraway voice. "What is to become of us, Lydia?"

I felt a tight catch at my heart. Indeed what was to become of us? Great God, I had no idea. I moistened my lips, arranged my mouth in a smile and was about to say something of a reassuring nature when the door all at once flew open. Annabel and I turned in unison.

There, poised on the threshold was the pinch-faced urchin of a Dickens novel: Head shorn; jacket dwarfing him; too-short trousers and black boots which appeared far too large for the feet I knew to be small and narrow. Edwin's feet.

Annabel scrambled up and shrieked his name. I flung my arms wide, laughing as he clumped across the room, threw himself at me and hung on for dear life. Sobbing into my neck, he stammered, "They told me … I would … never see you again … that you had … gone across the ocean in a ship and ---"

"Who told you?" I extricated myself and held him at arm's length, taking in the scar at his temple, pink and raw-looking.

He drew in a shaky breath. "Two of the bigger boys."

"Two of the bigger liars I should think, who need their ears well and truly boxed." I took Edwin's face between my hands and gazed into his tear-filled eyes. "We have no intention of leaving you, dear heart. You are our treasured brother … our only brother. And when we do sail on a ship, the three of us will go together."

"Why do we have to be separated, Liddy?"

"Rules. Much as we may dislike them, I am afraid we must adhere to them."

"They are hateful." He sniffed back his tears and fished a handkerchief from his trousers pocket while Annabel patted his arm in a comforting gesture. After a moment of nose-blowing, he returned the handkerchief to its place and said, "I missed you both so much. Why did it take so long for you to come and visit me?"

"We had to wait for permission," Annabel answered with a disgruntled twist to her mouth.

I added an explanation about the every-other-Sunday visiting rules and then said, "I came to see you a week and a half ago when you were in the infirmary."

"You did?"

"Yes, but you were sound asleep."

"Lydia complained to me that you were snoring like a hippopotamus and making all the dishes rattle," Annabel said, straight-faced.

Edwin tipped his head and peered at her for a long moment. Then he grinned. "She did not, you big story-teller. Did you, Liddy?"

"No, dear heart," I said, grateful for the familiar banter between the children. "I certainly did not." I embraced Edwin again and thought with alarm how insubstantial he felt. "Sit here"—I patted the seat of the armchair I had vacated—"and let me have a good look at you."

Annabel settled sidesaddle on the arm of the chair while I knelt down in front of Edwin. I reached out and touched his scalp. My sister followed suit. The stubble had softened and felt like the fuzz on a baby's head. "It will soon grow back," I said.

"They will not let it," said Edwin, matter-of-factly. "All boys must have their heads shaved. Otherwise we would be creeping with lice."

"I think you mean crawling, dear." I shuddered. God in Heaven, will they shave our heads, too?

Annabel began to scratch herself all over. With her vivid imagination she would soon have herself alive with the creatures.

I gave her a nudge and frowned in disapproval. "What are you doing?" I asked.

"Nothing." She stopped raking herself and folded her arms across her ribcage. "Just listening is all," she said.

Anxious to change the subject, I said to Edwin, "Your cheeks are rather hollow. Are you getting enough to eat?"

"What about *my* cheeks, *Lydia*?" Annabel pursed her lips and sucked in hard, her eyes bulging with the effort.

"No change," I said. My sister's face was plump and rosy as ever.

Ignoring her loud exhalation and the look of disappointment that followed, I returned to the question at hand. "So, are you eating properly, Edwin?"

He grimaced. "I do not like the food, Liddy. It is all so plain and stodgy."

"I know, dear. But I am afraid you are going to have to make the best of it. And you must eat. You will need to be strong for our next adventure." Lord, there I went again with that deuced word adventure. How I overused it. But at least, for now, it had brought a smile to his lips and a sparkle to his eyes.

"Have they had you working?" I asked.

"Yes. But not outside. They say it is far too cold at present."

"I should say so. There must be six inches of snow on the ground and the ponds are all frozen over. So what have they had you doing?"

"Black-leading the kitchen range, cleaning the lamps in the lamp room, polishing Mr. Jellicoe's boots."

"Who, pray tell, is Mr. Jellicoe?"

"Our teacher. See, Liddy." Edwin held out his hands. "My fingernails are horrid, black as a chimney sweep's. I have scrubbed and scrubbed them, but I cannot get them clean."

"Cutting them will solve the problem. I will see if I can procure a pair of nail scissors before our next visit. What about your head? Does it hurt?"

"No, not a bit." He reached up and ran his fingertips over the scar as if to prove it.

"May I feel?" asked Annabel.

Edwin nodded yes.

"Has the doctor been to see you recently?" I asked.

"Yes. He came once … or was it twice?" He pressed his thumb to his lower lip and chewed on the nail for a time, his attention finally drifting to the contents of the shelves. "Are those games?"

"Yes," said Annabel, brimming with enthusiasm.

"You are not sure?" I said.

Annabel clicked her tongue against her teeth. "Yes, of course I am. Miss Dunn told us they were and you can see for yourself, Lydia."

Now, I made an irritated sound. "You will please watch your tone with me, young lady. I may be acting the part of a child, but I am very much your elder and you will show me the proper respect. For your information, I was speaking to Edwin about the doctor's visits."

But clearly Edwin had no interest in pursuing the subject. He got up and eased by me, intent now on Annabel and the games.

I rose and stood in front of the fire warming my posterior, and a discomfiting question entered my mind: Was it possible that my inquiries about Doctor Latham had more to do with my own interest in the fellow than in my brother's health?

Of course not. A ridiculous notion if ever I heard of one. I was thinking only of Edwin's well-being.

"Liddy. Will you come and play drafts with us?"

Thank the Lord. Salvation from my unsettling thoughts. "Of course, dear. But give me a moment."

After stoking the fire with coal from the bucket on the hearth, I removed a taper from its holder and lit the pair of candles on top of the bookshelf. Then I drew the curtains against the frigid day and joined my brother and sister at the table.

Blue flames licked up the chimney and the coal snapped and popped a cheerful song while we played drafts, then Happy Families in the candles' golden light. We bantered back and forth; we laughed uproariously. And when I produced from my skirt pocket a twist of paper containing the three mint humbugs Posy Paxton had procured—by fair means or foul ... I was not certain—and insisted I bring with me this afternoon, we sucked with gusto, manners be damned.

If someone had looked in on us, I dare say they would have thought what a charming tableau we presented. Happy. Loving. Delighting in each other's company. Not a worry in the world.

And their observations would have been right ... except for the last one.

I would always worry ... every day of my life ... until we were all together again under one roof. Living our own lives. Deciding our own fates.

"It is your deal, Lydia." Annabel's impatient voice intruded on my thoughts.

"Very well," I said, picking up the deck and absently shuffling.

Like it or not, I thought, the only course open to me now was to let the cards fall where they may.

## CHAPTER TWENTY-THREE
### *April-October 1888*
### *Brackford House, Yorkshire, England*

Edwin's eighth birthday—the fifteenth of April—fell on the Sunday designated for our visit, and it saddened me no end that all I could give him was a kiss and an embrace, along with a promise of a grand celebration of all our birthdays once the three of us were together again.

At least with the advent of spring and an improvement in the weather, we were allowed to visit outside in the acres of grounds, within the confines of the high, stone wall which divided the two wings.

We wandered along the paths which dissected carefully-tended flower beds filled with daffodils yellow as egg yolks, and pure white narcissi which gave off a delicately sweet aroma. We discovered an ancient orchard where bluebells grew in wild profusion among the gnarled old apple and pear trees. We chattered back to the chaffinches, imitated the trill of the yellowhammers and called out to the cheeky little blue tits who flitted from branch to branch. We were as carefree as children in a storybook with a happy ending.

One Sunday afternoon in May as we were setting out for our stroll under a pristine blue sky, a tall, corpulent man with a shiny bald pate suddenly appeared at our side and said, "Wait a moment children."

"Mr. Hazelhurst," Edwin whispered to me as we came to a stop. "The superintendent."

I well-remembered the name from Edwin's haircutting episode. My hackles rose and I eyed the fellow with suspicion.

"A perfect day for croquet," he said, shading his eyes against the sun. "Are you three interested in the game?"

I lifted my shoulders, uncertain how to respond.

Annabel said, "I am very interested. And Edwin piped up, "I am bound to say, sir, that I am a player of great skill."

"Well, young Mister Fullerton"—the superintendent gave a stiff little bow —"and I assume these ladies are the Misses Fullerton, there is a set available over there in the shed, should you wish to avail yourselves of it."

I could scarcely credit it. This man with the benevolent face and manner, whom I had judged to be an ogre had turned out to be nothing of the sort. "Thank you very much, sir," I said.

From then on the *thwack* of mallet on ball, the music of the children's laughter and their silly banter rang in my delighted ears every other Sunday afternoon. Spring gave way to yet another summer of record-breaking heat, and the lush green lawn on which we had begun our sport turned into a brown and desiccated expanse, mangy-looking as an old dog's coat. But it mattered not one jot to us. Nothing could mar our pleasure.

I became twenty-one years old on the fifteenth of July, but at Brackwood House my *fourteenth* birthday passed without fanfare. Posy got wind of the occasion, however, and presented me with half a dozen humbugs from her hoard, which of course, I shared with Edwin and Annabel.

Posy was a generous girl and I wished I could have done something in return. I expressed this thought to Annabel who—after several minutes of pacing and rumination—said, "I have an idea. We can ask Matron if she will permit Posy to join us on our Sunday afternoons with Edwin."

I doubted very much that such permission would be granted, but Annabel went ahead with the request anyway. She heard nothing for weeks and had almost given up hope when the surprising response from Matron came. "Mr. Hazelhurst and I agree that Posy Paxton may participate in your Sunday visits with your brother throughout the month of September."

I thought to remind my sister that Posy would be gone by mid-October, that she should be loosening—rather than strengthening—her ties to the girl. But I held my tongue. There was little enough joy in Annabel's life, I decided; let her take pleasure in this friendship, short-lived or not.

In truth I, too, enjoyed Posy's company; her presence enlivened our croquet games considerably. And at the end of each day before the lights were extinguished she would entertain us with the latest morsels of gossip. One such evening in early October, Annabel and I were seated on the edge of her bed chatting, when the girl said, "The doctor's been away this past week. 'aint been the same without 'im."

My ears pricked up. I had seen neither hair nor hide of him in weeks. I had heard no mention of him, either, until now. "Really," I said.

"Been to visit 'is in-laws, 'e has."

"In-laws?" My tone was sharper than I intended. "But I could have sworn you said he was not married."

"'e ain't."

"Well, how on earth---"

"'old on. I ain't finished yet. 'twas Nurse Jamieson what told me. "'e went up ter London ter see 'is wife's—she died five year ago 'avin' their baby which di'n't live—ma an' pa." Posy exhaled a long breath.

"I see." The world was full of sad stories, I thought.

"'e goes three or four times times a year," Posy went on. "By the way, 'e asked me yesterday, if I thought you an' Annabel might be int'rested in 'elpin' out in the infirmary? Reckon 'e knows I'll soon be off. Only a fortnight, now, an' I'll be sailin' the seven seas, so ter speak."

Annabel's face fell and her eyes filled with tears. "I shall miss you so, Posy. Perhaps, since you cannot write yourself, you will be able to persuade the persons with whom you are billeted to send a letter to me, and I shall immediately write back to you."

"Can't read, neiver," Posy said. "So I should 'ave ter ask them ter read whatever you 'ad writ." She heaved a sigh. "An' I dunno if they would."

"It is a difficult situation," I said, placing an arm about Annabel's shoulders, unable to think of anything of a reassuring nature to add.

"I hate it," she said.

"I know you do, dear." I patted her hand. And then I once more turned my attention to Posy. "Tell me again, if you will, what the doctor asked you."

When Posy reiterated the doctor's inquiry about our working in the infirmary, Annabel said with a shudder, "No, not me, that is for certain. I have no desire to see blood or any of the other nasty things one sees in an infirm ---"

"Don't be daft. 'e don't mean in the 'ospital. 'e means in 'is surgery. Like I told you 'afore. With the bandage-windin', the pill-countin' an' such like."

"I still would not be interested," said Annabel.

"I should have to give it a great deal of thought," I said.

"'course, yer'd 'ave ter get permission from Matron first," Posy said.

I fully intended to do so the following week, having thought long and hard about the wisdom of working with the doctor, and having decided that an occasional change from the daily grind to which I was subjected would be most welcome.

But what I learned from Edwin that second Sunday in October changed everything.

It had been only a fortnight since I had seen him, but it suddenly occurred to me how much he had grown. "Stand back-to-back with me," I said. And when he did, I said, "Annabel, look. He used to be about six inches shorter than me. How much shorter is he, now?"

Annabel folded her arms and rested her chin on one hand. "Oh I do not know. Maybe ---"

"I have grown, Liddy. Doctor Latham said if I kept it up I would soon be as tall as he is."

I stepped away from Edwin. "When did he say that?"

"The day before yesterday, when they took me to his office and he ---"

"They have had you to the doctor?" I touched his forehead with the back of my hand. No fever. "Have you been poorly?"

"No, not since they cut my head." Edwin wandered over to the games table and sat down.

"So what reason did they give you for the visit?"

Edwin lifted his hands palms-up and shrugged.

Annabel came and sat opposite him, and as if I needed a translation, said, "He does not know, Lydia."

"They just took me there, Liddy," Edwin went on. "And the doctor said he was going to give me a good going-over, rather like the one he gave me at

Great-Aunt Ernestine's. And he looked in my ears and my eyes and tapped on my chest and made me touch my toes and ---"

"Did he explain why?"

"No."

"Did he …?" I stopped myself. Of course, he would not say anything of consequence to an eight-year-old child. But what was it all about? Why had they singled out Edwin when examinations were normally reserved for those embarking for Canada? I beat a tattoo on the tabletop. It made no sense. Was there something wrong with Edwin? I swallowed, my throat clogged with fear. That had to be it. Something was wrong and they were keeping it from me.

I shot to my feet. As his sister, I had a right to know exactly what was going on. And by Jove, I would get to the bottom of it.

I strode to the door. "You two stay here and do not move until I return. I have important business to attend to."

## CHAPTER TWENTY-FOUR
### *October-November 1888*
### *Brackford House, Yorkshire, England*

I heard the muffled sound of a clock striking two as I approached the closed door of Phillip Latham's office. Earlier, when I had passed by en route to the boys' wing, the door had been ajar and I had seen the doctor bent over his desk, clearly absorbed in his work.

According to what Posy had said at breakfast this morning, the doctor's plan was to head for home after two or three hours in his office and not return to Brackford House until Tuesday.

Hoping against hope that he had not already departed, I tucked an errant wisp of hair behind my ear, smoothed my skirts and knocked loudly and with purpose.

His immediate, "Come in," made my heart thump. I slumped against the wall, hands pressed to my breast, waiting for my heartbeat to return to its regular rhythm.

"Come in," he said once more, louder this time.

Again, I started. Again I calmed myself. My courage was ebbing fast. I must act NOW. A swift inhalation of air to fortify myself and I flung open the door, whereupon it struck the wall behind it with a resounding—and utterly mortifying—crash. Lord in heaven, if I had fired off a cannon I could not have done a better job of announcing myself.

"Well 'pon my word"—Doctor Latham lowered the newspaper he had been reading and inspected me over its top—"Miss Lydia Fullerton as I live and breathe."

I felt my face flame. "I am most terribly sorry." I advanced into the room and stopped within a foot or so of his desk. "An accident, of course." I glanced back over my shoulder. "I do hope I have not dented your wall."

He took an inordinate amount of time folding and placing his newspaper on the desktop, resting on his elbows, leaning towards me and fixing me with the sternest of looks. "If you have done serious damage," he finally said, pausing as if to give the speculation more weight ... perhaps even to add to my discomfort, "then we shall keep your maladroitness between the two of us."

Maladroitness indeed? Did he think to flummox me with his long words? In one breath I felt a fresh wave of heat rise up in my face, in the next I willed it away. *Remember, you are a thirteen-year-old ... no ... fourteen-year-old, with a limited vocabulary. Put on a bland face now. Pour on the obsequiousness.*

"Thank you, sir." I actually dipped a small curtsy. "You are most kind."

"Think nothing of it." He gave the desktop a slap with the flat of his hand. "Now, to business. I assume you have not come here merely to pass the time of day with me, that you have something of significance to discuss, so please, child, do not stand on ceremony. Take a seat." He signalled me to the chair across from him.

As I subsided into it, my eyes lit on the newspaper's blaring headline—RIPPER STRIKES AGAIN—and I temporarily forgot both my irritation and my mission. "The Whitechapel Murderer," I said with a shudder.

"How on earth do you know about such things?"

"I read," I said haughtily.

One of his dark eyebrows rose. "Read what?"

"Newspapers."

Phillip Latham creaked back in his chair and clasped his hands behind his head. "And where on earth does a girl like you find newspapers?"

*A girl like me? And what sort of a girl might that be, pray tell?* "Matron and other members of the staff often leave them lying around."

"I see." He lowered his arms and rested them on the desktop once more. "So, you know all about the murders, then?"

"Not all about. But as much as anyone else who reads the newspaper." The horror of what I had garnered thus far on the subject made me forget myself. "The victims may well be women of ill repute, but they are human beings. And their killer is nothing less than a fiend."

"Women of ill repute, you say. And what sort of women would those be then?"

Ye gods, was that a smile twitching the corners of his mouth ... and what a well-formed mouth it was? For once I had my wits about me. "I really cannot say. It is a description I have read, and heard. I suppose they could be footpads, out-and-out robbers, or those who have not paid their debts."

I knew full well what women of ill repute were, had known since I was fifteen years old, having received my education on the subject of ladies of the night from a young woman congregant of Papa's—how he would turn in his grave if he knew. She had spent her summer in London with two male cousins of a decidedly lascivious bent. I blush to think about it now, but I learned a great deal from her about whores who would spread their legs for sixpence and of the various—and astonishing—ways they serviced their customers. I learned also—and again I blush to think about it—that a *prick* can be something other than what one does to one's finger.

Ye gods, my nether regions had grown warm and strangely heavy. I squirmed in my seat. I had best turn my mind to purer thoughts ... and quick about it.

The doctor was tapping on the desktop with the handle of a letter-opener. He angled his head and frowned at me. "I must say, Lydia Fullerton, you are a most unusual child."

*While you, sir, are a most tiresome fellow.* I felt his discomfiting stare and itched to tell him his manners were appalling. But instead, I said, in as sad a tone as I could muster, "I am just like all the other children here, sir. A poor orphan left homeless in a cruel world. Condemned to a life of ---"

"We still have not talked about what problem brings you here. Are you feeling bilious after today's roast beef? Or is it the ague?" He dipped his chin and lowered his brow, I supposed for a better view of me.

"No, sir."

"I must say you do have a feverish look about you." He made a move to rise. "Perhaps I should check ---"

"No." I sat bolt upright and waved him back as if he were something evil. "I am neither bilious nor feverish. I am perfectly well, thank you. It is my brother, Edwin, I have come to inquire about. May I know, sir, what ails him."

"What ails him?" Phillip Latham retrieved his pen from the inkstand and made a show of studying the nib. "Nothing, as far as I am aware." He passed a distracted-seeming hand across his mouth then through his thick, dark hair and something in the way his eyes moved over me made my skin tingle, my pulse quicken.

I took a moment to collect myself, reaching to my nape and tidying my bun and wishing all at once that I had retained the childish ringlets. Then I sat forward and gripped the edge of the desk. "Then why, sir, was it necessary for you to examine him earlier this week?"

The doctor's gaze fell on my red, chapped knuckles and broken nails. I snatched my hands back and dropped them to my lap, and he said in a crisp voice, "If you come to the infirmary next week, I will give you an ointment that will be of help."

Annoyed at his sidestepping of the subject, I looked up into his now-solicitous-looking face. "Thank you. But you have not answered my question. Why was Edwin subjected to an examination?"

He made an exasperated sound. "Because Matron—for reasons to which I was not made privy—ordered it."

I refused to be put off. "How could you not be privy?" I asked.

Phillip Latham rotated his chair to face the window, giving me the benefit of his back. His broad shoulders rose and fell as if he were breathing deeply ... as if perhaps he were struggling with some dilemma, and a long elastic moment passed before he turned to face me again.

For an instant I was tempted to point out his rudeness. But I caught myself, and meek as a dormouse, said, "May I please have an answer, doctor?"

After adjusting the stickpin in his cravat, then flicking what was certainly an imaginary speck from his jacket lapel, he regarded me in a strange, cool manner that forbade further discussion. "You have it. Now, run along, child." He waved a dismissive hand. "I have work to do and quite enough of this Sunday afternoon has already been wasted."

———

The sting of that brusque dismissal stayed with me for days, at times overshadowing my anxiety about Edwin. Hovering at the back of my mind had been the faint hope that in Phillip Latham I had found—if not a saviour—at least an ally. I had seen him ministering to Edwin, I had heard through Posy of his many virtues and I had—up until this last one—relished our few encounters.

Now I had to face the fact that the man was a liar. His eyes had told me he was hiding something ... most certainly something to do with Edwin.

But during the Sunday visits that followed, everything appeared to be perfectly normal as far as Edwin was concerned. He had had no more contact with the doctor, he said. Nothing further of an untoward nature was mentioned and so, as the weeks passed, I felt able to put my worries on that score behind me. It was not long, however, before I was beset with worries about Annabel.

Even though she had expected Posy's mid-October departure for Manitoba, when it actually happened Annabel took it badly and descended into a state of utter dejection. I could have told her she had me, that I was her very best friend and that we, of course, would never have to part company. But I bit my tongue and let her be, showing my love and concern for her with an occasional arm about her shoulders, a stroke of the back of her hand or a gentle pat on her cheek. And finally, one day towards the end of November, when we were in the library methodically, almost unconsciously dusting dozens of leather-bound books, a miracle happened, and as if a sorcerer's wand had been waved over her, Annabel suddenly turned back into her old cheerful self.

She clapped a book to her chest and with great drama said, "I shall miss Posy dreadfully and I will never forget her. But I am bound to make more friends."

"You certainly are," I said, breathing a sigh of relief. "But not here at Brackford House."

Annabel wrinkled her nose and regarded me with a quizzical expression.

"Remember, in another two months we, too, will be embarking on our journey across the ocean and the friends you make will be at your new home."

"On the prairies?"

"Yes, I imagine so."

"Perhaps I will befriend a Red Indian girl."

Visions of marauding savages and wild cowboys and stampeding buffalo rolled across my mind. "Perhaps," I said.

"I think I should rather like to learn to ride a horse and maybe become a cowgirl."

"You know, we really do not know what we are going to be facing, Annabel ---"

"And I think," Matron's deep voice suddenly sounded from the doorway and we both started, "it will be woe betide you girls if you do not attend to your work."

"Thank you," I said, grateful for the interruption, and she looked at me as if I were daft.

But I had come dangerously close to putting a damper on Annabel's dreams. And that was the last thing I wanted to do.

### CHAPTER TWENTY-FIVE
#### *December 1888 to January 1889*
#### *Brackford House, Yorkshire, England*

Before we knew it, the festive season was upon us and Brackford House underwent a transformation. A few days before Christmas Eve a couple of the gardeners brought in from the grounds a tall, freshly cut fir which they placed in a large sand-filled tub in the entrance hall. After that, the men returned with holly boughs laden with red berries and armfuls of evergreens with which they set about decorating the entire house. Holly sprigs were tucked behind picture frames and arranged in bowls and vases. Mantelpieces, shelves, archways and doorways were festooned with greenery whose wonderfully-pungent aroma filled the air.

We Fullertons had always had a Christmas tree at the rectory, even after Mama's death. But many of Brackford's orphans had never before seen such a thing, nor had they ever been instructed in the art of red-and-green-paper-chain and tiny-lantern-making, as they were during lessons the same day the tree was put up.

When we assembled in the entrance hall the next afternoon with our chains and lanterns, Nurse Jamieson, Amelia Dunn and Miss Hubbard were on hand to help us climb up onto stools and stepladders, and once we had finished hanging our handiwork we stood by and watched the three apply strands of silver tinsel, artificial snow made of cotton wool, German glass balls and strings of tiny glass beads—apparently from Matron's personal collection— and several dozen small reflective metal candleholders containing red candles which we were told would be lit on Christmas Eve.

Sure enough, an hour before bedtime on Christmas Eve we were summoned to the entrance hall for the tree-lighting which was performed by one of the gardeners under Matron's watchful eye. After a great deal of "oooohing and aaahing" from all present, Miss Hubbard led us in carol-singing. And finally, Mrs. Jamieson served each of us a mug of the most fragrant and delicious hot spiced cider.

And as if this were not enough, Matron announced that Brackford's twenty-five boy orphans had been invited to join our celebrations here in the girls' wing on Christmas Day, Boxing Day and New Year's Eve.

Needless to say, standing together, arms linked, Edwin, Annabel and I were beside ourselves with joy on Christmas morning when Matron and Mr. Hazelhurst jointly handed out to each orphan an apple, an orange and a handful of nuts. And later on, we sat together in the dining hall savoring first the exquisite aromas, and then the taste of golden-skinned roast goose, of roast potatoes and gravy and carrots, followed by rich plum pudding with custard sauce and silver threepenny bits—so we were told, but did not bag—hidden within its fruity depths.

Edwin was with us again on Boxing Day when the Bishop blessed each one of us, then presided over a special tea where we were served—among other things—mince pies, Christmas cake and trifle. And after tea on New Year's Eve, the three of us, along with all the other boys and girls were allowed to congregate under the tree again, toast each other with cups of cocoa and sing Auld Lang Syne. Immediately afterwards, the boys were herded back to their quarters and we girls were hustled off to bed.

The next day—New Year's Day, 1889—we returned, of course, to the status quo, with the rule of segregation once again enforced and visits limited to every other Sunday.

We saw Edwin on the sixth of January, and then, to my surprise, Annabel and I were summoned to Matron's office immediately after breakfast on the ninth—a Wednesday. I felt certain a miracle had occurred and she was going to tell us that from now on we would be allowed to see Edwin every weekend.

But on that score my hopes were quickly dashed. No sooner did we enter her domain than Matron said with a nod in Annabel's direction, "You will spend the day in my quarters where I have a number of chores for you to attend to. While, you, Lydia, will go about your usual tasks until four o'clock, at which time you will come to my dining room. I will be entertaining guests at tea and will require you to wait on us."

"Very well, Matron," I said, disappointed that there had been no mention of Edwin, but pleasantly surprised by the news of my assignment.

"Be sure to make yourself thoroughly presentable; shoes polished, apron clean, hands and face clean, fingernails clean."

*Bottom clean?* I suppressed a smile at my own private joke.

Thrice before I had served at Matron's soirées. And, in truth, of all the tasks I had been called upon to perform during my stay at Brackford House, I had found this the most tolerable. Depending on the guests, the conversations were often interesting, and if the partakers-of-tea retired to Matron's drawing room for sherry afterwards, chances were there would be sandwiches hardly-touched and the remains of cakes and biscuits left on plates. These could be handily slipped into a serviette, popped into my apron pocket, and in the dormitory later on, shared with Annabel and whomever else of the pleasanter girls might be at hand.

When I knocked on the dining room door at precisely four o'clock, I was smiling to myself in anticipation of the hours ahead. But seconds later, after I had answered Matron's, "Enter" and stepped across the threshold, the smile froze on my lips and I stood rooted, gaping in utter bewilderment.

There, seated around the table—looking mightily pleased with themselves and tucking into an assortment which included sandwiches, pink blancmange, red jelly, petit fours and other cakes—were Matron, Annabel, Edwin, and a couple who were strangers to me.

The middle-aged pair were a study in contrasts. The woman was large-bosomed and wide-shouldered, her complexion dark, her nose narrow and long and her black hair was pulled severely back into a stingy bun at her nape, making her unusually high forehead seem even higher. The man was a slight, inconsequential-looking sort, pasty-faced, with bony cheeks and a near-bald head reminiscent of a baby's with its wisps of pale blond hair.

"Do not just stand there gaping, girl." Matron wiped her mouth on her serviette and gestured for me to come forward.

I stopped by her chair and, as if through a fog, observed Annabel tongue a blob of jam from the corner of her mouth while Edwin licked butter cream from the cake layers he had taken apart. They each slanted a glance in my direction, but were clearly far too involved with their meal to be concerned with me.

"Say good afternoon to my guests, Mr. and Mrs. Chistlegate," Matron said, with a grandiose-looking gesture in their direction, "and go and stand over there, close to them, so they can get a good look at you."

"Afternoon," I said with reluctance under my breath, making my way to the far end of the large, oval table. A frantic tom-tom beat in my chest. There was something dreadfully wrong with this scene of conviviality ... something dangerous about this couple whose eyes were now roving over me, making me feel as if I were an animal on the auction block on market day. I balled my fists at my sides, straightened my spine and like a fighter challenging an opponent, I tipped my chin and skewered each of them with a stare of such belligerence that I fancied them scorched by it.

Mrs. Chistlegate's response was to purse her lips in a mean little smile, while her husband averted his eyes and turned his attention to the slice of cake on his plate.

Continuing to smile, the woman said, looking across the table at Matron, "Oh my, not this one, I fear. Entirely unsuitable." She elbowed her husband and he jumped to attention. "Do you not agree, Thomas?"

"Yes dear, of course, dear," he said.

Matron dipped her head in acknowledgment. "I understand. Positively too much to hope for, I suppose. But at least you will have the two." She beckoned to me. "Come back over here, child. I have something of considerable importance to impart."

I did not remember moving, but I must have, for the next thing I knew I was beside Matron's chair again. "Now"—she took my hands and covered them with her own—"what I have to tell you is most exciting. Mr. and Mrs. Chistlegate have been visiting us on and off for quite some time now. And after careful consideration, they have made a very important decision about Edwin's future ... and as of today, your sister's also."

I felt dizzy, but Matron's grip on my hands kept me steady.

"Not only have they agreed to take Edwin," she continued, "but mindful of the pain caused by the separation of brother and sister, they have most generously agreed to include Annabel, too."

"Take?" I nodded dumbly. "Take where?"

"Into their home ... to bring up as their own."

I snatched my hands away as if scalded and backed up several paces. It could not be. No ... no. It could not possibly be.

"How fortunate a girl you are, knowing that while you still have your *Great Adventure* ahead of you, in Canada, your sister and brother will be here in England, safe in the bosom of their new family."

Fortunate? Great god in heaven. Blood drummed at my temples and I grasped my head between my hands. My brother and sister were to be taken from me. An ocean would separate us. I would never see them again.

Matron was all at once up out of her seat and at my side. She pulled my hands away from my head and said under her breath, "Do not do anything foolish, girl. Had you been less recalcitrant, you, too, would have been chosen by the Chistlegates."

Not wishing to alarm the children who were clearly oblivious of the drama being played out here and were happily continuing to fill their bellies, I kept my voice low. "You cannot," I said. "You promised. Do you not remember?" In spite of my resolve, my voice rose a notch. "No separation you said."

With an apologetic glance at the couple, Matron said, still in a low voice between her teeth, "That is quite enough of that, miss. You will behave yourself and serve us tea, now. And, if it is your desire to participate in this final visit with your brother and sister—to say your farewells and wish them well—you will exhibit no further rudeness or ingratitude. Do I make myself clear?"

*This final visit.* The words pierced my heart, the pain so searing I could hardly breath.

"Well, do I?" Matron gripped my arm.

"Liar," I mumbled.

"What did you say?"

I wrenched free of the woman and shrank from her. "I said you are a liar," my voice climbed the scale. "A damned liar whose word is not worth muck."

Matron stood stock still, her mouth slack. Out of the corner of my eye I took in everything at the table: Mr. Chistlegate's fatalistic shake of his head; his wife's delicate cough behind her serviette; Edwin's wide, frightened eyes; Annabel's reassuring pat on his arm.

*Oh my dear, dear loves. What are they doing to us?*

"You cannot take them. I will not let you." My heart pounded so hard I felt faint. I took a great gulp of air that in the silence sounded like a death rattle. "You cannot give my sister and brother away to those dreadful people," I prattled on. "I promised ... and you said ... together ... we were to stay ..." I paused for breath again, my head spinning, my ears ringing.

Matron clearly saw her advantage. She grasped me by the shoulders and whirled me about, shoving me towards the door.

I tried desperately to free myself, but Matron was too determined, too strong, too livid. Trapped in the vice of the woman's muscular hands, my feet barely touching the floor, I felt myself propelled ahead.

"You are finished here, little miss foul mouth." The vitriolic whisper burned like acid into my scalp. "And that, I can assure you, is no lie."

Finished here? *Oh dear God, help me, help me. What have I done?* "I am sorry, Matron," I called over my shoulder as I was thrust through the open door and into the hall, "I know I was terribly rude ... I did not mean to ---"

"Too late." Matron prodded me on with her knee. Then a few feet along the hall she suddenly stopped and spun me around. Hands clamped on my shoulders, she leaned down and said, "You stupid, stupid girl. It is far too late for apologies. Never mind burning your bridges ... with that disgusting outburst of yours, you have blown them to utter smithereens." Her mouth curved in the parody of a smile. "And what a shame, when I was all set to tell you that you would be allowed to stay in touch with your brother and sister by letter. Now, of course, no communication whatsoever will be permitted."

I saw the look of cruel triumph behind the woman's eyes, the cold fury on her face. I gave a strangled cry. Merciful Heaven, the nightmare was reality. And there would be no redemption.

*It will be up to you to hold the family together.*

*Oh, dear God, forgive me, Mama...*

"Please, Matron," I extended my hands palms-up, like a beggar, "let me at least say goodbye to them."

The clamps were on my arms again. "Positively no communication, I said."

"But I must ... I will." I turned my head and screamed over my shoulder, "Annabel, Edwin. I promise we will be together again. I promise I will not forget you. Wherever I am, I will ---"

Matron's hand covered my mouth. "And I promise, you will do nothing of the sort. It is The Punishment Room for you, girl." Her angry spittle showered my face. "I promise you, too, that you will *never*"— she punctuated the word with a particularly vicious squeeze of my upper arm—"see your brother and sister again." She paused in triumph and I put up a final, desperate struggle for freedom, flailing, kicking, trying to bite the hot, fleshy gag that threatened to suffocate me.

But I was helpless against the woman's strength. And when she said, "If it is the last thing I do, I shall make sure that you, you little vixen, are on the very next ship that leaves for Montreal," I realized the futility of it all, stopped struggling and quietly wept.

## CHAPTER TWENTY-SIX
### *January-April 1889*
### *Brackford House, Yorkshire, England*

In the flower bed outside The Punishment Room's cobweb-festooned ground-level window, the snowdrops carpeting the frosted earth lifted their heads to the anaemic morning sun, and on the handle of a trowel left there by a forgetful gardener, a robin redbreast perched, its tiny throat vibrating with its song.

From the edge of the cot where I sat swaddled in a rough, woolen blanket, I leaned forward and cocked my head straining to hear the melody. At the first, barely discernible flute-like notes, the corners of my mouth curved upwards of their own volition. Two of Mama's favourites -- the charming flower she had always considered a harbinger of spring; the little bird she had thought so cheerful a fellow and so full of hope, somehow.

As swiftly as my smile had bloomed it faded. Spring would find me leaving behind everything I held dear and crossing a vast expanse of ocean to God knew where. And as for hope …? I followed a cynical snort with a long sorrowful breath and the reek of the place—the mold and mildew and fermentation—made me feel slightly nauseated. I should have eaten more of the breakfast that had been delivered earlier. But the lumpy porridge and dry slice of bread had appealed to me not one jot.

This was Saturday, the twelfth of January, the third day of my imprisonment. Soon—tomorrow, the next day, a week hence … Matron had not been specific—I was to be transported to Liverpool. Once there, she had said, I would be installed in a boarding house of the type reserved for immigrants where I would remain until the sailings to Montreal resumed in March.

The sound of the key scraping in the lock interrupted my thoughts, and I turned in time to see Amelia Dunn entering the room.

"Morning, Lydia," she said, closing the door after herself. "How are you?"

Anyone else and I would have made some scathing remark. But the young woman had always been pleasant and considerate. "As well as can be expected," I said.

"I have news." Miss Dunn crossed the stone flags and sat down beside me. "We are leaving Monday morning."

"We?"

"I am to accompany you on the journey to your accommodations in Liverpool, make sure you are properly settled in, an' the next day, introduce you to the agent who will be in charge of you during your crossing."

"You will be staying with me?"

"For one night, yes."

"What do you mean by the agent?"

"Matron contracts with certain persons to accompany her children."

Her children. How innocuous she made it sound.

"You have been supplied with a new wardrobe an' I have taken it upon myself to pack your suitcase with the various items."

I was about to make an acerbic comment about Parisian couture, but thought better of it and instead, said with only a hint of dryness while passing a hand over the drab green fabric of my skirt, "Does this mean I will be able to dispense with this fashionable gown then?"

"Indeed, it does. You will have three new frocks; two serviceable everyday ones an' a better one for Sundays an' the like. You will also have new night attire, underwear an' a new pair of boots."

"Really?" I said, without enthusiasm.

"They want you to have a good start," said Miss Dunn.

With no attempt at a smooth conversational transition, I asked, "Have you heard anything of Annabel and Edwin?"

"No." Miss Dunn rose and stood looking down at me, her expression troubled. "Nor am I likely to. I feel badly about your separation from your brother and sister, Lydia. But I am afraid I can tell you nothing about the whys and wherefores of the situation. I follow Matron's instructions and that is that."

"May I ask you one more question?"

"Of course, then we must talk about the arrangements."

"Has Matron done this before?"

"Done what?"

"Given orphans to families here in England?"

"From what I understand, every so often a Brackford child or two gets adopted by a family here."

"Does anyone know where they go?"

"No, Lydia. None of us do. I suppose there must be records somewhere but Matron is the only one privy to them." She placed a gentle hand on my shoulder. "Anyway, there is no point in your worrying yourself about such things."

"No point?" I said with angry disbelief.

"Right. You are going to have to accept the situation and just get on with your life, dear."

"I have no life," I muttered.

If Miss Dunn heard me she did not let on. She brought her hands together in a decisive gesture and said, "Attend to me please, child, whilst I tell you about the plans for Monday."

———

A little over a year had passed since I had endured the joys of second-class train travel in a compartment open to the elements. On this Monday morning, my teeth once again rattled; my posterior bounced on the seat's hard wooden slats; the bitter wind whistled in my face and the sleet beat upon my bonneted head. Oh and the ungodly racket ... the soot ... the clouds of belching steam.

Miss Dunn had instructed me to sit tight against her, so that we might benefit from each other's body heat. We both kept shifting our feet on the foot warmers she had hired at York station. The square, metal bottles had been filled with boiling water, and if we were lucky they would stay warm for the duration of our journey.

Amelia Dunn gave me a nudge and leaned in to make herself heard over the din. "At least our feet will not freeze."

I nodded in agreement.

"An' we shall not go hungry." She indicated the portmanteau on the seat next to her and chuckled. "I do not know what came over Mrs. Jessop an' made her suddenly so kind, but there is enough here to feed an army. I asked her if she might be able to prepare a sandwich or two for us, an' the next thing she was parceling up slices of cold roast beef an' ham, almost half a loaf, a big chunk of cheese an' a good-sized slab of Madeira cake."

I responded with a weak smile. At present, food was the last thing on my mind.

But three hours later, I was starving, and said so.

"No wonder." Miss Dunn began rummaging in the portmanteau and extracting various paper-wrapped parcels. "We have put out as much effort as a good day's work with all the bouncing around and clapping ourselves on the arms and rubbing our hands together we have been doin'. Here." She had spread out the booty between us on the seat. "Tuck in."

After we had eaten, I drew up my collar, pulled my bonnet down as far as possible over my face and astonishingly—despite the buffeting about and the icy blast and the infernal racket of the train on the tracks—I fell asleep.

The next thing I knew I was being shaken awake, and Amelia Dunn's face swam into focus.

"We are here, Lydia."

I peered from beneath the brim of my bonnet. "Where?"

"Lime Street Station, Liverpool."

I sat up straight.

"Get a move on, now, and grab your luggage. We do not want to be left behind."

On the platform moments later, I stood in awe amongst the maelstrom of embarking and disembarking passengers, gazing up at the vast glass dome of a roof with its supporting iron ribs.

"Quite the architectural masterpiece in its day, from what I understand," shouted Miss Dunn over the din of hurrying footfalls and excited voices and rumbling wheels. She clutched my arm and urged me along, yanking me out of the way of a porter pulling a handcart loaded with suitcases. "You must watch your step, dear. An' stay close, whatever you do. It would be woe betide me if I lost you."

Perhaps if I had been able to muster the courage, I would have fled right then, disappeared amongst the crush of bodies. But I felt beaten down, dependent, and I hung onto Miss Dunn's arm with grim determination. Lord, was the entire population of Liverpool here at the station? I had never before seen so many people in one place. How I longed for quiet again, and for the solitude—ironic or not—to which those long hours in The Punishment Room had acclimatized me.

The ride in the hansom cab provided some insulation from the clamor of the outside world, although for the first few minutes of our journey the cabbie —an Irishman by the sound of him—kept opening the little trap door that separated him from us, and conversing with Miss Dunn. This meant I had to contend not only with their chatter, but with the rattling of the vehicle's wheels and the snorting of the pair of horses and their clip-clopping over the cobbles.

Eventually, we came to a halt outside a three-storey house in a long, curving terrace of what looked like identical houses. "Sure an' yer a lucky lass ter be stayin' in such grand diggin's," the cabbie said with a thick brogue, handing me down from the hansom.

Grand? I hardly thought so. I regarded the home's brick façade which must have been bright red at one time, but now was dull and grimy and clearly engrained with soot. In fact, I could taste soot on my tongue, feel its grittiness in my eyes. And no wonder. From every chimney on the street thick black smoke spiraled up.

"Most o' the immigrants end up in The Courts, so they do," the cabbie said, placing our luggage on the pavement, then taking the coins Miss Dunn proffered. I had not been heeding his and Miss Dunn's conversation, but she must have told him about what lay ahead for me. What in creation did he mean by The Courts? I asked myself, envisioning a bewigged judge wagging his finger at me and berating me for some crime or other.

Miss Dunn was clearly as perplexed as I. "I am afraid I do not comprehend," she said. "What courts are you talking about?"

The cabbie climbed up into his seat and shouted down to us, "Sure an' aren't they the slums, then. Great tall an' terrible 'ouses packed together on top o' one another, wi' nary a glimpse o' sun or sky."

"Ah," said Miss Dunn, nodding her understanding.

"Not fit for a beast ter live in," the cabbie went on, picking up the reins and murmuring soothing-sounding words to his horses. "Wi' dozens o' poor souls crammed in together, an' with only one privy fer the whole street an' them landlords gettin' sixpence a night off 'em … my own countrymen most of 'em."

"You are certainly correct, then, about the grandeur of this place," Miss Dunn said, turning to me for apparent confirmation.

I shrugged, but did not respond. It depended on one's perception.

Grand or not, the place did prove to be spotless we discovered, once the proprietress—an extremely tall, whippet-thin woman who introduced herself as Miss Waterhouse—responded to Miss Dunn's ringing of the doorbell and admitted us.

In an odd, stiff-lipped, manner which matched her ramrod straight back, the woman said, "Your Mrs. Bell made a wise decision in selecting Number Thirty six for her children. You will be pleased to know that unlike a great many other establishments, here we have no lice, no fleas, no bedbugs, no rats, no mice."

"A most comforting thought," said Miss Dunn catching my eye and clearly doing her best to suppress a smile.

I maintained a poker face. *Twice as nice, no lice or mice. Pray do you have a single vice?*

"Now, if you will pick up your luggage and follow me upstairs, I will show you to your room," Miss Waterhouse said. "Tea is at five. Second door to your right when you come back down." She took the two flights of stairs at a fast clip and we had to struggle to keep up.

Finally, we reached the room which was to be my home for close to two months and Miss Dunn's for one night. Sparsely-furnished with a double bed, chest of drawers and one chair, its scrubbed pine floor smelled of carbolic soap, which reminded me of the infirmary at Brackwood House, and inevitably of Doctor Latham.

While Miss Waterhouse and Miss Dunn conversed, my mind wandered. Did the doctor know I was no longer there at Brackford House? Did he care? Did I care whether he did or not?

"Lydia." The sound of my name being called and the snap of fingers next to my ear returned me to the present, and I found myself staring into Miss Dunn's face. "Time to come back to earth, Lydia. Miss Waterhouse tells me tea will be served in half an hour, so we had best see to our unpacking an' freshen ourselves up a bit. I see there is water in the jug on the chest of drawers over there."

"Cold water," I said, with a grimace.

"Better than nothing. Besides it will wake you up. Shake a leg, then, child."

I headed for the near side of the bed, she to the far side, and we each hoisted our suitcases up onto it. I had barely opened mine and dipped into it before Miss Dunn said, "Oh I almost forgot. I have a present for you Lydia. I have had it for years an' never used it, an' I suddenly thought you might find it useful."

My curiosity piqued, I stretched my neck for a view of the mysterious object. After a minute or two of rummaging, Miss Dunn said, "Here we are. Hold out your hand, child."

"What is it?" I asked, gazing down at the small, square, leather-covered box.

"You will see. Push the little metal button on the front and then lift the lid."

"Oh my. Edwin would have adored this," I said, regarding—nestled in its purple velvet bed—a diminuitive silver-cased carriage clock with open glass sides, exposing the various cogs and wheels of its brass workings.

"Never mind Edwin," said Miss Dunn. "What about you? Do you like it?"

"Oh yes. I love it. Thank you very much indeed."

"We will wind it now an' you can put it on the dressing table. An' when we come back after tea I think you an' I should have an early night. We have our meeting tomorrow with Mr. Benjamin Vye, Matron's agent, an' after that I have another long journey ahead of me back to Brackford House"

Matron's agent. I was no fool. I was a commodity that needed guarding and she could not risk my running off.

The following day I was sorry to see Miss Dunn leave. She had been a good and—of late—generous friend to me. "You take great care of my young charge here," she had told Mr. Vye, who turned out to be a jolly, corpulent fellow with beetling brows over sharp little eyes. "Make certain nothing untoward befalls her during the crossing, an' be sure an' keep those dreadful

Irish away from her."

Her words made me uneasy. But Mr. Vye put my fears to rest. "I will treat you like my own, little lady," he said. "'tis my job to make sure you arrive in Montreal in one piece, an' that you most certainly will do."

"I should hope so," I said with cynicism, "I am valuable cargo," whereupon he threw back his large head with its mane of thick white hair, and roared with laughter.

My life at Number Thirty-six was dreary, to say the least, the monotony stultifying, but Mr. Vye's weekly visits saved me. He thought me the image of his grand-daughter who lived all the way up in Scotland in the back of beyond and whom he rarely saw, so he made me her proxy. Insisting I sit on his knee —which turned out not to discomfit me at all—he regularly performed tricks with a gold sovereign, using astonishing alacrity in order to make it appear and disappear in various odd places such as the cuff of my boot, the back of my collar, and in my hand.

"You an' I shall be the best of friends, little girl," he often said, his coarse, white side whiskers grazing my cheek.

One week dissolved into another. March gave way to April and I began to wonder if I would ever leave. By now I could not wait to depart. I was to be forced to give away five years of my life. Let me get on with it, then live for the day I could return to England and search out my dear ones.

At last, on the morning of the twentieth of April, word of the irrevocable day of my departure arrived. "You and I, m'dear one," Mr. Vye said as soon as I answered the door to him, "are all set to sail for the port of Quebec, on Thursday, five days hence, on The Allan Line Steamship, *Parisian*."

———

With shoulders and elbows, Mr. Vye cleared a pathway for me through the mob on the morning of the twenty-fifth. I scuttled alongside him, my ears ringing with the shouts of men and boys, the shrieks of women and children, the rumble of the wheels of carts—two-wheeled, four-wheeled, large, small— and the rolling over the cobbles of hogsheads and various other-sized barrels. The reek of unwashed bodies and tobacco smoke and a sulphurous odour like boiled cabbage made me want to hold my nose. But I was too busy to do so, having to dance a jig of sorts in order to avoid the stevedores carrying on their backs and in their arms, sacks of grain and bolts of cloth and boxes and baskets and all manner of supplies destined for the steamer on which I was to travel.

Earlier, while Mr. Vye waited outside, I had been shepherded into a warehouse and lined up with dozens of others for a medical examination. A nameless doctor had made a perfunctory check of my ears, nose, teeth and throat and applied his stethoscope to my chest. "Pass," had been his verdict.

Now, borne along in the crush of bodies, I felt Mr. Vye's ham of a hand grasp mine. "'ere she is, all four 'undred and forty-odd feet of 'er," he said, indicating the great iron hull of the ship anchored alongside us at the wharf. Men were swarming like insects all over of the decks, readying the vessel for departure, I assumed.

"A right beauty, ain't she?"

I nodded. Not exactly my idea of beauty, but nevertheless an imposing steamer. My stay on it, however, was bound to be a nightmare. I had heard enough about steerage class conditions on board these immigrant vessels to know what horrors were in store for me.

But praise be, I was wrong. The thoughts had hardly crossed my mind before Mr. Vye said, "By the way, little one, you shall not be travelin' steerage. I 'ave arranged for you ter have a cabin all to yerself."

I was speechless at this fortunate turn of events, so used had I grown to the misery of my life without my dear ones. I reached up and planted a light kiss on my benefactor's cheek, and he tucked my arm through his, and smiling from ear to ear, escorted me up the gangplank of Her Majesty's Steamship, *Parisian.*

---

Admittedly, I was beset with misgivings later that afternoon once I was installed in my cabin and mulling its many comforts. Had I been too forward? Would my actions be misinterpreted? Had I been naïve? Did I need to call to question Mr. Benjamin Vye's motivation?

I felt a sudden vibration beneath my feet. No doubt the engines were being tested to ensure that they were running properly. I glanced at the little carriage clock on the nearby dressing table. It was only half-past three … an hour-and-a-half before our scheduled departure, and three-and-a-half before Mr. Vye would come by to escort me to dinner.

How on earth was I going to kill all that time? I was not allowed to go wandering about the decks, that was for certain. "You must stay put until I come an' get yer," Mr. Vye had said. Stay put and do what, though? I exhaled a long, bored breath. The cabin lacked a porthole for me to look out of. I had no cards with which to play Patience. I *did* have three or four old *penny dreadfuls* in the bottom of my suitcase, but I knew I would not be able to settle to reading. With another long sigh, I regarded my bunk. A nap appeared to be the only alternative left to me.

I had barely laid my head on the pillow before someone rapped on the cabin door and made me almost jump out of my skin. I clapped a hand to my chest over my fast-beating heart. It could only be Mr. Vye; I knew no one else on the ship.

"Coming," I shouted in answer to a second knock, which was delivered with considerably more force than the first. "Patience old man," I said under my breath, scrambling down from the bunk and stomping across the cabin. I took a moment to collect myself, then heaved open the door and said in the sweetest of tones, "Is there something you forgot, Mr. Vye?"

"Indeed there is," said the deep, musical voice.

I clutched my throat and like the heroine in a melodrama, let out a little gasp.

But this *was* a melodrama, for I was staring into the golden eyes of Doctor Phillip Latham.

### CHAPTER TWENTY-SEVEN
### *April 1889*
### *On Board the "S.S. Parisian", Liverpool, England*

"Doctor Latham?" I shook my head in astonishment. "What in creation are you doing here?"

He doffed his hat and smoothed back the swatch of dark hair that fell over one eye. "Looking for you, you poor child, having heard from Amelia Dunn just two days ago about the sorry state of your affairs."

So now I was not only a child, but a poor child.

Looking beyond me into the cabin's interior, he shrugged out of his topcoat and asked, "May I come in?"

I nodded, stepping aside to make way for him, detecting in his wake the subtle scent of lavender and vanilla that must have been his cologne.

His eyes cut to the armchair. "Mind if I sit?"

"Please do." I took his hat from him and placed it on top of the chest-of-drawers while he draped his coat over the chair's back and sat, exhaling a long, grateful-sounding breath. "I have had one devil of a time following your trail and getting here on time, and am about ready to drop."

Feeling thoroughly discomposed, I crossed to my bunk and settled on its edge. Whatever his reason for being here, he needed to look sharp or he would find himself in Quebec along with the rest of us. "You do know the ship is readying for departure?"

He drew a weary hand across his forehead. "Indeed I do, Lydia. Heard it from the first-officer, in fact, when I received dispensation from him for this visit." He felt inside his jacket and extracted a pocket watch. "In exactly one hour and five minutes, if my information is correct. So we had best be quick about our business."

Our conversation had an odd sort of formality about it, and—contrary or not—I did nothing to counteract it with my, "I am afraid you have me at a disadvantage, doctor."

He tilted his head, appraisingly. "You look thinner. Have you not been eating properly?"

I answered with a lift of my shoulders.

"Perhaps your frock is creating the illusion. You are not wearing the rather tent-like Brackford issue, I see."

I smoothed the skirt of my purple-and-green tartan. "I was given a new wardrobe. I suppose they want me to look presentable for my owners."

"Hmmm ... yes, I suppose they do." The doctor stared off for a moment, his expression grim. Then he returned his attention to me and with a sorrowful shake of his head, said, "Helluva business this separation. You, dispatched without so much as a by your leave, your siblings sent god knows where."

"I am surprised Matron did not tell you all about it."

"Believe me, Lydia, I have little contact with the woman. She is the Queen Bee as regards the operation of Brackford House. I answer to the Board of Directors and run my surgery and the infirmary as they require. And I can assure you"—his voice took on a slight edge—"Mrs. Bell and I do not sit around drinking tea and gossiping about the children or the staff. I can assure you, too, that were it within my power to free you, I would. But you are unfortunately, the property of the powers-that-be at Brackford House, at least for the next five years, and there is not a deuced thing I can do about that."

I flushed and tightened my lips at what I felt was a rebuke. I fiddled with a loose thread on the counterpane, my agitation growing by the minute. *Why on earth did you come here, then? For pity's sake put me out of my misery and tell me.*

Seconds later, as if Phillip Latham had read my mind, he leaned forward, elbows resting on his knees, and said in a soft voice, "I am here to help you, Lydia, my dear girl."

The dam broke then, and tears spilled from my eyes. "How can you help?" I said through my sobs. "Can you stop them from sending me to Canada? Can you reunite me with Annabel and Edwin? Have you any idea where they are? Will I ever see them again?"

Apparently unfazed by my outburst, he was all at once on his knees in front of me, my hands captured in his, his breath warm on my face. "No, I cannot stop them sending you away. No, I cannot reunite you with your brother and sister. And no, I have no idea where they are. But you will see them again. By God you will, if I have anything to do with it."

"But how?"

He released my hands and placed them in my lap as gently as if they were two newborn kittens. I stared down at them and said in little more than a whisper, "What can you possibly do?"

Scrambling to his feet, he fished a handkerchief from his jacket pocket then bent over me and dabbed away my tears. "There, there, my dear," he said, thrusting the white cotton square upon me. "Be a good girl now. Dry your eyes and blow your nose."

Mortified, I blotted, sniffed delicately—I would not stoop to blowing— and castigated myself. Ye gods, I had exhibited all the panache of a five-year-old and was being treated like one.

"Alright, now," Phillip Latham had risen from his knees and was looming over me, "make room for me to sit down beside you."

I felt my eyes grow wide. Lord save me. The stuff of my dreams ... my almost twenty-two-year-old dreams. I was to have this man beside me in my bed ... not exactly in, but certainly on. Feeling a little breathless, I budged along and he sat next to me, his long legs stretched out alongside my considerably shorter ones. At least mine were slender and shapely and, yes, I did have well-turned ankles and dainty feet worthy of a gentleman's attention. *Piffle. What nonsense is this?*

Phillip Latham placed a long-fingered, well-shaped hand on my knee and a tiny shudder went through me. "Although I cannot perform miracles, Lydia, I do have a plan of sorts."

"Really?" He had withdrawn his hand, but I still felt its warm imprint.

"Yes. I am going to give you my home address so that you may stay in touch with me by letter."

My heart fluttered. "You are?"

"I am certain, given time, that I shall be able to find your Edwin and Annabel."

"You are?"

"Yes. So, as well as writing to me I want you to write separately and regularly, to your brother and sister."

"Then when"—I did not want to say *if*—"you find them, depending on the time it takes you to do so, you will have either a few, or a great many letters to present to them."

"Precisely." He suddenly rose and fumbled in his inside jacket pocket. "Here is my address, Lydia. Please be sure and put it in a safe place."

I too got up. "I will, later on, I promise." For now, I folded the paper and put it in my skirt pocket. "I am perfectly happy to write both to you and my siblings. But how, exactly, will you go about looking for the children?"

"I have not yet refined my plans, Lydia." He grasped me by the shoulders and regarded me as I imagined an artist might regard his model, his eyes moving over every contour of my face, lingering on my cheekbones, the bridge of my nose, the curve of my lips.

Faint with expectation—of what I had no idea—I held my breath and in that moment I felt the tenor of the engine's vibrations all at once alter. I exhaled shakily, sensing a kind of urgency to the thrumming. Apparently so did Phillip Latham. He dug into his pocket and brought out his watch again. "Good Lord." He moved swiftly about the cabin, retrieving his hat and coat and donning both. "I had best get off the ship and fast, or they will be arresting me as a stowaway."

I stayed put, unsure of what to do.

"Come here, Lydia," he said, shocking me with his outspread arms.

After a moment's hesitation I went to him, and it felt like the most natural thing in the world to be cradled against him, with the rough tweed of his jacket grazing my cheek and his heart beating beneath my ear. "Remember, my dear, dear girl, you have my solemn promise that I will find your siblings."

I hardly had time to respond with a dreamy, "Thank you," when the ship's horn sounded a couple of horrendously loud blasts which so startled us that we sprang apart.

I stood, arms limp at my sides, dizzy from the embrace and its sudden interruption.

Phillip Latham took a step towards me and looked down at me with an unfathomable expression on his face. "I must go now, Lydia." He brushed my cheek with the back of his hand, letting it linger there for an instant. "Remember," he said, turning on his heel, "write to me."

"I will." I watched him hurry for the door. Seconds later it thudded shut behind him. I remained motionless for a time, my irrational mind telling me that a miracle might occur, that he would come charging back to the cabin and say there had been a mistake and that he could, in fact, save me from my fate.

Gradually, my senses returned to me and I trudged to my bunk. I lay down on my side, clutching the pillow to my middle, and began to sob.

I must have dozed off, the movement of the ship lulling my senses. By the time I came to, half an hour had passed and my tears had ceased flowing. But when I got up and went to the dressing table mirror I was appalled to see how red and swollen my eyes were. Ye gods, I would need to repair the ravages before Mr. Vye came to collect me in approximately one hour. The last thing I wanted was his scrutiny and sympathy.

On top of the nearby washstand was a large water-filled jug and a bowl. Attached to each side of the stand were racks from which towels and a flannel hung. This latter I soaked in cold water and wrung out, then I returned with it to my bunk and lay down, applying the compress to my puffy eyes. Over a period of half an hour I repeated the process several times then dressed in the best of my three new frocks, so that by the time I opened the door to Mr. Vye's knock another half hour later, I felt I looked reasonably presentable.

"Ready, little one?" he asked, apparently noticing nothing amiss about my appearance.

I pasted on a smile. "Yes."

"Quite the adventure this. A voyage on a grand steamship to start with, an' a safe one at that. 'tweren't too many years ago—1864 or 5, if my mind serves me proper—that the Allan Line's *Bohemian* which were bound fer Portland, Maine went down. Two 'undred poor souls lost."

I glanced up at him in horror.

He must have felt my eyes upon him for he said, "Sorry, lass. Did I frighten yer?"

*Oh no, not at all. I find your rhetoric most reassuring.*

"Do not fret. 'tis a sturdy vessel, this 'un. An' yer'll be on a train that's just as sturdy, later on—after yer stay at the Distribution Centre in Ontario—when yer carry on ter Regina ---"

"That is where I am to be sent?"

"So they tell me, little lass." He patted my shoulder. "As I was sayin', when yer carry on to Regina, yer've a grand journey in store fer yer on the mighty Canadian Pacific Railroad. An' what a wonder that is, spannin' the country from east to west. A regular miracle-worker, is that Mr. Van Horne." He slanted a sidelong glance at me and apparently wanting to ensure that I had all the facts, added, "'e's the chap what thought up the idea of layin' the tracks for all them 'undreds o' miles. Got 'imself a regular army o' chinks ter do it, 'e did."

"Chinks?" I wrinkled my nose in puzzlement.

He tucked my arm through his and hustled me along with him, doffing his hat to this person and that as we approached the dining room. "Chinese, lass. Coolies. Work like that is all they're good fer."

"I see." Thank God I was English.

"Excited, are yer?"

*Positively beside myself actually. The Grand Tour has always been a dream of mine.*

Clearly, he had not noticed my lack of response. "There's not many a lass 'as the chance ter travel the world like yer goin' ter be doin'."

*No. Not many at all. Only hundreds and hundreds of Home children— slaves really, like me—who are regularly being shipped out to Canada,*

*Australia and the like.*

"Sorry I can only go with yer to Quebec. Then there'll be others to make sure yer get on the train ter Sudbury." The old fellow squeezed my arm tight against his side. "If I could keep yer I would, little lass."

I rolled my eyes. *Never mind keeping me. I would much rather you got yourself a parrot. You have been kind to me, yes. But if I had a way of escaping you I would. Get off this deuced ship. And run ... run ... run ... Run where, though, that is the thing?*

"I have no idea," I said out loud.

"What was that, Lydia?"

"Nothing, Mr. Vye."

"Dinin' room's coming up, little lass. Ready for dinner, are yer? May as well enjoy it while yer can, for yer never know what weather's in store for yer crossin' the Atlantic. The roughest seas yer'll ever see, that's fer certain. Almighty storms ... waves as 'igh as a house. Gales fit ter blow yer ter Kingdom Come"—he chuckled—"an' if yer lucky, bring yer back again. An' everybody from the captain on down sick as dogs." Releasing my arm, he took my hand in his sandpapery one and lifted his big, bulbous nose, sniffing noisily. "'ere we are, now. Just smell that grub. By Jove, makes yer mouth water, don't it? Did yer say yer were 'ungry?"

"No I did not. I believe I might have been earlier, but now—for some untold reason—my appetite has completely deserted me."

"Huh. I cannot fer the life o' me fathom that."

Mentally, I shook my head. The world was full of things I could not fathom. I was like a boat without a rudder ... without a sail ... without a compass.

My brother and sister were lost to me. Although we had agreed to write, Phillip Latham might well be lost to me. My home, my country were lost to me. Everything I held dear was lost to me.

*But you are still here.* The voice in my head was clear, resounding. My own or Mama's, I did not know, but in my mind I answered it. *You are right. I am. And it is for certain I am no namby-pamby. I am strong. I have a good brain. I will prevail. Whatever it takes ... slaving away like those poor Chinese, saving every cent, stealing, if necessary, I will survive. And by God, I will reunite my family.*

"I will, I absolutely will." Without realizing it, I had spoken out loud just as we were being seated at our table.

Both the waiter and Mr. Vye gave me a quizzical look.

"Yer will what, little lass?" The old fellow asked.

I squared my shoulders and straightened my spine. "Nothing," I said, gazing beyond the porthole and the roiling waves of the Atlantic to the far horizon, ready now to face my future head on.

# *Part Three*

## CHAPTER TWENTY-EIGHT
### *August 1889*
### *The Prairies, District of Saskatchewan,*
### *Northwest Territories, Canada*

My slippered feet flew as I circled the maypole, my scarlet ribbon intersecting Annabel's yellow, Edwin's purple, Mama's pink and Papa's green. We were reunited, disbelieving, tears of joy coursing down our cheeks, our heads thrown back in delighted laughter.

The laughter was still on my lips, the tears still wet on my cheeks, when the dream all at once aborted and I returned to my body, my befuddled mind registering the fact that I was fully-clothed but in a bed of some kind, and that whoever was jiggling the lumpy, straw-filled thing, was clearly determined to dislodge me.

On my side, knees drawn up, and with my head buried beneath the covers, I scrunched my eyes closed and feigned sleep. Ye gods and little fishes, always some slave-driver tormenting me. Why could I not for once be left in peace? This merciless rattling of my bones hurt, for pity's sake. "Go away, please," I muttered into the bedclothes. "Let me sleep just a little longer. I will rouse myself soon, I promise."

But pleas and promises flew in the face of this tormentor. Suddenly there came an almighty jerk. My eyes flew open, my heart somersaulted in my chest and I threw myself on my back, tensing myself for disaster.

Merciful heaven, it was dark as a sealed tomb, and from somewhere below came hellish sounds … grinding and rumbling and groaning sounds. Where in creation was I? In my bunk on the *Parisian* in the midst of a storm with the ship about to break up? I sniffed tentatively. No stench of vomit. No salty air.

Whatever the source of the cacophony, it lulled me and was soon replaced by a different sound. *Da-da-da-dum … da-da-da-dum … da-da-da-dum.* I was on the train, the famous train someone—Why could I not remember who?— had told me was the brainchild of some famous engineer. The noisy monster chugged along the sweeping curves of an enormous lake, clinging to a shoreline guarded by ancient, scarred rock masses on which perched ugly, raggedy-looking pines of some sort. *Da-da-da-dum ... da-da-da-dum ... da-da-da-dum.* Onward ... faster, faster, across infinite expanses of bleak wilderness then ever onward through a vast sea of tall, golden grass. *End of the line*, came the voice in my head. And once again, I returned to reality.

Had I been able to see my knuckles they would have been white, so fiercely was I was gripping the sides of the bunk, or whatever it was on which I lay. I cocked my head. The ungodly clamor had not abated while I had been off on my flight of fancy. Cringing, I strained to identify the sounds. No, not a train or a ship. Oh my Lord, what in creation was it then? Some sort of cataclysm? Had the end of the world finally come?

"*Mein Gott!* Johann drive like a fiend, tonight."

It took only seconds for me to recognize the female voice, then several more for a bell of recognition to ring in my head and return me fully to my senses. I burst out laughing. I was not going to come to a dreadful end after all, unless of course, Johann's fiendishness landed the three of us at the bottom of a ravine.

The Johann in question was my new employer, Mr. Brecht, and the voice I had just heard belonged to his wife. As for the hellish noises—now thankfully transformed into rhythmic, wheel-turning noises—they were those of a wagon, a covered wagon no less, and somewhat a relic of a bygone era from what I had been able to gather.

I had no idea what day it was, but I remembered it was the second week in August and I knew we were somewhere in the southeastern part of the District of Saskatchewan in Canada's Northwest Territories and in the midst of a two-day trek from the railway station at Regina to the Brechts' farm. Mr. Brecht had had business in the city; otherwise they would have had me continue on to the railhead at Blackstone, which from all accounts was about forty miles west of their home.

What was in store for me there was anybody's guess. It surely could not be worse than the several weeks of drudgery—far worse drudgery, mind you, than at Brackford House—I had experienced at the Distribution Centre in Sudbury. Some children were lucky—or unlucky enough in some cases—to be selected for apprenticeship to a family immediately after their arrival. I, however, was the runt of a very large litter whose members were, for the most part, tall, strong, brawny girls and boys, extremely well suited to farm labour.

Thank God for Mr. Brecht whose letter had arrived two months into my stay at the centre. He had expressed a desire for a girl experienced with baby care. And as it happened, I was the only one.

I wriggled into a more comfortable position, getting a whiff of myself as I moved. I wrinkled my nose in distaste. Lord, there were parts of me that had not seen soap and water in weeks.

Oh for a bath, a long, hot, fingertip-wrinkling, lavender-scented soak. And afterwards, a freshly-washed night dress of smooth, soft lawn, with the smell of the sun still on it.

Oh for home ... for England. Oh for my two darlings. Oh for life as it used to be. Instead of this ignominious trek to God knew where.

"Are you awake, Lydia Fullerton?"

I started, collecting my wits again, and rolled my eyes. Really, of all the asinine questions. With this kind of commotion, rigor mortis would have to have set in for me not to be awake. I turned in the direction of the disembodied voice. "Yes, ma'am," I said long-sufferingly, "I am indeed."

"When we take trip, Mr. Brecht always in a great hurry to get back to farm."

All well and good, I thought, shifting uncomfortably on my sore bottom and spine. But what about stopping and camping for the night? Surely that was what sane, normal people did when crossing this godforsaken land? At least then one could find a tree or bush or boulder behind which to relieve oneself. Although even that was a doubtful proposition given the apparent sparseness of vegetation. Oh the indignity of having to squat over a metal slop bucket, as I had earlier today and on several other days, hoping against hope that the wagon would maintain a steady course while one did what one had to. Not to mention the struggle afterwards to replace the lid without it sounding like the crash of a cymbal. Thank the Lord the use of that communal slop bucket had been limited to myself and Mrs. Brecht. God alone knew where Mr. Brecht did his duty. Although one hardly had to be of superior intellect to guess. I made a wry face. At least at Brackford House, everyone had had her own chamber pot, likewise on the steamship, and later, at the Distribution Centre. Ah well, what was one more indignity to add to the many? This was, after all, the wild west.

Ye gods and little fishes, that I should have come to this —mulling over the merits and demerits of chamber pots and slop pails when my life was in chaos and my family had been ripped apart.

"Lucky we still have our teeth, *ya?*" Mrs. Brecht's voice rose out of the darkness again.

"What? Oh ... yes." Lucky we have a single intact bone in our bodies. "Is it not dangerous," I said, "driving at night like this, it being so pitch dark? I mean, how can your husband possibly see where he is going?" Struggling to a sitting position, I yanked at the quilt covering me and once I had it free, wrapped it around myself like a shawl. Lord almighty, trying to keep your balance with all this buffeting about was akin to being on a circus high wire.

"*Ach mein* husband knows trail like he knows way to outhouse in snow storm. And we have lanterns on front of wagon. Besides, tonight the moon is full. See." Mrs. Brecht lifted the canvas close to her and a yellow shaft of light momentarily carpeted the space between her bed and mine.

"What you feel is wheel going into rut; it not come off this time, *Gott* be praised." She lowered her voice. "Once when it do, I must help Johann with putting back on and because I am tall, he thinks I am strong as man and says pull this and push that and hold this up and whatever you do, do not let go." She paused for breath. "And all of it such a struggle, I think I will die. But wheel go back on and I do not die and Mr. Brecht think ... well, it is hard to know what Johann think."

Unsure whether or not a response was in order, I coughed by way of acknowledgment. Reading the mind of the taciturn Mr. Brecht certainly would be a challenge. To call him a man of very few words would be an exaggeration. So far, all the man had said to me, his round face flushing all the way up to his hairline, was a guttural, "How do you do, Miss?" when I had first identified myself to the couple at the railway station the previous day.

What a striking pair they were. Vikings, with white-blonde hair and ruddy complexions. Both with the lightest of blue eyes. Mrs. Brecht a strapping woman of perhaps twenty; Mr. Brecht, certainly not more than a few years older, taller by about a foot-and-a-half, but soft-looking and surely ill-suited to farm labour.

"Johann think women have far too much to say." Mrs. Brecht spoke so softly, I had to strain to hear. "But I think to myself, how can I have too much to say when there is no one to say it to? He is working, working, working. I am working, working, working. We eat. We sleep. Ah well, that is life, *ya*?"

I raised a cynical eyebrow. It certainly did not sound as if theirs was a match made in Heaven. Perhaps it was not a love match, but a mail-order mismatch.

I had first heard of the practice of mail-order purchasing during my stay at the Distribution Centre. According to the information imparted by a young Canadian woman who worked in the kitchen there, and with whom I had become acquainted during vegetable-peeling duty, you could buy whatever your heart desired through the Eatons' Catalogue, which was a thickish book full of illustrations and descriptions of items and their prices. All you had to do was make your choice, send in your money, and the item would be posted to you. From what she had heard, the young woman said, the same held true for brides, although of course, you could not order them through Eatons'; they were ordered through special brides' catalogues, and, of course—and she had clearly thought herself quite hilarious, here—they could not be wrapped in brown paper and sent through the post.

I made a wry face. Mail-order brides. Home children. What was the difference? Chattels all of them. Ordered to certain specifications, and returnable, too, from all accounts; at least Home children were, from what I had heard. People expected value for their money and naturally, if the merchandise was defective, they had every right to return it. Not that it meant, of course, that you would be returned to England. If such were the case I would go out of my way to prove myself worthless. You would be sent back to the Distribution Centre and put on the shelf, so to speak, until another order arrived for someone matching your specifications.

Thank the Lord I had met the Brechts' specifications, otherwise I might have languished at the Distribution Centre for months, years, a lifetime even. It did not bear thinking about, and I was grateful when Mrs. Brecht spoke again.

"I hear you sleep talk earlier, *ya*?"

"I might have." I lay back down, tired of trying to balance myself. "If I did, I am sorry. I did not mean to disturb you."

"*Ach*, 'tis nothing. I, too, sleep talk sometime. *Herr* Brecht, also." The woman dropped her voice to just above a whisper. "And he grunt and groan like buffalo *mit* arrow in behind."

The image made me smile.

"Johann kick, too, in sleep. One night I am so ... vexened ---"

"Vexed," said.

"Right ... vexed, that I kick him back. And he wake up and shout, "*Gott in Himmel*, what was that?" Mrs. Brecht snickered. "So I snore very loud, and he has no idea I am awake."

I answered her with a soft chuckle.

"Johann calls you my servant."

Bosh to that, I thought, making a disdainful face.

"He picks you for me because they tell him you are good with the child-caring and you have schooling, too."

"How many children do you have, Mrs. Brecht? Is someone looking after them? They said nothing about it at the Distribution Centre."

"No child yet. But soon ... four months I think. Nobody can see under skirts, but I *haf* bump ... very large bump." She laughed. "Big baby ... strong baby. By the time he ... she comes we will be moved into town ... to Plenty. Johann says enough of farming. Since eighteen-eighty-three we have depression, so it have been hard and Johann says it will be over soon and that general store will be good thing for us. When he was a boy, his papa have store in the old country.

I turned on my side, facing the woman. "You are to be shopkeepers, then?"

"*Ya*. Store is bought already from the Gavins. They go back to your country end of September … start of October. Someone there … *die mutter* … *der vater* of missus is very sick, dying I think."

"And your farm, is it sold?"

"*Ya*." Katerina Brecht plumped her pillow and shifted about for a time. "Buyers say they can wait until we are moved. You think, maybe," she went on, "you can teach me the speaking of good English. I think it good for store, and customers will like it, *ya*?"

"Yes. Absolutely. I would be most happy to do so," I said. After all, I could not very well refuse. "Are you glad to be moving, ma'am?"

"*Ya*. It will be fine, I think. In November, when baby due, there is much snow, sometimes no way for help to come to farm. A neighbor woman die last winter, her baby, too."

"How sad." I was tempted to begin the English lesson immediately and instruct the woman on the correct use of tenses. But I thought better of it.

"Johann want son. I think he will be sad if daughter comes. But I will be glad, whatever baby is."

The wagon seemed to be on smoother ground, now. It swayed gently and I felt my tension ease.

"I say before that Johann call you servant," the woman carried on. "But I would like us to be friends. I have no friends here … only in old country, and them I know I will never see again, so I must make new life."

"You have family in Europe, then, Mrs. Brecht?"

"Katerina. You call me Katerina when there is no Johann to hear. And *nein*. No family in Austria. All dead. I am alone, now. Except for husband. But Johann … well, it is not the same." She fell silent for a time, then surprised me with, "I am eighteen, you are fourteen, *ya*?"

"Fourteen? Me? Erm … yes."

"Not a great many years between our years. So no reason why we cannot be friends, *ya*?"

"None at all, Mrs. Brecht."

"Katerina … remember? Except when Johann about. Then I must be Mrs. Brecht, and you must be servant. Our secret, *ya*?"

I shrugged. "Of course."

"Now we must sleep again." The woman yawned loudly. "So, I say goodnight once more. And when we wake, we will be only one day away from home."

Your home, not mine, I thought, swallowing hard. I am four-thousand, five-hundred miles from *my* home.

Country living or town living would make not a jot of difference. I could never feel at home here, so dreary was the landscape, with its endless vista of prairie, clothed in buffalo grass. Everywhere yellow and brown and dust gray. Relieving the monotony, an occasional sad-looking wolf willow or bluff of box elders with leaves like a sycamore, but hardly a hint of green. The air dry and burning and always abuzz with mosquitoes and black flies and other winged tormenters.

Here there were no hedgerows, no towering oaks. No thatch-roofed cottages, only houses of sod with tar paper roofs. No scent of lavender or honeysuckle. No thrush or blackbird song or cuckoo call, just the cries of coyotes, mournful as a mother whose child has died.

Oh, and the wind, the relentless wind, hot and biting during the day, bone-chilling after sundown. Just thinking about it made me shiver. I burrowed down under the covers, my teeth chattering. I must think about somewhere warm and pleasant. Ah here we are … the rectory garden on a summer afternoon … Annabel and Edwin tearing about in it.

Lord, but it was hard tonight to conjure their faces. I felt a thrust of fear. What if I forgot them and they mine. Thank God for the image of Mama. I felt for the pouch at my waist; at least *her* face would not fade into oblivion. I tossed and turned, my chest aching with loneliness. How I missed my two darlings, and how I worried about them. And how frustrating not to be able to at least try and contact them.

All well and good to say write, as Doctor Latham had on the ship. All you needed was a pencil or pen, ink, paper and an envelope, as well as the appropriate postage. Simple enough. Unless you were a Home child.

How many times these past months had I tried to accomplish my goal of writing, only to be thwarted at every turn?

"Oh, they do not let you lot write letters; if yer can write, that is, an' there ain't many who can," my know-it-all acquaintance from the distribution centre's kitchen had told me. "Yer will not see so much as a slate or a piece of chalk 'ere, 'cause it ain't a school, yer know. An' th'only ones that does any letter-writin' are the supers tellin' various folks about what great little workers all of y'are."

"Pen and ink … is that too much to ask for?" My eyes flew open at the sound of my own impassioned plea, and my heart skipped a beat when Katerina Brecht answered with a perplexed, "You wish for pen and ink right now?"

I covered my mouth with my hands. The frustration of it all was making me lose my mind. Ever since the ship I had developed a penchant for talking to myself. "No, I am sorry," I said sheepishly. "I did not realize I ---"

"Tomorrow, when we get to farm"—Mrs. Brecht yawned loudly—"you shall have pen and ink."

"I shall?"

"*Ya.* As much pen and ink as you want."

"Really?"

"Really. Now you sleep, please."

I made a prayerful steeple of my hands. "Oh yes, Mrs. Brecht … Katerina. Now, I shall sleep."

## CHAPTER TWENTY-NINE
### *August 1889*
### *The Brechts' Farm, District of Saskatchewan,*
### *Northwest Territories, Canada*

True to her word, Mrs. Brecht supplied me with the pen and ink I had asked for, as well as a serviceable pine desk in a room of my own on the second floor of their poplar log house. But it was soon clear to me that it would be some time before I had a chance to use the implements.

On the twenty-second of August—a Thursday and my third day at the farm—Katerina Brecht informed me that the next day three couples of their acquaintance would be visiting. Arriving after breakfast and departing after supper, they would spend their time making sausages and hams and lard and all sorts of edible oddities I had never heard of.

At the time, the whys and wherefores of the production of these foodstuffs did not cross my mind. I was far too busy scouring and scrubbing what appeared to be every bowl, crock, dish and platter in Mrs. Brecht's kitchen. "We have much preparing to do," she told me. "Everything must be clean as *vistle.* And afterwards, we make bread. Johann's favourite, *sauerteig* rye."

"What on earth is *sauerteig*?" I asked.

"It is what I think you call sourdough. It starts bread." She scratched her blonde head and frowned. "You know leavening … like in Bible?"

I lifted my shoulders. Of course, I knew what leavening was. But …

"Wait … I show you." She went to the cupboard and returned with a small bowl covered with a cloth. "In here I put cupful brown bread dough, rub lard over and let sit for days in kitchen until I need." She pushed the heels of her hands against the tabletop and squeezed her fingers against her palms. "And today I knead." She looked at me poker-faced, waited a tick and then chuckled. "You know I make joke, *ya*?"

I laughed and nodded my head. "I certainly do, Katerina.

———

At four o'clock that afternoon I sat in utter exhaustion across from Mrs. Brecht at the enormous rectangular pine table in her blast furnace of a kitchen. The open door offered not one whit of relief temperature wise, but at least I felt saved from a feeling of suffocation.

My young employer's perspiration-saturated hair lay plastered to the sides of her face, while my hair—with its natural wave—had turned into a wild, damp frizz. We were both dusted with white and rye flour from head to foot. My back and arms ached from hauling sacks of the deuced stuff and punching and kneading dough, as well as from the endless stoking required to satisfy the voracious appetite of the cast iron wood stove's firebox. I raised a weary arm and swiped the back of my hand across my eyes; they burned from squinting at the stove's draft controls which required continuous adjustment and from the salty invasion of sweat.

And all this for six loaves of bread. Dark, crusty, mouthwatering bread, granted, with the most heavenly aroma – yeasty and rich and tangy. Hours of labour had left me famished. If I had my way I would grab one of those loaves, tear a chunk off, slather it with butter and stuff it down. But this was Johann's bread and I would have to be satisfied with the three-day-old white bread Katerina Brecht had earmarked for today's tea.

By the time we had the meal on the table and sat down to eat, I was so tired I could hardly keep my head up. But I managed to down a cheese sandwich followed by a slice of the honey cake Katerina had made earlier and put in the oven to bake with the rye bread.

"You get us water, please, Johann," Katerina said. And her husband obliged by filling two cups from the bucket he had just brought in from the well and serving us both. "You must drink much in this heat," he said to me, with a shy smile, the only words he had spoken to me since my cow-milking lesson two days earlier. He kissed the top of his wife's head. "I have more work outside, *liebling*. You go up to bed soon, *ya*?"

"I will. Soon as Lydia and I have cleared table and washed dishes."

We worked in silence, both too tired to talk. Once our tasks were completed, Katerina said, "I go to bed, and you must go also. Gallop along, now, child. Tomorrow is big day and we must be up before daybreak.

Any other time and I would have said, "You mean run, Mrs. Brecht. But the poor woman was worn out, so all I said was, "Let me help you, Katerina," tucked her arm through mine and ushered her towards the stairs."

———

"Wake up, Lydia."

I forced my way up through murky layers of sleep and reached the surface, my heart beating so hard I could hardly breathe.

"What?" I sucked in air, rubbed my eyes and struggled to a sitting position.

The first thing I saw was a protruding belly, the next, the rest of Katerina Brecht. "You must get up right now."

I swung my legs over the side of the bed and stood groggily.

"We have visitors this morning and Johann have made fire in *meagrope* when we are sleeping, and now we must stoke it so water is boiling good while we have breakfast. Eight eating – four men and their wives. You eat first, though."

"Very well," I said, having no idea what this *meawhatsit* was.

Hastily dressed and washed and in the kitchen moments later, I asked Mrs. Brecht to please explain.

"You go to window and look outside," she said, as she set the breakfast table and tended to the bacon sizzling in two large pans on the stove top.

I stretched my neck and surveyed the yard.

"You see barn, *ya?*"

"I do." The building was silhouetted against a sky streaked with the yellow and gold of daybreak.

"And next to it you see brick wall ... square, like pen?"

"An enclosure, you mean, with brick walls around it?"

"*Ya. Meagrope* inside that."

"But what is it, exactly?"

The clatter of pottery and cutlery came from behind me and I turned, my mouth watering, my nostrils quivering at the delectable aroma. I certainly hoped some of that bacon was destined for my stomach.

"It is large iron kettle with iron jacket which have little door where one push in wood to feed fire below."

"For what purpose?"

"You will see. Now we go outside."

In this post dawn hour, it was surprisingly chilly. But several minutes of shoving pieces of wood through the little door I had been told about and feeding the roaring fire warmed me from top to toe.

When I stood and helped Katerina up, I heard the most dreadful sound ... an awful high-pitched squealing. "Ye gods"—I folded my arms across my chest—"whatever is that?"

"They have no supper last night," Mrs. Brecht said. "If we feed them, they are full of gas when we open them and stink is something fearful."

"Feed what?"

"The pigs, child."

"Oh Lord"—I made a prayerful gesture with my hands—"that is what you put in your *meagrope*?

"*Ya.*" She actually laughed. "But we kill them first."

I looked at her dumbstruck. The unremitting screams kept up and I wondered as we continued stoking the fire if they were the screams of the starving or of the fearful, somehow privy to their fate.

Throughout breakfast, the raucousness and merriment of the Brechts' acquaintances thankfully drowned out the poor creatures' squeals. And my relief knew no bounds when the meal was over and the men rushed to the slaughter like knights off to the Crusades. At least, soon, the hapless animals would be put out of their misery.

As the shouts and laughter diminished, the women drew me into their giggling, jabbering German-speaking coterie. "We have chat," Katerina said. "Rest a bit until men finish."

Even raised, the female voices were insufficient to muffle the animals' frenetic screams. I could not help myself. I clapped my hands over my ears and pressed so hard, my head hurt. The women—except for Katerina— elbowed each other and roared with laughter. Katerina had the good grace to *shush* them, lay an empathetic hand on my shoulder, and after a long moment mouth, "It is over."

And when I uncovered my ears, for a time the silence was so utter, it seemed as if everything in the world had been killed.

But the uneasy peace was short-lived: seconds later, in burst the blood-spattered pig killers, as wild-eyed and euphoric as warriors returning from the fray, and lugging between them a great tub full of the animals' intestines and hearts and livers and other equally disgusting-looking insides.

I was conscripted, and spent the next few nauseating hours up to my elbows in offal, my hands moving of their own accord. And the only way I was able to endure the ordeal was to turn my mind to those long-ago afternoons at the rectory, when Mama's friends would visit and discuss the affairs of the parish over endless cups of tea, while I—attentive yet unobtrusive—sat off to one side on a favorite little blue velvet-covered footstool and worked on my embroidery, dreaming about the time when I would be entertaining my friends in my parlour while my husband was off doing grand and glorious things.

Katerina's excited voice brought me back to reality. "See what we have done today?"

I stared perplexed, first into her pale blue eyes then at the tabletop, focusing on the spoils of the day's slaughter. Had I actually participated in this? I massaged my temples as if to coax forth the answer. I must have, I supposed. And look at it all. I wrinkled my nose. A regular banquet.

There were crocks full of lard, rendered in the *meagrope*, and of *greavi schmolt*, made from the lard sediment and used like butter. Head cheese, made from ground head meat and rind. Big rings of liverwurst. Astonishing how I knew all the names. They must have inserted themselves into my brain while I was thinking about tea at the rectory. Ye gods, look at those two large crocks on the floor containing a horrid concoction of cooked pigs' feet, heart, knuckles and tongue, weighted down under brine.

"You have done great work, Lydia." Johann Brecht this time.

"Thank you," I said. "May I please go to bed?"

## CHAPTER THIRTY
### *August 1889*
### *The Brechts' Farm, District of Saskatchewan,*
### *Northwest Territories, Canada*

On the Sunday morning three days after the pig-killing Katerina Brecht said, "Today we give you afternoon off to be left to your own vices."

I laughed inwardly. A vice or two might make for a far more interesting life. But in truth, all I wanted was to be allowed the opportunity to write my letters.

"You will have tea ready for us when we return, please. Five o'clock Johann say. We go to neighbours' farm, ten miles distant. We have church service there in barn. Lay preacher comes tomorrow for baptizing of two little ones."

They departed at a little past one o'clock. I stood at my bedroom window watching the couple trundle off in their two seater buggy drawn by a couple of their horses—the black one, *Thunder*, and the white one, *Lightning*—both astonishingly born during storms, according to Katerina. After a time, all I could see of them on the trail that snaked into the distance was the cloud of dust left in their wake.

I sat down at my desk and extracted several sheets of note and blotting paper from my writing case. Hopefully Mrs. Brecht would suffer no ill effects from the trip. For certain, jiggling about in a cart on a rutted trail did not sound like the wisest course for a woman in her condition.

And she would surely swelter, as I was now. Perspiration trickled down between my breasts, dampened my armpits, made my drawers adhere to my posterior and my thighs stick together. No earthly use opening the window; more heat and humidity would pour in. So I undid the buttons on my bodice, held the fabric away from my body and used a handkerchief to pat my various parts dry. Then I exhaled a couple of strong breaths, directing the flow up over my face, resolving to ignore the discomfort as best I could and apply myself to the task at hand.

Scooting my chair closer to the desk, I took up the dainty pearl-handled pen and prepared to dip it into the cut glass inkpot. How incongruous these objects looked in a room with white-washed walls, a plain desk and chair, a chest of drawers with the paint peeling off it and a rust-pitted iron bedstead on which there rested a straw mattress covered with a faded, threadbare quilt. As incongruous as the dainty little carriage clock Amelia Dunn had given me, which I had set on top of the chest. I chuckled and shook my head. As incongruous, surely, as I was.

I dipped the pen in the pot and let it rest there. No matter. This afternoon I would be erudite, amusing … inserting a *bon mot* here, a *bon mot* there, and I would impress the doctor no end with my bravura. I withdrew the pen from the ink, wiped off the excess on the bristles of a small silver pen-wipe and in a meticulous hand wrote across the top of the sheet of notepaper in front of me, saying the words out loud, "Brecht Farm, Middle of Nowhere, Canada." I dipped again, added, "Sunday, 25th August, 1889." And a couple of lines below that, I penned, "Dear Doctor Latham."

"Dear Doctor Latham what?" I wrinkled my nose, sighing and replacing the pen in the inkpot, then staring out of the window at the endless sweep of land, and beyond it on the far horizon a towering bank of dark gray storm clouds which might—with a stretch of the imagination—be taken for a mountain range. Mountains were non-existent here, of course. As were hills … and knolls … and dips … and valleys. The terrain was utterly flat. Comprising green grasses and grains and wild flowers in a myriad of colours, all of it windswept into waves, the prairie was a sea of sorts. And by summer's end when the wheat and barley and oats were ripe, it would turn to gold, Mrs. Brecht had told me.

Despite the loneliness, the emptiness the view evoked in me, it continued to hold me in its thrall for several more minutes, until a fly buzzed around my face and broke the spell. I swatted the pesky thing away, glancing at the clock as I did. Ye gods, three-quarters-of-an hour had passed since the Brechts' departure. I had best look slippy if I were to get my letters written.

"Dear Doctor Latham," I said, taking up my pen again. "I am sorry it has taken me so long to write." After I had explained the reason, I went on to tell him how letters were picked up at, and delivered to the post office in Plenty, the nearest town, on Tuesdays and Thursdays only.

I told him Mrs. Brecht was in that certain condition, which had prompted the couple to sell their farm and purchase the General Store in town. I said they seemed a kind couple, and that unlike many a Home child, I was certain not be beaten.

"I realize I am supposed to be schooled until I am fifteen, but there has been no mention made of it yet," I wrote. "From what I gather I will be expected to assist in the store and Mrs. Brecht has hinted at the possibility of a small remuneration. This pleases me no end, for needless to say, I shall save every last cent of it towards the time when I am free of this bondage and able to return to England and my dear ones."

I felt a tear roll down my cheek and wiped it away with my sleeve. I blotted the paper, set it aside and smoothed out another sheet. I re-dipped my pen in the pot. "I do hope and pray," I wrote, "that by now you have been able to locate the children and that Mrs. Bell has relented and will no longer prevent you from establishing contact with them."

I blotted again and carried on. "In any event, I trust you will do your utmost to deliver to them the enclosed letter. I do not have a great deal to tell them at present, but as my life here evolves, I will describe every last detail of it, so that if God forbid, our separation is a protracted one, we shall not end up strangers to each other."

I added, "Please answer as quickly as possible. Any news of my dear ones, however inconsequential, will sustain me," then I signed, "Yours in gratitude and hope, Lydia Fullerton."

Setting aside the first letter, I wrote to the children. It was three o'clock by the time I had finished the epistle. I sat back in my chair and read it out loud in order to make sure it sounded the way I wanted it to.

"My Dearest Annabel and Edwin, at long last, glory be, I am able to write. How very much I miss you both, and how sad I was not to have been able to say a proper goodbye to you. I want you to remember that every night I am gazing up at the same moon and stars you are and holding you both in my thoughts and prayers, and I want you to believe with all your hearts, that we will be reunited.

I am so very sorry I missed your ninth birthday, Edwin. I thought about you constantly on that Sunday in April and I remembered the special teas we used to have and hoped your day was being celebrated in grand style. Another few months and you will be thirteen, Annabel dear. Imagine that.

You must not worry about me. I have been placed with a couple of German heritage who are treating me kindly. I trust the Chistlegates are taking good care of both of you and that you are taking care of each other.

I am praying that you will be allowed to write and I expect you, Annabel, to provide me with every last detail of your lives so that I shall not miss what I cannot experience with you. I, in turn, will tell you about my life here. This way, your education—which I suspect will have come to a full stop—will continue and you will at least have a geography lesson of sorts, and a far more interesting and accurate one than those delivered by Miss Bamford at the rectory.

For example, Indians are not red, as she led us to believe; they are extremely brown and extremely curious. At least, the one who came to the door yesterday was. He traded my employer several dead, grouse-like birds he had strung together, for a bag of flour and a couple of dozen eggs. From all accounts, this trading is common. Anyway, when the Indian saw me he stared open-mouthed, then pointed at me, laughing and jabbering. Mrs. Brecht—who understands something of the Sioux language—said the fellow had never seen anyone with such pale skin and with hair like fire. I would hardly call chestnut brown fire, but these savages clearly have a different view of things. Imagine the consolation I derived from Mrs. Brecht's assurances that soon my hair would be dulled by the sun and the wind, and my skin would be as burned as everybody else's. Needless to say, I have no intention of letting that fate befall me. Mama always stressed that to be ladylike one must be pale, and ladylike I am determined to be despite the crude surroundings in which I find myself.

My employers have a farm consisting of one-hundred-and-sixty acres, which makes them sound frightfully rich. But they are not. Like thousands of other settlers, Mr. Brecht received his land free from the Canadian Pacific Railway. All he had to do was agree to live on the land six months out of each of three years and this he did several years ago.

Their two-storey house is built of poplar logs and is white-washed inside and out. It is very-strongly constructed in order to withstand the vicious weather winter will bring. Many of the homes hereabouts are made of sod. Imagine it -- clods of grass-covered earth inches thick are ploughed up from the prairie and then used like bricks, one piled on top of the next.

Every day brings another strange sight or new experience. Two days ago I milked a pair of cows. After Mr. Brecht demonstrated, I mastered the technique in short order, and soon the milk was merrily squirting into my bucket. Later on, Mrs. Brecht showed me how to turn the cream into butter by using a churn containing wooden paddles that one vigorously stirs.

Whilst on the subject of butter, I do hope you are being well fed. I am sure, like me, you face fresh challenges every day. But be brave. And behave well for the Chistlegates; that way, they will have no cause to prevent you from sending and receiving letters.

I must stop my ramblings now. My employers will be home soon."

I signed the letter and glanced at the clock. Ye gods. I scrambled to my feet. I had only one hour left.

---

Once I had the wood stove stoked and the kettle on it, I stood in the open kitchen doorway, fanning myself with my apron skirt. Lord knew why, for it was doing me not one whit of good. How positively asinine, keeping a fire going in this scorching mid-summer heat, but there was no such thing as coal gas available here, and if one wanted kettles and the like heated, then one had to suffer.

Giving up on the fanning operation, I returned to the task at hand, unfurling a folded tablecloth and flapping it about like a bullfighter's cape, then smoothing it over the rough-hewn table's surface.

Would Phillip Latham think me a silly little chit doing my best to sound like an adult? I wondered as I set out the white ironstone service, the cutlery, butter, cheese, and raspberry jam. And if so, did it matter? After all, at this juncture, his only purpose was to be a go-between, was it not?

I spooned mustard pickle into a bowl and set it down next to the cruet. To be sure, he had been kind to me, made promises that were above and beyond the call of his doctoral duty. But before that last meeting on the ship, on those other occasions our paths had crossed, had he not proved himself to be somewhat of an odd bod with his peculiar mood changes? And had I not found myself annoyingly flustered around him? I gave a decisive nod. Yes, on both counts. Still, whatever the reason, I hoped my letter would sit well with him.

Earlier, I had debated whether or not to reveal the truth to him about my age, but I had resisted the temptation, afraid he might view the subterfuge in a negative light and be unwilling to help me.

"Pretense, pretense, pretense," I said between clenched teeth. Being someone you were not, watching your every word—spoken or written—was dreadfully tiresome.

I headed to the pantry and focused unwilling eyes on the spoils of the past week's slaughter. What should I put out? Liverwurst, that was it, Johann's favourite, according to Katerina. I grabbed one of the fat rings and clicked my heels together like an officer, bringing the sausage to my temple in a smart salute. "Johann," I sang out, "*lufs* his *livervurst*. And *ve* must alvays give *Herr* master *vot* he *vant*s."

"But *vot* if *vot* he *vonts*"—I held the sausage aloft, my mouth curled in disgust—is VILE?"

I got no further. Laughter suddenly exploded like magma from beneath my rib-cage. Out of habit, I tried to stop it. But after a few tortured seconds of lip-biting and breath-holding, I surrendered to the paroxysm. Doubled over minutes later, tears streaming down my cheeks, I hiccuped into silence.

Ye gods and little fishes, I had forgotten just how painful laughter could be. Liverwurst in hand, I straightened. I had to be going mad, not only talking to myself, but finding my own antics so hysterically funny. I wiped my streaming eyes. Mad or not, though, I still had my work to finish.

I turned my attention to a loaf of the rye bread I had helped make earlier in the week, the best Johann Brecht had ever tasted, according to his wife. "You must have magic in your hands, Lydia," she had said. "Johann eat so many slices he almost burst."

Sawing like a lumberjack through the dark, heavy-textured loaf, now, I harrumphed. Magic? It had been unadulterated anger, unhappiness over my situation ... pure frustration that had gone into my bread-kneading. I had pummeled and pounded and punished the dough as if it were something that needed destroying.

I thought, all at once, about our cook, Mrs. Dixon's soft, white, golden-crusted loaves, whose yeasty aroma used to waft through the rectory, and of her homemade lemon curd with its lovely sweet tartness.

The sound of boiling water sputtering on the stove-top cut short my nostalgia. I moved the kettle to one side, castigating myself for becoming maudlin about food, of all things, when I had Edwin and Annabel to think about.

I pulled my collar away from my sweaty neck and flapped it about, trying to create a breeze. Lord, how could anyone think in this heat? Another minute of it, and I would surely faint.

Outside was no better. The sky had the look of hot cobalt glass. The air hung about me like a suffocating shroud. At half a mile distant, the creek was no earthly use to me. But the well was just feet away.

The lunacy of it struck me the moment I poured the first bucketful over my head and lost my breath to the water's icy slap. But the relief was so profound, my only thought was to extend it. And so I hauled up another bucketful and another and unceremoniously doused myself with the contents.

Eyes closed, I tipped my chin and held my arms out at my sides, windmilling them in order to create a breeze. The blessed coolness seeped into my pores, and I felt a pleasant giddiness, a sense of separation, somehow, from my body.

How had it been possible, I wondered later, for me to be on my feet yet lose consciousness not only of time, but of my surroundings, and to such a degree that I did not hear the horse's hooves across the dried ruts of the yard.

By the time I came to my senses, it was too late.

The Indian stood not six feet from me. Holding out a string of the same pathetic-looking birds he had brought here to trade with the Brechts on my first day, he smiled and jabbered and gestured at my soaking wet form.

My heart in my mouth, I backed away.

For every step I retreated he advanced. He was pointing, touching his head, then pointing again ... at ... at my head.

Now he was almost upon me, those dreadful birds ... rank, smelly creatures thrust in my face. His mouth split in a wide smile, his big, jagged tobacco-stained teeth like the fangs of a wolf.

He extended a quick hand and touched my hair.

"Go away ... go away ... GO AWAY." He did not.

So I screamed.

And screamed.

And SCREAMED.

## CHAPTER THIRTY-ONE
### *August 1889*
### *The Brechts' Farm, District of Saskatchewan,*
### *Northwest Territories, Canada*

"Lydia ... Lydia. Everything alright. You are safe." The woman's voice came to me as if from a great distance and when I slowly opened my eyes I found myself staring up at Katerina and Johann Brecht.

I looked frantically about. The buggy was parked by the fence, both horses tied to it by their reins. "The Indian," I said. "He ... I ... he tried to ... my hair ... and the birds."

"He is gone." Katerina said, gently taking my arm. "Come inside. You dry off and change clothes, then we have cup of tea."

When I came downstairs from my room later, I found the couple seated at the table talking in low voices and chuckling as if they were sharing a private joke. The conversation abruptly stopped as soon as they saw me. No doubt they thought me an utter nincompoop. "I am sorry I acted so hysterically before," I said.

"*Ach*, it is no matter," said Mr. Brecht.

Katerina motioned me to the chair opposite her. "Sit and drink tea I have just poured."

As I prepared to do so, Johann Brecht said, "You do fine job with table."

Katerina licked her lips. "*Ya.* All this good food make my mouth weep."

"I hope I remembered everything," I said, taking a gulp of tea.

Mr. Brecht made himself a sandwich of a couple of slices of rye bread and a slab of cheese and between bites said, "You make good *hausfrau* when you grow up."

"Never mind *hausfrau* when she grow up." Grinning, Katerina slathered a thick slice of bread with butter and jam and invited me to do the same. "Lydia become bride right now today if she want."

"Bride?" I replaced the butter and jam dishes on the table. "What on earth do you mean, Mrs. Brecht?"

"You have what do you call it?" She pulled on her lower lip for a moment and then said, "Suitor I think."

I wrinkled my nose. "A suitor? How on earth could I have a suitor?"

"You have Indian ... Sioux who make you scream." She giggled. "He want you for his wife."

Johann Brecht leaned forward, elbows on the table, his broad face earnest. "Katerina is right. Indian bring birds in trade for you."

"Birds ... for me?" I felt my eyes stretch wide and hot blood rush to my cheeks. "Ye gods and little fishes. You mean to say he thought he could have me in exchange for those ... those dreadful putrid ---?"

"Not so putrid when roasted and on table," Johann said with a slight note of disapproval in his voice.

"*Ya* he did. He want you." Katerina's throat worked, her cheeks grew redder and redder, her eyes bulged. Finally she could contain herself no longer and let out a great howl of laughter. "*Ach* you should see your face. What picture it make."

I bristled. Bad enough that I had been frightened half to death by that savage. Now I was to be subjected to ridicule too.

"Enough *leibling*," Mr. Brecht said. "You make the child not comfortable."

"So sorry." Katerina smiled apologetically. "I not mean to disturb you, Lydia."

She had disturbed me, but I was not about to say so. I merely lifted my shoulders in response and turned my attention to the bread and jam on my plate.

We ate in silence for a time, all lost in our own thoughts. Mine turned to the promised trip into town tomorrow. "Johann do chores here while we go to post office and store," Katerina had said. Thank God. I would at last be able to send my letters.

I took a drink of tea and glanced surreptitiously at the young woman. A wistful smile played at the corners of her mouth as she passed her hand over the mound of her belly which seemed to be expanding by the minute and must surely contain an extremely large baby.

In a sense she and I were kindred spirits. Living in an alien environment, having no family aside from a somewhat taciturn husband and no apparent friends, unless one counted the pig-killing contingent, she surely must have felt the same desolation as I did.

But clearly such was not the case this afternoon. "We go to parlour now," she suddenly said, rising awkwardly from her seat. "Johann play organ."

"I do?" Her husband looked as surprised as I felt.

"*Ya.*" She waddled across the kitchen. "And I sing. Come along, husband."

The big man lumbered after her as she called over her shoulder, "You come too, Lydia."

"But I have the table to clear and the dishes to see to."

"They wait for you. They not run off across prairie."

Despite the fact that Johann opened the parlour windows, the room was stifling and we were all awash in perspiration by eight o'clock, when Katerina pronounced the concert over and the couple headed for bed commenting on how long their day had been.

My day was even longer. By the time I had cleared the table, washed and dried the dishes, filled the kettle for morning and generally tidied up, the clock was striking nine.

As I laboured up the stairs, oil lamp in hand, I thought about how pleasant an interlude the concert had been. What surprising skill and emotion Mr. Brecht had exhibited in his organ-playing. How sweet and clear Katerina's voice had been, despite the fact that I had not understood a word of what she had been singing. I cocked my head and frowned. What was that sound now? Was it a trick of my exhausted mind? "Johann." I heard the name called out clearly. Katerina's voice. I climbed, listened. "Johann." Again she said his name. I quickened my step, reached the top of the stairs. "Johann." A higher, louder, longer note. Was she in some kind of trouble?

"Katerina … Katerina." I stopped dead, one foot on the landing. Mr. Brecht's voice this time, a strange, low rumble. I held my breath. A small stifled sound followed, then another … and several more, interspersed with odd-sounding grunts.

I held the lamp aloft and saw that the door to the Brechts' bedroom was ajar. They always closed it when they went to bed. Perhaps the catch had not worked this time. The hairs on the back of my neck rose and I felt a trickle of sweat between my breasts. Unaware of my reason for doing it, I turned down the wick and extinguished the light, advancing slowly, stealthily.

Something told me I should pass their door as quickly as possible and on no account look. But the temptation was too much. I peered into the room through the darkness and what I saw made me powerless to move.

Facing the doorway, Katerina lay naked on her belly, splayed across the bed. Her eyes were scrunched closed and she writhed and moaned, but her face—visible in the play of candlelight and shadow—bore an expression not of pain, but of ecstasy as her equally naked husband kneaded her buttocks and thrust into her, again and again and again, crying out her name.

The muted explosion of my own breath suddenly freed me from the thrall of the scene and I bolted, almost dropping the lamp in my haste to escape.

Once in the safety of my room, I sat on the edge of the bed. God save me, my heart was beating so fast I could scarcely breath. My blood was racing through my veins. I felt a burning heat and an aching heaviness between my thighs. Great God, what ailed me? Visions of that coupling … that rutting … with no more tenderness than a stallion for a mare or a bull for a cow, kept running through my head like a Magic Lantern show.

I threw myself back on the bed and lay there in a fever tossing back and forth as if the physical effort would cleanse my mind of the images.

But they would not be erased. And in the end I surrendered.

My hands explored, soothed, stroked, and a different picture emerged in my head, of a slower, gentler coupling.

And I whispered into the darkness, "Phillip … Phillip … Phillip."

## CHAPTER THIRTY-TWO
### September 1889
### Latham Residence, Yorkshire, England

Phillip Latham sat forward in his chair, elbows on the desktop, and smoothed out the sheets of stationary.

"Nineteenth September, eighteen-eighty-nine, etcetera etcetera," he read in a low voice. "Dear Lydia, I had almost given up hope of hearing from you when your welcome letter arrived a week ago and I am most grateful to hear that thus far you are surviving the rigors of prairie life.

I would have written back immediately, but I wanted to wait until I had something concrete to report. Now I have it, and I am delighted to be able to tell you that I know the children's whereabouts.

They are living in West Kirby, a pleasant sea-side resort on the Wirral Peninsula, bounded by the River Dee on one side and the River Mersey on the other. I gather the Chistlegates own a boarding house there, in the vicinity of the promenade, so the children will be getting plenty of good fresh air.

I recruited an amateur sleuth—a Josiah Trotter whom I have known for several years—to find the children. He is a retired bobby and likes nothing better than ferreting out information. He did not actually see Annabel and

Edwin, but through whatever means he uses, was able to positively ascertain their presence at this boarding house.

Within the fortnight I plan on travelling to West Kirby and booking in—incognito, of course—for a day or two. How providential that the children should have been billeted at a boarding house where the comings and goings of strangers are nothing out of the ordinary. Providential, too, that my path did not cross that of the Chistlegates on their numerous visits to Brackwood House.

Frankly, I would have preferred to delay writing until after this visit, but I felt the wait might be too torturous for you.

At least by the time you receive this letter I will have seen the children and with my next letter will come detailed news of their circumstances. Whether or not Annabel will have a chance to pen a few words to you during my stay there, I have no idea, but in any event, she will at least know that the communication lines to you are open.

Try not to worry, Lydia. Easier said than done, I know. But things do not look half as black as they did. At least we know the children are in a decent spot, not some filthy factory town where their health might be jeopardized. And under the law, they must be sent to school, so no doubt they will make friends, and perhaps enjoy a far better life than they would have had they been shipped off to Canada. Perhaps, too, the Chistlegates will not turn out to be the ogres we thought them and there will be no necessity for subterfuge regarding your keeping in touch with your siblings. After all, it was not the Chistlegates, themselves, who were responsible for the severing of the ties, but Mrs. Bell.

I wish, with all my heart, that I could perform miracles and bring you all together again immediately. Orphans such as you three, who have only each other to depend on should not be separated.

I really must close now if I am to get this letter in this morning's post. I trust you are well. I am your friend, Phillip Latham, etcetera etcetera."

A soft cough sounded from somewhere close by and he glanced up.

His sister, Delphine, was looking at him with an amused expression. "Taken to talking to yourself, have you?"

"Not at all. I was merely reading what I had written."

"To the child?"

"Yes, if you must know."

Delphine rustled about his study, rearranging a book here, a figurine there, then smoothing the white linen antimacassar on the back of the overstuffed chair in front of the window.

As always, his sister's presence was soothing, unobtrusive. Tall and slender, she reminded him of a nun gliding about the hallowed halls of a convent. She had the look of a nun, too, with her high, unlined forehead and a smooth, untroubled face that belied her thirty-five years, a face whose soft, pale planes were totally unlike his own. Delphine had their mother's features; he had his father's. The only physical characteristics he and his sister shared were the hazel eyes, although hers were wider, larger than his.

Phillip leaned back in his chair and hooked his thumbs under the armholes of his waistcoat. "Yes, I decided not to keep the poor girl on tenterhooks. She must be beside herself waiting for news. It is the very least I can do."

Delphine refilled his coffee cup from the silver pot on the desktop and then added two teaspoonfuls of sugar. "You have really taken an uncommon interest in this one."

"This one? You make it sound as if we are discussing a horse or a hunting dog." Phillip spoke with a sharpness he did not intend. "Her name is Lydia."

Delphine raised an eyebrow. "Lydia Fullerton." She smiled her gentle smile and smoothed a flyaway strand of straight, golden-brown hair behind one ear. "You do know you have spoken of nothing else—or should I say, no one else—these past weeks?"

"Really?" Phillip took a sip of his coffee.

"You cannot afford to become emotionally entangled with these children. I feel for them, too, you know I do, but …" She let the sentence trail off, her shoulders raised in a helpless gesture.

"What?"

"Never mind. Drink your coffee before it goes cold."

"Yes miss, three bags full, miss."

Delphine sat across from him. "It is high time you thought about circulating … getting out and about and meeting people. You have become a social hermit since Georgina's death. You are still eligible and young. What are you now, twenty-nine?"

"Twenty-nine and five months, as a matter of fact, almost in my dotage," Phillip said acerbically. "And 'struth, I meet people every day, scores of them. You know how busy the practice is; if they are not falling ill or worse, they are mangling fingers and toes, breaking arms and legs. Not to mention Brackford House and the children there."

"I am not talking about the children, or the practice. They are patients and that is a different thing altogether." Delphine toyed with the ivory paperknife on the desktop. "I am talking about your finding a nice young woman and settling down."

"And you, Delphie? What about you? When will you begin circulating, as you put it? When will you think about settling down? All you do is work. Either about the house or in the surgery … with a once-in-a-blue-moon trip to the theatre. How many years has it been, now? Fourteen? Fifteen?"

He caught the flicker of pain in her eyes and momentarily closed his own, castigating himself for his thoughtlessness, his stupidity. In all this time they had never once discussed the tragedy of Stanley Moreton's death. An avid huntsman, he had been one month short of his twenty-seventh birthday, three months short of his wedding to Delphine when his horse had thrown him and the poor chap's neck had been broken. Phillip reached across the desk for Delphine's hand and patted it awkwardly. "Sorry old thing. Unforgivable of me."

Delphine freed her hand and gave him a reassuring smile. "I know you have avoided mentioning Stanley all these years—and incidentally, it has been fifteen and two months—for fear of opening up the wound, so to speak. But, really, the subject is by no means sacrosanct. In fact, I should rather like to talk about Stanley from time to time, as I am sure you would, Georgina."

Phillip shifted in his seat. In truth, these days thoughts of his deceased wife were few and far between. "Quite so," he said.

Delphine stared off for a time and then refocused on Phillip. "Anyway, dear, I am perfectly content with my memories and my life here. I find it very rewarding, actually, and I have absolutely no need to circulate. But you, Phillip, you really must start thinking about the future … a wife, a family."

Again Phillip shifted. He had had a wife. He had lost a wife … a child, too. He had no need of another one. He could satisfy his lust with the occasional visit to Mrs. Latch's fine establishment. Dash it all, Delphie meant well. But …

"If you ask me," his sister pressed on, "you are letting yourself become far too embroiled in the affairs of the Brackwood children, especially this girl."

*This child-woman who makes your heart beat faster.* "You may well be right. But this whole affair with the Fullertons stinks. The way those two younger ones were turned over to that abominable couple is beyond the pale. I did not met them, thank God, but I heard all about them from Miss Dunn and she has a suspicion that money may have changed hands, although she has no proof of this as yet. In any event, there is something decidedly fishy about the whole affair and I am determined to do everything I can to remedy the situation."

"By going, as you said earlier, to ---"

"West Kirby. Yes."

"You are not thinking this through clearly, you know."

Phillip drained his cup and replaced it in its saucer. "I beg to differ. I have worked everything out. It is just a matter of ---"

"You will be recognized."

"Nonsense. The Chistlegates have never laid eyes on me."

"But the children have. And what, pray tell, do you think they will do the minute they set eyes on you, their adored doctor? Acknowledge you, of course, and in no uncertain terms. Scream your name at the top of their lungs, I should not doubt."

Phillip slapped his forehead with the heel of his hand. "Lord … you are absolutely right, of course. So what on earth am I to ---?"

"I shall go in your stead," Delphine said matter-of-factly. "The weekend after next should work quite nicely, I think. They do not know me from Adam —or should I say Eve. And I shall use a pseudonym. Smith … Jones … something along those lines." She clasped her hands beneath her chin and grinned. "You know, I think I shall rather enjoy this adventure."

## CHAPTER THIRTY-THREE
### *October 1889*
### *West Kirby, Northwest Coast, Cheshire, England*

Once the cabbie had deposited Delphine and her suit-case outside 55 Boyle Road—or *Sea Winds*, as the sign on the brass plaque alongside the front door read—she took a moment to observe her surroundings.

The Chistlegates' home was not right on the sea front, as she had expected, but halfway down this long, straight side road. At one end she saw shops with striped awnings over their windows, at the other the promenade, with an iron railing separating it from the sea front. Like every villa on the street, this one was detached and three-storied with wide bay windows on the first and second floors and on the third, dormers beneath a red-tiled roof.

Delphine inhaled, savoring the tang of salt and seaweed, thankful for the unusual balminess of this early October afternoon. Phillip was right; this was a capital place for the Fullerton children to be. The clean, well-kept looking house was only a few years old judging from the bright, pinkish-brown of the sandstone. She stepped onto the terra cotta tiled rectangle which served as a front garden, although garden was hardly the word for it since it was completely lacking in vegetation. Even the white-painted, campana-shaped cast iron urns flanking the front steps she was about to mount were devoid of flowers or greenery. She nodded to herself in disbelief. At home, her own contained a magnificent show of scarlet and white geraniums.

Within seconds of pressing the bell, Delphine caught the muted sounds of a raised female voice, followed by scurrying feet. The door swung open, and on the threshold stood a maid. Lace cap askew on her wavy brown hair, she was clad in a high-necked, long-sleeved black frock far too large for her bony frame. Over it she wore a voluminous bibbed white apron whose hem she had raised to her eyes. Dabbing with it and sniffing loudly, she said, "May I help you, madam?"

"You most certainly may."

The maid lowered her apron, and Delphine found herself looking into the pallid, tear-streaked face of a mere child -- a gangly child of perhaps twelve or thirteen who shifted from one foot to the other, clenching and unclenching her fists and biting her lower lip in an obvious attempt to compose herself.

Delphine frowned. Whatever had possessed the Chistlegate people to employ so young a servant? She answered herself with acerbity. The same madness that from all accounts possessed half the population.

The girl sniffed again, and grimaced apologetically.

Delphine fished a handkerchief from her reticule and handed it to her. "Blow your nose, child, and put the handkerchief away in your pocket when you are finished with it."

The girl did as she was told, then cleared her throat and squared her shoulders, making her cap teeter even more. "Can I help you, madam? Do you have a booking? May I have your bags brought in?"

The rapid-fire delivery would have been comical had it not been for the anxious, still-tearful expression on the girl's face.

Delphine answered her gently. "Yes, you can, dear; yes I do, and yes, you may. And I am getting rather tired of standing on this step. So"—she eased by the girl into the oak-paneled hall—"you may tell your mistress that Miss Jones has arrived for her two-day stay, and you may have your porter or whomever is responsible, bring in my luggage. But before you do so, dear, let me help you with that silly cap of yours." Delphine started to unbutton her gloves. "A few hair pins clipped here and there should do the trick."

"Please do not trouble yourself, Miss Jones. She is quite capable of seein' to 'er own cap." The woman who had suddenly emerged out of the dim passageway and caused both Delphine and the girl to jump, dipped her head in greeting. "Gladys Chistlegate, madam, proprietress."

She looked to be in her forties, and was a big-busted angular woman with small, deep-set eyes and dull black hair scraped back into a bun. She smiled obsequiously. "May I say 'ow extremely delighted we are to welcome you to *Sea Winds*." Her smile fell away when she turned towards the girl. "'op it now, sharp like, an' fetch Mr. Chistlegate. Tell 'im Miss Jones's cases are to go into number four." She nodded in the direction of the curving staircase off to her right. "An' after that, make yourself available to our guest. Make sure she 'as ---"

"Oh, please, it is not necessary." Delphine kept her voice level, although inside she was seething. Nasty woman. Lord, how she would love to give her a good dressing down. And it was ludicrous the way she spoke, trying to sound so upper-crust, but unable to disguise her thick, north country dialect.

"I insist." The counterfeit smile came and went, the small eyes narrowed with determination.

Delphine was about to protest again, when Mr. Chistlegate appeared with her luggage in hand, and the maid following. He was an inconsequential-looking sort, pale and soft, and decidedly uncommunicative. A brief, "How do you do?" and he scuttled off upstairs with the girl in tow. Moments later, he briefly reappeared, the girl too, and then they made themselves scarce.

"We do not do dinner at night, 'ere, as I am sure you know from when you made your booking." Mrs. Chistlegate ran a fingertip across the top of the nearby gate-leg table, obviously testing it for dust. "But we do tea at five, madam, in the dining room to your left, there. We only 'ave two other guests—gents both o' them—at present, so go to whatever table you want. Meanwhile, the maid will come up to your room in a bit to 'elp you unpack, and do whatever else you may require of 'er."

"Thank you," Delphine said, heading for the stairs. "Since it is going to be a while until the meal, I should rather like a cup of tea, and perhaps some biscuits, in my room, if you do not mind."

"I want tea, too," a child's voice piped from the top of the stairs. "Tea and biscuits." The voice was that of a slight and very pretty boy of about eight or nine, who slid down the bannister with a shriek of delight and almost bowled over Mrs. Chistlegate with his clumsy landing.

Amazingly, she did not chastize the lad, but mussed his dark red curls and said, with a smile that illuminated her sour face, "Did my little man finish 'is lessons an' did Mr. Biddle leave?"

"Twiddle Biddle fiddle. I hate him. I hate his lessons. Why do I have to do the horrid things?"

"To make you cleverer than you already are, dear one." She tweaked his cheek and he gave her a thunderous look.

"You really are a rascal," she said with mock severity. "What is Mother to do with you?"

"Give me biscuits ... cream biscuits and tea. I want tea." The boy rolled his eyes as if he thought her stupid. "I told you."

"And you shall 'ave it my darling boy, just as soon as Mother is finished. This 'ere is Miss Jones. Can you be a young gentleman, and say 'ow do you do?"

"No." The boy lifted a defiant chin.

Mrs. Chistlegate shrugged and a beatific smile lit her face. "My boy ...

'e's full of spirit, an' no denyin' it."

"Quite so." Delphine bit her bottom lip. Full of downright naughtiness if the truth were known. Her son, the woman had said. But Delphine could have sworn Phillip had said the couple was childless? She must have been mistaken. Lord, but the poor Fullerton children were all the more to be pitied; imagine being billeted in the same household as this young charmer.

"Biscuits, biscuits, biscuits," he suddenly shouted at the top of his lungs, his face turning crimson. "Tea, tea, tea. Now, now, now."

Gladys Chistlegate lifted her shoulders. "Knows 'is own mind does my Edwin."

Her Edwin? But that was the Fullerton boy's name. The shock of it made Delphine catch her breath. Great jumping Jehosaphat, this hellion of a lad yanking on the Chistlegate woman's sleeve and the poor little chappie Phillip had spoken of as being so badly done to, had to be one and the same.

"Will you hexcuse me while I see to 'im, madam?"

"Yes ... of course." Delphine unconsciously waved Mrs. Chistlegate off. What about the girl ... the sister, though. Where was she? "You must not you keep the little chap waiting."

"I am not a little chap." The boy scowled at Delphine. "I am a big fellow."

Delphine acknowledged him with a crisp, "Indeed you are." And then, seemingly of its own volition, the question, "And is he to have tea with his sister?" slipped from her mouth.

Warily, the woman said, "Edwin is an only child. There is no sister."

"Sister," the boy said. Then again, in a high, strident voice, "Sister. I want my ---"

"What you want"—Gladys Chistlegate took him by the shoulders and turned him about-face—"an' what you shall 'ave this very minute, are biscuits. Off you go to the kitchen, now, and get out the tin."

Once the lad's eager footsteps had faded, she refocused on Delphine. "I shall send the maid up with your tea, madam. Number four, as I said, top of the stairs. Now, if you will hexcuse me, I 'ave my son to attend to."

But what in Hades have you done with the other one? Delphine wanted to say. Where is Annabel Fullerton?

## CHAPTER THIRTY-FOUR
### *October 1889*
### *West Kirby, Northwest Coast, Cheshire, England*

Delphine removed her long, tortoiseshell hat pin and took off her straw hat. "Have you worked here very long" she asked the maid who had just entered the room and set down a tea tray on the parlour table in front of the bay window.

"Not very. Shall I take care of those for you, madam?"

Following hot on the heels of the answer, the question caught Delphine unawares. She stared, nonplussed, for a few seconds, until the girl prompted her with, "Your hat can go on the shelf in the wardrobe, and your pin in the holder on the dressing table. Your jacket can be hung in the wardrobe, too, if you would like."

"Yes." Delphine smiled. "By all means." Goodness, the girl certainly seemed to have regained her composure and a modicum of maturity into the bargain. Now, she seemed more young woman than child, despite her oversized garb and the still precariously-perched cap on her head.

What an educated-sounding voice she had, too; she must have had schooling of some kind. Perhaps she had been taken under the wing of a previous employer and been tutored. Or maybe her family had been a respectable one that had fallen upon hard times and been forced to put their child into service. Delphine reined in her wandering thoughts and focused on what the girl was saying about there being hot water in the basin on the wash stand, and the tea being ready to pour.

"Will you join me?" Delphine asked after she had washed her hands and was toweling them dry.

Now it was the girl's turn to look blank.

"For tea and biscuits." Delphine nodded towards the table.

"Oh no. I could not possibly do that." The maid bit her lower lip anxiously. "Mrs. Chistlegate would not … I mean, I would be wasting time when I am supposed to be helping you with your unpacking and ---"

"Nonsense. I am perfectly capable of doing my own unpacking, but positively incapable of drinking tea alone. So, be a dear and bring the beaker off the wash stand. There is plenty of tea, but I see only one cup on the tray."

Once the girl had sat opposite her, Delphine asked, "By the way, what is your name?"

"Er … er"—she cleared her throat—"Jane." She looked at the floor and then out of the window. "Jane Black, madam."

Delphine poured and milked the tea and then with tongs poised over the sugar basin said, "One lump or two?"

Jane lifted her shoulders, ran the tip of her tongue across her lips, and said hesitantly, "Three?"

"Three it is." Delphine proffered the biscuit plate, sugared her own tea and added more hot water from the pewter-lidded jug to the pot. "So"—she took a couple of sips and returned her attention to the maid—"exactly how long have you been here, then?"

The girl did not answer. She was clearly too involved with her biscuit for the question to have registered. Having separated its halves and eaten the plain one, she was now intent on nibbling all around the edges of the cream side.

Delphine bit back a laugh. So where was the self-possessed young woman, now? "Jane," she said firmly.

The girl froze, the biscuit clamped between her teeth, a rosy flush spreading up her neck and into her cheeks.

"Gracious, dear, no need to look so mortified. Finish your biscuit—I always save the cream filling until last, too—and tell me how long you have worked here."

Jane giggled then quickly finished eating. "Several months, madam."

"And do your duties include taking care of the boy?"

The maid's eyes widened. "No ... she will not ... I do not ... I mean, I cannot." She paused to clear her throat and drink the rest of the tea in her beaker. "Only Mrs. Chistlegate takes care of Edwin."

"Perhaps that is just as well, given his rambunctiousness. He is the only child, is he not?"

Instead of answering, Jane said vehemently, "He is a little beast. It is absolutely horrid what she has done to him."

Delphine leaned forward. "Done to him? What do you mean?"

"Nothing." The girl jumped up, knocking the empty beaker over in the process, then quickly righting it. "I am sorry, I should go." Her nervous eyes darted about, and she covered her mouth with her hands like a child who had said something naughty and knew she would be reprimanded.

"You can tell me, Jane."

The girl gave a vigorous nod of her head. "No, I cannot."

"Does she hurt the boy?"

"No, she never hurts him."

"What then?"

"She will not let me have anything to do with him."

"And you want to?"

"Yes. He is ... he is." Jane shifted from one foot to the other and wrung her hands.

"What is he?" Delphine prompted in a gentle tone.

"She has ruined him. He was always so sweet before. Now, he is positively ---"

"Horrid?" Delphine filled in the blank. "What do you mean by before? I know he is adopted—I will tell you in due time how I know—that Mrs. Chistlegate brought him here in January, I believe. But ---"

"I came with him in January." The girl's eyes glistened with unshed tears. "They brought us both here from an orphanage, although I know they really only wanted Edwin. He is my brother, Miss Jones. Edwin is my brother." Now, she began to sob quietly, desperately. "But she will not let us speak to each other. She tells him he has no sister, he must call me the maid and I must refer to him as young master Edwin, and she says if I do not do exactly as she says, she will send me away"—she stopped to suck in air—"and if she did, then I should never see Edwin again and I said I would always take care of him … I promised our sister ---"

"Lydia. Right?"

The girl's eyes widened and her mouth fell open.

Delphine rose and went to her. "And you, my dear, are not Jane, you are Annabel." She took a handkerchief out of her skirt pocket and gently dabbed at the child's tears. "And I am not Miss Jones. Come"—she took the girl by the elbow and steered her back to the table—"sit down, now, and let me tell you who I am and what I am doing here."

## CHAPTER THIRTY-FIVE
### October 1889
### West Kirby, Northwest Coast, Cheshire, England

Delphine checked her watch. Eight. Any minute now, if everything worked according to plan, and Annabel should be returning.

The girl's rap on the door came at a little before ten past, and was so loud and purposeful-sounding that even though Delphine had been expecting it, she almost jumped out of her skin.

She showed the girl to the parlour table by the open window. "Sit here while I get the letter. There is still sufficient daylight left for you to read by."

"What about the mending job, Miss Latham?" Annabel held up a sewing basket. "Should I get started?"

"That will not be necessary, dear. What *will* be, however, is for us to keep our voices down, just in case your employer is hovering in the hall."

Annabel nodded, wide-eyed.

"Another thing that will not be necessary is for you to wear that silly cap. Take it off and put it down on the floor, there, beside the basket."

"Yes, Miss Latham."

"Very good. Now, sit back—you look positively worn out—and enjoy the fresh air." The net curtains flapped suddenly, as though in encouragement. "But first peep in the serviette on the table; there were far too many *petit fours* at tea, so I popped a couple in my handbag for you."

"For me?" Annabel licked her lips. "I never get cake."

With a soft laugh, Delphine said, "Absolutely for you. Every last crumb. So tuck in, now."

Delphine felt in her suit-case's side pocket for the envelope from Lydia Fullerton, smiling to herself as she thought about the fit the Chistlegate woman would have if she knew the half of what was going on.

First of all there had been Delphine's teatime tardiness. Knowing full-well that five was the appointed hour, she had put in an appearance in the dining room at half-past.

Unctuous to a fault, Gladys Chistlegate escorted her to her table and said, "Madam must 'ave misunderstood when I told 'er what time tea time was, or p'raps madam fell asleep. Anyway, I shall be 'appy to send up the maid, tomorrow, to remind madam of the time."

"Thank you, but that will not be necessary. Actually, madam did not misunderstand or fall asleep." Delphine took her time in making her selection from the plate of sandwiches on the table in front of her. "Madam was late because of the unfortunate mishap that befell her. You see, there is rather a nasty little metal curlicue on the towel rail on the side of the wash stand in my room, and the deuced thing caught on my frock and ripped the skirt right off the bodice." She had let the silence hang, then, for added drama.

A wary veil dropped over Mrs. Chistlegate's face. She clearly had no idea in which direction the discourse was headed, so she kept quiet.

Delphine touched her serviette to her lips. "Not that I hold you at all responsible for that mean little hook, Mrs. Chistlegate. It surely was my own clumsiness that caused the mishap, and my own foolishness that has put me in such dire straits, now." She shook her head heavily. "You see, I did not pack sufficient frocks that I can do without the one in question. So"—she drained her tea cup, set it down and blotted her mouth again—"I should be most appreciative if you would allow me to borrow your maid, assuming, of course, she is handy with a needle and thread and that you can spare her later on this evening."

A moment of silence, a flickering back and forth of those calculating eyes and then a brilliant smile had almost split the woman's face in two. "Spare 'er? Habsolutely, Miss Jones." The woman's relief had been palpable. Clearly, no aspersions were to be cast on her fine establishment. "A right marvel with 'er needle an' thread, is our Jane," she had said.

"By the time I was finished with your mistress," Delphine told Annabel now, "she was trilling your praises."

"She told me it would be woe betide me if my work did not please you, Miss Jo ... I mean, Miss Latham," the girl said, wiping off her sticky fingers with the serviette and giggling, "I know it is terribly wicked of me, but I think it is wonderful what you did, and ever so clever."

"Thank you, my dear." Delphine handed her the envelope and went and sat on the edge of the bed. "Rather wicked of me, too, to have spun such a yarn. But I did it with the very best of of causes in mind -- that, of course, of yourself and your siblings. So, take your time, now. See what your sister has to say. And then we shall work on your response."

Annabel made no move to open the envelope, but clutched it to her chest and looked over at Delphine with anxious eyes. "I feel sort of frightened. I mean, what if it says something dreadful? What if Lydia says we shall never see each other again?"

"I am sure it will say nothing of the sort. Just open it, child."

Annabel did so, smoothing out the pages in her lap with tremulous fingers and then fortifying herself with a deep breath.

Beyond the window, a pair of gulls rode the thermals, their mournful cries punctuating the ensuing silence.

Her brow furrowed in concentration, Annabel started to read, the gamut of emotions playing like light and shadow across her face. When a smile tweaked the child's lips, Delphine felt her own mouth curve up. And when tears spilled down Annabel's cheeks, Delphine felt a lump rise in her own throat.

Lord, but what on earth had come over her, she thought. All these years of managing to stay outside of things, of keeping emotions in check—not to mention her chastisement of Phillip for his over-involvement with the Fullerton children—and here she was guilty of the same misdemeanour.

Feeling foolish, she rose and went to the dressing table. There, she busied herself with her hair, removing the pins and laying them tidily in the porcelain tray.

She had just about finished when Annabel blurted, "Oh mercy, Miss Latham, Lydia says there are Red Indians there. I am certain I read or heard somewhere that Indians scalp people."

"Nonsense." Delphine loosened her hair about her shoulders and continued with conviction, "They are not savages anymore, dear. We have long-since civilized them." Lord, but she certainly hoped it was true.

Truth or not, Annabel seemed reassured and returned to her reading.

Delphine checked the clock. It would not do to keep the child up too long. Nine—another half-hour—and she must dispatch her. "Are you at the end yet, dear?" she asked.

"Almost. There … now I am." Annabel flopped back in her chair, the letter clutched to her chest once more. "I shall look at the moon tonight." She smiled a faraway smile. "The stars, too. Lydia says that is what she does every single night."

"All well and good, young lady, but before you start your moon- and star-gazing, come over here and write your letter." Delphine had unpacked her leather writing slope which held all the necessities. The room contained no desk, so the dressing table would have to do.

Once seated there, Annabel said, "But what shall I write about? You said I must not worry her. And if I tell her the truth, she will ---"

"White lies, dear, mixed in with the truth. They are quite permissible when used to good ends. Tell her you are well and that Edwin is prospering ... in your own words, of course."

Annabel made a face. "But Edwin is getting beastlier by the day."

"I know." Delphine touched her shoulder reassuringly. "But you must not mention that, it would upset her. And you must remember what a nice little chap he was before, and have faith that he will be again."

"Very well."

"And you have no need to speak of your present lack of schooling or your unhappiness with these people, of course. You can put the emphasis on how much you feel you are going to learn from what she has to impart. That sort of thing."

Annabel sighed. "Very well." She stared dolefully at her reflection in the mirror. "It will be most dreadfully hard, though."

"But you can do it, dear, I know you can. You will doubtless have to face many more difficulties, but everything will sort itself out in the end, you will see."

While the child wrote, Delphine went to the window and looked out into the gathering dusk. Lord, what on earth had possessed her, giving such assurances, when she had not one whit of an idea how the situation was going to be resolved?

It had been compassion that possessed her, she suddenly realized. Phillip was absolutely right; the lot of the Fullerton children was a dreadful one. And for her part, she would do her level best to help put things right. How, though, that was the thing? There were just so many problems to sort out.

---

"It is a little complicated," Delphine said to Phillip over dinner the following Monday evening. She had been home two hours when her brother came through from the surgery where he had just seen his last patient off. He had started quizzing her immediately, but seeing how tired he looked, she had said, "Food first, then my regalement."

As soon as Mrs. Entwistle, their housekeeper, had cleared away the dishes, Delphine launched into her tale. Phillip listened intently, elbows on the table, chin cupped in his hands.

"So, there you have it." Delphine slumped in her chair, tired from the telling of the tale.

Phillip rose. "Come on … into the drawing room. You look done in."

At the sideboard, he paused to take a drink of the brandy he had just poured. "I would say the first thing on the agenda is for you to become a regular visitor at the Chistlegates. That way, we can keep the lines of communication open."

"I have already set the wheels in motion, brother dear," Delphine said. Despite her exhaustion, she could not resist stopping to rearrange a couple of roses in the vase on the mantelpiece, before she sat down.

Phillip handed her a glass of sherry and sank into the armchair across from hers. "In what way have you done that?"

"I have convinced Gladys Chistlegate that I am a woman of delicate constitution who has been advised by her doctor"—she tipped her head deferentially in Phillip's direction—"that she must have regular doses of sea air … even during the winter." She chuckled. "So, I told her I should like the same room made available to me once a month for the foreseeable future." She sipped her sherry. "And, no, I told her there was no necessity for me to leave an address. If there were to be any changes in plans, I would get in touch with her."

"Good for you, Delphie." Phillip raked his thick hair back and grinned. "A spy in the enemy camp, eh?"

Delphine smiled briefly. "And a spy who does not know what on earth she is going to do except deliver and pick up letters. What will we do, Phillip? I mean, for one thing, the boy really seems to have developed into a regular little horror. And for another, if Gladys Chistlegate got wind of anything, I feel certain she would have no compunction whatsoever about getting rid of Annabel."

"Getting rid of her? Good Lord."

"Not literally, of course. But the girl is a commodity as far as that dreadful woman is concerned, and valuable only as long as she is of use to her."

"We shall have to careful then, old thing. And as far as young Edwin is concerned, we shall have to undevelop him. After all, it is a question of influence, is it not?"

Delphine did not answer him. Instead, she said, "I feel so sorry for poor Annabel, not being allowed to talk to the little chap. I would dearly love to be able to bring them together. I am sure he misses her just as much as she misses him."

"Indeed he must. And he must be a very confused and angry little fellow. But whatever you cook up—and knowing you, the pot is already simmering— I should tread very softly, Delphie."

"Oh I shall, of course. Now, what you said before, about Edwin ... the question of influence part. What exactly---?"

"I mean the the little chap was perfectly all right until that Chistlegate woman got hold of him." Phillip drained his glass and then beat a tattoo on its edge with his nails. "So, were he to be removed from that influence, there is no reason to believe he would not be perfectly all right again."

"Removed?" Delphine sat forward. "What do you mean by that?"

Phillip hitched his shoulders uncertainly. "I really have no notion. I was just thinking out loud." He put the glass down on the table beside him. "All I *do* know is, I am going to help those children. Do whatever it takes. And hopefully a clever plan will reveal itself in the very near future."

"At least you have news for the sister. And Annabel's letter to send along."

"There is nothing in it that would alarm Lydia, is there?"

"Not a word. Annabel did a capital job."

"And I shall do an equally capital job when I write to Lydia again, this evening." Phillip got up. "And when I have finished, you and I will put on our very deepest thinking caps, Delphie."

## CHAPTER THIRTY-SIX
### *October, 1889*
### *The Brechts' Farm District of Saskatchewan,*
### *Northwest Territories, Canada*

Up at first light on that Tuesday in late October, I brewed a pot of strong tea, downed a well-sugared and milked cup of it along with a slice of bread and jam, and then began the task of boiling, scrubbing, bluing, starching and wringing out a mountain of garments and bed linens. By the time I had finished my hands were red-raw and I felt as if all the muscles and bones in my body were crying out in protest.

I had not played the role of lone washerwoman before. Normally, this was a two-woman job, but Katerina had finally given in to her husband's request that she stay in bed late and leave the work to me.

At eight o'clock, after I had placed the laden laundry basket by the back door, I heated up the kettle and made a fresh pot of tea, leaving it to draw while I settled on a stool in front of the stove. Massaging the ache in the small of my back, I rotated my shoulders and stretched. Steam rose from my

*166*

garments, misting about me as I toasted myself. I closed my eyes, exhaustion wiping out all thoughts …

"Good Morning."

My eyes snapped open. My heart skipped a beat and I almost fell off my perch.

"So sorry to startle you, Lydia." Mr. Brecht loomed over me. Pointing to the teapot on the table, he said, "If you have tea, I have a quick cup."

Collecting myself, I started to rise. "I do, it is freshly-made."

"You stay where you are. I help myself. Shall I pour a cup for you?"

I demurred and silence hung between us while he drank. Finally he said, "I go into town. I have much to do there. You will please keep an eye on my wife until I return?"

"Of course."

He had hardly closed the door after himself before he reopened it and stepped inside. Indicating the basket with a tilt of his blond head, he said, "It is heavy, *ya*?"

"*Ya*," I almost said, feeling peevish after my struggle with it. "Yes," I said, "it certainly is, Mr. Brecht."

"You will want it by clothes line, *ya*?" He was already halfway out the door with the basket before I had a chance to say, "I will. And thank you."

Minutes later I ventured outside clad in the heavy tweed coat Katerina had given me. I snugged the collar up around my neck and tugged my woolen hat down as far as it would go, saving my face from the sting of the icy wind. Glancing up at the gunmetal sky, I shivered. Winter was already on its way. I had been so wrapped up in my worries, I had hardly been aware of the changing seasons. I gave a doleful shake of my head. Nine months since I had laid eyes on my dear ones. Almost two months since I had heard from them. So much for the continued communication the good doctor had promised me.

I set down the heavy basket, loosened a sod with my boot toe and gave it a vicious kick. In the next instant one of the resident barn cats—a great fat tabby whom I knew to be a tom—pounced on the clod of earth and began to bat it around as if it were some creature bent on escape. After a minute or two, he lost interest in the game and sauntered over to me, wrapping himself around my legs. "Silly cat," I said, bending down and scratching him behind the ears. His steam engine of a purr made me smile in spite of my woes. "You certainly are a funny fellow. Do you know, you have cheered me up no end?" The cat meowed what sounded like a response, and I burst out laughing. "You are just what I need, puss," I said, hefting the basket. "Come along. You can keep me company while I do my work."

—

Katerina and I ate leftovers from Sunday's roast beef at mid-day. For me the meal was a rushed affair, for I still had to sweep and dust upstairs and change the beds, and then, of course, later on I would have the washing to bring in and dinner to prepare.

By one o'clock I had finished my upstairs chores and when I came downstairs I found Katerina, clad in her husband's coat—the only one that would fit her burgeoning body—by the back door with the laundry basket in her arms.

"What on earth are you doing?" I asked.

"I bring in wash. It should be dry by now. We have sun two or three times and much wind blowing."

"The laundry is my job." I helped her out of her coat, took her by the arm and guided her back to her armchair.

"You are bossy girl," she said serio-comically as I propped her swollen feet up on a footstool. "I have fidgets. I must do something."

"You can help me fold the washing later. You need all your strength for the baby." Although there had been no discussion of a due date, Katerina had grown so enormous, it surely had to be within the next few weeks. "Not to mention the move, which is only a fortnight away."

"*Ya*, I know it. Lucky I have this chair to sit on. Johann have taken so much of the furniture already." She looked thoughtful for a moment, then said, "You think I can lend one of your penny awful books. Is good for my English practice, *ya*?"

"Of course you may borrow my *penny dreadfuls*." I drew the two words out and raised a questioning eyebrow at Katerina, waiting for comprehension to dawn on her face.

And in a few seconds it did. "*Ach*, yes," she said. "I borrow, you lend the dreadfuls."

Early on I had explained how the books helped me forget my troubles and I had decided they were the perfect vehicle for Katerina's lessons. So far, we had had many a laugh over the overblown prose. But she continued to learn from it, too.

Sometime later I left her contentedly browsing through the stack of dog-eared volumes while I headed outside and retraced my steps to the washing line behind the barn.

I set down the laundry basket beneath it and watched a sudden gust of wind come up and send the bed sheets slapping about in a blue-white frenzy. Pillow slips and towels waved like frantic flags of surrender. While alongside them a pair of long johns performed a manic dance, and the image came unbidden of Mr. Brecht half-clad in the undergarment, ramming into Katerina.

I tutted at myself. What on earth ailed me that I would allow myself to revisit that July night? Was I a deviant? No, of course not. One saw something and then one thought about something relating to it. At least there would be no encore performances, now, with Katerina being so enor ... I let the thought trail off and shook my head in vigorous disapproval of my prurience. Ye Gods, what was I coming to?

I battled with the flapping garments on the line, unpegging each and dropping them and the pegs in the basket. I came to one of Katerina's aprons and smoothed my hands over the cold starched length of it. Poor dear, she was worn out. I exhaled a long sigh. She was not the only one. I was worn out.

In addition to the household chores and the sewing of the baby's layette— a challenge when your fingers were rough enough to sand a board—Mr. Brecht had had me chopping kindling, mending sections of fence that had been blown down in the last storm, helping him with the mucking out of the pig pens and cow sheds, also the currying of their six horses ... not to mention the riding of one of them, too. I slumped with my back against the post on which the washing line hung, exhausted by the mental litany.

What a surprise the horse affair had been. "When we move to store in Plenty," Johann Brecht had told me one morning when we were in the stables, "I may need you to make deliveries. So, I think it a good idea you learn to ride."

"Horses?"

Mr. Brecht's pale eyes twinkled and his mouth twitched at the corners. "Yes, Lydia, horses. We leave the buffalo to the Indians."

My stupidity made me blush.

"But first I think you should learn about tackle. What is called what," he smiled, "and what goes where."

"You mean the saddle, the bridle, the stirrups?" I had said, anxious to prove I was not completely stupid when it came to equestrian matters.

"*Ya*, all that. And other what you would call"—he tugged on his lower lip as if to bring forth the phrase—"bits and pieces. And when it is all learned, I teach you how to saddle horse. Then tomorrow, you ride around paddock, and each day afterwards you ride maybe ten minutes. What do you say, Lydia?"

"Will I be required to ride side-saddle?" I had asked him, envisioning the women riders in the hunts at home, hobbled by the dictates of fashion.

"*Ach* No. We will find trousers for you among friends who have boys. Until then, you will have to borrow pair of mine." He was doing his best not to smile, I could tell. "We put string around to hold up. How is that sounding to you?"

What else could I say but, "Fine."

And it had been, surprisingly … after the initial couple of days wearing Mr. Brecht's trousers. I had taken to horse-riding rather well. And now, I actually looked forward to my daily canter around the paddock, although I had yet to venture out into the countryside and test my skills to the full.

My posterior had suffered at first, of course, from the constant bouncing up and down. I felt a slight twinge in my right buttock, now, as I straightened and moved away from the post. I had slight twinges everywhere, I thought, returning to the clothes line and unwrapping a bed sheet twisted around it by the wind. My arms ached from the effort. But at least they were strong. Strong? Ye gods, I had muscles no self-respecting woman would admit to having.

A fortnight from now, when the move to the general store in Plenty occurred—assuming by then I had not expired from overwork—Mr. Brecht would doubtless have it in mind for me to be a loader and hauler of furniture, too. And Lord knew what else.

I dropped a handful of clothes pegs into the basket. How lovely it would be to hear something like, *I think we should let Lydia have a holiday now we have had her work her fingers to the bone. Or, Why not give her enough money to take her back to England and her family?*

I laughed out loud at my own silliness, and was still chortling seconds later when I rounded the corner of the barn and barged with considerable force into Johann Brecht.

Thank God I managed to keep the basket upright. At least the washing was saved. What was he doing? Spying on me … making certain I was not idling? Even as the thought formed, I decided it was not at all the man's style.

"I have been searching for you," he said. Clearly flustered, his face blotched crimson, he dusted off the front of his coat, even though he had no need to. It was not as if he had fallen down; I and my basket had merely set the fellow back on his heels. "Here," he finally said, reaching into his pocket. "You have letter … from old country."

"A letter," I sang out. Of course, Tuesdays and Thursdays the post was delivered in Plenty, and today was Tuesday.

He dropped it in the basket and I stared down at the worse-for-wear envelope. "You go now." He tipped his head in the direction of the house. "Leave washing for me to bring in. You catch your death standing out here."

I needed no further urging and set out at a trot. Once inside the kitchen, I sloughed my coat, thrust my hat and gloves into the pockets and hung everything up on the hooks by the door. Clutching the envelope to my chest, I rested my back against the wall, my heart hammering as much from excitement as from exertion. I had managed only one deep, calming breath when Katerina lumbered in from the direction of the pantry, bearing a glass jug containing buttermilk. "So, you did not get the washing?" she said.

"Your husband kindly offered to carry it in for me."

"It is dry?"

"Some, but quite a lot is still damp."

With difficulty, she sat down at the table, poured herself a glass of buttermilk and offered me one, which I declined. Between gulps she said, "Soon as Johann comes in I will have him set up racks in front of the stove. Then everything soon will be dry."

The subject of laundry was of absolutely no interest to me at present. I dipped my head in acknowledgment, and unable to contain myself a moment longer, said, "Look."

"At what?" Katerina put down her glass and wiped away a mustache of white foam from her mouth with the back of her hand.

"The letter your husband picked up for me in Plenty." I wafted the envelope a couple of inches in front of Katerina's nose and she crossed her eyes comically.

"From my doctor friend," I said. "And a nice fat one."

"*Ya* ... I mean, yes ... I see. Fat, as you say." She rubbed her stomach. "Just like me."

At that moment, the back door banged open and Mr. Brecht came in. "Where would you like?" he asked his wife, nodding at the basket in his arms.

"You put by the stove. Then you get the drying racks, please, and Lydia will hang everything later."

Wanting to remain unobtrusive, I had gone to sit on the stairs.

Once he had done as Katerina asked, Mr. Brecht said, "I go to Rempels this afternoon. I must return the tools I borrow from Walter many weeks ago. You will be alright while I am gone?"

"I will be fine. I have Lydia."

Mr. Brecht glanced over at me and I raised a hand in confirmation.

"Tell Walter and Sara I send regards," Katerina continued. "You bend down, please." When he complied she kissed him lightly on the lips.

"You watch she does not do too much, Lydia," Johann Brecht called over his shoulder as he exited the kitchen.

"I certainly will."

Katerina took a sip of buttermilk, dabbed at her lips with her fingertips and said, "Where were we?"

I came to life, pirouetting across the room and waving the envelope like a semaphore flag. "My fat letter. Which doubtless means there are two ... a note from the doctor and several pages from the children. Oh I know I have the vegetables to peel and chop for the stew and the washing to finish seeing to, but may I please take a few minutes to read it?"

"Of course." Katerina pushed her dank, blonde hair back from her forehead and waved me off. "You have waited much, much time to hear news of them." Wincing, she rose laboriously now, her hands cupped beneath her mammoth belly as if she were afraid it might drop to the floor.

For one crazy moment, I imagined it doing just that, slipping like some gigantic pumpkin from beneath the skirts of her voluminous linsey-woolsey frock, and rolling across the pine boards. No sooner had the uncomfortable image formed, however, than I blinked hard and managed to banish it and return Katerina's belly to its rightful place.

Mama had been nowhere near this size. But then, unlike Katerina, she had been small-boned and dainty, and had done everything possible—as was customary—to disguise her *certain condition.*

Katerina groaned and stretched as best she could.

Noting her pallor, I asked, "Are you all right?"

"*Ach,* yes." She waddled over to me. "Tired is all. And I have pain right here." She knuckled her lower back.

"Have you seen the doctor recently?"

"No, not for a while. I have no need to see doctor all the time. I see him at the start. And I am strong woman, he says. I see him at the end, maybe. Anyway"— she massaged her back again—"uncomfort is to be expected when few weeks left." She flicked my arm. "Off you go, now. I will go to parlour and lie down. At least Johann has left alone the furniture there until day before we move, he says. If he have his way"—she made a disgruntled face—"he would have taken everything out of house and loaded it onto wagon already and we would be eating and sleeping on bare boards."

That I very much doubted, I thought, as I bounded up the stairs. From what I knew of Johann Brecht he was a considerate and kind man. "I shall only be a few minutes," I said. "Be sure to call if you need me."

Halfway up, I ran out of steam and heaved a loud sigh, aware again of my dull little aches and pains and my bone-weariness. I would have to guard against the siren song of bed when I reached my room.

Once there, and comfortably settled on the edge of the bed, it took only a minute or two for me to digest Phillip Latham's first letter and to scan his second note, which he finished with, *Do take good care of yourself, and rest assured I shall see no harm comes to your siblings.* Harm? What harm? Feeling anything but reassured, I unfolded Annabel's letter with shaky fingers.

Seconds later, my trepidation had turned to elation, for Annabel sounded positively in the pink; full of the place and how pleasant it was, and of all the interesting people she was meeting. I unlaced my boots and slipped them off, then pulled the quilt over myself and took up the letter again.

No mention of the Chistlegates … nothing about their treatment of Edwin and herself, no clue as to whether or not they were kind, unkind or indifferent. Which, really, was reassuring, since Annabel had never been reluctant to bare her soul and her miseries. No mention of her schooling, either. But then her head had doubtless been filled with all the other tidbits she had wished to impart. And there were plenty, especially those surrounding her new ally, Miss Latham, Doctor Latham's sister.

And, ye gods—I plumped my pillows and settled my aching back against them—just look at this news of Edwin. Fancy his having a tutor at his disposal. What a wonder, when he might well have ended up sweeping chimneys or scaring crows from the fields, or slaving away in a match or glue factory. Or worse yet, he might have turned into the street Arab of Ernestine Hadfield's nightmares, stealing at every turn and picking pockets.

Thinking of Great-Aunt Ernestine reminded me that I still had the children's shillings. I must remember to mention them when I next wrote, assure them that their money was still safe.

I hugged myself and laughed out loud. My darlings, praise be, were all right. And Phillip Latham, dear, dear man … miracle-maker, had fulfilled his promise.

I turned and looked at my mother's portrait on the candle stand beside the bed. "He is such a fine man, Mama," I said, trailing a fingertip over the tiny image. "Such a wonderful friend to have. And no, the children and I are not yet together as a family. But at least we have made a start—Phillip and I—in the right direction."

I stared up at the ceiling, marking the slow progress of a tiny spider across its white-washed expanse. The feather bed felt like a cocoon. I snuggled further into it, breathing deeply, my tension slipping away. The ceiling wavered. When I tried to blink it back into focus, my eyelids felt as if someone had put weights on them and hard as I tried, I could not stop them from closing.

### CHAPTER THIRTY-SEVEN
#### *October 1889*
#### *The Brechts' Farm, District of Saskatchewan,*
#### *Northwest Territories, Canada*

When I next opened my eyes a shivering sense of premonition hit me. An odd keening—no longer evident even when I held my breath and strained to hear it—had drawn me to the surface.

I sat up, instantly orientated to my surroundings, but befuddled by the fact that the clock on the chest of drawers—whose ticking seemed loud as a drumstick on a cymbal—registered half-past two. I rubbed my eyes and stared beyond the window. The sky had lost it earlier flat, gray look and was now full of angry, scudding clouds that every so often obscured a watery sun.

Waiting for the fuzziness in my head to clear, I yawned and stretched for several seconds. Then, like the slap of a wet towel on my face, reality struck. I clapped my horrified hands to my mouth. Ye gods and little fishes, I had come up here just after half-past one. I had slept for an entire hour.

I scrambled out of bed, threw on my boots and made for the door. I scuttled along the landing, tucking errant strands of hair into my bun, smoothing the creases in my apron. Not that Katerina would give a fig about how I looked. But she certainly would care about what had kept me up in my room all this time.

At the top of the stairs, I paused to compose myself. Then I heard it again, the eerie keening noise that had awakened me. Held in its thrall, I tipped my head and listened.

Silence. Except for the rasp of my own breathing and the soughing of the wind against the house. But only for a moment. Then the banshee wail started somewhere below, curled up the stair well, and formed itself into a single heart-stopping word:

"HELP."

Great god. Katerina.

Skirts hitched up, I took the stairs two at a time, barely managing to keep my balance. Once down them, I stumbled along the hall, calling out at the top of my lungs, "Coming, Katerina, coming."

When I burst into the parlour, the sight of Katerina on her back on the rag rug in front of the fireplace stopped me in my tracks. Stupefied, I steadied myself against the door jamb, my eyes registering a scene that transported me back in time. Merciful heaven … Mama all over again. Mama clutching her belly … uttering those heart-wrenching sounds. Mama thrashing about in agony."

"Lydia."

The sound of my own name pulled me back to the parlour, to Katerina. "*Gott* be praised, at last you are here," she said, her arms stretched out like those of a supplicant.

"Oh yes, I am here," I said, as much to ground myself in the present as to reassure Katerina. "And I am sorry, so very sorry." I swiftly crossed to the fireplace and knelt beside her, grabbing a cushion from the nearby armchair and slipping it under her head. "Lord, what in creation happened?"

"I called and I called"—Katerina's lower lip trembled—"and when you did not come, I thought you had run away."

"Run away? Why would I run away? You and Johann are so good to me." I dabbed ineffectually at Katerina's flushed, tear-wet face with my apron hem. "I was reading my letters and the next thing …" Lord, this was no time for explanations. "Did you fall? Are you hurt?"

"I was going to sofa and a pain come, a very big pain"—she clamped her teeth over her lower lip and scrunched her eyes shut for a moment—"and it take away my breath. So I think I must lie down, but I fall."

I slipped off my apron and blotted Katerina's brow with it. Merciful heaven, the baby was much too early. "You had just one pain?"

"*Nein.* One before you came, one a quarter-of-an-hour before, I think. And before that"—she rolled her head fretfully from side to side—"I do not know. There is no clock. So ---"

"But regular pains?"

"*Ya.*" This baby comes soon, Lydia." She pulled herself up on her elbows and exhaled a long, noisy breath. "You must fetch Johann, now. And you … he … somebody … must get word to doc ---"

"I cannot get Johann, Katerina, dear." I sat back on my heels. "He is positively miles away. Even if I ran like a jack rabbit, it would take me hours. And I cannot possibly leave you alone that long."

"You take *Thunder.*" Katerina gasped through another pain. "He is fast as racehorse."

Ride *Thunder*? I felt my jaw drop. I had ridden him only twice and that had been just around the paddock. "Katerina, I do not think I ---"

"Aaaaaaaah." Katerina fell back, suddenly, brought her knees up and began to pant. "Go. Please. Get Johann. Doctor. Mrs. Rempel. Now. You go NOW." She screamed the final word.

I clambered to my feet and stumbled for the door.

God help me.

And God help Katerina.

## CHAPTER THIRTY-EIGHT
### *October 1889*
### *The Brechts' Farm, District of Saskatchewan,*
### *Northwest Territories, Canada*

Considering my lack of expertise, the speed with which I managed to saddle *Thunder* astounded me. Within five minutes of leaving Katerina's side,

I was astride the animal and urging him on with a flick of the reins and a frantic, "Go boy, go."

He must have recognized the panic in my voice for he gave a loud snort, tossed his mane and leapt upward, raising his hind legs an instant before his forelegs came down in a great curvet. I shrieked, grabbed onto his mane as well as the reins, and hung on for dear life as he curveted once more and then shot out of the stables, across the yard and through the gates which I had thought to throw open moments before.

Once we had turned right onto the trail, I gave the horse his head. I felt his muscles bunching and tensing and thrusting under my legs. He was like the Pegasus of Greek mythology — a winged creature, flying, racing untrammeled. Faster. Faster. I bent low over his sleek, outstretched neck, feeling his mane whip my face, praying for the strength to stay on him.

The horse and I became one, hoofbeat and heartbeat marking off the seconds, the minutes of a somnambulistic race where time had no meaning. Only when the horse's gait suddenly changed from gallop to canter did I return to earth. I sat upright in the saddle and reorientated myself to my surroundings. Astonishingly—without benefit of direction from me—we were through the gates to the Rempels' ranch and heading up the rutted drive. "Whoa there," I said, with a tug of the reins that slowed the horse to a trot and finally brought him to a halt at the front of a white clapboard house.

I had no idea how long the journey had taken. The first thing I said when Mrs. Rempel answered the door in response to my frantic knocking was, "What time is it, please?"

Three apple-cheeked replicas of the tall, hefty woman—two boys and a girl—popped up from behind their mother's skirts like startled gophers. "Time?" She shook her gray head as if to clear it. "Lord o' mercy, girl," she glanced back over her shoulder, "'tis nigh on four. But what in tarnation d'yer want to know fer, and what are yer doin' hereabouts lookin' like yer've been dragged through a tumbleweed backards? Aren't yer that Fullerton girl ... that Home girl that come from ---?"

"Yes," I cut in. "I am the Brechts' Home girl. And I need to see Mr. Brecht, urgently, please."

"Lord"—the woman passed a large hand over her plump face —"somethin' wrong is there?" She did not wait for an answer. "Mr. Brecht," she yelled over her shoulder, using her wide hips to shove the three children aside, "wanted y'are, urgent-like."

After that, chaos reigned for a time, with everyone talking at once and the children whining and pulling on their mother in a battle for her attention.

At last—thanks to Mrs. Rempel—a plan evolved. Mr. Brecht would saddle one of the Rempels' horses and ride to Plenty in search of the doctor. Walter Rempel would take care of the children and the horse, ensuring he was properly cooled down and stabling him for as long as necessary. And in the meantime, Mrs. Rempel would hitch up their wagon and drive herself and me back to Katerina's.

"There is nothing much at the house, ma'am," I had the forethought to remind the woman, just before we set out. "I do not know what you need, but almost everything is packed up for the Brechts' upcoming move into town."

Betsy Rempel patted my arm. "Lord o'mercy, 'tis good yer've a brain in that head o' yours, Lydia Fullerton, or yer poor mistress would be in a sight bigger pickle than she is already. Let me just run upstairs and put the necessaries in my case."

Mrs. Rempels' pair of grays had none of the speed of *Thunder*. By the time the wagon rolled into the Brechts' yard it was almost dark.

Leaving Betsy Rempel to follow, I scrambled down and raced for the front door. Thank God there was still sufficient light to see by.

"Katerina, we are back," I shouted, pulling off coat, hat and muffler as I entered the house. "I have brought help."

"Lydia?"

Faint. Ghostly. Katerina's voice seeping along the hall like smoke. I tipped my head and froze. Mama's voice … the life almost gone from it. Dear God, the voice, surely, of a dying woman.

I felt dizzy. "Hurry Mrs. Rempel," I called over my shoulder.

"A body could not hurry any quicker," she said from behind me as she came huffing through the door, "if a wolf was gnawing at her behind. Take this, girl." She thrust her suitcase at me as she doffed her coat and bonnet and tossed them over the newel post at the bottom of the stairs. "Now, show me where she is."

I nodded in the direction of the slightly-ajar parlour door.

"It is Betsy Rempel, Mrs. Brecht," she said in a loud voice, "here with your girl." The woman nudged me into motion. "Look sharp now, missie"— she shoved ahead of me—"we've a birthin' to see to. I know yer've not helped bring a young'un into the world afore, but it is a purely natural event"—she pushed the parlour door wide—"and nothin' at all to fuss ab …" Her voice sputtered away like a lamp out of oil. She brought one hand up to her mouth and extended the other behind her in a staying gesture.

Under her breath, just loud enough for me to hear, she said, "Oh Lord have mercy on the poor, dear soul."

## CHAPTER THIRTY-NINE
### *October 1889*
### *The Brechts' Farm, District of Saskatchewan,*
### *Northwest Territories, Canada*

My heart threatened to beat out of my chest and only an effort of will kept me upright. "Is she dead?" I craned for a view of the parlour's interior, but Mrs. Rempel's large frame filled the doorway.

"Kitchen. Hot water … plenty of it." The woman's voice was full of urgency. "Make sure the stove is well-stoked. Sheets. Clean rags. Whatever yer can lay yer hands on. Blankets, too. Sharp like. When yer come back, knock an' wait till I say it's alright fer yer to come in."

I whirled about the kitchen then up and downstairs in a state of automatism, returning to the parlour door some time later with a couple of blankets, an assortment of linens and an oil lamp which I set down on the demilune table at my elbow.

With trembling fingers I extracted a match from the box I had brought from the kitchen and lit the lamp. Then I knocked loudly on the door.

Interminable seconds passed. In my agitation I danced about like a child needing the commode. I heard murmers—one voice or two, I could not tell— and the snap and crackle of kindling from the fireplace. A shaft of light came from under the door. Mrs. Rempel must have lit the lamps. Why in Hades did she not answer?

I tried again, pounding this time, and almost fell on my face when Betsy Rempel flung the door wide.

"Lord o'mercy, girl, I said ter knock." She spoke in a low voice. "Not ter beat down the door. Hand me them linens, now, an' that lamp, an' wait there."

Reluctantly, I did as I was told, and in a minute Betsy Rempel reappeared. "Have yer no sense, makin' such a racket?" I bit back my irritation. "I wanted to know what was going on and if—"

"Lydia? Is that you?"

"Katerina?" I frowned, head tilted, and looked up at Mrs. Rempel for confirmation.

Vaguely, I heard her say, "Wait there. I am not ready for yer yet … I 'ave not had a chance ter …"

But I had been forestalled long enough and elbowed my way past the woman.

Barely into the room, I halted, my knees threatening to buckle. Only the sound of Betsy Rempel's voice commanding me not to dare faint kept me on my feet.

I had no eyes for anything but the blood. A dust storm of thoughts about Indian massacres swirled in my head and I half-expected to see a brave leap from one of the shadowed corners, tomahawk raised.

Everywhere blood, illuminated by the lamp- and firelight. Too much. Far too much. Splotches and spatters and streaks of it across the floor's white pine boards; an island of it with a ragged coastline set against the pale blue sea of curtains that someone had ripped from the windows and tossed across the sofa. Shockingly scarlet like the blood on Mama's nightgown that I had not been supposed to see. My heart pulsed at my temples. And in my head birth, blood, death danced a macabre minuet.

I inhaled a harsh breath and the coppery smell made my gorge rise.

"Lydia".

I started. My gaze unconsciously moved to the sofa and the source of the voice, and after a long moment of puzzlement, the eyes sunk deep in their smudged sockets and the pale blonde hair clicked like kaleidoscopic pieces into place and became Katerina's features.

"Did you see him?" The weakest of smiles touched her lips; her eyelids fluttered, then closed. "Is he not beautiful?"

"The baby? Oh, great god, Katerina, you had the ---"

"Shush." Betsy Rempel's voice came from behind and I swung about. "An hour since she had the little chap. Brung 'im into the world all by 'erself, she did. So, leave 'er be, now. See, she 'as dropped off, poor soul. Come. Over here, in front of the fire. Took the drawer out of the sideboard, I did. 'twas the best I could do since I seen no cradle nowhere."

"The cradle has gone. Mr. Brecht already moved it into town," I said, kneeling beside the drawer, my heart in my throat, as I gazed down on the baby's blood-streaked, wizened little face. "Is it alive?" I asked.

"Him … not it. Yes … 'e is." Betsy Rempel struggled to kneel beside me. "Look, yer can see the poor little mite breathin'. Once we get sorted out, we shall get 'im cleaned up."

"But why is he not crying?"

"I reckon he's done all 'is cryin' for now, gettin' into this world. An' with no one but 'is poor Ma ter help 'im, neither."

"Is she all right? Kat … Mrs. Brecht?"

Mrs. Rempel frowned and glanced over at the sofa. "I dunno, dear. Somethin' a bit peculiar goin' on there. But never you mind, 'twill all be ironed out when the doctor gets here. Lord o'mercy, where is that man, anyway?"

I cocked my head. "Outside, I think."

"Run along, then, will yer, an' stop 'em afore they come bargin' in."

I met the men by the front door and blurted, "The baby is here."

"Here? *Mein Gott,* we have our baby?" Johann Brecht raked back his hair and laughed.

"Where is the lass?" Dr. Purdy was already striding by me as I nodded towards the parlour.

"Is it girl or ---?"

"A boy," I told Mr. Brecht. "And according to Mrs. Rempel, he is fine."

"He is that." Betsy Rempel came puffing along the hall, carrying the makeshift cradle. "Doctor says fer yer to take the mite into the kitchen, now."

Johann Brecht took the drawer from her. "My son," he spoke in a soft, awed voice, looking dazedly down at the sleeping infant, and then up at me and Mrs. Rempel.

"Yer missus was a proper soldier. Brung the young'un into the world all by 'erself, bless 'er heart."

"I must see her."

"Afraid that is out of the question, old chap," Dr. Purdy said. "At least for the time being."

"I do not understand."

"One moment, sir, and you will. Now, Mrs. Rempel, if you would be so kind as to step back into the parlour, I am in need of your help."

"What about me?" I pushed forward. "Can I ---?"

"Lord no, lassie." Dr. Purdy looked at me as if I had lost my senses. "You certainly canna."

"Why don't yer go and make a nice pot o' tea," Mrs. Rempel said kindly. "Yer can help later on."

"Doctor. Why can I not see my wife," Johann Brecht said. "Is she ---?"

"All right?" Dr. Purdy finished his question for him. "At this point, old chap, I canna say. What I can tell you, though, is that she has a sight more work ahead of her. There is another wee babe to be born, you see."

## CHAPTER FORTY
### *October 1889*
### *The Brechts' Farm, District of Saskatchewan,*
### *Northwest Territories, Canada*

I remembered how Papa had paced, grim-faced, during all the hours Mama had laboured to bring Edwin into the world. But Johann Brecht sat in silence by the kitchen stove, still as an effigy, staring down at the sleeping newborn in the makeshift cradle which he had balanced on two chairs.

I had boiled the kettle and made a pot of tea, cringing at the sounds of

Katerina's moans, holding my breath between each. Now, I added milk to the cups and reached for the sugar basin.

"Twins. I cannot believe it."

I started. These were the first words Mr. Brecht had spoken since our banishment to the kitchen half an hour earlier.

"Nor can I." I dropped two sugar lumps into his cup, stirred the steaming brew and took it to him. I had just returned to my seat and was about to sugar my own tea when a scream lacerated the quiet. Johann Brecht's head and my own came up simultaneously and our horrified eyes locked.

I wanted to cover my ears, but the sound held me transfixed. On and on it went until I thought my head would explode. Then as suddenly as it had begun, it ceased, and absolute silence ensued.

I did not realize I had been holding my breath until I heard its ragged expulsion followed by Johann Brecht's *"Mein Gott"*. Like a puppet whose strings had been suddenly pulled, he got up. "You watch the child, please," he said. "I cannot sit here while …"

Just then the door opened.

Merciful Heaven. I rose, hammers still beating at my temples. Framed in the doorway, looking as dishevelled and blood-splattered as the survivor of a massacre, stood Doctor Purdy.

He cleared his throat and ran a distracted hand through the tumble of his white hair.

Dear God. I gripped the edge of the table, concentrating on his lips.

"Dreadfully sorry, old chap."

My heart plummeted and I sank back into my seat.

"I am afraid we lost her."

## CHAPTER FORTY-ONE
### *November 1889*
### *The Brechts' Farm, District of Saskatchewan,*
### *Northwest Territories, Canada*

Johann Brecht was adamant about it. There was to be no laying out of the body, he told Betsy Rempel when she offered her services. Nor was there to be a funeral. "I will bury her here," he said without expression, over Doctor Purdy's protestations.

"But you have sold the place, man," the doctor said. "What of the folks who have bought it; what will they think? Besides, would you not sooner take her into town and have her near you?"

"Where the body lies is of no matter to the Lord or to me." Johann Brecht spoke in a flat tone, with no sign of emotion. But his eyes held volumes of pain and grief. "Nor do I care what folks think. What does matter is that the body goes into the ground right away. So, you will please leave, doctor, and let me get on with my work."

"And Lydia, will you please go upstairs and stay with—"

"Of course."

Upstairs, moments later, I turned down the wick on the oil lamp, making the light in the bedroom dim. Then I watched from the window as Mr. Brecht headed with a lantern, pick and shovel to the rear of the barn. Clearly, his plan was to dig the grave in the garden patch back there, close to the grove of poplars. The earth had been turned earlier on, making it more easily workable than the ground elsewhere, now that the winter freeze had begun to set in.

Sometime later, I saw him making his way to the barn. I recalled hearing him say to Katerina a few weeks ago that he would keep a hammer, saw and nails here in case of any last minute repair jobs. He had also mentioned that he planned on leaving behind the stack of pine boards which were apparently left over from the construction of the farm house's floors. I chafed my upper arms. He had everything on hand for the construction of a coffin.

The hammering went on for what seemed an eternity, and by the time it stopped and the light in the barn was extinguished, it was too dark for me to see any outside activity.

I sank into a nearby chair and waited, my heart in my mouth.

Eventually I heard the sound of movements in the hall below. I wrapped my arms tightly about myself. Dear God … it was time.

My eyes took in the still form in the bed, and the pine drawers set on the trunk at its foot. Sleeping in one was newborn William, his pink flower of a mouth making soft little sucking noises.

I tiptoed to the bedside and gazed down into his mother's face, the face that was Katerina's and yet was not, so shocking in its whiteness, the bones standing out sharply, as though hewn from marble.

Poor dear. I leaned over and gently smoothed back the pale hair. Katerina's eyes suddenly opened wide and focused on me. "Two babies," she murmured, a faint smile on her lips. "How good of God to give me two babies."

I took her hand and caressed it, my ears attuned to the heavy footfalls on the staircase. "Go back to sleep," I said softly.

She did, thank God.

Otherwise, she would have seen her husband in the doorway, their daughter's coffin in his arms.

## CHAPTER FORTY-TWO
### *December 1889*
### *West Kirby, Northwest Coast, Cheshire, England*

Delphine stood at the window of her room at the Chistlegates', looking out. The sleet-laden wind off the Irish Sea lashed the panes, making visibility almost nil, so she returned to the chintz-covered armchair by the fire, castigating herself for having lost her wits.

Who else but a fool would opt for a sojourn at a northwestern seaside resort in December, and on such a weekend as this one?

Someone kindhearted, perhaps? She made a derisive sound at the back of her throat. Or someone—with her offer to trek here, in the first place—too deucedly impulsive for her own good. Not that the planned monthly visits had worked out as envisioned, anyway.

October's had been an exercise in futility, with Annabel absent the entire three days. "I've lent 'er out," Mrs. Chistlegate had said in answer to Delphine's casual inquiry. Something to do with one of the woman's acquaintances being in a pickle and needing extra help ... willing to pay dearly for it, too, and business was business.

Then last month, Delphine had earmarked the middle weekend, had her bags packed and everything arranged, but a telegram had arrived from her Aunt Bea's housekeeper in Manchester, saying her aunt had fallen and broken her arm. Clearly, there had been nothing else for it. Delphine had left immediately and spent a week nursing the dear, old soul.

Delphine leaned into the fire and warmed her hands. At least she was getting a little respite and would doubtless return home refreshed on Monday. She had plenty of books with her; she could catch up on long overdue correspondence, if she had a mind to; she could work on her needlepoint. Or she could do absolutely nothing ... except fret about the situation.

If only she could pack up both children and flee with them. She harrumphed at herself. Then what? If she and Phillip at least had a concrete plan, she would feel heaps better. "This is all we can do for now, Delphie," he had said as she was leaving for West Kirby. "Just keep an eye on the children and let Lydia know they are safe.

She gave the fire a poke and then sat back in her chair. Later this evening she would be busy with Annabel. She had seen nothing of the girl today, and yesterday she had been able to exchange only the briefest of greetings with her. When Mr. Chistlegate answered the door and ushered Delphine in, Annabel had been scurrying by. At least she had paused long enough to wave and say, "Hello", and for Delphine to see the pleased look on the girl's face.

The child could just as easily have been angry or at the very least, disappointed. After all, Delphine's talk about being a regular visitor at *Sea Winds* must, by now, have struck the child as bunkum.

Delphine shrugged her shawl about her shoulders. Thank the Lord there would be ample time to explain herself this evening. Orchestrating an hour or two with the girl had been a simple proposition. It had merely been a matter of playing to Gladys Chistlegate's greed.

"I should be most obliged," Delphine had said as she was about to leave the tea table earlier on, "if you would send your maid up about eight o'clock with a pot of cocoa and perhaps a few biscuits."

"You did not get enough to eat, miss?" Gladys Chistlegate's perplexed gaze had rested on the empty plates that had borne scones and sandwiches and slices of cream cake—most of which were wrapped in a serviette Delphine had hidden in her reticule.

"Oh, my goodness, yes. My affliction and my doctor require me to eat enormous quantities of food and with a frequency that is positively unseemly. But I ask you, what is one to do under such circumstances?"

"Has you're told, of course, miss," Gladys Chistlegate had responded with her customary obsequiousness, her eyes moving like the beads of an abacus, clearly calculating the increase in Delphine's bill.

"Oh, and one other thing," Delphine tossed off as she rose from the table. "I have rather a difficult time getting to sleep, so if I might impose upon you to allow your girl to read to me for about half an hour, I should find it wonderfully soothing. Assuming, of course, she knows how to."

"Habsolutely, miss. I made sure of it when I took 'er on."

"Very good. So you would have no objections?"

Of course the woman had. The set of her mouth and the subtle change in her expression told the story. But before she had a chance to thwart the plan, Delphine continued with, "It goes without saying that I should be more than happy to compensate you for your maid's time."

There was nothing subtle about the avarice at the back of the woman's eyes. "No objections whatsoever, miss. Your sleep is most himportant to your 'ealth. Keep 'er with you for as long as you like."

Delphine had smiled her most beneficent smile and said, "How very kind you are."

"And how very devious you are, Miss Latham," Delphine said out loud, now, leaning back in the armchair and closing her eyes.

"Were you talking to me?"

"What?" Her eyes snapped wide and she clutched the chair's arms, slowly turning until she had the door in her sight. She had left it open in the hopes of catching Annabel between chores, and reminding her to bring with her, later on, any letters she had managed to write to Lydia.

"Who is there?" Even as the words slipped out, she thought how foolish they sounded.

The grandfather clock on the landing answered with seven sonorous booms. And after the last one had died away a high, thin voice said, "I am a ghooooo-oooooo-ssssst."

Several seconds passed before the revelation hit. Then Delphine's tension came out in a whoosh of laughter. Of course. Annabel, bent on having a little sport. "Well ghost," Delphine called out, "if you are clever enough to materialize, let me have a look at you."

Silence.

Oh, so the game was to continue. Delphine carefully got up and tiptoed for the doorway. Biting back a chuckle, she eased her head out, steeled for Annabel's *Boo*.

And a *boo* came. Not from Annabel, however, but from the girl's brother.

Delphine's mouth fell open at the sight of him, with his back pressed up against the wall to her right. "Gracious," she said, "it is Edwin, is it not?" Lord, but what a silly question. And it would probably bring an equally silly— or downright rude—response.

But surprisingly, all the boy said was, "Did I frighten you?"

He stepped out into full view, and on his face was such a look of hopeful expectancy, that she said, with a good deal of sighing and eye-rolling, "Indeed you did, young sir. I do not think I have been so thoroughly petrified in my entire life."

His grin almost split his face in two. "Really?"

"Really. Do you remember who I am?"

"Er ... Miss ... Miss ...?" Edwin winced apologetically.

"Jones," Delphine said, thinking this was not the Edwin she had met previously. Here was a different boy altogether – a solemn, almost winsome boy, with the same aura of loneliness about him she had observed in many of the Brackwood House children.

Lord, but how providential to have him to herself for a time, free of the influence of that dreadful Chistlegate woman. She must make the best of it, let things play out and see where they led.

"So, what are you up to, young man?" she asked.

The boy lifted his shoulders and made a sad face. "Nothing. Father is asleep in front of the parlour fire, and snoring so loud it makes my ears hurt. Mother has gone to church with my ... with ... er ... the maid."

"Church on Saturday?"

"There is a meeting of the Aid To The Heathens Society."

"Will they be long, do you suppose?"

"An hour and a half, Mother said. Tonight they will be exceedingly busy parcelling up Bibles to send to the savages across the sea."

"And Jane is assisting?"

"Yes." Edwin gnawed on his thumbnail for a time. "And if she tears a page, as she did last time, Mother says it will be woe betide her. I hope she does not get …" He caught himself and trailed off.

"You hope she does not get what?" Delphine said.

Edwin started, looked through her for a moment, then picked up her cue. "Nothing. I … er … nothing." He ran a reflective hand over his nose and mouth and then said earnestly, "Miss Jones, how do you suppose savages read Bibles?"

For some untold reason, the very seriousness of the question tickled Delphine's funny bone, and she burst out laughing.

Edwin regarded her as if she were demented, his eyes growing wider and wider. And the more he stared, the harder she laughed.

Her ribs were aching and she was gasping for air by the time Edwin succumbed. One minute he was almost glassy-eyed, the next his face turned crimson, the veins swelled at his temples and he exploded with sounds that were so loud, so raucous, they stopped Delphine in her tracks.

The hairs on the back of her neck rose and she clapped a hand to her mouth. Merciful Heaven, this was not laughter. This was a horribly dissonant, uncontrollable sort of braying.

"Stop," she heard herself shout. And when the boy did not, she grabbed him by the shoulders and shook him, calling out his name.

He fixed her with a blank stare for a few seconds, uttered one final peculiar bellow and then, thank the Lord, hiccoughed into silence, tears making twin tracks down his cheeks.

"Do you have a handkerchief?" Delphine asked.

He nodded that he did.

"Then wipe your eyes … your nose, too."

Gracious. She exhaled a long breath. Laughter must have clearly become so foreign to the lad that once it started he was helpless to stem its flow.

Afraid she might set him off again, she did not pursue his Bible and savages question, but instead, asked, "How would you like to play cards?"

Quivering with excitement, he stuffed his handkerchief into his trousers pocket. "Oh, I adore cards. Do you have *Happy Families*?"

"As a matter of fact, I do."

"We used to play it all the time," the boy said wistfully.

Delphine gestured for him to precede her into the room, indicating the table by the window. She closed the door. "So, you and your mother and father played?"

"Not father. He was always too busy. And Mama died when I was very small. But with my sist ---"

"Your sister? Goodness, I had no idea you had a sister. I have not seen her when I have come here to stay. Is she away?" Delphine got the cards out of her suitcase and brought them back to the table.

"I ... er. I did ... I do not ..." The boy stammered into silence, staring down into his lap as if he were afraid his face might reveal something. Several seconds elapsed before his head jerked up and, like a medium summoning an entity from the other side, he was transformed. But not completely, for although it was Edwin Chistlegate who said with a defiant thrust of his chin, "I thought you said we were going to play cards", it was Edwin Fullerton whose gray eyes brimmed with tears and whose bottom lip started to tremble.

Delphine found it all too much. She had no more stomach for playing cat to Edwin's mouse, and baiting him with questions designed to trip him up. "It is all right, dear," she said gently, reaching across and squeezing his shoulder. He stiffened under her touch, and she withdrew her hand, adding, "I know all about Annabel and Lydia."

Edwin sucked in a breath, his eyes widening with fear.

Perhaps her instincts to tell the boy the truth were wrong. She forged ahead anyway. "I am a friend, Edwin," she said, "a friend who has talked to your sister, Annabel. A friend who is delivering letters from your sister to Lydia."

"Really?" He scrubbed his eyes with the backs of his hands.

"I am not Miss Jones, but Miss Latham. Do you remember Doctor Latham?"

Hesitantly, the boy said, "Yes."

Well, I am his sister."

"You are?"

Delphine nodded. "Annabel already knows all this."

"She does? I miss my sister. Even though I see her every day, I cannot play with her like I used to. Anyway, I am so beastly to her, she must hate me." Edwin fought for control, clenching his fists, biting down on his under-lip. But in the end, he lost the battle. "I am bad ... ever so bad. I shall go to Hell when I die."

"No, no, you are not bad, dear, nor will you go to Hell. You are just a little boy who has had to do as he was told. And you will return to being your old nice self when this is all over."

"Oh I will, I will, I promise." He began to weep wrenching sobs, and Delphine felt her throat tighten. She let him cry for a time, then rose and went to him. "Come along now. Get out your handkerchief, child, and dry your eyes," she said, standing quietly by.

Once he had finished, she urged him up out of his seat. "Things are going to be just fine, Edwin. Come and sit with me by the fire and I will tell you everything that has been happening with Annabel and we will talk about what we are going to do."

## CHAPTER FORTY-THREE
### December 1889
### West Kirby, Northwest Coast, Cheshire, England

The clock in the hall was striking quarter-to eight as Delphine prepared to send Edwin on his way. "Best you go back downstairs, now, to Mr. Chistlegate. That way there will appear to be nothing untoward when Mrs. Chistlegate returns home."

"Must I?"

"I am afraid so. And do remember to keep our meeting secret."

"Oh I will, Miss Latham. I am very good with secrets." He lowered his voice to a whisper. "Annabel and I have been keeping one for Lydia." He looked up at Delphine, saucer-eyed. "A positively enormous one."

What a little dramatist, Delphine thought, mussing his curls. "I am sure you have, dear. We will chat about it later." She gave him the tiniest of pushes. "Off you go, now."

An expression of recalcitrance flashed across his face. "She was just pretending," he called over his shoulder as he made his way to the top of the staircase.

"What was that you said?"

The thump of the boy's feet as he descended the stairs made it difficult for Delphine to discern his next words, but she thought she heard, "She is really a grownup. Ask Annabel. She will tell you."

Delphine made a disbelieving sound at the back of her throat. Ask Annabel, indeed. She had quite enough to talk to Annabel about without adding the boy's nonsense to the mix.

The girl appeared at Delphine's door half an hour later, bearing a tray with the requested cocoa and biscuits. "It has been a positive age since I last saw you, dear," Delphine said, directing her to the table in front of the window. "When I came here in October, you were nowhere to be seen."

"I was lent out," Annabel said with a disgruntled twist to her mouth.

"So I understand." Delphine sat opposite the girl. "I am dreadfully sorry I missed my November visit to *Sea Winds*. My elderly aunt had an accident and needed nursing for a week."

"Oh," was all Annabel said.

"Be a dear and pour us both a beaker of cocoa. And help yourself to the cake and scones." Delphine indicated the smuggled slices of cream-and-jam sponge and the scones laid out on a serviette.

"Thank you, but I am not hungry."

"Not even for cake and scones?"

"No. I am sorry."

Dear me. Something must really be amiss. "No need to be sorry, child. Are you ill?"

Annabel had her beaker raised halfway to her mouth. She held it there long enough to say, "No," and then took a quick gulp of cocoa.

The child was clearly in the doldrums. Time to help her snap out of it. "You will never guess who came to visit me this evening."

"Mr. Chistlegate?" Annabel said in a disinterested tone.

"No, my dear. Your brother."

Annabel appeared to snap out of her torpor. "Edwin was here?" She put down her beaker. "Mercy, did he barge in on you, Miss Latham?"

"No, not at all. I saw him out on the landing. We talked and then I invited him in."

"And was he a positive horror?"

"Quite the contrary. He was charming. He and I had a perfectly jolly time of it. He was delighted, by the way, to hear all about Lydia and the letters. Incidentally, did you have a chance to write to her?"

Annabel nodded in the affirmative, fumbled in her apron pocket, and passed an envelope across the table.

Seeing the words Lydia Fullerton all at once made Delphine think about Edwin's earlier prattlings. "Your brother is quite the dramatist. He said something rather startling about your sister."

"Startling in what way, Miss Latham?"

Delphine laughed. "He said she was just pretending. And if I am not mistaken, I thought I heard him say as he was charging down the stairs, something about your sister really being a grownup and that I should ask you about it."

Annabel sat up ramrod straight in her seat and said through clenched teeth. "The little horror, I could strangle him. He was sworn to absolute secrecy."

Confused, Delphine massaged her temples with her fingertips. "I am afraid you have lost me, dear." She took a sip of cocoa. "But I dare say you will find me again if you tell me what this is all about."

Annabel shook her head heavily. "I was sworn to secrecy, too."

Delphine reached across the table and gently patted the girl's hand. "Sometimes, Annabel dear, secrets can become a dreadful burden. Far be it from me to encourage you to ---"

"What my brother said is right, Miss Latham. My sister is a grownup. She was twenty-two on the fifteenth of July."

"Twenty-two? Good Lord," said Delphine. How in creation had the girl— or rather, the woman—managed to bamboozle Phillip? He would be flabbergasted when he heard the news. "But what on earth prompted such a pretense?"

"It was the only way she was able to stay with us when our great-aunt— who told us she was too old and poor to keep us—turfed us out and sent us to Brackwood House. They do not take children older than fourteen there."

"You are right; they do not. Your great-aunt, then, must have been a party to the whole affair."

"If you mean, did she help? Yes, ma'am, she did. Once she knew about the promise Lydia had made to our mother on her deathbed."

"What promise was that, dear?"

"That Lydia would always keep our family together."

Delphine shook her head sadly. "And, of course, all that changed when Mrs. Bell entered the picture and sent you two here and your sister off to Canada."

"Lydia never would have deserted us," Annabel said vehemently. "We were going to stay together forever."

Delphine sighed. What a sorry state of affairs it had turned out to be. But how very admirable of Lydia Fullerton to do her utmost to keep her promise. "I find it astonishing that your sister managed to pass herself off as a child and that the ruse was not discovered."

"She is small and dainty and a good deal shorter than I, even though I am so much younger. She dressed in one of my outgrown frocks and arranged her hair in ringlets and she made her voice sound childish." Annabel gave a rueful laugh. "I have always been the big one in our family, the buxom one, my father used to say."

Delphine took a slice of cake and popped a piece of it in her mouth, chewing thoughtfully. The poor girl was no longer buxom. Tall, yes, but bony and hollowed-out looking. "Your sister's age has no bearing on your situation, now, Annabel," she said.

"I know. But you will not say anything to anyone, will you, Miss Latham?

Lydia would get into trouble if ---"

"The only person I will tell is my brother, Doctor Latham, and I assure you he will guard your secret with his life. Now, let us forget about secrets and talk about what else transpired during my visit with Edwin."

"I hope he did not continue to show off."

"No, he did not. The poor boy was full of remorse and confusion. You see, children need discipline, Annabel, and when they do not get it they become unmoored, without direction, like a little paper boat bobbing about in an enormous ocean." Delphine took up the chocolate pot and poured herself and Annabel more cocoa. "But do rest assured dear, the boy loves you and misses you dreadfully."

Something resembling a smile flickered across Annabel's lips. But she appeared to be too busy squirming about in her seat to comment.

Delphine felt a stab of irritation. "Whatever is it, child?" she asked.

"Do you mind if I stand, Miss Latham?"

"Stand?" Delphine blinked in bewilderment.

"I have done something to my ..." The girl trailed off, wincing and starting to rise. Looking everywhere but at Delphine, she carried on. "I tripped on the stairs and slid down them on my ... er ... on my bottom."

So that was it, Delphine thought. No wonder the poor child did not seem herself. "Well dear, you certainly could not help it, could you? It was not your fault. How would it be if we finished our visit sitting on that nice soft feather bed."

Annabel nodded her agreement.

"But first, I have a little something for you ... for Edwin, too, for Christmas." She went to the dressing table and retrieved her reticule, then dug around in it for a moment. "Something practical. There is absolutely no point in giving you some geegaw or other that might be commandeered by the Chistlegates."

Annabel's mouth dropped open when she saw the shiny, silver coins. She raised wondering eyes to Delphine and said, "Two florins, Miss Latham. That is a fortune."

Delphine laughed. "Not quite. One for you and one for Edwin. You may hold onto it for him, for the time being. But you must be certain, of course, to keep the coins well hidden from the Chistlegates."

"I will."

"I would have preferred to give you something more personal, but"—she made a palms-up gesture—"under the circumstances ..."

Annabel had already pocketed the money and was patting the spot as if to reassure herself of its safety

All this time Delphine observed, and Annabel still had not smiled. It certainly would not be the first time a girl had been afflicted with melancholia. She would doubtless soon snap out of it. "To the bed," Delphine said brightly, removing her slippers and indicating Annabel should follow suit with her boots, "and our much comfier conversation spot."

Propped up against pillows and a long bolster, they settled side-by-side against the bed head. Annabel raked her hair back off her forehead just as Delphine slanted a glance at her. Good Lord, the girl had a black-and-blue duck-egg at her temple. "How on earth did you manage to do that?" Delphine asked, pointing to the lump.

"I ran into the door ... forgot it was closed," Annabel said quickly, her eyes filling with tears. "I am most dreadfully clumsy sometimes."

And no wonder, Delphine thought, with that odious Chistlegate woman certain to be watching her every move. "I doubt that, dear. Accidents happen to all of us. I swear there are times when I am forever knocking into things or tripping over them." She patted Annabel's hand, then contemplated her own stocking-clad feet, allowing the girl time to collect herself .

But instead, she almost frightened the life out of Delphine by suddenly clutching her arm and saying in a frantic-sounding voice, "Miss Latham, I have to get away from here. May Edwin and I come and live with you?"

Blindsided by the question, Delphine removed Annabel's hand from her arm. "Calm yourself, dear."

"May we, please? I hate it here."

"I know you do," Delphine said, castigating herself for her part in the drama. If she had not become so chummy with the girl, then all this may not have happened.

"We would be ever so good. And we would work very hard, honestly, we would."

Delphine gently covered the girl's rough, red hand with her own. "I am so sorry, child, it is just not possible."

Annabel snatched her hand away as if stung and scrambled off the bed. "I have to go," she said, sniffing back her tears as she bent to put on her boots.

By the time she had them on, Delphine was by her side. "I am so sorry," she said. "It is just too complicated ... too ..."

"Too much trouble. I should have known," Annabel said, stumbling for the door.

She was through it and had slammed it behind herself before Delphine could think of a response.

## CHAPTER FORTY-FOUR
### December 1889
### Latham Residence, Yorkshire, England

"You can imagine how dreadful I felt." Delphine spoke over her shoulder to her brother as he steadied the stool on which she balanced.

She had returned home from *Sea Winds* that afternoon and after dinner she had conscripted Phillip into helping her put up the Christmas decorations. "What made it even worse," she continued, tucking a couple of holly sprigs behind the portrait of their father, "was that I had not one second alone with Annabel for the rest of the weekend. Clearly, she was doing her level best to avoid me."

"You did the right thing, Delphie," Phillip said. "The only thing, in fact. Giving the girl false hope would have been downright cruel."

Delphine sighed. "I know you are right. But it does not make me feel any better. Perhaps if I had been able to finagle some way of bringing the two children together it would have helped. And it would have made a lovely Christmas present for them … in addition to the money, I mean."

"I think you did the only thing feasible under the circumstances. And when you return there in January—"

"I do wish I could go there sooner. But, aside from the fact that I shall be frightfully busy here, Gladys Chistlegate made it clear she does not take guests during the festive season."

"As I was saying … when you return there in January, you can explain things to her. She seems like a reasonable girl and an intelligent one. She is bound to understand."

"I am not sure about that. It will depend on what I tell her. And I have no notion what that will be until you and I have worked it out."

Phillip dipped into the basket he held, selected another berry-laden spray and handed it to Delphine. She tucked it behind their mother's portrait, studied the effect and adjusted it to her liking. "At least, now, Edwin is in the picture, so to speak."

"Yes, and certainly a much happier chap for it." Phillip helped her down and returned to the chair behind his desk. "An entry or two in this deuced ledger," he said, "then you will have my undivided attention again, I promise."

Delphine settled in the seat across from him. Poor dear loathed the paperwork involved in his practice, but if he did not keep up with it, then it would fall to her to do it and she had quite enough on her hands, as it was. How weary and disheveled he looked. He was jacketless, his shirt sleeves rolled up, his waistcoat front smudged with the blood of the obstreperous inebriate who had been his last patient of the day.

"I swear," he said, blotting the entries he had just made in the thick, leather-bound book, "if that chap shows his drunken face in my surgery again, I shall boot him out, for certain."

Delphine smiled to herself. Of course, he would do no such thing. Phillip was far too dedicated a doctor and too gentle a soul to ever turn patients away, whatever their proclivities. She should know; she had answered the bell to enough of them these past few years. Hard to believe it had been four years since he had set up practice here and two since he had started at Brackwood House.

The ticking of the grandfather clock on the nearby wall, the scratch of Phillip's pen across the ledger pages and the soft hiss and crackle of the fire lulled Delphine. Her eyelids felt heavy and she began to drift. But this was the moment Phillip chose to slam the ledger shut.

"Lord"—she clapped a hand to her bosom—"you almost gave me a heart attack."

"Sorry old dear. Just so happy to have it finished." He clasped his hands at the back of his neck and swiveled in his chair. "Now, where were we?"

"Discussing Edwin," Delphine said. "It really is outrageous for those Chistlegate people to place such a burden on his shoulders. Fancy telling him he must forget his entire family. Not to mention all the bribery involved … giving the boy whatever he wants in exchange for his affection.

"Of course, bribery inevitably leads to corruption," Phillip said. "And from what you have told me it has already begun where young Edwin is concerned. Do you think he will be able to keep up the pretense with Gladys Chistlegate?"

"Of continuing to play the little horror, you mean? I should think so. He seemed to relish the idea of our secret pact. Seemed to fancy himself something of a *Scarlet Pimpernel* type, I think."

"And, of course, he knows how high the stakes are. Any blabbing from him or from Annabel and ---"

"Connections between the two would instantly be severed. They are both acutely aware of that. They are amazing children, Phillip." She exhaled a doleful breath. "But I worry about Annabel."

"You mean that she might let something slip."

"No, not that. She seems so frail and I do not think she gets enough to eat … or enough sleep, for that matter. I mean look at the fall down the stairs I told you about and the bump on her head. And her reaction when I said living here would be impossible. Maybe if I had had a letter for her from her sister, it might have … Oh Lord, what an addle-brain I am. I just remembered. I have something rather startling to tell you about Lydia Fullerton."

"That reminds me." Phillip clearly had not been listening. He shot out of his chair and made for the door. "I saw the postman heading down the drive about an hour ago."

In a minute or two he returned, grinning from ear to ear and brandishing an envelope. "From Lydia," he said, ripping it open as he went back to his seat.

Delphine got up. The news she had to impart about the girl could wait. If she told him now, he would want to know all the ins-and-outs and she had neither the time nor the energy to pursue the subject. This evening she had guests arriving for the annual Christmas dinner party. She tapped on the desktop in order to get Phillip's attention. When he looked up she said, "I shall leave you to your reading, then."

"No, hold on, Delphie. Sit down. No need to go flitting off yet."

"Flitting off? In less than three hours our guests are due to arrive. One of the women Mrs. Entwhistle hired from the village sent a message that she cannot come, so Mrs. Entwhistle is positively run off her feet." Delphine felt her heartbeat quicken with the thought of the thousand-and-one tasks not yet completed.

"Yes, yes." Not raising his eyes from the page he was reading, Phillip made an irritatingly dismissive gesture. "I am sure it will all work out."

"Not if I sit here twiddling my thumbs."

Her brother was oblivious. He said, "I tell you, Delphie, no one should have to endure what this poor girl has to. Listen."

With a long-suffering shrug, Delphine said, "Very well. But it better not take too long."

"It is dated the twenty-sixth of November and postmarked Plenty, the town they have recently moved to. Anyway, I shall skip the first part about how much they could have done with my presence there and ..."

"They?"

"Mrs. Brecht, actually. The woman had twins, apparently, and almost died during the confinement. The first was a healthy boy. The second—a girl—was stillborn. Listen.

"So I was left with Mrs. Brecht and newborn William while Mr. Brecht went out into the night and by lantern- and moonlight, buried the other little mite."

Phillip shook his head while turning the page. "I tell you, Delphie, this Brecht chap must be a peculiar sort. Instead of taking the responsibility, himself, of relaying the news to his wife, he had Lydia do it. There is more ..."

"And now Katerina cries when she thinks no one is looking. Of course, she does her very best to mother little William, but her grief over the dead baby is heartbreaking. And poor Mr. Brecht does not know what to do about it.

"I had wanted to write much sooner, but have been prevented by the events outlined here and the press of my new responsibilities in the general store and with the baby, Mrs. Brecht not yet being strong enough to work.

"Needless to say, I was elated to hear that you are in touch with Annabel and Edwin and hope you have more news of them and have seen them since September. I have been thinking about the Christmases we used to have at the rectory, and of the kissing bough Mama would make with rosy apples in the middle and candles and home-made ornaments and mistletoe, and how we would gather beneath it and sing carols. Oh, such happy times those were.

"There will be carolers in Plenty, I am sure. And if I have my way, the store will be festively decorated. But it will not be the same. I shall have to be content with my memories until Annabel and Edwin are with me again. I wish I could have sent them a little something, but I have yet to be paid for my efforts and therefore have no funds on hand. And I am loath to touch on the subject until Mrs. Brecht is well-recovered. The letter I enclose is all I can offer my two darlings.

"I must finish up now. I wish you and your sister a very happy Christmas and the fulfillment of all your hopes and dreams in the New Year, eighteen-ninety.

"Yours etcetera etcetera"

"She certainly has backbone," Delphine said.

"Huh?" Phillip stared uncomprehending until she repeated herself. Then, he said, "You are right. And such unusual maturity for one so young."

Nowhere nearly as young as you think, Delphine thought, wondering how he would take the news of his protégée's true age. Had he not gone rushing off to the post and then taken up her time with his letter-reading, she would have told him earlier. Now, she had neither the time nor the inclination. He would have to wait until after their dinner guests departed this evening.

"Sounds as if she could do with a little cheering up," Phillip said. "I must get a letter off to her right away, tell her about your visit to West Kirby and what happened with Edwin."

"But not now, Phillip." Delphine rose and smoothed out her skirts. "The dinner party? Remember?"

"Oh yes. That. Did I mention, by the way, that I had invited Matron's assistant, Miss Amelia Dunn?"

Delphine rolled her eyes. "No you did not."

Phillip knew how delighted she had been to hear that Mrs. Bell was away for a fortnight visiting relations, so they were spared the necessity of inviting her. "I believe you met the young woman once," he said.

"Yes, I did. She seems a nice enough person. But I am not sure why you would---"

"Pure deviousness, old thing. She is the keeper of the accounts at Brackwood House, and a veritable fount of knowledge. There is something decidedly fishy going on there. And, from what I hear, after a glass or two of spirits our Miss Dunn becomes more than a little talkative. Which should prove rather handy when it comes to my questions."

"What sort of questions?"

"We will discuss that later." He came around to Delphine's side of the desk and put an arm about her shoulders. "It is all for a good cause."

"Speaking of good causes"—Delphine slanted a look up at him—"did I tell you that I had invited Charity Melham to the party?"

"No, you did not."

"And before you ask me why, she is a charming young woman, and I thought to make the numbers even." She made for the door. "Now, of course, with your latest invitee, they no longer are. Our nice tidy dozen has turned into thirteen … not an omen, I hope." In addition to Charity, she had invited the squire and his wife, their banker and chartered accountant and their wives, her elderly-but-lively widowed cousin Margaret, the bishop and the newly-appointed curate. She turned and added, "Charity is not only charming, she is uncommonly pretty."

But Phillip did not comment.

He had gone to the window and stood looking out, his mind clearly elsewhere.

## CHAPTER FORTY-FIVE
### *December 1889*
### *Latham Residence, Yorkshire, England*

On all counts but one the dinner party was a resounding success.

The guests were interesting. The conversation flowed. Throughout the evening an atmosphere of conviviality prevailed. And from soup to sorbet, the eight courses were enough to tempt the most finicky of palates. But to Delphine's chagrin—and thanks to Phillip—he and Charity Melham hardly exchanged a syllable.

With something akin to sleight of hand he had, at the last moment, switched the name cards Delphine had strategically placed, so that Charity ended up between the bishop and the curate at one end of the long, rosewood table while he positioned himself at the far end next to Amelia Dunn.

Then he had charmed her. Every time Delphine glanced in their direction, the woman was fluttering and simpering like a debutante, or the pair—heads together like conspirators—were conversing in irritatingly low voices. A question or comment from Phillip and off she would go, her lips reminiscent of a tent flap on a windy day.

Of course, her wine glass was never empty. Phillip seemed to be forever giving the nod to the village woman hired for the evening, to top it up. And this topping clearly had a lot to do with Miss Dunn's mood.

Phillip confirmed as much after the last guest had departed and he and Delphine were in the drawing room, seated in front of the fire's embers, and engaged in a post-mortem of the evening's events.

Once he had unfastened the stud on his starched collar and loosened his bowtie, he said, "Wine works wonders."

"For you?" Delphine asked, taking up the chocolate pot Mrs. Entwhistle had brought in earlier and pouring herself a cup of cocoa.

Phillip chuckled. "No. For tongue-loosening."

"I suppose you mean one tongue in particular … that of the delightful Miss Dunn?"

"I do indeed."

"I have to tell you, I thought you devoted an uncommon amount of attention to the woman. I know you said you had questions for her, but surely you could have been a little more sociable where our other guests were concerned."

Phillip raised an amused eyebrow. "By our other guests, you mean Charity Melham, of course. You are absolutely right about her, Delphie. She is charming … and pretty, if one is partial to that soft, round, pink look. But she is of no interest whatsoever to me."

"You have been a widower for far too many years, dear brother. You need to ---"

"Do take off your matchmaking cap, old girl." Phillip slumped back in his chair and stretched his long legs out, resting his feet on the brass fender. "Ask me about my conversation with Amelia Dunn, who, incidentally, is a very decent young woman."

"Very well, consider yourself asked."

"First of all, one of the questions plaguing me was this: What prompted Mrs. Bell to turn over the two Fullerton children to the Chistlegates? I mean, it was certainly a deviation from the norm, in that the Home's sole purpose is to take in orphans, train them, and then ship them off to Canada." Phillip reached for the poker, stirred the embers with it and then returned it to its stand. "We know, of course, that Brackwood House has a board of governors and operates under the auspices of the charity that was set up decades ago, that it is not a profit-making venture and is in large part dependent on donations."

"True," Delphine said.

"So, I asked myself this: Was the whole thing a result of orders from the charity's hierarchy, or were things done at the behest of an important benefactor, connected in some way with the Chistlegates? Or was it—unlikely as it may seem—a question of Mrs. Bell's compassion for a childless couple?"

"That woman has not a drop of compassion in her," Delphine said.

"My conclusion, too. Anyway, back to Miss Dunn and the ultimate solution to the riddle."

Intrigued and temporarily forgetting the news about Lydia Fullerton she had for Phillip, Delphine sat forward.

"It turned out to be quite simple: money was the sole motivator. Four hundred pounds to be exact."

"Good Lord, you mean ---?"

"I mean, Mrs. Bell sold the children to the Chistlegates for a total of four hundred pounds. One hundred for Annabel and three hundred for Edwin, according to Amelia Dunn."

"Great God, that is nothing short of ---"

"Slavery," Phillip said. "And Lord knows what else. There apparently is evidence of the receipt of the funds, but no sign of any deposit into Brackwood's accounts."

"And the Dunn woman volunteered this?"

"Yes ... eventually. Thanks in large part to the wine. Making me privy to all her secrets seemed to be a source of great delight for her."

Delphine took a quick sip of cocoa. "Well I never."

"The picture we all see of a devoted employee is farcical. Amelia Dunn clearly despises Mrs. Bell. And no wonder, considering what that woman has apparently been up to. Seems Miss Dunn has been keeping a mental dossier on Matron for years ... to what end, I have no idea."

"You mean, there have been other activities?"

Wearily, Phillip brushed his hair back from his forehead, rotated his neck and rolled his shoulders. "I should say so. Donations intended for the inmates funneled into Mrs. Bell's own coffers, for instance, and a few misappropriated legacies, along with other questionable practices which I shall not go into at present."

"So, what do you plan to do about it? Expose her?"

"No, I do not believe so. Not yet, anyway." Phillip strummed on his lower lip for a moment. "To be honest, I have not had a chance to absorb all this yet... to think it through. But one thing I know, Delphie; I shall use the information I have garnered to my advantage."

"Your advantage? Surely you mean to the advantage of the Fullerton children?"

"Absolutely. And of the other Brackwood children, who deserve far better than they have been getting."

"I should say so."

"And I will tell you this, too"—Phillip sat forward, hands on his knees, his eyes blazing in his tired-looking face—"my New Year's resolution will be to beat Mrs. Bell at her own game. And I shall do it well and truly, you mark my words."

In the midst of digesting what her brother had told her, Delphine all at once remembered the news she had to impart. "Oh my Lord," she leaned forward and touched the back of his hand. "I almost forgot."

Distractedly Phillip said, "What?"

"I just discovered something about your friend, Lydia. Something quite shocking, in fact."

## CHAPTER FORTY-SIX
### *February 1890*
### *Plenty, District of Saskatchewan, Northwest Territories, Canada*

The thirteenth of February was a frigid day in Plenty. By noon the clearings proprietors had made in front of their places of business were hidden under a fresh counterpane of snow, as were the tracks left by sleighs and hooves and by the boots of those brave enough to venture out.

At a little after half-past twelve I was alone in the J. & K. Brecht General Store where it was hot as a foundry thanks to the pot-bellied iron stove at its hub. Warm from toasting myself in front of it, I returned to the back corner where I had been rearranging bolts of flannel, worsted and velvet before the mid-day closing.

During lunchtime I had gone to the living quarters at the rear of the store, and into the kitchen. There I had helped myself to the stew I had prepared before breakfast and left simmering on the hob.

The Brechts were nowhere to be seen. As was their custom every afternoon, Katerina and three-month-old baby William were upstairs napping in one of the three bedrooms. Mr. Brecht was across town seeing to the excess goods he kept in his recently-constructed warehouse. If true to form, he would appear just before closing to check the day's take.

Earlier, he and his cronies who represented a cross-section of Plenty's burgeoning commercial enterprises had been gathered, as usual, about the stove, drinking coffee and talking their important talk, as Katerina called it. "*Ach*, 'tis always about money, money, money," she had told me.

Now, thankfully all was quiet. The only sounds were the crackling of logs in the stove and the creaking of the pine boards under my feet as I wandered among the fabrics. I inhaled the aromas of coffee and burning logs, and of dried lavender and furniture polish. A rare sense of contentment filled me and I hummed softly, smoothing and pinning and tucking the various bolts of material.

The cavernous log building, with its high ceiling supported by massive, rough-hewn beams, reminded me of St. John's Church. It had the same feeling about it, too. Comforting ... restorative. The potpourri of aromas, the play of light through the stained-glass window above the double doors, the hushed atmosphere made me forget my worries. The phrase, *The peace that passeth all understanding* came to my mind.

The atmosphere was usually anything but peaceful. Had the weather been decent, a mob of yattering customers would have been waiting to be served, and none would have left empty-handed. I looked around. One thing I had to give Johann Brecht credit for was that he knew what to stock ... what people needed, wanted. Here, there seemed to be something for everyone.

J. & K. Brecht General Store was a regular tinker's cart, overflowing with pots and pans of gleaming copper and brass; with picks and shovels and rakes and hoes; with gingham shirtwaists, corsets, flour sack aprons and blue denim overalls stiff enough to stand on their own; with shiny hightop boots and dainty kid slippers, caps and flowered and feathered bonnets; with enormous jars of candies; with tins of coffee and aromatic spices; cigars and soaps and polishes and sticky flypaper; buckets and brooms; with lotions and potions and ointments designed to cure every ill imaginable ... and some unimaginable.

The responsibility for shop-keeping had landed in my lap shortly after our move here, when it became clear Katerina was not yet up to it and Mr. Brecht seemed to think I was. "I have hired a woman to help my wife with the house-cleaning while you work in the store," he had told me. "When Katerina is better, then you will be able to return to your household duties full-time."

In truth, I much preferred my work here in the store. It had surprised me how quick a study I had been when it came to learning the fine points of running it. Luckily, on Wednesday and Friday afternoons I had Sally Porter to help me. A broad-beamed and gregarious Welsh woman—daughter of the local undertaker and a spinster in her mid-twenties—she had been bequeathed to the Brechts by the previous owners. As generous in nature as she was in size, she clearly relished her role as tutor and was delighted to share her expertise with me, as well as her friendship.

I wandered over to the roll-top desk behind the counter, now, dipped into a candy jar on the counter's top close by, and popped a mint humbug in my mouth. Then I riffled through the sheaf of papers next to the ledger on the desk top. Here, waiting to be processed, were I.O.U's, notes accompanying payments, letters of intent to pay, letters of apology for not yet paying. Poignant chronicles of disillusionment and dashed hopes.

Canada had been in the throes of depression since eighteen-eighty-three, and then last year at harvest time, the hot winds had blown in again and many farmers had experienced crop failures. Despite all this, the influx of immigrants—both from overseas and from the East—had continued. Lured by posters, pamphlets, newspaper advertisements and touring exhibits touting the wonders of the Golden prairies, dozens of people arrived in Plenty with their heads full of ideas far too grandiose for their near-empty pockets.

As yet, the town had no bank, at least not a formal one. But it had Johann Brecht, general store-owner, warehouse-owner, land-owner—rumor had it his holdings had increased to several hundred acres of prime real estate—and money-lender. New immigrant, business venturer or down-on-his-luck farmer, it made no difference. If Mr. Brecht thought them capable of paying within a reasonable period and at the interest rate demanded, the funds were theirs.

Every day the money—or explanations for its absence—arrived from near and far, either delivered in person or in the twice-weekly post. Recently, the responsibility had fallen to me to count it, check it against the accompanying paperwork, enter the appropriate credit in the ledger, and then place the funds in the oak cash box in the cupboard below the counter, and lock it up.

Concealed from prying eyes under my cotton waist and denim apron-top, the key hung from a long chain around my neck. It puzzled me no end that I— a Home girl, and in Johann Brecht's eyes a mere fourteen years old—should have been charged with this task. Sometimes I saw my guardianship of the key as a mark of his trust in me, implying a belief in my honesty and reliability. At other times, I doubted trust was involved at all and convinced myself—despite the man's kindness to me—that it had more to do with his convictions about his ownership of me than anything else.

"You must always keep the key hidden, Lydia, and you will please on no account transfer money to the cash box with a customer looking on," he had said.

As if I would, I had thought, irritated by his obvious view of me as a dimwit, albeit a trustworthy one. "Oh, and while I am at it," I had wanted to say to him, "shall I tell the world you have a safe hidden somewhere in your quarters that must be positively overflowing with all the money you are taking in?" At the end of each day, he emptied the till and the cash box contents into a large canvas bag, disappeared with it into the back and returned some time later with the empty bag.

*More and more money into Johann Brecht's coffers and not a jot of it to you,* my inner voice derided. *You were supposed to be paid ... remember? A decent wage. How else are you ever going to get away from here ... do what you are supposed to do ... make good on your promise to your mother?*

How else, indeed? I bit down on my lower lip. I kept meaning to ask Mr. Brecht. But every time I saw his sad face my resolve evaporated. "I shall ask him tonight," I suddenly said out loud, my voice echoing in the silence. "No ... I shall demand it."

One of the shop's double doors rattled suddenly, as if in response to the vehemence in my voice, and I almost jumped out of my boots. Lord, but it was one o'clock already and time to open up again.

The frost on the glass had finally begun to melt, and through the thawed circles and against a backdrop of snowflakes drifting like feathers from a pillow fight, I could see Ena Hall, the post mistress, fidgeting about to keep warm, and clearly impatient to be let in.

As soon as I opened the door, the wisp of a middle-aged woman skittered by me like a shore bird, making little pecking motions with her head, and leaving in her wake an overwhelming scent of lavender.

"Six payments by the look of them. I do declare your Mr. Brecht is keeping this town alive. Hardly a person I know is not beholden to him."

"As in owing him money, you mean?" I could not help myself. "And he is not *my* Mr. Brecht," I added under my breath.

Miss Hall appeared not to notice the comment. Her focus had shifted to the one envelope she still had. Holding it up like a proclamation, she said, "Another letter from your gentleman friend."

I had never divulged the letters' source. But Miss Hall—like all good and nosy post mistresses who lived vicariously through their customers—had drawn her own conclusions. "An uncommonly faithful letter-writer, I must say," she said, her eyes flashing over the tops of her spectacles.

*And I must say that if your nose grows any longer, you will trip over it.* I extended a hand and smiled my sweetest smile. "May I please have my letter?"

"Of course, dear. I hope it is good news. One hears of such monstrous happenings." Miss Hall seemed unaware that she was being ushered towards the door. "I heard tell this morning of a fellow who lost his foot the other night over at ---"

"I am sure my news will be a sight better than that." I opened the door, grasped the postmistress by her elbow and propelled her outside. "Thank you for the delivery, Miss Hall. I know you must be anxious to be on your way."

I was tempted to lock the door after her in case she felt compelled to return with more of her gossip. But were I to slide the bolt against the woman or any other customer, it was bound to get back to Mr. Brecht. And that would never do.

At least for the present I had the luxury of being alone. I returned to the desk behind the counter, smiling to myself. Not a thing or a soul to distract me from my letters.

Phillip Latham's was peppered with phrases like, *We are closer to a solution ... Events seem to be taking a turn for the better.* What surprised and pleased me most about the letter was the signature it bore -- his Christian name only. He asked me, also—and I knew it would take me a while to get used to the idea—to please address him in future as Phillip, not Doctor Latham. And, it may have been my imagination, but I detected a subtle change in the tone ... something in the vocabulary, the less-simple sentence structure ...almost as if he knew I were not the child I purported to be, which of course, was ridiculous. How on earth could he?

The children's letters were, as usual, guileless, and filled with their yearnings to see me again. Edwin's penmanship showed vast improvement. Annabel's hand, however, had deteriorated, making the deciphering of several of her sentences an impossibility.

Up to this point, the news from England had always been a comfort to me. But today, for some untold reason all I could think about was my own inability to improve the situation. Clearly, Phillip Latham was endeavouring to instill hope in me and do his level best to help me. But the trouble was, I had come no closer to a solution.

Indulging in a moment of self-pity and forgetting those less fortunate, I railed at the world and my lot in it, wondering if I would ever escape from this servitude. I toyed with the chain at my neck , trudged over to the till and opened it. The coins glinted enticingly; I scooped up a handful, letting them trickle through my fingers. So much money. So many coins.

*None of them yours.*

*But they should be. No one would be any the wiser if maybe six or seven made their way into your ....*

*Lead us not into temptation.*

But I was already led.

Within the blink of an eye, I turned into a thief.

I pocketed six half-dollars and oddly enough, felt no remorse.

## CHAPTER FORTY-SEVEN
### *February 1890*
### *Plenty, District of Saskatchewan, Northwest Territories, Canada*

Hardly had the loot found its home in my capacious apron pocket than my conscience returned to me with a vengeance. Guilty tears sprang to my eyes and my fingers trembled as I sought to retrieve the coins and return them to their rightful place in the till.

Once I had accomplished the task I closed my eyes and slumped against the counter, weak with repentance and relief.

"Are you ill, child?"

I snapped to attention, eyes wide.

Mr. Brecht stood at my elbow. I had been so absorbed in consideration of my malfeasance I had not heard his approach. Ye gods, had he arrived any sooner he would have seen me commit my crime. "Oh no, I am perfectly fine, thank you. I just ---"

"How were sales today?"

"Rather slow, I am afraid."

"*Ach*, that is the way sometimes," he said, pulling out the canvas bag from under the counter.

At that moment a thought struck me: If he had just paid me, as promised, I would not have turned into a thief, albeit a short-lived one. I straightened my spine, inhaled an angry breath and with its expulsion blurted to Johann Brecht's back, "I must have a wage ... and a decent one. I was promised it. I deserve it ... I ..." All of a sudden my bravado deserted me and I clamped my mouth shut. I shifted from one foot to the other, cringing at the creak of the floorboards. What kind of a fool was I, asking him today of all days, when the only thing I had sold had been a ten-cent packet of sewing needles, a few pounds of sugar and a corset?

Mr. Brecht tucked the canvas bag with its meagre take under his arm and turned to face me, his pale blue eyes inscrutable. "A wage?" he said, playing with the pencil-thin line of the mustache he had recently grown.

"Yes." My courage—or was it recklessness?—returned to me, gathering momentum like a brush fire. "Actually, I could just walk away from here ... find a job elsewhere. I am certainly well-qualified and at twenty-two years of age, quite capable of taking care of myself."

"Twenty-two, you say?" Johann Brecht felt for the high stool behind him and sat on it. His feet easily reached the floor, and he crossed them, leaning back slightly, arms folded. His forehead puckered and he shook his head in obvious confusion. "But I have your birth certificate, Lydia, along with the other papers that came with you. Fourteen, they show you to be."

Ye gods and little fishes, something in the way he said, *that came with you* made me feel as if I were a piece of merchandise for his shop. I lifted my chin like a boxer waiting for the next jab. "Well that one is a fake. The one I possess is the genuine article. Mrs. Brecht has seen it"—I paused for effect —"and it vouches for the fact that I was born in eighteen-sixty-seven."

When I saw his eyes widen slightly I drove my point home. "I will be happy to show the document to you if you wish. You will have no doubt as to its authenticity when you see it."

Nerves taut as the strings of a harpsichord, I waited for his response.

But Johann Brecht remained mute. He merely contemplated his crossed feet. Something worked in his throat, and I could see the veins throbbing at his temple. An ominous feeling rose in the pit of my stomach. He had thus far seemed a reasonable sort, but everyone had his breaking point. What if he had reached his? *For mercy's sake say something,* I willed him.

After what seemed an interminable time, he brought his head up and pinned me like a butterfly on a specimen tray with a transfixing stare. When I finally managed to break free of it, I said, "If you bring me the Bible, I will swear to all this."

The reference to the *Good Book* seemed to return him to his senses. He blinked and massaged the back of his neck with a distracted hand, and as he rose from the stool and brushed by me said, "Wait here, Lydia, if you please."

I settled into the desk chair and in a moment heard the sound of voices, punctuated by bursts of crying from William. Ye gods, I should be taking care of the little mite. And 'struth—I brought my hand to my mouth—why had I not thought things through before I blabbed on? Mild- mannered or not, Johann was certain to be angry at Katerina for keeping my revelation from him. What sort of trouble had I landed her in? As if the woman did not have enough to contend with.

*Never mind Katerina ... what about you?* My inner voice pulled me up short. *You have done it now, for certain. Proved yourself a liar ... a cheat. Who in his right mind would have someone like you working for him? Never mind giving you a wage, he will doubtless turn you out on your posterior. And then where will you be, you and your high and mighty notions?*

"Stop," I said out loud, covering my ears with my fists and scrunching my eyes shut.

"Get up, please."

Eyes still closed, I lowered my hands and tipped my head. I could have sworn I ...

"I said, get up."

I flashed open my eyes.

Johann Brecht stood over me. "You will go to the kitchen now, Lydia."

I scrambled to my feet. Katerina was doubtless all set to give me a good dressing down.

"My wife waits for help with tea and with William."

"But what ---?"

"You are not paid to stand about," he said brusquely.

In one instant I felt myself bristle; in the next, the realization of what he had just said flashed upon me. "Did you say *paid,* Mr. Brecht?" I asked.

The semblance of a smile tipped the corners of his mouth. "A dollar a week, starting tomorrow. Off with you, now."

Hardly able to credit my good fortune, I slid by him, stammering, "Thank you ... thank you very much." Not that a dollar was a fortune. But at least it was a start.

"One more thing," Johann Brecht said as I reached the door.

I turned. "Yes."

"The birth certificate I have is a forgery, *ya?*"

"Yes," I said uncertainly.

"Forgery is a crime ... a serious crime. You agree?"

I felt the bones of my spine grow rigid, my jaw tense. I nodded yes.

"Persons go to jail for such crimes, *ya.*"

I wagged my head in the affirmative.

"As you will go to jail," he continued, his pale eyes turned to ice, his expression stern, "if I turn over your forgery to the mounted police. And if you ever run away, I will do that. And they will bring you back. You are bound to Katerina and me for five years. Your indentureship papers from the Home say so. You understand?"

I swallowed hard, my insides chilled by his announcement. Clearly Johann Brecht was not the milquetoast I had thought him.

"I mind not," he continued, "if you are twenty-five ... thirty-five ... as long as you do your work. And I mind not who knows your age. In fact, 'tis good that customers know they have a woman waiting on them and not some child without experience. So"—he made an expansive gesture with his hands —"you may tell the world, Lydia, if that is your wish."

Feeling thoroughly deflated, I said nothing.

"As for your wage, I shall expect much for it. You are, as you say, a woman, and duties of a woman are much more than duties of a child. *Ya?*"

I lifted my shoulders in a lacklustre response.

"We are your family now, Lydia, my wife and I." His tone softened. "You are important to us. Katerina needs you. Your sister and brother have their own family in old country. This is your country now. Your home. Until your five years have passed. You understand, *ya*?"

*Nein... nein ... nein. Annabel and Edwin are my family. England is my home.* "I understand," I said in a dark and bitter-sounding voice I hardly recognized as my own.

## CHAPTER FORTY-EIGHT
### *February 1890*
### *Brackford House, Yorkshire, England*

"Doctor Latham, do you have a moment?"

Phillip groaned inwardly. Bad enough that it was one of those dreary, late February days when the dampness seemed to seep into your bones and you wondered if you would ever see the sun again. Now here was Amelia Dunn poking her head around the door. Not that she was an unpleasant young woman. But he just was not in the mood for chit-chat.

Ever since the Christmas dinner, she had been a regular visitor. Amazingly —in her cups or not that night—she had remembered their conversation almost word-for-word, and these past weeks had made him the depository for every scrap of information she could dredge up about Mrs. Bell's activities, nefarious or otherwise.

Unfortunately, none of it so far had triggered in Phillip any brilliant plan vis-a-vis the Fullerton children. So much for his spoutings to Delphine about his beating Mrs. Bell at her own game, he thought with disgruntlement.

He gestured for Miss Dunn to enter and take the seat opposite him. "I am afraid one minute is all I can spare," he said, gathering together the notes scattered about his desktop. "I have a full contingent of patients waiting in the infirmary."

It was true. Nurse Beasley had just been by to fill him in. Two brothers— new arrivals—infested with head lice; the sweet little Garrett girl who had started to cough up blood a couple of days ago, and was still doing so; a boy with an abscessed tooth which would have to come out; two ear aches and an assortment of cuts and bruises and grazes; not to mention the splinter in the rump of a great hulk of a lad called Tiny Malloy, who seemed incapable of resisting a bannister when he came across one.

"Now, Miss Dunn"—Phillip lined up the corners on the sheaf of papers in front of him—"what exactly have ---?"

"Do you remember, doctor, the children we discussed over dinner?"

"You mean the children in general?"

"No, doctor. I mean the pair Mrs. Bell sold. That nice girl, Lydia's brother an' sister."

Phillip sat forward in his seat. "What about them?"

"Well, doctor"—she turned her head slightly to one side, tucked in her chin, and regarded him over the top of her spectacles—"a letter came, you see."

"From whom, Miss Dunn?"

"I happened upon it this mornin' when I was doin' a spot of ... er ... tidyin' up. I remembered your mentionin' these particular children, so I ---"

"But who was the letter from?" He said it slowly, deliberately, as if she were dim-witted.

"Mrs. Chistlegate." Amelia Dunn rummaged in her skirt pocket. "I have it right here, doctor. Not the actual letter, of course, but a copy I penned since I thought it a little too risky to remove the original missive from Mrs. Bell's desk."

Bristling with impatience, Phillip smiled pleasantly and said, "May I see it?"

"I copied it exactly. Dreadful grammar ... spellin' ... punctua ---"

"Thank you," Phillip cut in, whipping the letter from her outstretched hand.

It read:

*"Albert an me shud like our one undred pounds back regards our adopshun of Annabel Fullerton plus the five she stole from the tobacco jar on the mantelpeace afore she left. Run off she did. Bin gone 4 days since. Good ridance we say er bein a theef an never much good to us anyway bein a weeklin in the first place an havin too much to say for erself as well. An as you will remember we did not want the girl but took er out of the goodness of hour earts. We wud take another girl in er place if you ave a strong an relible one hoo is not a theef. Hutherwise pounds will do. Rite away hif you please an let us know wen we can expect our muney back or another girl.*

*Yurs faithful,*

*Gladys Chistlegate."*

No sooner had Phillip absorbed the final word than he was on his feet. "God in Heaven." He struck the desk top with his fist and Amelia Dunn jumped so hard her spectacles slipped off her nose and fell to the floor.

Phillip did not pause to do the gentlemanly thing and help her retrieve them. He strode for the door. A trumped up story? Of course not. No one would be that stupid.

God, but it was a disaster. He could hardly abandon his patients and do the job himself. Trotter—sleuth extraordinaire—must be notified. One of the lads needed to be sent to Delphine with a message asking her to get a telegram off to the fellow.

At least it was a place to start. Where would it finish, though, that was the thing?

## CHAPTER FORTY-NINE
### *April 1890*
### *Brackford House, Yorkshire, England*

"Good mornin', doctor." Amelia Dunn popped out from behind a pillar directly in Phillip's path.

He had been six thousand miles away from the quadrangle he was traversing at a little before eight in the morning. He returned to it, now, with such a jolt that the sheaf of case notes he had tucked under his arm went flying. Several pages landed around his feet on the gravel pathway, the rest on the surrounding dew-soaked grass.

"Oh I say, I am sorry."

Phillip gritted his teeth, aware that if he voiced his thoughts he would singe the woman's ears. He closed his eyes against the infuriating sight. His nerves were frayed enough as it was after last night's supper with Josiah Trotter at the *King's Arms*. Not to mention the hours of tossing and turning and floor-pacing that had ensued. All he had been able to think about was the fact that the second week in March had come and gone ... twenty interminable days had passed since Annabel Fullerton's disappearance, and Trotter—despite his week or so in West Kirby and surrounds—had been unable to unearth a single clue as to the child's whereabouts."

And as if that were not enough, Edwin was now ill, according to Gladys Chistlegate's tearful revelation to Josiah Trotter, alias Mr. Flynn, travelling salesman, who had repeatedly lent an empathetic ear during his stay.

"Were the lad's symptoms mentioned?" Phillip had asked.

"Aye," had been the taciturn Trotter's response. Conversation was not his strong point; listening, observing, analyzing were. And he was a good chap with a kind heart, Phillip knew from past dealings. Eventually Phillip had elicited the news that Edwin was neither eating, speaking nor leaving his bed, and naturally, the Chistlegate woman had no explanation for the boy's behavior, nor did she want anything to do with Trotter's suggestion that she call in a doctor.

Clearly, Phillip had thought, the boy was pining away. And who would not be, given the circumstances. A mother gone, a father gone, and now the second of his precious sisters lost to him. And pining should never be taken lightly; its effects could be devastating.

A tap on Phillip's arm drew him back from his mental meanderings and Amelia Dunn's face loomed. "Oh I do hope I did not cause you too much distress, doctor," she said.

He rolled his eyes. Too much distress? Lord, he could have cheerfully strangled the woman. *My papers, damn it,* he railed inwardly, *just look at my papers.*

Amelia Dunn's gaze followed his and at least she had the good grace to take the hint, scuttling to retrieve them and looking suitably sheepish when she handed them back. Although, God alone knew how he would manage to decipher his notes; dew and ink were decidedly incompatible. He managed a tight-lipped, "Thank you," followed by a hasty, "I must get along, I am afraid. I have a thousand-and ---"

"She is not goin' to do a thing about it, doctor." Hobbled by her skirts and reminiscent of a participant in a three-legged race, Miss Dunn trotted alongside Phillip, doing her best to keep up with his long stride. "She is positively livid, in fact." Her spectacles slid down her nose and over the top of them she slanted a look up at Phillip, waiting for his cue.

Immediately, he made the connection. "You have seen Mrs. Bell's response to the Chistlegate woman. And in effect, she has told her to go to ..." He caught himself and slowed to a halt. "She has refused to provide a replacement. Is that about it?"

Looking deflated, Miss Dunn said, "Well, yes ... in a manner of speakin'." She repositioned her glasses on her nose. Her dark, little eyes darted back and forth for a few seconds, then refocused on Phillip. "It is nothin' to do with her, she says. The girl was delivered in excellent condition, an' if they have lost her, it is entirely their own fault. As it is their fault, also, if they were fool enough to give the girl access to their cash." She paused long enough to pull up her coat collar against the chill. "Of course, we all know this will not be the end of it. The Chistlegates will doubtless be just as livid as Mrs. Bell. 'an, who knows where that will lead." Amelia Dunn could barely suppress her glee when she added, "To a battle royal, I should not doubt."

Who the deuce gave a hang for their squabbles, thought Phillip, suddenly striding off again, leaving Miss Dunn to catch up. When she did, she said breathlessly, "You do wish me to continue to keep you posted, doctor, about the situation?"

"Yes." Phillip stopped in his tracks again. Annoying or not, Amelia Dunn seemed to be his only resource at present. And she was a decent enough young woman. "Anything you hear, however trivial, please do let me know right away."

But what he heard towards the end of the following week was anything but trivial, and its source was not Amelia Dunn but Josiah Trotter.

He showed up on the Thursday evening shortly after dinner. Delphine was out at the theatre with friends and Phillip had just settled himself in the drawing room in front of a roaring fire and was trying to distract himself with the latest issue of *Punch*, when Mrs. Entwhistle announced the sleuth.

His appearance had no doubt boded him well during his career, for he was a nondescript-looking chap in his fifties, of average stature, with sparse, sandy-colored hair and pale gray eyes.

Declining a brandy—he had apparently taken *the pledge* within the past year—and opting to keep his coat on since he was unable to stay long, he said, he took a seat by the fire opposite Phillip and said in a grave tone. "Know where she 'as been, your girl."

"Been?" Phillip rose, a chill overtaking him, and stood with his back to the fireplace. "You mean is."

"Naw. Been. Dunno where she is now, doc. Left already."

"Left? Left where?"

"Liverpool," Trotter answered.

"'Struth."

"Spent a night at Maisy Pollard's, the young miss did."

Phillip frowned. "A boarding house?"

"Naw." Trotter fingered his side whiskers. "Not a boarding house, doc. A bawdy house -- one of Lime Street's oldest and best-known."

"Good god, man, what are you saying?"

"That one of Maisy's girls found the young miss wanderin' about. Been knocked about by a couple of sots, she 'ad."

"Annabel had? How badly was she hurt?"

Trotter shook his head sadly. "Bruised something fierce. Lip cut. Eye blacked. Clothes ripped to shreds."

"Anything else, man? Did those louts ---?"

"Dunno, doc. Maisy said the young miss would not say a word, would not let her or any of 'er girls touch 'er ... help 'er clean 'erself up, that is. So they gave 'er a room and a bed. Hot water, clean clothes. Maisy thought she would quiz her the next day. But when she checked, the followin' mornin' the lass was gone."

"God in heaven." Phillip sank into his chair. "What on earth are we to do then, Trotter?"

"Keep lookin', I reckon." He stared into the flames for a long moment, seemingly mesmerized by them, and then lifted his eyes to Phillip's. "I will tell you this, though, doc. Liverpool is a snake pit if ever there was one. It does not look good for the girl. Not good at all."

## CHAPTER FIFTY
### *May 1890*
### *Plenty, District of Saskatchewan, Northwest Territories, Canada*

"So, what do you 'ear from England, Lydia?" Sally Porter had just dragged a sack of potatoes across the shop floor on this balmy May morning, ready to fill the bins lined up against the wall. She took a moment to get her breath, swiping her crimson face with her sleeve, then huffed to the counter where I stood.

"Nothing for almost two months." I looked up from the catalogue I was perusing. "However, the last letter sounded very hopeful. And I cannot spend all my waking hours worrying, can I?"

"I should say not." She braced herself on her plump, freckled arms. "But you can spend some of them dancin', can't you, though?"

"Dancing … whatever are you talking about?"

"The Anglicans are havin' a social an' dance a fortnight on Saturday. Bet you 'ave not had a good laugh or a good dance in years."

How right she was, I thought. It had been six since I had attended Georgina Hartwell's sixteenth birthday party. And what a caution that had been. Ten hitherto sedate young ladies partnering each other and dancing the polka like dervishes. Ten spotty-faced boys regarding them with the superciliousness of adults who thought them demented, yet far too gauche to disguise their interest in the froth of petticoats and the silk-clad legs.

"You 'ave to go to it with me, don't you though?"

I had learned soon after meeting Sally that her constant *Isn't that-rights* and *Don't you thoughs* were merely an idiosyncracy of the Welsh dialect, and one was not required to agree or disagree. Still, I often found myself nodding first one way, then the other, when Sally and I conversed.

"Perhaps," I said absently, chewing on my lower lip, gazing unseeing at the images on the page, my mind having returned to the children and Phillip Latham. Why had there been such a lapse in communication? Lord, what a great lonely hole it left in me.

When Sally hauled the next sack into place, I said, with a distinct lack of conviction, "There is absolutely no point in fretting about it."

"The dance?"

"No. The letters … or should I say, the lack thereof."

"But no news is good news, isn't it though?"

No news is room for worry. A foolish exercise for certain. After all worry did absolutely nothing for you except feed upon itself. And there came a point where you had to put a stop to it and plumb the depths of your faith in yourself. You had to find something to hold onto. Or go mad. And you had to be thankful, too, for the progress—however infinitesimal—you were making towards your goal, however unattainable that goal might seem.

The hollow rattle of the biscuit tin in the drawer of the night stand beside my bed attested to my fortune, grown now to the magnificent sum of eleven dollars, thanks to my constant frugality. Resisting the shop's tempting array of goods, I had purchased not so much as a ribbon in all these weeks. Luckily, the Brechts had given me new boots for Christmas and shortly after, Katerina had passed on three of the frocks she had worn before the birth of the twins. She had neither the desire nor the energy to make them over for herself, she had said, but I was welcome to use the new sewing machine Johann had bought her.

While practice had certainly not made me perfect, hour upon hour of it had at least made a decent seamstress of me. By mid-March, I had managed to transform the voluminous garments into two frocks, two basques and a walking skirt, made according to the Butterick patterns carried in the store, and fashionable enough to garner me compliments from customers every time I wore them. Donning something I liked that I had made myself and that actually fit me, as well as being given responsibilities I enjoyed and a wage, made me feel worthwhile … more a regular young woman, less a Home girl.

Granted, I was bound as inexorably as ever to the Brechts, still theirs to command and with the ever-present threat hanging over me of Mr. Brecht's exposure of my crime to the authorities. But show me a woman who was not bound to some person, some state or other, whether it be to a husband, a father, a brother, a guardian, to privation or abuse. At least I had been spared the latter. I had not been beaten or starved as had many a Home child. Nor was I worked like a slave, although my duties were sufficient to keep me busy from dawn until dark six days a week.

Since I was free to do as I wished on Sundays as long as I had tea on the table at the usual five o'clock hour, I fell into the habit of going with Sally to the community hall which had been made temporary headquarters for a burgeoning group of enthusiastic Anglicans. Despite my sporadic relationship with God, I found the familiar hymns and the age-old litany comforting. And when the collection plate was passed around, and I was able to add my contribution—albeit a meagre one—I felt a great sense of satisfaction.

Occasionally, I did insert a prayer into my bedtime rituals, which included counting my money and laughing at myself for the Shylock I had become. The biscuit tin was the next-to-last thing I looked at every night before I blew out the candle. My dear mother, gazing out at me from the little, silver oval, was the last. And every night I made the same affirmation: "I shall reunite the three of us, dear Mama, I promise."

"So what do you think then?" Sally's voice returned me to the here and now.

"I think I am taking a holiday from worry." I snapped the catalogue shut and gazed beyond the window for a moment, at the clear skies. "It is far too nice a day for it."

"I meant about the dance."

"I think I shall think about it," I said teasingly.

"'twould do you good, wouldn't it though?"

I nodded this way and that. "I just wish I had heard from them."

"From what you 'ave told me, the young ones are farin' quite well, isn't that right, though?"

"I suppose it is."

What I had told Sally during these past weeks had been a précis of my life before Plenty. Confiding in the jolly young woman had seemed the natural thing to do. Her warmheartedness and ready laughter buoyed my spirits as they had not been buoyed in years.

Katerina had the opposite effect on me. After seven months spent empathizing and trying unsuccessfully to cheer her up, I felt enervated around her, irritated, too, of late. Whatever happiness I had managed to glean here in Plenty was hard-won, and I resented having Katerina's melancholia constantly impinge on it.

Certainly, she had suffered a terrible loss. But loss was a part of life. Children lost parents; parents lost children; husbands their wives; sisters their brothers. So it went. And in truth, Johann Brecht was right: Katerina still had William and, no doubt, would go on to have other children.

My emotions ran the gamut where Katerina was concerned. And in the wake of anger, impatience and resentment came the inevitable guilt. After all, Katerina had become my dear friend, my confidante. A deep affection had developed between us. But of late, it seemed to have become one-sided, with Katerina's self-absorption leaving little room for thoughts of anyone else.

Things had come to a head one morning back in March when Johann departed at first light for a meeting at his warehouses across town, leaving Katerina and William sleeping.

Charged, as usual, with the running of the shop, I had eaten breakfast early, made my preparations for the day's meals, banked the fire and cleaned up the kitchen by eight o'clock, when I settled myself at my desk in the shop. Poring over the account books some time later, I heard William crying. No matter, I thought. Katerina would see to the baby. But after more than five minutes and no cessation of the cries, I was no longer able to endure it and went to investigate.

By the fireplace, in his cradle, I found William, fists pummeling the air, legs flailing and his little face purple from screaming at the top of his lungs. Katerina, however, was nowhere to be seen.

I scooped up the baby and held him close, making soothing sounds, stroking him, rocking him until his cries dissolved into shuddering sobs. He clung for all he was worth to my bodice, his plump little hands striped white with the effort. "It is all right," I kept saying. "Everything is all right."

Such trust in those wide, blue eyes searching my face. For a moment the face became Edwin's when he was this age, and I was a young girl pretending to be his mother. Tears pricked my eyes and I felt a tightening in my throat. I nuzzled William's soft neck, breathing in his scent as if I were inhaling perfume and drawing comfort from it. He half-sobbed, half-giggled and I kissed the top of his head and said, "Now, let us go and find your mama, shall we?"

I was astonished to find Katerina upstairs in her bedroom, seated in the chair by the window, rocking back and forth, back and forth, staring ahead, as if in a trance. Beside her on a small table I noticed a half-empty, unstoppered bottle—sans measuring spoon—of the popular *Priors Magic Cordial* Johann Brecht stocked in the store — a supposed cure-all for a plethora of ailments which included black moods, sore throats, female troubles, piles, rheumatism, poor eyesight, gout and headaches. Clearly Katerina had been seeking solace from this elixir.

Balancing William on one hip, I grabbed the chair's arm, stopping the motion. Katerina started and looked up at me, her face blank, her eyes slightly glassy. I said her name.

"What is it?" she asked slowly, dully.

"What is it?" I stifled the urge to shake her. "Your baby, Katerina." I kept my voice modulated so as not to alarm William. "What on earth possessed you to leave him alone like that?"

"*Ach,* but he was crying again, and I could not stand it." Katerina pushed back a matted string of hair. "He would sleep, I thought, if I left him. I would sleep, too. I am so weary, Lydia." She pouted like an unhappy child. "So weary of life ... of this place ... of Johann. What is the point?"

"The point?" I rolled my eyes in frustration. "You have a beautiful baby, here." I placed William in her lap. "You are his mother. He needs you."

William looked up into Katerina's face. Then he reached for her lower lip and plucked at it, breaking into chuckles at the slurping sound it made.

There is nothing more infectious than a baby's delight. But Katerina was immune to it. Her only response was to capture her son's hand in her own and utter a sharp, "*Nein* … no."

William's bottom lip began to quiver. His eyes welled with tears and he started to whimper. Katerina picked him up and held him away from herself as if he were contaminated. "You take him," she said, yawning. "I am just too weary."

It had been, thank the Lord, one of Sally's two full work days. So we had managed between the two of us to keep things running smoothly in the shop and take care of the baby.

Johann Brecht had been furious when he came home halfway through the afternoon and saw what the situation was.

Whatever he said to his wife must have made an impression on her, for she appeared in the shop sometime later, washed and dressed and at least wide awake enough to reclaim William.

Since then, she had done an adequate job, both in the running of the household and the care of her son. But there still remained a listlessness about her that made me want to grab her by the shoulders and shout, "Be glad for the family you have, you foolish woman."

I could just as easily have sunk into despair over my loss. But I chose to get on with life and try to enjoy myself anytime the opportunity arose.

"So what do you think, then?"

The sing-song voice again intruded on my reverie.

"Think, Sally?" I busied myself with the ledger, smoothing out a page and running my finger down a column of figures. "About what?"

Sally flopped into the chair opposite and raked her wild red mane back off her face. "The social."

"Do they polka there?" I asked.

"Do all sorts there," Sally said with a chuckle. "At the one In January Walter Strunk proposed to Lizzie Hodges, didn't 'e, though? Right after the last waltz when everyone was gettin' their coats. 'course, we didn't know, did we though, what 'e had said to 'er till later? Anyway, started carryin' on somethin' fierce she did ... jumpin' up an' down an' shriekin' like a banshee. Bein' as it was a barn once, before it was turned into the community hall, an' there bein' plenty of creatures lurkin' in all the nooks and crannies, we all thought somethin' had bitten 'er on the you-know-what, didn't we, though?"

Chortling, I nodded in agreement.

"Turned out it was 'er way of sayin' yes, wasn't it though? Never saw a girl as excited as Lizzie, nor a fella as frightened as poor Walter looked. Must've thought 'e'd proposed to a loony." Sally rested her elbows on the counter and cupped her full, rosy cheeks in her hands. "Then, chances are I'd act like a loony, too, wouldn't I though, if somebody proposed to me?" She sighed. "Not that anyone ever will." Her expression held a wistfulness I had not seen before.

"Oh, Sally," I said, "of course they will. You would make a wonderful wife."

"All the good ones are taken, aren't they, though?" She stared off for a time. "Like Mr. Brecht. Lovely man, isn't 'e though? Give my eye teeth I would, to have somebody like 'im."

"You would?" I said, surprised that Sally would see the man in such a light. But then everyone's perceptions differed.

She straightened and glanced down at herself. "Leastways any man who took me would get 'is dollar's worth, wouldn't 'e, though? If they sold me by the pound I would be worth a mint. Anyway, what about you? You must've had dozens of proposals, mustn't you, though?"

"Hardly," I said dryly. "My life has not exactly been conducive to romance."

Sally leaned across the desk, her hazel eyes alight with mischief. "No one who ever took a shine to you?"

"No."

"What about the doctor?"

"Doctor Latham, you mean? He is ... he is ---"

"A right handsome chappy the way you describe 'im, an' ever so nice from what you 'ave been tellin' me. A proper knight in shinin' armor, isn't 'e, though?"

"I suppose you could say that." I stretched a kink out of my back. "But you do not understand, Sally. There is not one jot of romance here. Phillip—Doctor Latham—thinks of me as a child. A fourteen-year-old."

"Sure of that, are you now?"

"Of course, I am. And even if things were different and there had been no subterfuge on my part, rest assured my only interest in the man would be—is—as a means to an end. He is my link to Annabel and Edwin. And that is all there is to it."

Sally stopped running her fingernail along a crack in the desktop and slanted a look at me from beneath her lashes. "Hmmm," she said, smiling knowingly. "We'll see about that, won't we though?"

I glared at her and shook my head. Such nonsense. Lord, it almost smacked of perversion, Sally speculating about a man who had to be in his late twenties having an interest in a girl he thought to be fourteen. Granted Phillip Latham was everything Sally had said, and more. Granted thoughts of him had a way of insinuating themselves into my mind and I could see his face quite clearly. The way his hair fell over one eye and he had to keep brushing it back;

the fine bones; the crease in the middle of his chin. And I could recall vividly the way he had held me in the cabin, the feel of him, the scent of him. Still, the idea of any romance was unthinkable .

"Sally Porter," I said, "you really are incorrigible. We will have no more such talk, do you hear?"

"Oh yes, ma'am, indeed I do ma'am," Sally answered in a tone of mock servility.

"So, let us discuss this social you have been talking about."

"You are goin' to ask, then, if you can go?" Sally sat up straight in her seat, all agog.

"I am," I said. "And I see no earthly reason why I should be refused."

"Oh it will be great fun, won't it though? You an' me in all our finery."

"I do not know about the finery, but yes it will be fun. I shall take your advice, Sally, believe my *friend*—I emphasized the word—Doctor Latham, trust all is well in England, and partake of a little jollity for a change."

### CHAPTER FIFTY-ONE
### *May 1890*
### *Plenty, District of Saskatchewan, Northwest Territories, Canada*

The next morning after breakfast—with Johann in the store and the baby upstairs asleep again after a restless night—I sought Katerina's permission to go to the social.

An odd metamorphosis occurred in her, the change so sudden it made the hairs on the back of my neck rise. In what seemed like the blink of an eye the listless, brooding Katerina of the past months transformed herself into a vivacious woman of quick, light movements whose eyes burned in their sockets and whose pallid cheeks took on a vivid pink hue.

"Of course you must go," she said, pouring herself another cup of tea and dropping a fourth sugar lump in her cup. "And you must have a new gown. Nothing made over. Something *modisch* ... stylish I think you say. You will have to sew it yourself, though, for there is not time to send for something made up already. But you can choose from the materials in the store ... sateen I think, and lace, much lace. You will look ... how do they say? *Divine*. And you must have ribbon trim and those what do they call them? *Rosettes* ... that is it ... much rosettes.

On and on she went like a runaway wagon. And in a while my brain stopped processing the words. Between sips of tea, I stared over the top of my cup fixated on the movement of Katerina's mouth, which in my imagination had become a snapdragon flower. As a child I had loved picking the blossoms and entertaining Annabel and Edwin by playing puppeteer and manipulating the flowers up and down and from side-to-side as if they were lips talking.

The snapdragon all at once turned back into Katerina's mouth. She raised her cup to it and drank thirstily. I waited only long enough for her to return the cup to its saucer, knowing that if I did not speak now, it would be like trying to catch the train after it had pulled out of the station. "I cannot possibly afford the material for a new frock," I said, having already concluded I would have to make do with what I had even if half the world had already seen it.

"Afford? What is this afford? I shall pay for the material and pattern. All you have to do, *liebchen*, is pick them out...choose what you want and ---"

"Oh Katerina, that is awfully kind of you. Are you sure?"

"*Ya*, of course I am sure." She made a steeple of her hands and pressed her lips to them, her eyes focused on a spot beyond my shoulder. "I used to love the dancing, you know, when I was growing up. We had festivals and everybody came from miles around. I was pretty, then, the prettiest girl in ---"

"You still are pretty," I said.

Katerina lifted her shoulders doubtfully and continued. "And all the boys wanted to dance with me. One of them—I cannot remember his name now ... Pieter, it might have been—told me he loved me and I believed him and I thought we would marry and I would stay in the village and he would take care of me since I had no one but my old auntie and uncle." As she spoke, the color seeped from her face. And by the time she finished with, "But they sent me away and there was Johann looking for wife ... and here I am, *ya*?" her cheeks were as pale as her flour sack apron.

I said nothing, thrown off guard by Katerina's reversion to form, at least her form of the past few months. I did not know whether to empathize or cajole. Neither, I concluded after a few seconds, choosing instead to attempt to keep the conversation light. "I had no idea you were allowed to dance," I said. "I had imagined things were very strict where you came from."

"*Ach* it is true. Many things were *verboten,* but not the dancing and music." Katerina drained her cup. "You must dance your feet off, Lydia, and make the hearts of all the young men beat faster. "*Ach*"—she threw up her hands, her face all at once animated again, her cheeks flushed—"but you cannot dance in boots. You must have shoes ... pretty ones ... like the ones in the store that came from Montreal, *ya*?"

"But Katerina, surely I need to ask your hus ---"

"No buts." Katerina raised her hands in a staying gesture. "And no need to ask Mr. Brecht. In this department, I make myself boss." She was silent for a few seconds, picking at a spot on the back of her hand. Then she looked up, her expression pensive. "I wish you to have joy I cannot now have myself,

Lydia. Not for long, long time I think. Perhaps years. You understand?"

I nodded that I did, filled with a sense of sadness that this hitherto lighthearted young woman—my good friend—was so weighed down by her grief.

But what saddened me even more was Katerina's revelation three weeks later on the Saturday evening of the social.

I was at my dressing table putting the final touches to my coiffure when she came to my room. I had swept my hair up into a cushiony bun on top of my head and secured it with pins and two tortoiseshell combs. "You are vision," Katerina said, standing behind me and studying my reflection in the mirror.

"Hardly," I said, embarrassed. "Just well-scrubbed is all and with tidy hair for once."

"Your gown?" Katerina asked.

"Over there on the bed."

"Such a fine job you have done," Katerina said, reaching down and running a reverent hand over the pale, apricot-colored sateen.

I rose and joined her. "I am afraid I can take only the tiniest bit of credit for it. It is almost all Sally's handiwork. Remember, I told you she steered me to her Eatons' catalogue and helped me pick out a design—one for herself, too?"

Katerina scrubbed at her scalp. "*Ya* ... that is right."

"She had both gowns completed in a week. Hers is in that lovely deep green brocade that---"

"*Ach* I know the one. I am surprised there was enough left on the bolt."

"Just enough. Sally said when she was finished she had only a few scraps left over."

"I did not know she was magician with needle and machine."

"Nor did I," I said, gazing down in awe at Sally's magnificent creation. The gown had a high neck with ivory lace trim and ivory lace covered the bodice then extended down to form an overskirt with a complicated sort of drapery creating five-pointed sections, all edged with gathered flouncing. The sleeves were of a fashionable three-quarter length with a slight puff to their tops. A ribbon bow with streamers ending in tassel-like ornaments decorated the base of the front pearl-buttoned closure and the same kind of bow, streamer and tassel arrangement embellished the centre back where the bodice ended.

"You do not think it is too much, do you?" I asked Katerina. "After all it is just a church social, not a coming out ball. Perhaps I should have made something plainer."

"I do not know this *coming out*. The frock is beautiful ... not too much at all, I think. You will be what do they say? *Belle of ball.*"

"That I very much doubt," I said, returning to my seat at the dressing table where I patted the coil of my hair, making sure the pins and combs were secure.

Meanwhile, Katerina began bustling about, doing nothing in particular.

Ye gods, the air seemed brittle with this newfound energy of hers, a peculiar unsettling sort of energy that made me feel nervous. I reached for the bottle of lavender water, dabbed a little on each wrist and inhaled deeply until my heart took up its regular beat.

"Let me help you lace up," Katerina said, "and fix bustle and put on the gown. I am wanting to see you in it."

I would have happily foregone the corset; I had not worn one since I had left home. But Katerina insisted. Slender or not, I must have the right foundation for a dress as fine as this.

As for the bustle—all the rage again after a several-year hiatus—there was no getting away from it if one wanted to appear fashionable. And I did. If this meant I was shallow, then so be it. I was weary of fretting over the future and Annabel and Edwin and where all our lives were going. For once, I wished to think only of myself.

I positioned the corset about my rib cage, waist and hips. "I am ready for the torture," I said, already conscious of the bones digging into the underside of my breasts. "Not too tight, though, please, or I swear I shall faint away and never even make it to the social."

"*Ach*, not you." Katerina tugged at the laces and instructed me to hold my breath. "You are little wisp of thing, *ya*, but you are strong as poplar tree, I think."

After the corset came the attachment of the bustle. Once Katerina had it positioned over my buttocks and tied the tapes around my waist, I donned the gown. Then with each other's help we drew the bulk of the skirt material to the back and draped it over the steel cage. Although I was no stranger to the bustle —it had been a standard part of Mama's attire—I had never had to wear one myself, being too young when they were last in vogue.

Lord, but how peculiar all this corseting and bustling made you feel, I thought, turning this way and that in front of the mirror. And what an odd silhouette it gave you—your bosom preceding you like the prow of a fattened Christmas goose, your posterior feeling as if you were carrying the week's washing along with you. "Ye gods, Katerina," I said, "how in creation I shall be able to dance with this infernal contraption in my wake is beyond me. I shall doubtless be knocking people over at every turn."

"*Ach*, you will be fine," Katerina said. "You will become used to it."

"I certainly hope so." I narrowed my eyes and studied my reflection. What an odd sensation ... akin to looking at a photograph of someone else ... someone who bore a striking resemblance to Mama. A fashion plate for certain, in her apricot and ivory frock. Lord, I hoped Katerina was right ... that I would not walk into a sea of denim and homespun and made-over flour sacks, and feel as overdressed as a duchess in a workhouse.

Katerina's squeeze of my arm delivered me from further fretting. "One more thing you must have," she told me.

"My shoes? My shawl? They are over there, Katerina."

"Not shoes, not shawl. This." She pressed a narrow, rectangular, leather-covered box into my hand. "Your birthday present."

"But Katerina my birthday is not until July."

"So?" She turned her hands palms up.

"I do not know what to say."

"That you are pleased with it, I think. But first you must open it, *ya?*"

When I did I gasped. Resting against a bed of cream-colored velvet was a necklace of faceted oval citrines, interspersed with tiny dots of gold on a seed pearl chain. "It is beautiful," I said, "positively beautiful."

"My grandmother's, then my auntie's, then mine. Put it on."

I looked up at Katerina. "Not an heirloom like this. It should stay in your family."

"I do not wish to wear jewelry, now."

"But in the future you may feel differently. Things may change. Remember how you told me that once wedding rings were not allowed in your religion and that now they are? You should save this for a daughter ... you are bound to have anoth ... I mean, you will have more children, I am certain, and the necklace should be passed on to ---"

"No. No more children. William is only one. I will have no more. If I do I die."

I set down the necklace on the dressing table top. "Die? Whatever makes you say that? Oh Lord, Katerina, did the doctor tell you?"

"No. Nobody tells me." She twisted her hands. "I have seen it in my dreams. I know it to be true."

I had a flash, suddenly, of myself at the rectory, eavesdropping on Mrs. Dixon, our cook, and Gwen Jones—who occasionally came to help in the kitchen—my eyes growing bigger by the minute, my heart beating high in my throat as I listened:

*I mean men ... all alike they are. Bishop or butcher, makes no difference. Now, would you not think him bein' a man of the cloth an' all, that he would 'ave let her be, kept his thing in 'is britches and not gone jumpin' into 'er bed like he must have? If you ask me Gwen, 'tis that what killed 'er.*

I blinked hard and shook my head, quashing the memory. "But Katerina, what about your husband? How can you avoid ---?"

"There are ways."

"What do you mean?"

"You have seen the Assiniboine woman, *Anna TwoBears*, who comes into store with her remedies, *ya*?"

"The Indian, you mean?"

"*Ya*, the Indian. She has given me what I need." Katerina gripped my arm. "Not a word, mind you, to anyone. You promise?"

I nodded dumbly. "I promise." I had heard such things rumoured ... that there were ways of preventing conception. "Perhaps you will feel differently later on. You have not been at all well and ---"

"No. Never." Katerina closed her eyes, held up her fists and then punched the air. "Never ... never ... never," she said, her voice growing louder with each repetition. She opened her eyes. "Now, please, you take my gift. You are my friend, *ya*? I want you to have it." She removed the necklace from its case and held it aloft. The citrines reflected in the lamplight and looked like tiny golden campfires.

There was such pleading on her face that I lifted my shoulders in a helpless gesture and took the jewelry from her. I could no more deny Katerina her wish than I could deny baby William the comfort of my arms when he cried out to be held.

The necklace was so delicate, so lovely. My throat tightened as I clasped it about my neck. It did not feel right for me to have it. By accepting it I felt as if I were accepting Katerina's hopelessness and helping seal her fate. Tears came to my eyes and Katerina must have thought I was overwhelmed by the gift. She smiled and said, "You are pleased, then?"

*Pleased? No, I am not pleased,* I wanted to say. *If you must know, I am afraid . Afraid for you ... afraid for little William ... afraid for your husband. And, yes, afraid for myself. For, like it or not, what affects this family affects me.*

But all I could bring myself to say was, "Thank you, Katerina. I will always treasure it. And I will always think of you when I wear it."

## CHAPTER FIFTY-TWO
### *May 1890*
### *Plenty, District of Saskatchewan, Northwest Territories, Canada*

It was half-past seven on the last Saturday night in May and Sally and I had just arrived at the community hall. Our aim, now, was to reach the couple of vacant seats we had spotted on one of the benches against the far wall.

"Causin' quite a stir, aren't we though?" Sally chuckled in my ear as she ushered me through the noisy crowd assembled around the edge of the dance floor.

"And no wonder," I said under my breath. It was not every day that two grandly-attired ladies arrived at a function in a hearse. Sans coffin, granted, but a hearse nevertheless. The odd thing was, Sally clearly saw nothing untoward about our mode of transportation "Pa wanted to drive us," she had said. "Got 'imself all duded up, too, in his top an' tails. Said he wanted to make the evenin' special, didn't he, though?"

Special? I grimaced to myself as Sally nudged me along. Why had he not loaded a few corpses into the hearse while he was at it? Then we really would have caused a stir.

I shrank into myself, now, trying to appear inconspicuous. But the popping eyes of the two old codgers and a quartet of men up ahead swiftly dispelled that notion. Had they not been taught it was rude to stare? And just look at the knowing nods and nudges and behind-the-hands whisperings of the Misses Bletherall and McKnight. Ye gods, my worst fears were being confirmed. Everyone clearly thought we were ridiculously overdressed.

"Sally." I had to raise my voice to make myself heard. "We should go home ... change into something simple."

"Rubbish. We should do no such thing."

"But people are gawping."

"'course they are. An' why wouldn't they be?"

I tipped my head questioningly.

"We are a picture, aren't we, though, you in your apricot sateen an' me in my green brocade. Never seen anythin' like us, 'ave they though, all decked out in our frocks? It is admiration, isn't it, though? You will see I am right when the music starts"—Sally prodded me on—"an' all the lads who 'ave been eyeing us come flockin' around and askin' us to dance."

We had reached the bench, now. Sally's face flamed and she sat, with a relieved sigh, and fanned herself with her hand. Then, smoothing her skirts, she patted the spot alongside her. "Hurry up and sit yourself down before somebody else does."

My bustle forced me to perch on the bench's edge. "Deuced contraption," I muttered. "I never should have let Katerina talk me into it and I never should have let you construct my gown to accommodate it."

"Oh but it looks a proper treat on you," Sally said.

"Where is yours, then, that you are so enamoured of them?" I asked.

"Mine? Right here, isn't it though?" She patted herself on her posterior and chuckled. "With a beam as broad an' round as mine I 'ave no need of such an annoyance, do I though?" She gave me a gentle jab in my ribs.

"I should have worn one of my everyday frocks and ---"

"Rubbish." Sally waved me off and craned for a view of the stage at the far end of the hall. It was flanked by tubs of flowers, and crepe paper streamers in every hue imaginable festooned the wall behind it.

"Look," Sally said, "the Ohland brothers and Charlie Chester ... gettin' all set with their fiddles. Wait till you hear them. A proper treat they are. When they are not tunin' up, that is." Sally snorted with laughter and covered her ears for a few seconds. "Remind you of a bunch of coyotes, don't they though?"

I could not help smiling. A trio of cats with their tails caught in the door, had been my thought. "They do rather. Sally, I still think we ... I should ---"

"Sound champion, they do," Sally cut in, "once they get goin'. You will not be able to keep your toes from tappin', I tell you." She glanced behind me and snorted again. "And that bustle of yours will be bouncin' for all it is worth, won't it, though?"

Mentally, I threw up my hands. It was for certain I would get no sympathy from Sally. So there was clearly nothing else for it but to stop worrying and enjoy the evening.

I focused on the stage. "That is Mrs. Fletcher, is it not?" The woman settling herself at the piano was a regular customer at the store.

"'tis indeed," Sally said. "Just wait till you see 'er play. Pounds the keys like she is killin' a bunch o' varmints, doesn't she though, an' throws 'erself about something fierce? Must fancy 'erself one o' them concert pianists playin' for the la-di-da crowd."

"Oh and look," Sally continued, "'ere comes Jed Traske with his banjo. Everyone is here now, who is supposed to be. So they must be about ready to start."

And start they did, with a rollicking piece that had everyone—myself—included—tapping their toes. Soon the floor filled up with dancers of all shapes, sizes and ages. Forming two long lines opposite one another, partners stepped forward and back, forward and back, and then the couple at the head of the column met up once more, grabbed each other's hands, and did what looked like a cross between a gallop and a jig down the central aisle while the rest of the dancers whooped and whistled and clapped encouragement. This routine progressed, with each couple peeling off, meeting up and gallop-jigging to the far end until all the pairs had switched places and the nearest had become the farthest and so on and so on.

"Didn't I tell you, though?" Sally shouted over the din.

"What?" I was intent on the dancers.

"That they'd be flockin' to ask us."

"Huh?"

"Our admirers."

I refocused on Sally in time to hear her add, "The three boys over there."

They were not boys, that was for certain, I thought, nor were they men; they were awkward youths who wore their bodies like ill-fitting suits, constantly shifting, rolling their shoulders, stretching their necks and feigning self-assuredness. One was big and soft-looking, one short and slight, the other of medium build.

"Been tossin' a coin, they have, to see who gets the first dance with one of us."

"They could be wagering about any old thing."

"Well, we will know soon enough, won't we though? Here comes Duffy Pierce, now."

A surreptitious glance told me he was the medium-sized fellow. "He is no doubt going to ask you," I said.

But he headed straight for me, swallowed hard, said not a word and yanked me to my feet. The shock of it rendered me speechless, and it was not until he had hauled me onto the dance floor that I found my tongue again. "What in Hades do you think you are doing?" I asked, snatching my hand free of his.

His face turned crimson and he touched my arm in what appeared to be reassurance, then pulled back his hand as if scalded and said, "Oh Lord, Miss I am sorry. I ... er ... I should 'ave ... will you ... can I ... may ...?"

All at once I felt sorry for the poor fellow. His bravado—if in fact he had had any in the first place—had clearly deserted him. I touched his arm and smiled up at him. "Yes, you may have this dance," I said.

The dance happened to be the fiddler's slow, sawing and whanging version of a waltz, thank the Lord, and although Duffy was a bit on the clumsy side, I emerged at the end of it unscathed.

Duffy smiled the smile of the beatified as he escorted me back to my seat. Would I dance with him again, later? he stammered. I said I would, but had barely sat down beside Sally than I was whisked off again by another young man, then another after that, and another and another. And so it went all evening long, with hardly a moment for Sally and I to chat, until the musicians took a break.

I was delighted to hear that Sally, too, had had a succession of partners. It was no surprise that her love of fun and her empathetic ear made her popular.

"Men like nothin' better," she said, when we were comparing notes, "than talkin' about themselves, isn't that right, though?"

I laughed. "I should say so. My ears are well and truly bent." By this time I had been regaled with accounts of the hopes and aspirations of at least twenty of the men in the hall.

"So, has anybody tickled your fancy yet?" Sally rolled her eyes wickedly.

"No. A couple of fellows were really quite handsome ... several were very charming and said terribly flattering things, which, by the way, I took with an enormous pinch of salt, especially the proposal."

"Lord love us. You mean one of them proposed? Which one?"

"I have no idea. I have danced so much, I have listened so much, my brain is completely addled. But do you know, Sally, one thing strikes me."

"An' what is that?"

"Not one of those chaps asked me anything about my hopes and dreams."

"Never do, do they, though?"

A picture of Phillip Latham flashed across my mind. Now there was a man who was concerned for the dreams of others. What a fine figure he would have cut here, tonight.

"They think all you are good for," Sally chattered on, "is lookin' after them an' havin' their children—if you are married, that is. An' you are bound to be before too long."

"What positive piffle. That is the very farthest thing from my mind. I have one goal and only one -- to work like a pack mule, save every last cent I am able and get away from this place and back to England and the little of my family I have left."

"I understand." Sally gave me a couple of little calming pats on my arm.

"Besides, I am as good as an indentured servant, with the remains of a five-year term to fulfill."

Sally frowned in puzzlement.

"I am caught in the web of my own lie ... the one about my age, remember?" I had done nothing to hide my true age since my conversation with Johann Brecht wherein he had encouraged me to make it known to the world.

"I came to the Brechts last year," I reminded Sally, "supposedly as a fourteen-year-old child. That I am actually twenty-three in July, and they know it, means absolutely nothing. Legally, I am bound to them for another four years. If it were up to Katerina, my period of servitude might well be shortened. But unfortunately it is not."

"Oh things will buck up. Knowing you, you will find a way out of it, won't you though?"

I contemplated my lap. "I have no free will, Sally. I belong to the

Brechts."

"She is right, she does."

At the sound of the masculine voice, I went very still, thinking I was hearing things. But when Sally said, "Good Evening, Mr. Brecht," I knew this was no hallucination and I slowly turned, frowning in bewilderment, and looked up into my employer's face.

His blue eyes held mine for a second and then swept over me. "She belongs to the Brechts," he said under this breath, "and this Brecht has come to fetch her."

"Is it William?" I asked, panic suddenly washing over me. "Or Katerina?"

"No. Nothing is wrong. I am sent by my wife to transport both you ladies home." He nodded first at me then at Sally, telling her, "I have spoken to your father, Sally, and received his permission."

Her throat worked and she seemed a little tongue-tied. Finally, she managed to say, "You mean we don't 'ave to ride in the hearse again?"

"Correct. I am also instructed by my wife to have one dance with each of you."

"With us?" Sally said, blushing scarlet.

Incredulous, I said, "You dance?"

Johann Brecht did not answer me. The musicians had resumed playing and he cocked his head for a moment, listening. Then he extended a hand to Sally, palm-up. "It is polka, *ya*? May I have the pleasure?"

Her eyes round, her mouth splitting into an enormous smile, Sally rose. "Indeed you may Mr. Brecht."

And off they whirled while I sat watching, open-mouthed.

Some five minutes later, Johann Brecht delivered a red-faced, beaming Sally to her seat. Between the risings and fallings of her bosom, she gasped, "Thank you very much, sir. Lovely that, wasn't it though?"

Looking slightly discomfited, Johann Brecht adjusted his shirt collar. "*Ach*, I am how do you say? Rusty, I think. It has been many years since I ---"

"Take your partners ladies and gentlemen," the voice from the platform interrupted, "for the last dance ... a waltz."

Mr. Brecht signaled me to rise and then he took my arm and steered me towards the dance floor. We stopped at its edge. "Polka I know well. But the waltz I know little. It is one-two-three, one-two-three, *ya*?"

I nodded.

"I put my arm around your waist like this. I hold your hand like this, *ya*?"

Again I nodded.

He held me firmly and I felt the heat of his hand burning into my back through the thin material of my gown. He moved me with him, repeating under his breath, "One-two-three ... one-two-three."

His voice faded. The sounds of fiddle and piano and feet upon the floor faded. My mind whirled. And soon I was no longer in Plenty, District of Saskatchewan, Northwest Territories, but six thousand miles away, clasped in the arms of Phillip Latham.

## CHAPTER FIFTY-THREE
### *May-June 1890*
### *Plenty, District of Saskatchewan, Northwest Territories, Canada*

At five past ten Mr. Brecht and I dropped Sally off at her parents' house. A few minutes later we were home and while Mr. Brecht saw to the parking of the wagonette in its allotted outbuilding, I headed inside, exhausted.

All I wanted was my room, my bed and solitude. But no sooner had I entered the hallway leading to the quarters at the rear of the shop than Katerina appeared at my elbow and began a rapid fire salvo of questions.

Did everyone admire my frock? Was anyone else wearing anything similar? Was this person or that person at the social? What was the music like and who played which instrument? How many dances did I dance and with whom? Did I meet anyone who particularly took my fancy?

My heart took on the rhythm of the verbal bombardment and its assault made my head throb. But I could not bring myself to disappoint Katerina and spoil her vicarious enjoyment. So I let myself be propelled to the kitchen table and a waiting cup of tea and then did my best to recall each question and address it. I was about to answer the one about dance partners, when Johann Brecht poked his head around the door and said, "Katerina, you stop now with the questioning. We must not wear Lydia out. I think she has had very much excitement for one night."

Grateful for the interruption I flashed him a brief smile. "Indeed she has," I said, rising from the table. The animation drained from Katerina's face. But I was too tired to try and boost her spirits. I merely laid a hand on her arm and said, "I appreciate your waiting up." Then I thanked Mr. Brecht for the waltz and the ride home and bid the couple goodnight.

The next morning—Sunday—when I descended to the kitchen at a little past eight, I was surprised to find Katerina seated at the table, nursing William. Fingers of sunlight poked through the gap in the partially-drawn curtains at the window, dappling the tablecloth with light and shadow and every so often diverting the baby's attention from his hungry suckling.

I felt a stab of envy at the sight of mother and child. Katerina the pale Madonna, William the rosy cherub. They reminded me of one of the Old

Masters hanging above the staircase at Hadfield Hall. I lowered myself into my seat, rested my elbows on the table and cupped my chin in my hands, expelling a soft sigh. Was there anything more beautiful?

Would I ever love a man and bear his children and be sitting at a table or by a hearth somewhere with my baby at my breast and four or five little ones gathered about my knee?

*And two or three dead and you worn out and a man who cares about nothing but his own desires. Look at all the unfortunates you have seen thus far in your not-too-long life. Back home in the village; on the streets of Liverpool; on the immigrant ship; at the Distribution Centre, not to mention right under your nose here in Plenty.*

I blinked and sat up straight. Ye Gods, where had that litany come from?

I studied Katerina. Judging from the dearth of talk and the dismal expression on her face, her mind had clearly moved to that other place—that black place it so often occupied. Oh what a see-saw my friend rode, between enthusiasm and utter gloom, I thought with a prick of impatience.

"Has Mr. Brecht had his breakfast? I asked, uncomfortable with the long silence.

"He is away for day," Katerina said, wearily. "He will not return until after sunset, he says. He does not tell me reason for his going but I think it is church business."

Having no desire for her mood to infect me, I focused on the baby. "Good morning, little man," I said. He stopped sucking and stared at me long enough to make a sound that was somewhere between a chuckle and a coo, then his eyes once more followed the progress of the sunbeams across the checkered linen of the cloth.

Uplifted, I smiled as I poured cream on my porridge, sprinkled a heaping teaspoonful of brown sugar on it and dug in. Katerina continued to stare off, wincing every now and again when William drew too strongly on her nipple.

At seven months, he was the prettiest of babies. Small for his age and dainty, he had pink cheeks and dimples when he smiled, and his corn-yellow curls hugged his perfectly shaped head. And thanks to me and my attention to him, his mother insisted, he was no longer the fretful infant he had been for the first three or four months of his life. In truth, the baby slept for hours upon end, so deeply sometimes it was nearly impossible to wake him.

I poured myself thick, strong coffee from the pot on the trivet close by, then milked and sugared it. Circling my hands about the cup, I savoured the rich aroma and watched William's eyes—the same pale blue as those of his parents—grow large with fascination as they now followed the dance of sunlight across the ceiling. I had just taken a drink when Katerina came back to earth. Shifting William to her other breast, she said with a long-suffering sigh, "I am cow. Do not be surprised if I next say Good *mooing* and not Good morning."

I burst out laughing and the sound was clearly so alien to William he did not know what to make of it. He stopped feeding and twisted so as to observe me, his concentration on me so fierce it made me laugh even harder, whereupon his frown deepened, his eyes grew wider and his mouth began to quiver.

Oh Lord, I was clearly frightening the little fellow to death. I pulled myself together and leaned across the table. "There, there, sweet baby. I have not gone completely mad. It is just that your mama is so very funny."

Katerina sighed and shook her head. "Not funny. Weary. Come, child, get on with your breakfast, then I can rest." She adjusted her neckline and was repositioning her breast when I saw the bruise. "Ye Gods," I blurted, "what on earth have you done to yourself?"

Katerina's dull gaze followed mine to the area a couple of inches above the nipple William had latched onto. She stared down for an instant then rearranged the folds of her dressing gown so as to cover the crimson mark. "*Ach* that. It is nothing."

"Did William ---?"

"No, not William. Babies are not only ones who like the breast."

Perplexed, I tipped my head.

"Men, too." William had apparently fallen asleep; Katerina got up and placed him in the cradle by the fireplace.

When she returned to her seat I said, "Men too, what?"

Katerina leaned on her elbows and sat forward. "Men too like the breast." She closed her eyes momentarily and a little tremor shook her. "*Mein Gott,* how Johann forgets himself when the passion ... how you say? ... takes over him."

My shocked expression stopped her in her tracks for a second.

"*Nein,*" she went on. "You are not understanding. He is not bad man. He is just man." She lifted her shoulders in weary resignation. "He cannot help the wanting ... the lust, you call it. He needs me. I cannot refuse him and be good wife to him."

I squirmed in my seat. Lord, one minute Katerina was as tight-lipped as an oyster, the next forthcoming as a madam in a bawdy house.

She poured herself a cup of coffee, making a face when she tasted the stewed brew. "*Mein Gott*"—she shifted uncomfortably in her seat and put down her cup—"Johann must have me all night long, it seem. I try to think about other things, but he is big like bull and he is in me and in me and in me until I think he will go through me and come out other side."

The images the uninvited confidences evoked made me shudder. And if Katerina's expression was any indication there were more to come. I had had quite sufficient, thank you, and sought to forestall her. "Did I tell you I am to meet Sally this afternoon?" I asked.

It took time for Katerina to make the transition from last night to the present. Eventually she said with uncertainty, "No, I do not think so."

"We are going to take a picnic lunch down to the creek."

Katerina's face lit up. "*Ach*, I have always loved picnics." The longing in her voice was so palpable I found myself saying, "Come with us."

"You and Sally would not mind?"

"Of course not."

That afternoon Sally drove us in Mr. Porter's buggy which was built to accommodate two. That all three of us women and William squeezed into the seat made for a great deal of sport. By the time we reached the creek and parked in the shade of a grove of poplars, and then set up a lean-to of branches and blankets where we would take turns minding William, we were all giggling like girls let loose in a school for boys.

Once more, Katerina had transformed herself; this time, into her former self, with her endearing, self-deprecating humor and a jolliness that was more than a match for Sally's.

After a feast of cold chicken, potato salad, crusty bread slathered with butter, washed down with lemonade, we lay back, satiated as a pride of lionesses on the veldt, conversing in low voices and trading gossip about the local characters while William napped. Sally fell asleep first, then Katerina. I would stay awake, or so I thought.

Sometime later the honking of a *Vee* of geese overhead roused me. I yawned and stretched. Like Katerina, I too, felt myself suddenly transformed. For now I had sloughed the yoke of responsibility and felt carefree as a child again.

"How would it be if we left her to take care of William?" I said to Katerina, indicating a softly-snoring Sally wrapped around the baby like a large cocoon.

"It would be good, very good," Katerina said, following me through the shoulder-high grasses. At first I walked, then I trotted, then I ran full tilt and she kept up with me. I rolled down a couple of knolls and she followed suit. She sat on the bank of the creek, dabbling her feet while I paddled in the brown water enjoying the feel of the mud between my toes.

Another flock of wild geese flew over, honking, and Katerina and I honked back at them at the top of our lungs. Then we made a mad dash after a pair of prairie chickens headed in the direction of the wheat fields beyond the barbed wire fence. After a while, I gave up, realizing the futility of the chase, and collapsed in a hysterical heap, but Katerina kept on running ... running ... running as if she would never stop.

By the time I had stopped laughing and recovered my breath enough to get up, I could see no sign of Katerina. I called her name. "I am done in," I shouted. "Far too done in to play hide and seek."

"I could not play hide and seek if I wanted to," finally came the faint response.

"Why not?" I started moving in the direction of the voice.

"*Ach*, just look at me." Katerina limped into view. "I have argument with a piece of barbed wire. I rip my skirt and my leg."

"Ye Gods, Katerina." I rushed to her. "Let me see. You have blood all over your skirt. Sit down."

"It is nothing much." She sank to the ground with my help and grimacing, stretched out her legs and lifted up her skirts.

I kneeled. "Nothing much," I said, wincing. "It looks downright nasty to me. I think we should get you to Doctor Purdy's."

"Rubbish. I do not need a doctor. Just take me home."

"Very well," I said, uncertainly, "if you insist."

"I do. And Lydia"—she grabbed my arm—"this was best day I have in years. Thank you for it. And for your friendship."

I did not know how to respond except to smile, pat Katerina's hand and say, "Come along, then, let us get you home."

## CHAPTER FIFTY-FOUR
### *June 1890*
#### *Plenty, District of Saskatchewan, Northwest Territories, Canada*

"I have decided I shall open a shop when I return to England." I tossed a pebble into the creek's brown depths, thinking what a poor substitute it was for the clear, bubbling waters of the brook that had flowed through the field behind the rectory.

Sally followed suit with her own pebble, and said, "You have, have you?"

At a little past eleven on this Sunday morning the air was already stifling. I took off my wide-brimmed straw hat and fanned myself with it. "Lord, Sally, sinful or not of me to say it, I am so glad we decided not to go to church."

Sally had already doffed her bonnet. She blotted her flushed face with a handkerchief. "So am I," she said, lifting her skirts and flapping them about in an effort to cool herself. "Would have melted or passed out, wouldn't we, though?"

Our decision to forego morning service had been a last-minute one. A stroll to the same spot where we had had our picnic with Katerina the week before had seemed a far more attractive option. "At least with the water," I said, "and this bit of shade, we can fool ourselves into believing it cooler."

"Right about that you are." Sally continued her skirt-flapping. "So, tell me about this shop of yours."

"There is nothing much to tell, really. It is just that I rather like the idea of being a merchant." I checked the grass for ants and seeing none, sat. Then I took off my boots and stockings and dangled my legs over the bank.

Sally followed my lead, but noisily, puffing and panting, her plump cheeks growing redder by the minute. I had a difficult time keeping a straight face at the sight of my friend engaged in what looked like a battle with her hose and the tiny buttons on her boots. "Blasted things have to be the devil's invention, don't they though?" she said, finally flinging aside the second of her boots.

I carried on where I had left off. "Annabel would, I am certain, make a first-rate assistant. She is quite the talker, you know, and from what I hear from home, quite the worker, too."

"Had another letter, have you?"

"No. There has been, as I told you, a bit of a lapse in communication, with Phillip's sister being ill etcetera. Remember? She has not been able to visit the children for some time."

"*Phillip's* sister, is it?" Sally smirked slightly.

"He asked me to call him Phillip. What the deuce is so unusual about that? It is what friends do, Sally, call each other by their Christian names."

"All right. No need to get yourself in a tizzy."

"I am not," I said sheepishly. "Anyway, as I was saying, Delphine has been unable to visit the children. But I am sure everything is all right. They would tell me if it were not."

"Course they would. So about this establishment of yours, what kind will it be?"

"General merchandise I should think. Although I do love the fabrics ... the haberdashery ... that sort of thing. But, oh Lord, Sally"—I swallowed hard, feeling suddenly on the edge of tears—"I shall no doubt be in my dotage before I am able to do anything about it. Some days, I tell you, I am sorely tempted."

"To do what?"

"Take off."

"You mean run away?"

I nodded. "Idiotic idea, of course. After all, where would I go, what would I do? How long would the few dollars I have saved last me? Not to mention what Johann Brecht would do to me if I tried it and the scheme failed, which it doubtless would and ---"

"Do to you? He isn't goin' to beat you, is 'e, though? I mean, Mr. Brecht isn't like that. He may 'ave 'is funny little ways, but 'e's always been decent to me an' ---"

"You are right," I said. "He is basically a decent sort. The difference is, though, you work for him. I am owned by him."

Sally reached across and touched my arm, her expression at once sympathetic and mischievous. "Even so, we cannot have you runnin' off an' endin' up an Indian squaw, can we, though?"

"True." I smiled in spite of myself.

"Or in some pot cookin' over a fire, now that there is 'ardly a buffalo to be had"—Sally snorted at her own joke—"an' made into a nice tasty stew."

"What a thing to say."

"Only teasin' you, wasn't I, though?"

"But, really, it is no laughing matter, is it? I mean, I know they are heathens and all, but from what I have heard, they have had a terribly rough go of it. Disease. Starvation. The lot. Imagine having to resort to hunting gophers and rabbits to survive, when for centuries you have depended on the buffalo."

"I know," Sally said soberly, "doesn't bear thinkin' about, does it, though?"

We fell silent for a time, each lost in our own thoughts. Sally finally broke the quiet. "Changin' the subject," she said, "been meanin' to ask you. Had any more waltzes with Mr. Brecht?"

"Lord, no. Nor am I likely to. Monday he was all business; he would have ignored me I am sure, had he not felt compelled to tell me about his departure for Regina Tuesday morning."

"Regina?"

"Yes. A six-or-seven-day trip. The dearth of cash seems to have been much worse this past two or three months. You know how it has been, with everyone wanting to pay for merchandise with anything but money? I had a customer actually bring a Billy goat into the store last week and ask if it could be applied towards his account."

Sally slapped her thighs and roared with laughter.

"Anyway," I went on in a serious voice, "I said of course"—I paused for effect and Sally stopped in mid-laugh, her mouth dropping open—"we were happy to take goats, but only nannies, and that in his case we would require three."

"You never did?" Sally said in a stunned tone.

I stared back at her for a long moment. And then a great bellow of laughter surged up in me and I spluttered, "Oh Lord, Sally, you should see your face. It is an absolute picture. Of course I did not say that."

Sally clicked her tongue against her teeth. "Knew all along, didn't I though?"

I had one last giggle before continuing. "Anyway," I said, "getting back to where we were ... I gather Mr. Brecht has a surfeit of barter goods to dispose of ... far too many for those two chaps that show up every so often to buy from him."

Sally frowned. "Wonder if Mrs. Brecht will be all right while 'e is gone."

"What makes you say that?"

"Actin' proper peculiar she was, yesterday, in the shop. You were in the back seein' to the tea, so you wouldn't have seen it all."

"Katerina peculiar? In what way?"

"Oh I dunno. Floatin' off when she was talkin' to me, 'er eyes sort of wavin' around."

There was nothing particularly odd about that, I thought: Katerina's mind often wandered these days.

"An' I didn't realize it at first," Sally went on, "but she 'ad left little William by the bean sacks ... just laid 'im down on the floor there. An' of course what does 'e do but get all set to stuff a fistful of beans in 'is mouth? Well, Mrs. B... . she just watches 'im, doesn't she though? An' makes not so much as a move to stop 'im. Lucky I was there to see it. Or the little chap could 'ave choked."

I dipped my feet into the brackish waters, relishing the coolness for a moment. "Mrs. Brecht goes through her ups and downs, Sally, that is for certain. But, bless her heart, she does the best she can. And it has not been easy for her with one thing or another. I mean it has only been a few months since she lost ..." I stopped myself; gossip about Katerina was the last thing with which I wanted to involve myself. "So, you had to persuade William to relinquish the beans, then?" I said, attempting to bring a little levity to the conversation. "That must have been quite a challenge."

"I should say so. 'as a mind of his own, that one, 'asn't 'e, though, small as 'e is? 'ad a deuce of a time gettin' 'is little fist open. Surprised you didn't bring 'im along today, 'is Ma, too. Didn't she say anythin' this time?"

"I have not even seen her today. She called to me early this morning when I was passing her bedroom. Said she had had a restless night and would stay in bed for a time. Asked me to get William up—he is in his own room, now, next to theirs—and after I had seen to him to put him back in his cot for his nap which usually lasts an hour or so. I told her I would be going to church later and she said not to worry, she would attend to the baby when he woke up." I leaned over and plucked a flax flower, admiring its delicate blue blossom. "I imagine she will be expecting me to come home after church and then go out again in the afternoon with you."

"An' will you, then?"

I exhaled a gust of air. "Not today, Sally, if you do not mind. It is so deucedly hot, I think I shall stay in my room—with the curtains drawn and the lamp lit—and write my letters so that I have them ready for when Phillip's next one arrives. Unless Katerina wants to chat ... which is a distinct possibility. One nice thing about Sundays is that she prepares the dinner, does the dishes, too. Says nothing should interfere with my day off."

But there were no signs of dinner today, I was disgruntled to discover when I arrived home a little before half-past twelve. As I opened the back door I thought I heard William crying; uncertain from which direction the cries were coming, I hurried along the passageway to the kitchen.

Empty. Still. No evidence of its having been occupied during my absence, nor of any food preparation. Despite the heat of the day, I had chosen on rising that morning, to light the fire so as to boil water for coffee and cook a couple of eggs; the embers were barely alive. William's bottle—used now to supplement his mother's milk—was in the same spot I had left it after I had washed and dried it, on a tea towel on the table. A shiver touched the back of my neck and travelled down my spine. Odd, all of it.

A wail echoed through the silence and made my heart jump into my mouth. William. It had been his cries I had heard. And from upstairs. Here came another ... and another ...ascending the scale now, and culminating in a scream of such desperateness that it gave wings to my feet. I tore up the staircase, shouting, "Katerina, are you up here?"

"Yes," came the faint response as I reached the landing and William's screams abated for a moment, "but I cannot ... I have trouble, I need help. But the baby, help the baby first."

"Oh I will, Katerina, I will. Hold on. Just as soon as I have seen to him, I will help you."

I threw open the door to the infant's room and stumbled for his cot, terrified about what I might find. When William caught sight of me, he stopped in mid-scream and raised his arms to me, his tear-swollen face collapsing in on itself.

"Oh you poor little mite," I said, scooping him up ever so gently, not sure if he were injured in some way. A swift check of his little body told me he was not. The smile he gave me—such a heartrendingly-grateful one between his shuddering sobs—convinced me further. Filthy and foul-smelling, soaked in urine, snot oozing from his nose, and no doubt ravenous after all the hours he must have spent here, but thank God, all in one piece.

There was no time at present for anything but a quick kiss on the top of his golden head and a reassuring, "There ... there," as I made for the door. I needed to see to his mother.

Katerina tried to raise herself from her prone position when she saw me. "I am so sorry, it is my leg ... aaaaah ... the pain ... it is everywhere." She fell back as I reached her bedside. "*Ach, Gott* be praised, you have baby." I glanced down at him. Wonder of wonders, he was fast asleep.

"He cries and cries, but I cannot move," Katerina went on. "So hot." She pulled at the neck of her nightgown as if it were choking her and rolled her head back and forth on the pillow. She looked like a consumptive with her scarlet-stained cheeks and lips dry as parchment. "Water please, Lydia," she said, "you bring me water."

"In just a moment, Katerina." I felt her forehead. Burning hot. "I must take a look at your leg, first, though. Alright?"

I did not wait for permission, but lifted Katerina's nightgown. When I saw the leg, my heart stopped, my stomach heaved. Swollen to about four times its normal size, it did not even resemble a leg but some monstrous thing whose skin was about to burst. Around the spot where the barbed wire had punctured the skin the flesh was blood red and shiny, and inside the thigh area, it looked as if someone had dipped a pen in red ink and drawn a line which travelled up from the wound towards Katerina's groin.

Numbly and with the utmost care, I pulled down the nightgown.

Katerina groaned at the movement of the material over her skin. "Is not good, *ya*?" Her voice had a far-away quality to it. "Anna TwoBears ... maybe she can help me."

Perhaps the Indian woman could. But she was like a spectre ... showing up at the store once a month and then disappearing to God knew where. It would have to be Doctor Purdy, I thought with desperation. He was our only hope.

"You will be alright, Katerina," I gently touched her shoulder, I am going to get help. I shall have to put William down in his cot for a few minutes. He is asleep, now, so he should be fine. If you hear him crying, you must not worry. I shall not be long, I promise."

"Is cold, Lydia. So cold." Katerina's teeth were chattering now. She must have thrown off the covers; they were strewn about the floor beside the bed. I retrieved them and heaped them over Katerina's upper body, knowing that any weight on her leg would be agonizing.

God, how I hated to leave her like this. But there was nothing else for it.

And clearly no time to lose.

———

I had run through the streets like a mad woman, first to Doctor Purdy's—thank the Good Lord he had been home—then to Sally's. I could not possibly manage to take care of Katerina and the baby, and it was for certain once the doctor had done what was necessary with that monster of a leg—drained the poisons or whatever was entailed — there would be a good deal of nursing involved.

It was half-past four, now. William was in the kitchen with Sally and I. I had woken him up and brought him downstairs as soon as I had shown Doctor Purdy into Katerina's room. The doctor had been up there for what seemed like an age. But a glance at the clock on the mantel told me it had been less than half an hour.

Sally had resurrected the fire enough to boil water both for William's bath and a pot of tea. She had already bathed and dressed the baby and now she was feeding him his bottle while I poured the tea.

Standing at the table, too fidgety to sit, I took a drink of the strong, sweet brew and set the cup back in its saucer. "Thank the Lord for you, Sally. I do not know what I would have done without you."

"Managed. Always do, don't you though?"

"Do you think she is going to be all right?"

Sally lifted William to her shoulder to bring up his wind, and rubbed his back. "Oh I should think so. A strong woman, isn't she though? An' Doctor Purdy"—she paused to listen and tipped her head at a spot beyond my shoulder –"will be able to tell you, won't 'e though?"

I wheeled about and saw the doctor standing in the doorway. Thank the Lord. Finally, a progress report.

"You had best come upstairs with me, lassie?" the doctor said.

"How is she?" I mounted the staircase behind him. "Will she be all right?"

He said nothing until we reached the landing. There, he stopped. He turned around, put his hands on my shoulders and looked me straight in the eye. "Ya told me Mr. Brecht is in Regina, right lassie, an' that he willna be back until tomorrow or Tuesday?"

I nodded.

"That will be too late. I am afraid."

"Too late?" I squirmed under his big hands which suddenly seemed too heavy.

"Aye. 'tis blood poisoning. I am sorry but she is dyin' child ... your mistress is dyin' an' she is askin' for you. I 'ave given her somethin'; she is in no pain. So go into 'er now, will ya?"

"No ... no." I squirmed out of his grip. "How can you say such things? Katerina cannot be dying. I do not believe you." It was all a dreadful nightmare. In a moment I would wake up.

I shoved by the doctor and opened Katerina's door. "I am back," I called out. "I told you I would not be long."

"Lydia *liebchen* ... closer .... come closer. I cannot see you."

I had no consciousness of moving, but the next thing I knew I was at Katerina's bedside and gazing down on her face; it was that of a Madonna— smooth, transparently white, peaceful. And yes, full of joy ... the eyes shining with that same knowingness with which Mama's had shone.

And I knew then, with a terrible pain that seemed to pierce my heart, that what the doctor had said was true.

"She is here, Lydia," Katerina whispered.

I leaned in closer, tears coursing down my cheeks. "Who is here?"

"My sweet baby girl." Katerina smiled a beatific smile. "*Ach*, she holds out her arms to me, Lydia ... and she is so beautiful ... so like my William. She gripped my arm suddenly. "You will take care of him, my sweet baby boy. Promise me you will, Lydia. And my Johann. You will take care of him, too. He is good man."

I opened my mouth to speak, but her hand all at once went limp and fell away from my arm.

And with her last long, rattling breath, I realized I had been spared the necessity of another promise.

## CHAPTER FIFTY-FIVE
### *July 1890*
### *Latham Residence, Yorkshire, England*

Phillip found Delphine in the garden lost in admiration of a rose she had cut and was placing in her basket. She glanced up when she heard the crunch of his footsteps on the gravel path.

"Glorious afternoon ... splendid blooms," she said, indicating the contents of her basket as she came and sat next to him. "They have done so well this year. Just look at this one, Phillip." She proffered a perfect, ruby red bloom. "Smell it, the scent is exquisite."

Frowning, Phillip pushed her hand away and brandished a letter. "Sorry, not in the mood, Delphine. I just opened this." He waved a couple of sheets of paper at her.

"Oh, the letter that came in this morning's post. Upsetting news?" Frowning, she eased forward for a better view of Phillip's face.

"I felt like an utter cad before," he said, "with all the subterfuge and half-truths. Now, I feel useless, too."

"What on earth do you mean?"

"There were two letters enclosed, actually; the first written in early June expressing disappointment—and why would she not—about the lack of news from this end. The second penned a week later." He cleared his throat and began to read:

"Thursday, 12th June, 1889. Dear Phillip, I am heartsick. My employer—indeed my dear friend, Katerina Brecht—passed away last Sunday, the eighth, and is already in the ground alongside her baby girl. Blood poisoning followed what appeared to be a small wound—little more than a scratch, really—from a barbed wire fence. She had only twenty-two years on this earth. Far too few. I can make no sense of her cruel death which has left me to be mother to baby William.

I am numb. I have no cheerful words or uplifting thoughts for my dear Annabel and Edwin this time. Perhaps you will make something up on my behalf. And perhaps you will have letters from them when you next write.

I hope your sister fares better and is recovered from her ill health. I can say nothing more.

Yours in gratitude, as always.

Lydia."

Delphine set her basket down, drew off her gloves and placed them in it, then removed her wide-brimmed, straw hat, searching for the right words. But all she could think to say was, "It is all very sad, Phillip."

"Sad?" He sounded annoyed. "It is tragic, damnably tragic. And I have nothing to offer to help alleviate poor Lydia's suffering." He bent over, elbows on his knees, and propped his head in one hand.

Delphine felt a prick of resentment. She had scant time for herself these days with Phillip bent on driving himself harder and harder and taking her along with him. His surgery, here, was open weekdays nine until one, and she was at his beck and call for everything from wound-cleaning, bandaging and splinting to cajoling, comforting and admonishing his patients. After lunch every day he headed for Brackford House while she kept up the practice's books and organized the surgery for the next day.

Every so often Phillip would send one of the Home children over to help her with various tasks. Today a great lump of a lad had appeared on her door step and although his intentions had clearly been good, he had proved to be far more hindrance than help. By the time he left, she had been worn out and ready to snip at anyone who looked at her sideways.

But once in the garden, with the aromas of sun-warmed earth and roses all about her, she had felt her tensions slip away. Now, though, they had returned in full measure.

What more could she say to her brother? *It is not your responsibility, Phillip, to take on the girl's grief. It is dreadfully sad, for certain, that the poor woman died, but it has no bearing on the situation here with Annabel and Edwin and what we are going to do about things.*

She passed a distracted hand across her mouth. If Phillip felt like a cad, then she felt like a *cadess.* Although she had not put down the lies on paper, she was as much a part of them as he. In fact, it had been her suggestion to say she had been ill and unable to visit West Kirby, and to tell Lydia Fullerton that the illness might well prove to be a protracted one. And what about all the fibbing about Edwin?

Phillip sat back. "Deuce it all, if I had just told her the truth, she could have dealt with it by now and adjusted to it." He got up and urged Delphine to her feet. "Walk with me while I think things through."

She donned her hat and said, "But you agonized over it, remember? You decided the truth would be too much for her—what you thought to be—young ears."

Phillip studied the crazy-paved path under his feet as they walked. God, how he hated this subterfuge. He had thought it far better than devastating Lydia. Now, she was devastated anyway. What he would not give to tell her something that would bring a smile to her face. He expelled a loud breath. "You are right, Delphie, I did fret over it ad nauseum. But I had hopes back then that Annabel would be found. I had even convinced myself she would be all right ... none the worse for the experience. But, damn it, however this all turns out, there is no escaping the fact that she is bound to be the worse for it. I was a fool to think otherwise."

Delphine slanted a sidelong glance up at him. He looked worn out. God forgive her, but sometimes she wished she had never heard the name *Fullerton.* She touched his arm. "Everything you have done, dear brother, has been with the very best of intentions. And one thing you will never be is a fool."

"I do not know about that, Delphie, but I do know Annabel has been missing now for over three-and-a-half months. And every day that passes lessens the likelihood of her being found." They had reached the lily pond. Both stood contemplating the shiny, green pads.

"But there is always hope, Phillip. There really is."

He tossed a pebble into the water and said nothing.

Delphine touched his sleeve. "From what you have told me, Josiah Trotter has certainly not given up."

"No. But I have a feeling he is dangerously close to it." Phillip aimed another pebble at the narrow space between two pads and hit his target. "Once that point comes—and it cannot be put off too much longer—I am going to have to tell Lydia. And, Lord knows what the news will do to her, now."

"At least Edwin has perked up a lot." No sooner had the words left Delphine's lips than she regretted them. It sounded like the empty utterance of someone at a funeral telling the bereaved his or her dear departed was at peace.

"Thanks to you," Phillip said.

Delphine cocked her head. "We had best head back. I believe I hear Mrs. Entwhistle sounding the dinner gong." She tucked her arm through Phillip's. "You say thanks to me. But I, too, had to resort to untruths, as you well know. Had I not lied to Edwin, it is for certain he would have let himself fade away."

Delphine shivered despite the warmth, her mind returning to her weekend visit to *Sea Winds* in April.

A new maid—a smiling giant of a woman with a haystack of yellow hair and an abundance of rotten teeth—answered Delphine's knock. Without a word, she grabbed Delphine's suitcase from the waiting cabbie, shut the door in his face—thankfully he had already been paid—and made for the stairs. "Missus 'as told me yer room number," she called over her shoulder. "Says ter tell yer she'll see yer at teatime."

"Hold on." Delphine climbed the stairs after the woman.

"Proper panned out she is on account o' the boy bein' so poorly. She an' the mister are 'avin' theirselves a bit of a snooze down in the kitchen by the fire."

"Edwin is ill, you say?"

The maid opened the door to Delphine's room. "'as been fer weeks."

"What exactly ails him?"

"Dunno. Doctors dunno neither." She hefted Delphine's suitcase up onto the bed and opened it. "Want me ter take care o' yer things."

"No thank you. What is your name, by the way?"

"Frances, Miss."

"Well that will be all for now, Frances. I will ring for you if I need anything further."

She waited for the woman's footfalls to fade, heard the sound of a door closing downstairs, then headed for Edwin's room.

The curtains were drawn and a fire crackled in the grate, casting shadows on the walls and across the bed's white counterpane. "Are you awake, Edwin?" Delphine asked in a soft voice, moving with caution across the carpeted floor.

"Who is it?" came the thready answer.

"Your friend, Miss Latham; Annabel's friend, Doctor Latham's sister."

"Is she here?" The bedclothes rustled as the boy struggled to raise himself.

"May I open the curtains so we can see each other."

"Did Annabel come back?"

Turning from the window, Delphine drew in a sharp breath at the sight of Edwin. Face the colour of bleached bone, eyes dark, red-rimmed pits. Oh and his hair … those once lovely chestnut curls now dull and lank. She quickly crossed to him and helped him sit up, plumping the pillows behind him. Lord in heaven, he felt like a bird, all bones, hardly any flesh. His thin hand grasped her arm. "Did she come back? Did you bring her?"

"No dear, she did not."

Edwin's bony shoulders slumped and tears filled his eyes.

"But I have news about her."

"You do?" He swiped at his eyes and regarded her with rapt attention.

Delphine moistened her mouth so that the lies would more easily roll off her tongue, swallowed hard, then put on a bright smile. "Annabel is off on a wonderful adventure—just as Lydia is—and she sent you a message."

The boys eyes widened. "A message?"

"Yes indeed. Your sister is making her way in the world and becoming exceedingly prosperous, so prosperous in fact that she said to be sure to tell you she will soon be able to come back here and get you."

Miracle of miracles, a smile touched the boy's lips.

"And you, Annabel and Lydia will all live happily ever after."

Edwin's smile grew broader. "We will?" He licked his dry, cracked lips and Delphine poured water from the carafe on the bedside table into a glass and helped him drink from it.

"You will, indeed. But only if you eat and grow strong and healthy again. Annabel says she expects you to be a big strapping fellow by the time she returns."

"How long will it take?"

"Oh, not long at all." Delphine stroked his cheek and he leaned into it for a time as if starved of human contact. Eventually he said, "Do you think you could get me something to eat, Miss Latham? I think I am hungry."

Thank the Lord, she had thought back then. The boy would be all right.

Last month when she had seen him, he had put on weight and grown an inch, she was certain. Gladys Chistlegate had kept the boy to herself, and Delphine had managed to talk to him only once, and then for just a few minutes. More lies ensued, one building on the next, the fable of Annabel's adventures and the futures of the three siblings taking on a life of its own.

And she dare not ask the boy to pen a few words to Lydia. He would not be able to contain his excitement about what he thought lay ahead.

"It is all becoming so complicated, Phillip," she said, in the present once more, and glad to see they had reached the back door, for she was feeling exhausted.

Phillip slanted a glance at her. "You look done in."

"We are both tired." She gestured for him to hand back to her the basket of roses. "Let us put the subject of the Fullerton children aside for the rest of today. I mean nothing is going to happen tonight that will change a thing."

But halfway through dinner the door bell rang. "Josiah Trotter," Phillip said, dropping his knife on his plate and making Delphine almost jump out of her skin. "You made no mention of his coming here tonight," she said. "Perhaps it is one of your patients. An emergency of some kind."

They both stared at the closed dining room door, listening to Mrs. Entwhistle's approaching footsteps, then looking up as she entered.

"Miss Amelia Dunn, doctor. Waitin' for you in the drawing room."

"Oh Lord." Phillip clapped his hands to the sides of his head. "That deuced woman is haunting me. Did she say what she wanted?"

"Only that it was very important and she needed to see you right away."

Moments later Phillip found the woman standing in front of the fireplace staring up at the portrait of his mother. "So what can I help you with this evening, Miss Dunn?" he asked.

At the sound of his voice, she wheeled about. "It is not you who can help me, doctor. It is *I* who can help you."

"In what way?"

"You did say if anythin' came up in relation to the Fullertons, you wished to be inf ---"

"Another letter has come?"

"It has indeed."

Phillip folded his arms across his chest. He must keep himself in check and do this dance of words, he providing the prompts, she the information, but bit by bit like crusts of bread to the starving. Delphine ridiculously contended this longwindedness had to do with the young woman's admiration for him and her desire to prolong their contact. Mentally, he shrugged off the notion and said, "From the Chistlegates?"

"Oh no, doctor."

"From whom, then?"

"I am blessed with an extremely acute memory and am able to recall facts and figures from months, even years ago. And so, when I saw the name on the back of the envelope, I recognized it."

"And?"

"I am loath to admit it, but I steamed the letter open. And later on I spied on Mrs. Bell when she read it. She was beside herself, doctor. Ripped the missive to shreds. And no surprise when you cons ---"

"What? For God's sake, Miss Dunn, please do spit it out and be done with it?"

Looking flustered, she pushed her spectacles up her nose. "Oh ... yes ... of course. So sorry. The letter revealed the whereabouts of Annabel Fullerton, doctor."

## CHAPTER FIFTY-SIX
### Hadfield Hall, Sussex, England
### July 1890

"I am expected." Delphine held out her carte de visite and the elderly woman took it in her red-knuckled hand saying, "Boot, miss," as she closed the front door.

Glancing down at her own feet, Delphine said, "I beg your pardon?"

"Lord luv us." The woman made a sound that was part wheeze, part guffaw and clapped herself on her breast. "Not what is on yer feet, miss. 'tis me is the boot. Mrs. Boot. 'ousekeeper 'ere goin' on twenty year."

Delphine bit back a chuckle. "I see."

The woman coughed a deep chesty sound like a miner whose lungs were clogged with coal dust then drew in a rattle of a breath. "You was ter be showed into the drawin' room, mistress said. It is this way"—she indicated the dark-panelled hall to the right—"if yer'll just follow me."

Dust-mote-laden sunlight streamed into the capacious room through four tall, rectangular windows, none of which was open Delphine noted as she entered. The atmosphere was stuffy and the odours of furniture polish and spent fuel—coke or coal or firewood—mixed with that of mildew. A William Morris paper in its bold signature pattern of maroon, dark blue and green covered the walls, providing a splendid backdrop for a profusion of gilt-framed watercolors. A few feet to her right stood a grand piano whose top was draped with a multicoloured fringed shawl on which a clutter of knickknacks rested. An assortment of small tables, alabaster busts, embroidered footstools and at least three whatnots bearing yet more knickknacks gave the room the overcrowded style considered de rigueur these days. And clocks—Lord save her—there had to be at least four in this one room alone.

And there mounted on the wall by the fireplace was one of the fairly new-fangled telephones. In her telegram answering Phillip's of the same day, Ernestine Hadfield had provided her number for the device. "Ring me if you wish," she had said, but Phillip had opted for another telegram to inform the old lady of Delphine's expected time of arrival.

"If yer'll 'ave a seat, miss"—the housekeeper indicated two chairs flanking the fireplace—"I shall tell the mistress yer waitin' an' I shall make a nice potta tea."

*Not tea ... cold lemonade, please ... a gallon of it.* Delphine felt perspiration blooming under her arms and between her breasts. She found her handkerchief and blotted her moist face. *Lord, what in creation am I doing here? I am forever chasing here, chasing there. Oh these deuced stays ... I can hardly breath. Look at the clock on the mantelpiece ... the monstrosity with the gleaming brass pendulum. Listen to its tick and all the other ticks in the room. Watch the pendulum ... do what the mesmerists do ... concentrate on the rhythm ... and think cool, refreshing thoughts ... cool, refreshing ...*

"Miss Latham?"

Perched on the chair's edge, Delphine started and an involuntary "Yes," escaped her lips.

"Ernestine Hadfield." Aided by a cane, an ancient-looking silver-haired woman navigated her laborious way across the Axminster carpet and around the various furnishings, finally managing to reach the armchair opposite Delphine's.

"If you would be so kind as to help me into my seat," she said, her voice reminiscent of a rusty gate hinge. "I find sitting quite the deuce of a challenge. When I am up I cannot get down and when I am down I cannot get up."

Once Delphine had the woman settled, she reseated herself and after a minute or two of obligatory patter about the journey and the weather, she could contain herself no longer and asked, "I wonder when it might be possible for me to see Annabel, Mrs. Hadfield?"

"I am afraid she is not at all well," the old lady said. "Her nights are extremely restless and she sleeps a great deal during the day ... is asleep at present, in fact. I realize you have travelled quite some distance and your time is limited, but I believe we should allow her to rest a while longer."

"By all means," Delphine said. "Far be it from me to want to add to the poor child's problems. And actually time is of no great concern to me since I am booked in at the *Cottage Loaf* for the night, although I shall have to impose upon you to have your man drive me there later on, if you do not mind."

"Not at all. Now, if you do not mind, I should like to know exactly what your connection with the girl is, Miss Latham. I must say the whole situation has me thoroughly flummoxed. Of course, at my age"—she gave a little snort of derision—"a great many things are not quite as clear as they should be. You are sister to the doctor who examined the children three years ago and are sent in his stead, that much I do know. As for the rest …" She threw up her hands.

"My brother observed a great injustice, Mrs. Hadfield, and took it upon himself to do his best to right it. I volunteered to assist him in his efforts."

"Assist him you say?" Ernestine Hadfield raised her lorgnette to her eyes and peered through it. "Kindly explain yourself."

As quickly and succinctly as possible and in a tone that brooked no interruption, Delphine recounted the events leading up to Annabel's disappearance from the Chistlegates. During Delphine's narrative, the old lady sat ramrod straight and still, the widening and narrowing of her eyes, the only indication she was taking it all in. Once she realized Delphine had finished, the woman closed her eyes momentarily and said, "Dreadful, positively dreadful. The poor girl had clearly reached the end of her rope, otherwise she would never have considered leaving her brother. I observed them to be extremely close the short time they were with me. And you say those poor children were actually sold?"

"Yes. Edwin was the prize those reprobates really wanted, Annabel was included merely to serve them as a skivvy and as I said, she was treated abominably. And Lord knows what she had to contend with on her trek from the northwest to you here in the southeast."

"Dear God, I had no idea." The old woman pressed a hand to her meagre bosom and shook her head dolefully. "Clearly, when Annabel arrived here I knew something had gone awry and I immediately wrote to the matron at the Home—twice, in fact—but received no response. I decided I would wait and speak to the girl myself. But the problem is, she will not say a word to me. I understand she has spoken to the servants but has provided no information about her … misadventures."

"I am hoping against hope she will speak to me," Delphine said. "She and I have had many conversations over the months. I shall not belabour you with the content. Suffice to say we had established an excellent rapport until a misunderstanding upset it."

"Oh these misunderstandings. How they do affect our lives."

Delphine pursed her lips. *As do arbitrary decisions about helpless children.* "Of course I am not privy to the circumstances which led you to relinquish your kin to Brackford House in the first place," she found herself saying, "but I must tell you …" She paused to draw breath, aware that she was about to say something she might regret, and the old lady cut in with, "I do believe I detect a note of censure in your voice, Miss Latham."

"Forgive me, madam. It is not my intent, I assure you. I fear this whole affair has soured my mood and made me ---"

"I deserve censure." Ernestine Hadfield suddenly said in a surprisingly forceful voice.

Mrs. Boot chose that moment to enter, a laden tray in hand. The soul of discretion, she merely dipped her head in acknowledgment, poured, milked and sugared their cups of tea and then offered a plate of assorted biscuits without commentary.

Delphine drank thirstily, reminding herself of the adage that hot tea could have a cooling effect.

Ernestine Hadfield dunked a shortbread finger in her tea to soften it, took several rabbit-like nibbles and waited for the housekeeper to close the door after herself before she resumed her story.

"Oh the guilt. You cannot imagine it."

*Indeed I can,* thought Delphine, remembering her rejection of Annabel's plea that she and Edwin be allowed to live with the Lathams.

"The way Lydia looked at me that last morning," the old lady went on. "The children had no idea, of course, what was about to befall them. Lydia made sure of that. Such spunk that girl had ... has."

"Yes. I have not met her but I know quite a bit about her. And it is for certain she is not lacking in mettle. My brother and I are aware of her true age, by the way. Since she was exiled halfway across the globe, I do not think she saw any point keeping it a secret."

"Quite a clever ruse that was." She stared off for a moment and then turned to look at Delphine. "She chastised me, you know."

"About what?"

Mrs. Hadfield nodded ruefully. "About being a blind fool. And she was right. Had I not been, none of this would have come about." She gripped the arms of her chair and sat forward. "I fell in love, you see. Old and decrepit as I am, I fell in love"—her voice quavered—"and was foolish enough to believe my feelings were returned."

"I am sorry," Delphine said out of politeness.

"I have a great deal to account for, Miss Latham." She studied the carpet for a time then went on with, "Callenforth was his name. They did not care for him at all. And of course I thought their opinions of no importance whatsoever."

"I take it you are talking about Lydia, Annabel and Edwin."

The old lady nodded. "I had known the man when I was young." She gave a wry laugh. "We were star-crossed lovers, prevented from being together. Then lo and behold—miracle of miracles—all these years later he reappeared in my life. By then I had agreed to give the children a home. I could hardly refuse since my nephew had willed them to me. They needed to continue their lessons, of course, and I was considering hiring a tutor for them. But my paramour generously—or so I thought at the time—stepped in and offered his services."

"So he taught them for a time?"

"Indeed he did. And what a disaster that turned out to be. He could not stomach the children, nor they him. He was the one who eventually persuaded me to send them away to Brackford House. He loved this relic—"with hands to her bosom she indicated herself—"he needed me, he wanted me all to himself to adore, to cherish, he said, and this of course, is what he promised me when we wed."

"You married him, then?" Delphine said, immediately realizing she was asking the obvious.

"I did, old fool that I was." She sniffed and dabbed at her eyes with a tiny square of lace. And as you said earlier about your relationship with Annabel, I will not belabor you with all the details of my sorry association. Suffice to say I found out it was not I with whom he was in love, but my assets, limited as they were at that time. No sooner did he have the ring on my finger than he changed into a tyrant, giving me no say whatsoever in my affairs."

"If you do not mind my asking, where is your husband now?"

Ernestine Hadfield blew her nose, pocketed her handkerchief and then shocked Delphine with a wicked-looking smile. "Dead as a doornail."

*Oh Lord, did the old dear do the fellow in?* "I am so sorry. Did ---?"

"Heart attack two years after our wedding."

"How dreadful."

"No, no, my dear Miss Latham. Not dreadful … providential." She chuckled. "There is a delicious irony to the whole tale."

"There is?"

"My husband invested—some might say gambled with—the assets he stole from me and did quite nicely thank you. By the time he so very conveniently passed on, he had made me into an exceedingly wealthy widow. So wealthy, in fact, that it was an easy proposition for me to have my solicitors assist me in regaining the Hadfield name.

Delphine shook her head in wonderment. "Well I never," she said under her breath.

"Would you be kind enough to pour us more tea, dear?" Mrs. Hadfield asked. Once they had settled back with their refreshed cups, she said, "I do apologize for regaling you so when all you wished to hear about was Annabel's health."

"But what you have told me has great bearing on Annabel's situation," said Delphine.

Mrs. Hadfield regarded her quizzically over the top of her cup.

"I believe it means that the girl's presence here will present you with no hardship."

"You are right, Miss Latham.

"Has the child been looked at by a doctor?"

"My own ... the day after she arrived. He could find nothing in the way of a physical ailment although he did say she had an abundance of bruises."

"Did your doctor examine her *thoroughly*?"

"If you mean"—she pursed her lips and looked disapprovingly down her long nose—"in an intimate fashion, Miss Latham, no. Absolutely not."

"Of course not. Sorry." Delphine blotted her face with her handkerchief. Lord, what had she been thinking, asking such a question?

"It astonishes me how she found her way here," the old lady said. "And it astonishes me further that she would give me another chance after I sent her away. Although with her refusal to speak to me, perhaps she has decided not to."

"I am certain her sister would never have spoken ill of you, Mrs. Hadfield. As I said I do not know her personally, but I believe her to be an honourable woman."

"A sight more honourable than this foolish old woman."

"Did your doctor offer any opinions, ma'am, about Annabel."

"Yes. He feels there is a mental problem of some type. Hysteria was the word he used. But it is all rather beyond me, I am afraid."

"I do hope she will speak to me," Delphine said.

"She may surprise us all and chatter like a magpie when she sees you."

Delphine felt a trickle of sweat running down the side of her face; she blotted it with her handkerchief. She felt out of sorts all at once. If only she could forget the Fullerton children and their confounded problems. She should have put her foot down long since, told Phillip it was all none of their business. She exhaled a derisive little puff of air. As if she would. She had formed her own attachments to those children and she certainly could not blame Phillip. She could blame herself, though, for not recognizing the depth of Annabel's desperation. Maybe she should have spirited the girl away from that dreadful woman, consequences be damned. Then what, that had been the thing? Lord, it was all so complicated.

"A guinea for your thoughts, Miss Latham."

The old lady's voice brought Delphine back to the present.

"They are hardly worth that, Mrs. Hadfield."

"I must admit I did my best to expunge the memories of the children. I had no desire to spend my remaining days wallowing in guilt." She dunked a piece of biscuit in her tea again and took a few seconds to gum it. "There was positively no going back, I knew. So I forged ahead ... refurbished the entire place ... myself, also." She touched the lace collar of her fashionable gray and mauve frock. "Surrounded myself with everything you see here."

"None of it helped assuage the guilt, however. And then after my husband died and I was once more in control of my own funds I had a revelation. I would send money to Brackwood House to be forwarded on to the children. At least, wherever they had ended up, it would make their lives easier, or so I thought. The first time—I imagine it would have been about a year ago—the Bell woman wrote back immediately, saying all three children were doing exceedingly well and that I could be assured they would benefit no end from my generous contribution." She fell silent and fiddled with a feather of her silver hair.

"May I ask, Mrs. Hadfield, if you sent additional money?"

"Indeed I did, apparently more fool me. Quite a sizeable sum, in fact, and I think there is little speculation as to whose pocket it now resides in."

"You would have records, though, would you not? Evidence of your draft ... or some such---?"

Ernestine Hadfield's shoulders slumped. She shook her head sadly. "None, I fear. Cash-- crisp new bank notes, all of it. I have never been one to trust a bank with my money."

"I see." Delphine mentally shook her head. Fool that the old lady was, indeed. So much for recourse. There clearly was room for none where Mrs. Bell was concerned.

"The whole affair is an abomination, there is no question about it," Ernestine Hadfield continued. She raised her lorgnette and squinted through it at the mantel clock. "Is that twenty to four? I cannot quite make it out."

Delphine acknowledged that it was.

"Then I am sure Annabel will be rousing herself about now. You will find her room up the stairs you saw when Mrs. Boot let you in. The third door on the right."

Upstairs moments later, and outside the room in question, Delphine knocked, not expecting a response, but wanting to warn the girl she had a visitor. Entering hesitantly, she closed the door behind herself.

It was a pleasant, airy room with a brass bed. The wallpaper and curtains were decorated with garlands of red and pink roses and next to the window was a wing-backed chair upholstered in dusky pink moquette. Annabel was seated in it, her legs curled beneath her, a book open in her lap. She appeared not to have heard the door and kept on reading—or was it staring?—at her book.

"Annabel." Delphine spoke softly. "It is Miss Latham." She approached the chair. "How are you, dear?"

Nothing.

"I have been having a nice chat with your great-aunt. She thought that perhaps you and I might ..." Lord, the girl was like a statue, sitting there ... not a muscle moving, her chin on her chest, her hair a thick curtain covering her face. "Annabel, can you talk to me?"

Nothing.

At the chair, now, Delphine leaned down and touched the girl's arm. "I want to help you, dear. I know something dreadful must have happened to you. But no matter how awful, you can tell me. I am your friend, dear."

Nothing.

Delphine adjusted her skirts and knelt. She took the book from Annabel's lap and put it down beside the chair. Then she reached over and gently brushed Annabel's hair back and looked into her face.

She heard the sharp intake of her own breath. Great God in Heaven ... it was a spectral face, almost transparent in its whiteness. And the eyes, oh Lord, the eyes. Where was the life ... the spark?

Where had Annabel gone?

### CHAPTER FIFTY-SEVEN
### *July 1890*
### *Plenty, District of Saskatchewan, Northwest Territories, Canada*

Leaning over the side rail of William's cot, I kissed his cheek. The lavender scent of his night shirt mingled with the smell of goat's milk and of the cornstarch with which I had dusted him after his bath. In the waning nine o'clock light, I straightened and folded my arms, my head tipped in contemplation of this blond rosy cheeked cherub who not only smelled sweet, but looked sweet. "Good night, little man", I whispered. Already teetering on the edge of sleep, the baby gave a tiny smile, then his eyelids fluttered and closed.

The wide open window beyond whose screen the ubiquitous mosquitoes gathered provided not an ounce of relief. I exhaled forcefully, aiming the hot air up over my face. Ye Gods, I was sweating like a farmhand. I undid several buttons at the neck of my lawn shirtwaist and mopped my face and throat with one of the freshly-laundered muslin nappies from the stack on top of the chest close by. Then I lit the oil lamp and turned down the wick until the flame cast just the barest flicker of light.

The baby made a hiccoughing sound that struck me comically. A sweet-natured, contented little fellow, he often made me laugh. Without that laughter these past weeks, I surely would have descended into utter despair.

At nine months William was thriving, every day making the kind of strides babies make: discovering textures and tastes; exploring everything with wonderment in his blue eyes; testing the strength of his chubby legs. His gurgles were becoming words; the tiny white buds in his gums were turning into teeth.

I felt my throat tighten. All those strides, and no mother to see them. Sad ... so sad. Sadder still, the realization that he would never know his mama.

I settled into Katerina's rocking chair by the window and gazed out into the night. William and I were alone in the house. As usual, Johann Brecht had taken his meal by himself and left directly after it to go who knew where ... perhaps his offices over the warehouse. And if he proved true to form, he would return about eleven.

Mrs. Dykstra, the newest member of the household—albeit a temporary one whose tenure was anyone's guess—was out visiting her daughter and family across town and would not be back until late.

The middle-aged, spare and stern-looking woman belonged to the same congregation as Johann Brecht. Their recently-constructed *Tabernacle Of The New Life,* located five miles west of town and housed in a square clapboard structure bearing little resemblance to a church had become Katerina's final resting place. Her grave in the white-picket-fenced enclosure at the back of the building, and overlooking the vast and lonely sea of the prairie, had the dubious distinction of being the Tabernacle's first. Thank the Lord, I thought, rocking vigorously, she had not been afforded the same moon-and-lantern-lit farmyard burial as her baby daughter.

Clearly curious about the Tabernacle and its peculiar customs, almost every citizen in Plenty had attended the funeral. From all accounts, only marriages and baptisms were required to be conducted by the sect's Regina-based head pastor, so the burial service—short, simple and strange, without music, without flowers decorating church or coffin, and with none of the pomp and circumstance of the Church of England with which I was so familiar—had been overseen by one of the elders.

When Mrs. Dykstra had introduced herself after the burial, I recognized her—together with several others in the German contingent—as one of the women involved in last summer's pig-killing festivities at the farm. "*Mein* husband and I are friends of Mr. Brecht," she had said. "I come back for funeral tea, then I stay."

"Stay?" I had been unsure what the woman meant.

"*Ya.* I am to help with cleaning and cooking."

"And how long, may I ask, will you be staying?"

"*Ach*, 'tis hard to say. Maybe five ... six months, I think."

Hallelujah!. My relief was so overwhelming, my heart missed a beat. I would not, at least for the near future, be put in the position of living alone in the house with Johann Brecht. Not that I was afraid of him, or even uncomfortable around him. But simply stated, I was a spinster and he a widower and I had no desire to be the object of gossip. "I see," I said in a noncommittal manner.

"There are many young women of our congregation," Mrs. Dykstra went on, "who will be—how do you say it? Setting their bonnets for our Johann. *Ya,* six months, I think, and he will marry again."

"Marry?" Ye Gods, Katerina was hardly cold in her grave.

"In meantime, Johann call on me for the helping, thinking you will *haf* hands too full with baby and with store," the woman had continued. "*Ach*, but you are lucky Home girl to be in household of such a man."

*Lucky you say? What in Hades is lucky about being trapped in servitude and being parted from the people you love most and not knowing when, if ever, you will see them again and losing one of the few allies you have in the world?* "Indeed I am, Mrs. Dykstra, so lucky I am positively beside myself," I said in a voice whose sarcasm clearly went over the woman's head.

On the score of the hands too full with baby and store statement, Mrs. Dykstra had certainly been right, though, I thought now, bringing the rocking chair to a standstill. I rolled my shoulders and a band of pain ran from one arm across my back and down the other arm. My feet burned and felt too big for my boots; I unlaced them and eased them off, then wiggled my toes in relief. I had not realized until now just how weary I felt. Today, William had been particularly active and inquisitive. Every day after breakfast with his father the baby accompanied me to the store, where Sally and I took turns juggling customers and keeping an eye on him.

Feeling fidgety, I rose and stood at the window looking out. Faint strains of organ music drifted on the air; the choir practice at the new Congregational church must be running late. A pair of dogs yapped back and forth in an oddly lethargic manner; a horse and cart clattered over the ruts in the wide, dusty street. I heard children and in the waning light I managed to make out a couple of boys darting in and out of various shop doorways, eventually reaching the scaffolding in front of the skeleton of a two-storied, false-fronted building at the far end of the block, which once complete would house Plenty's first saloon.

Rumor had it the railhead—presently at Blackstone, some forty miles distant—might be extended during the next year to within half a mile of Plenty. Consequently, there were many more shops now than there had been six months ago. At the opposite end of the block from the saloon, a solicitor—whom Johann Brecht had already hired to represent his interests—had set up. A millinery and a feed store flanked Sally's father's undertaking business, while a cobbler's and a cabinet-maker's shops sandwiched the offices of the *Plenty Chronicle*.

A light went on in those offices now. I could make out the outline of the huge printing press which sat a couple of feet back from the store front's window and the silhouette of a man bending over it. Elijah Standish, no doubt, setting the type for tomorrow's issue.

*Untimely Death of Leading Citizen's Wife*, the headline had read that June Wednesday six weeks earlier. Untimely. I made a derisive sound at the back of my throat. Mama. Papa. And now Katerina. Yet another in a succession of untimely deaths.

I touched the carved crest of Katerina's chair, setting it in motion. After a moment or two of mournful creaking it came to a stop. And I remembered, with a lump in my throat, how Katerina had often looked sitting here, rocking aimlessly or staring off, with nothing but hopelessness in her eyes.

I sat back down in the chair, now, and gazed into the oil lamp's flickering flame. Katerina's life had not been all sadness. Before the babies, there had been good times. I felt a smile tug at my mouth. Oh the stories we had shared ... silly stories that had us giggling like school girls. And those English lessons ... how we had split our sides laughing at Katerina's outlandish pronunciations.

"Oh Katerina ... Katerina," I said out loud. "What a waste." I brought the chair to a halt and sat very still. Tears welled in my eyes and spilled down my cheeks. Too exhausted to play the stoic anymore, I gave myself up to my grief and sobbed quietly until I felt I had no more tears left to cry. Closing my eyes, I pushed off with my foot and gradually felt myself drifting ... drifting ...

*I stood on a clifftop pulling with all my might on a rope to which Annabel and Edwin were both clinging. The rope was slipping ... slipping ... slipping out of my grip. Frantic, I screamed, "No ... no." Then someone grabbed me from behind and yanked me back and I flailed my arms and screamed again, screamed and screamed and a far-off voice called, "Lydia ... Lydia".* And all at once, with a thudding heart, I was awake and I felt the rocking chair move beneath me.

A blinding light dazzled me and I brought my hands up to shield my eyes. "Mrs. Dkystra?" I said with a flash of annoyance. "Would you please move the lamp. I cannot see a blessed thing."

The light was instantly moved to one side and a face came into focus. Not Mrs. Dykstra's, that was for certain, but Johann Brecht's.

"You make strange sounds," he said, leaning in, holding the lamp high for a good view of me, his troubled eyes peering into my face. "You are all right?"

"Ye gods"—I shot a look at the cot—"did I wake William?

"*Nein.* He sleeps like angel." He went to the chest of drawers and returned the lamp to its usual spot. "Besides, the sounds you make are small ... what you call ... whimpers ... I think."

Whimpers? How odd, I thought. In the dream I had heard myself shrieking at the top of my lungs. "What time is it?" I asked.

"Just past quarter to ten?"

"Is Mrs. Dykstra ---?"

"No. Not yet. Not until eleven. I tell her tonight she is to take her time. Her son-in-law will bring her back here, she says."

He tiptoed to the cot-side and gazed down on his son. "He is a fine boy, *ya?*" he said softly.

"He is indeed." The room seemed more suffocating than ever, now, and I fanned myself with my hand.

"You are fond of him?"

*Of course I am fond of him. Why do you ask such a foolish question? And what are you doing home so early pestering me like this.* "Yes, of course."

Johann Brecht leaned down and pulled the sheet up over his son. "It cools off, now, I think."

I licked my sweat-salted lips and rolled my eyes in disbelief.

Straightening, turning back to face me, Johann Brecht passed a reflective hand over the moustache he had once again grown. "My boy needs a mother," he said. "Every child needs a mother."

From what Mrs. Dkystra had said, I thought, he would have no trouble finding one for little William.

"Do you not agree?" Johann Brecht fixed me with a disconcertingly piercing look.

"I do," I said uncertainly.

"Come, then." Johann Brecht returned to my chair-side and extended a hand as if he expected me to take it.

But I found the thought of my hand in his discomfiting. And so I swiftly rose and turned to face the window.

Johann Brecht touched my shoulder and said pleasantly, "We go down to the kitchen, *ya,* and have cup of your good, strong tea and talk about it."

I followed him from the room and suddenly bone weary, trudged after him down the stairs. What on earth did he mean ... talk about what? The merits of the various ladies of the congregation? The selection of Katerina's replacement? Surely he would not make me a part of such a decision.

At the kitchen table minutes later, he offered me a biscuit from the open tin.

"No thank you."

He did not take a biscuit either, but sipped on his tea and then leaned back in his chair and ran a hand through his pale hair, his eyes fastened on mine. "Do you know why I have hired Mrs. Dykstra?"

"To help alleviate my workload. And I am most grateful." I drummed on the tabletop, feeling unaccountably nervous.

He edged forward and rested his elbows on the table. "No ... not the workload, although I am glad to be of help and pleased by your gratitude. She is here, Mrs. Dkystra, to still the tongues."

As if I did not know. "The wagging tongues," I said.

"*Ya.* You understand. But Mrs. Dylkstra tells me today she cannot carry on here for more than two or three months. She has sick child who is in need of its mother. This makes ... what you call ... dilemma, *ya?*"

I almost responded with, "*Ya,*" but caught myself. "It does indeed," I said.

"I am respected member of community. You are respectable young woman ... chaste young woman"—he strummed his bottom lip, not taking his eyes off me for an instant—"and I of course would not wish your reputation to be ...how do they say? ... compromised."

I shifted uncomfortably in my seat.

"But I have solution, Lydia." He reached across the table suddenly and captured my hands in his, so shocking me that for a moment I could not move. "Solution for me ... solution for you ... solution for William." I eased from his grip and he flushed slightly. "Forgive me, I did not mean to startle you."

I made a show of brushing something off my skirt. "You did startle me," I finally said with an ill-disguised note of peevishness in my voice. I picked up my cup and sipped on the cold tea for a time. I was exhausted. The last thing I wanted was to sit here chatting with Johann Brecht.

"So sorry. I think you are tired. But I must tell you what I have decided."

"Very well, Mr. Brecht," I said wearily.

"Johann ... you must call me Johann, now."

My teeth clenched. *If you do not let me go to my bed, I will call you something a good deal different than Johann and you will think me anything but respectable and chaste.* "Very well, Johann."

He leaned back in his chair, hooked his thumbs under his lapels and looking mightily pleased with himself said, "When next the pastor comes through the district ... end of November ... beginning of December, you will become mother to my son ... and wife to me."

## CHAPTER FIFTY-EIGHT
### *September 1890*
### *Latham Residence, Yorkshire, England*

Unimpeded by corsets or bustle and wearing a walking skirt of her own design and construction, Delphine strode along the lane beside her brother. Every so often he slowed his pace, enabling her to catch up with him. They had left the house half an hour earlier—after their Saturday breakfast—agreeing that a walk on the common might help them sort out their thoughts.

Already Delphine felt energized by the crisp September air. She loved autumn. The smells of loam and damp foliage. The beauty of a landscape daubed with russet and crimson and gold. The rustling sound the thick carpet of fallen leaves made when she hitched up her skirts and kicked her way through them like a child.

A flock of noisy blackbirds swooshed across the clear blue dome of the sky. Every year at this time they returned from their summer sojourn on the Continent. Mystified as always by the uncanniness of this migration, Delphine stopped to watch them, and then had to run to catch up with Phillip who was waiting at a bend in the lane.

"So"—he smiled down at her—"did all that leaf-kicking and cogitating of the heavens trigger any great revelations?"

"Afraid not." She set off again and he followed suit. "To be honest, I was not even thinking about it all. But now I am. What about you? Have you come up with any brilliant solutions?"

"I am working on it, Delphie." Forging ahead of her, he thrust his hands deeper into his overcoat pockets and veered off onto a narrow path that wended its way over a sandstone outcrop and up the bracken-and-heather-covered slope towards a grove of silver birches. Presently, Delphine fell in behind him, stepping cautiously over roots and rocks. "I did tell you, did I not," she said, "that the old lady made it clear she was quite willing to have Annabel stay on with her?"

"Yes you did." Phillip said.

"Permanently, I mean."

"Yes." Phillip pushed his hair out of his eyes. "But the situation really is untenable. We have a very sick child. And we have a very elderly woman. I just do not see how Ernestine Hadfield can possibly ---"

"I agree, she cannot be counted on to continue to take care of the girl. But she certainly has the wherewithal, Phillip. I mean if there were someone that could be hired—an expert, perhaps, in the field of whatever it is we are dealing with—I know Mrs. Hadfield would be more than happy to foot the bill."

"Hmmm. An expert you say." Phillip indicated a fallen log alongside the path. "Time for a breather." He took off his scarf, spread it out on the damp bark and they sat.

"There must be someone who has had experience with this type of thing," said Delphine. "Hysteria, Mrs. Hadfield's doctor called it?"

Phillip tugged on his lower lip. "I read something recently about a French chap. Charcot was his name. Doctor Jean Charcot. He has been using hypnotism to treat this sort of thing."

"Mesmerism, you mean?"

"It is the same thing, Delphie."

"But it is all hocus-pocus, surely. Drawing room nonsense."

"Not necessarily. Some is bound to be, of course. After all, the world is full of charlatans. But hypnotism is gaining recognition, Delphie, as a valuable tool." He was silent for a time, then turned and glanced sidelong at her. "You know old thing, you just might have hit on something here."

Puzzled, Delphine lifted her shoulders. Before she had a chance to comment, Phillip continued.

"There is another chap, too—a Viennese doctor I know of ... a Josef Breuer—who takes an entirely different approach than hypnotism. He contends that if he can persuade patients to talk without inhibition about their experiences, confront the trauma so to speak, that led to their neuroses, then healing can begin."

"All well and good, Phillip, for someone who can speak."

"She can, Delphie. Remember, you talked to the housekeeper and cook at Hadfield Hall ... and the two servant girls. And they all said Annabel had exchanged a word or two with each of them. It is just a matter of getting her to really converse."

"Just? Hardly."

"Bad choice of words." Phillip passed a thoughtful hand over his face. "Do you remember Reggie Fardoe, the chap I roomed with at McGill?"

"Yes."

"I should see if I can get a number for him, and ring him."

Delphine chuckled. The fact that Ernestine Hadfield had a telephone must have made an impression on Phillip, for it was not too long after Delphine's visit to Hadfield Hall that he had decided to have one of the devices installed. "I swear you are besotted with that instrument," she said.

"I am impressed alright and no denying it. For one thing, think of the lives that are going to be saved. People can actually ring for me when there is an emergency."

"Only those with the money to afford the service, though, that is the rub."

"Oh, but soon—I read it somewhere—there will be public telephones accessible to all and sundry. Anyway, where was I? You have made me lose my train of thought."

"Annabel ... Reggie Fardoe. You should ring him, you said. But why on earth would you want to do that?"

"Brains, Delphie. He went into neurology, you see. If he cannot help, I am sure he will be able to recommend someone who can. And I warrant he is well up on the works of the good doctors Charcot and Breuer."

"If you *are* going to contact him—and it sounds like a good idea to me—you should do so immediately. I mean look at the amount of time that has passed. You cannot keep Lydia hanging on forever, can you? You will simply have to tell her something."

"I did send off a short note to her a few days ago."

"Really, you said nothing about it to me."

"It was not worth mentioning, Delphie. I wrote a lot of nonsense, actually. Said you had finally seen the children and that they were well, but that neither had been able to put pen to paper themselves. Felt like a rotter, lying like that."

Delphine got up, fidgety all of a sudden. "I know the feeling well. I cannot keep on lying to Edwin, either."

"I know." Phillip rose wearily. "Shall we go back? I have no more stomach for exercise."

Delphine took the lead. "If only we could get them together ... Edwin and Annabel," she said over her shoulder. "It is for certain having her brother at her side would do Annabel more good than any neurologist or mesmerist could ever do." She aimed her toe at a pebble and watched it sail through the air. "Whatever dreadful thing happened to her to render her almost mute, how could she not speak were her brother Edwin to throw himself into her arms. And then, after that, someone—perhaps Reggie Fardoe or another doctor ... a friend ... whomever she trusted enough—could do as your Viennese doctor does and help her exorcize her demons."

"Delphine"—Phillip stopped her with a hand on her shoulder—"you are a positive genius."

She looked up at him. "I am?"

"By Jove, you are. You have given us our solution." Phillip rubbed his hands together like Shylock about to count his shekels. "It is time for drastic action. Time to give the Mesdames Bell and Chistlegate a dose of their own nasty medicine. I say we kidnap Master Edwin Fullerton."

## CHAPTER FIFTY-NINE
### *Hadfield Hall, Sussex, England*
### *September 1890*

"So, may I ask if you are you in agreement with our plan, Mrs. Hadfield?"

Late on this Tuesday afternoon following the weekend Delphine and Phillip had hatched their plot, Delphine was once again in the now-familiar, cluttered and capacious drawing room, and about to partake of the tea, cucumber sandwiches and assortment of cakes set out on the table.

Delphine's telephone call on the previous Sunday had prepared the old lady for this latest visit. Her only proviso had been that this time Delphine stay the night at Hadfield Hall.

Delphine had just finished telling the woman of her plans to go to West Kirby three days hence. Some time on that Friday, she had told her, she would take Edwin aside and prepare him for what was to happen. Then on the Saturday morning, she would ask Gladys Chistlegate if she might take the boy for a walk along the promenade. Delphine had done so before, so it would not be deemed out of the ordinary. What would be out-of-the-ordinary, though, was that they would not return to *Sea Winds*. Instead, at a designated spot and time, they would rendezvous with the same hansom driver who had brought Delphine from the station the day before; he would transport them to Chester —a good twenty miles from West Kirby—and from there they would take the mid-day train south-east to Burgess Hill, and Hadfield Hall.

"Agreeable, Miss Latham?"—Ernestine Hadfield clapped delightedly—"I am so agreeable I am positively beside myself. Our young Edwin's place is with his family, certainly not with those despicable Chistlegate people."

Delphine let out a relieved breath. "Wonderful," she said, "I had hoped that would be your reaction."

"What about my great-niece, Lydia. Can we do something about her, also ... bring her back from that heathen backwater?"

"I really have no idea, Mrs. Hadfield. Phillip and I have had no discussion on that score yet. But I do know she was indentured for a five-year term, as are all the Home children. And I imagine breaking that indentureship would not be a simple proposition."

"Hmmm." Ernestine Hadfield nodded thoughtfully. "I never should have agreed to her deuced scheme. But she so desperately wanted to stay with them." The old lady made a steeple of her hands and pressed them to her chin. "Perhaps if I had insisted she go into service here, in the county, then it would have not been at all difficult to re-claim her. Ah well, Miss Latham, no earthly use dwelling on the past, eh? It is the future we are concerned with, now."

"Indeed it is."

"And will you tell the woman ... Gertrude ...?" Ernestine Hadfield tapped herself on the temples as if to free the thought.

"Oh, you mean Gladys Chistlegate. Absolutely. It may seem cruel, but I shall take great satisfaction in doing so. But not in person, of course. I shall leave a letter. I shall not go into great detail. I shall merely explain that the boy has been returned to his rightful place and include a few well-chosen words hinting at the illegality of trading in orphans. For certain, that will preclude any further actions by the Chistlegates."

"Will they not go running to the Bell woman at the very first opportunity, though? If nothing else, they will surely want their money returned."

Delphine had just taken a bite of her cucumber sandwich. She chewed quickly and swallowed. "Of course, you are right, Mrs. Hadfield. I had not even thought of that. But I suppose even if they do, our hand will not be revealed to Mrs. Bell."

Ernestine Hadfield leaned forward, her rheumy eyes all at once bright with curiosity. "Your hand, you say. Oh do tell what you have in store for that dreadful woman."

"Sorry, I am misleading you." Delphine dabbed at her mouth with her serviette. "There is, as yet, no hand to reveal. Oh there most certainly will be, if my brother has anything to do with it. But at present all our efforts are directed towards reuniting Edwin and Annabel."

"Quite so," Mrs. Hadfield said. "And speaking of Annabel, I did tell you did I not—when you telephoned—that I had something to report."

"Yes. But that you did not want to go into it over the telephone and ---"

"A useful instrument, to be sure," the old lady cut in, "but wearisome to someone of my years. When it comes to lengthy conversations, face-to-face ones are so much easier on the voice and ears."

Delphine dipped her head in agreement. "If you recall," she said, "I, too, mentioned that my brother had some new thoughts about the girl."

Finished with her tea, Mrs. Hadfield retrieved her lorgnette from her lap and regarded Delphine with a distinctly mischievous look. "Shall I tell first, or shall you? My news is quite interesting. But perhaps yours ---"

"Oh, no, please, do go on."

"Very well." The old lady shifted in her seat and then with a smile that could only be called smug, said, "Annabel is speaking."

Delphine moved to the edge of the settee. "Mercy, Mrs. Hadfield. To you? To whom ex ---?"

"To a dog. A rather odd little mongrel, actually."

"A dog? But what ... how ...?"

Ernestine Hadfield motioned her into silence. "If you would be so kind as to summon Mrs. Boot—the bell pull is over there by the fireplace—I shall have her give you all the details."

—

"So there we was stood by the lily pond with Annabel starin' into it with that proper queer, *gone off-somewhere* look about 'er an' me keepin' a weather eye on 'er o' course, like the mistress 'ere, says I should 'cause Lord knows what the young miss might take it into 'er 'ead to get up to ..." Mrs. Boot stopped for a wheeze of air, clapping herself on the chest as she drew it in. Next to her on the settee, Delphine touched her arm reassuringly.

"Take your time," Mrs. Hadfield said. "Have a sip of your tea."

"Thank you, madam." Mrs. Boot drank thirstily, not stopping until her cup was empty.

"Now, carry on."

"Then all of a sudden like, out of nowhere come this mangy-lookin' little black beast. 'Ardly 'igher than six pen'orth o' copper. A-jumpin' an' a-yippin' an' a-waggin' an a-tryin' to lick us faces, it was, an' stinkin' some'at fierce. All over the both of us, mostly young Annabel on account of I were shovin' the little varmint off me. Get away, you flea-bag you, I shouts—musta been fairly snewin' with 'em, the filthy state it were in—Get off 'ome where you belongs, I shouts." Mrs. Boot paused, sucked in air again, and nodded at the teapot. "I shall 'ave another spot or two, madam, if yer do not mind." Given the go-ahead, the housekeeper poured herself more tea and slurped it down. As she returned her cup to its saucer, Delphine prompted with, "And did the dog go aw---?"

"About to, 'twere. Tail atween its legs, them eyes all sorrowful, ears 'angin' ever so long, if yer know what I mean. Then all of a sudden like, young miss says, *No, let 'er be.* Could 'ave knocked me over with a feather, I tell you. 'an she picks that mutt up, 'olds the thing like a baby an' says, *'ello, you poor little dear. We must get you some food and clean you up.* An ', Lord love us, before yer knows it I am in the kitchen bathin' the beast. Took a right scourin' to get rid o' all them fleas, I can tell yer. An' she 'as got food an' water dishes an' a blanket all lined up, 'as Miss Annabel, an' she says, *I shall call 'er Dolly.*" It was time for another pause for air.

"Rather a sweet little thing, actually, is our mysterious Dolly," Mrs. Hadfield said. "Sent by Providence, I should not doubt."

Bemused, Delphine said, "She is still here, then, this dog?"

"Goin' on four weeks, now," Mrs. Boot answered.

"Thankfully, no one has come forward to claim the animal," Ernestine Hadfield added. "I say thankfully, because the two—Annabel and Dolly—are now inseparable."

"So, Annabel is conversing normally, now, with everyone in the household?" Delphine addressed both women.

The housekeeper opened her mouth to respond, but Mrs. Hadfield cut her off, asking her to kindly return to her duties.

Once Mrs. Boot had left the room, the old lady said, "To answer your question, Miss Latham, Annabel is conversing normally, but only with Dolly. She is forever prattling on to that little creature. But as a rule, only when she is alone with her. At dinner, as you will see for yourself this evening, Dolly or not, Annabel is far from chatty."

"So we are to come face-to-face again at dinner. Will she know me this time, I wonder."

"She has put names to our faces, now, so perhaps she will to yours, Miss Latham. Oh, and by the way, she *does* say a few words to us. *Thank you, Good morning, Goodnight* etcetera ... oh, and *fine* ... she is always fine when one asks her."

"What does she talk to this dog about, Mrs. Hadfield? Anything of consequence? Anything about what happened to her?"

"Lord, no. All idle chatter, from what we have have overheard. The weather ... a book she has read. A pretty bird or a butterfly she has seen ... where they will walk on a particular day ... how her embroidery is progressing. That type of thing."

"I see."

"Although I cannot vouch for the content of her conversation when she and Dolly are alone in the child's room. Call me a silly old woman, but I saw no reason to forbid Annabel from having the animal sleep with her."

"Nor would I, Mrs. Hadfield. She has found a friend ... a confidante of sorts."

"You are pleasantly surprised by my news, I trust."

"Oh, very much so. And it makes me think that my brother's ideas regarding Annabel—which I should like to tell you about—may have even more relevance, now."

———

"Pass the gravy to our visitor, child," Ernestine Hadfield said.

Annabel slid the boat across the damask cloth to Delphine, but not before she had dropped a sliver of roast beef into the mouth of the sleek-coated black dog sitting next to her. Mrs. Catterly, the cook, had served dinner to the three at the round and *much cozier*—in Ernestine Hadfield's words—oak table in the breakfast room, rather than at the dining room's nine-foot long rosewood table where conversation was a challenge, at the best of times.

So far, five minutes into the meal, Delphine had managed to elicit from Annabel a *Good evening*, a *Fine*, as well as several *Thank you's* in response to various passings back and forth of serving bowls and plates .

The *Good Evening* had followed Delphine's, "Do you remember me, Annabel?"

Foolishly, she had expected recognition to dawn in the girl's gray eyes. None had. And Delphine had felt a momentary rush of anger. She had wanted to shake the girl and say, *What silly game are you playing? Why are you trying to punish me? Please talk to me.*

But as swiftly as the anger had come, it left, replaced by compassion, hope, too, that Edwin's arrival here would bring Annabel back. Not to mention Phillip's experts. Mrs. Hadfield had thought the idea of bringing such a person here an excellent one. "But let us first see what influence young Edwin's presence has on her," she had said.

Delphine caught Annabel's eye again, now. Nothing but the mildest of ... what was it ... interest? Hardly. Acknowledgment then. But obligatory acknowledgment of a dinner guest with whom the child felt no connection whatsoever.

Mercy but these long silences were nerve-wracking. Mrs. Hadfield was clearly used to them and was concentrating all her efforts on her meal.

The situation was so bizarre, hurtful, too, if the truth were known. To think that she and Annabel had shared all those hours at *Sea Winds,* enjoyed each other's company so, developed such affection for each other, and the memory of it all had vanished or become locked away behind some impenetrable wall. Delphine took up her knife and fork and regarded the food on her plate, wondering how she would manage to eat with all these thoughts churning around in her head and a feeling in her stomach close to nausea.

Dolly came to the rescue. All at once her nose was in Delphine's lap, and not only was her stubby tail—which had an end on it like a flue brush— wagging, her entire body was. "Oh my goodness"—Delphine laughed and stroked the dog's head—"I have a friend."

"A little beggar more like it," Ernestine Hadfield leaned to one side for a better view of the animal.

"But a dear thing," Delphine said.

"You may give our Dolly a tidbit, if you wish."

Delphine looked up at Ernestine Hadfield, astonished. "Are you sure it is all ---?"

"It would make her very happy ... and someone else, also." Mrs. Hadfield did not need to say more. Delphine glanced in Annabel's direction. The girl perched on the edge of her seat, grinning, her eyes alight with interest, now.

"There you are, Dolly." Delphine popped a piece of beef in the dog's mouth. It was gone in a trice.

"Say thank you to the lady," Annabel said.

The jaws of both Ernestine Hadfield and Delphine dropped.

Dolly let out a little yip.

"Good girl," said Annabel.

And Delphine leaned down again and stroked the dog. Sent by Providence, for certain.

All that remained, now, was for Providence to smile on the kidnapping plan.

## CHAPTER SIXTY
### *September 1890*
### *West Kirby, Northwest Coast, Cheshire, England*

Edwin closed the front door quietly and tiptoed to where Delphine stood in front of the hallstand mirror adjusting the pins in her hat. "It is in the bush by next-door's gate," he whispered. "Nobody saw me leave it there ... I was ever so careful."

*It* was the small suitcase containing the barest necessities that she had brought with her the day before. She had planned on leaving it behind in her room so as not to arouse suspicion, but Edwin had come up with the idea of secreting the case for later retrieval. "This way you will not lose any of your things," he had said.

She mussed his curls. "You certainly are a clever fellow to have thought of hiding it. Now, get your kite, dear." Folded up and propped against the newel post at the bottom of the stairs, the toy was meant to give credence to this morning's jaunt.

"I have it, Miss Latham. Now may we please go?"

"Just as soon as we say au revoir to your ---"

"Jailer," Edwin cut in and then covered his mouth with his free hand as if he had said a dirty word.

Delphine patted his head. Thank the Lord he had developed not an iota of attachment to the Chistlegates. He really was an amazing boy. Comical. Affectionate. Resilient. And a born thespian.

"The curtain is about to go up Master Fullerton," she said softly, then she called out, "We are off now, for our kite-flying, Mrs. Chistlegate."

"I 'ave been givin' things a bit more thought," the woman answered, wiping her hands on her apron as she entered the hall from the direction of the kitchen. "An' I am not at all sure about you takin' my boy chasin' about down there on the shore with all them waves an' all that wind."

Delphine's heart missed a beat. Edwin's face fell. Nothing could have prepared either of them for this.

"I know I said hit was alright when you asked me last night," the woman went on, "but 'e's got a bit of a sniffle, 'as my little man."

"He has?" Delphine heard herself say. "He seems perfectly al ..." She stopped herself, glimpsing something at the back of the woman's eyes and in the next breath recognizing it as jealousy, pure and simple. Edwin had made no bones about the fact that he enjoyed—perhaps even preferred—Delphine's company. Lord above, that enjoyment might well prove to be their undoing. What to do, about it now though, that was the thing. Delphine cast about for something to say, but Edwin saved her the job.

"No," he said, marching over to Gladys Chistlegate. "I shan't stop in. You said I could go." He stamped his foot, barely missing hers and she backed away slightly. "You promised."

"Now *lambikins*"—the woman moved her hands in a placatory gesture —"Mother may 'ave said it but she did not hexactly promise. An' you know 'ow poorly you 'ave been an' ---"

"I have no sniffles." Edwin presented his nose for examination, pulling it up by its tip. "See ... positively no snot."

"Uh-hmmm." Gladys Chistlegate pursed her lips. "Mother sees."

"You never let me have have fun anymore." He hung his head, sniffed loudly and made a sobbing sound. "I shall probably die before I have a chance to fly my kite again."

"There, there, my little sweetling, do not take on so." She brushed away the tears that, amazingly, Edwin had managed to produce.

"May I please please"—he drew out the word—"go, dearest Mama?"

Clearly torn between the desire to assert her dominance and the need to have the boy's approval, she chewed on her lower lip for a long moment. Finally, she said, "Oh, halright then. Just as long as Miss Jones 'as you back 'ere in hexactly one hour."

Delphine caught Edwin's look of triumph as she said, "Of course, Mrs. Chistlegate. Rest assured, I shall take extra special care of your son."

"Au revoir, dearest Mama," Edwin called over his shoulder as he and Delphine exited the front door.

Moments later, they were down the steps. Edwin hurried to retrieve Delphine's suitcase. And then without a backward glance at *Sea Winds,* they set off along the street.

## CHAPTER SIXTY-ONE
### *September 1890*
### *Latham Residence, Yorkshire, England*

About the time Delphine and Edwin boarded the train on that September morning, Phillip headed down his drive to meet Harry Stratton, the postman.

"Another letter from Canada," the fellow called out. When he reached Phillip he did not immediately relinquish the envelope, but scrutinized it in his usual nosy manner. "Relation of yours?" he asked.

Phillip could have put him in his place and told him to mind his own damned business, but as always, the sight of the letter made his heart sing. "Something along those lines," he said, thinking that Lydia's letter must have crossed with the note he had sent her at the beginning of the month.

Once in his study, he settled comfortably in the armchair by the window, poured himself a glass of sherry, and with nervous fingers ripped open the missive. He read aloud under his breath.

"31st August, 1890. Dear Phillip, I have not felt like putting pen to paper for quite some time now since there have been no letters from you or the children to answer. I fear you may have abandoned my cause and I worry every waking hour about Annabel and Edwin.

Things have taken a turn for the very worst for me. Now I am well and truly trapped and what was to have been three years and four months more of this servitude has all at once turned into a lifetime. Several weeks ago Mr. Brecht informed me that as soon as the head pastor from the Regina headquarters of his church makes his semi-annual visit to Plenty in late November or early December, he will have him marry us."

Momentarily stunned, Phillip let the sheet of paper fall from his hand. "Marry us," he said, dumbly shaking his head. "Marry us," he repeated, his voice rising. "What in Hades …?" He took up the letter again and forced himself to read on.

"How could a child be made to enter into a marriage, you are bound to ask. The truth is I am no child, but a woman of twenty-three years as of this July." Phillip smiled in spite of himself. *I know that my dearest girl, have known it for months, now.* "I came to this place under false pretenses, having passed myself off at Brackford House—by means of a forged birth certificate and other subterfuges—as a thirteen-year-old. It was the only way, I thought, for my siblings and I to be able to stay together. Sometime last year, in a moment of rashness, I divulged my true age to Mr. Brecht and thus betrayed myself. Being indentured to him, I must obey him, of course. He is a decent sort and I have tried to persuade him these past weeks to consider one of the many eager female candidates in the town. But since I have been such a good mother to his child and he holds me in high regard, he says, he must have me for his wife."

Phillip paused long enough to drain the contents of his glass, then read on: "I see no possible solution. Escape is out of the question; I have no funds to pursue such a course. The few dollars I have managed to scrape together would get me no further than the railhead at Blackstone, some forty miles distant. And unfortunately, I have no rich friends on whose largesse I can count. If I had only myself to think about, I would run away, but if something unfortunate were to happen to me, where would that leave Annabel and Edwin? At least this way, they will know my whereabouts. I shall not give up. Perhaps I shall have a revelation and think of an answer to my dilemma. I am uncertain what this will mean to our correspondence. I pray you will not abandon me. Your friend, Lydia."

Phillip dropped the letter as if scalded. "Damn it to Hell?" He leaped to his feet and began pacing, raking a frantic hand through his hair. But she could not … he would not … Would not what? Allow it? But how could he stop it? It happened all the time, this subjugation of young women into marriage. And how could he—all these thousands of miles away—do anything about it? She might as well be marrying the *Man on The Moon.*

*Oh Lydia, Lydia, my dearest girl, what am I to do?* He hesitated in his tracks. *Thousands of miles away.* He massaged his temples with his knuckles. *Think. Think. You have brains. Top of your class at McGill. Finished medical school a year ahead of your peers.* He pounded a fist against his palm.

At that moment the telephone rang and his heart jumped into his mouth. He returned to his desk, taking a couple of calming breaths before lifting the receiver and stating his number.

"Oh so glad I caught you in."

Phillip groaned inwardly. No mistaking the deep female voice. Harriet Bell … the last person in the world to whom he wanted to talk. The person— damn it all—responsible for the wreckage of Lydia's life and that of her siblings. "What is it?" he asked, with no attempt at civility.

"Sorry to bother you at home, doctor. I know this is your Saturday off, but I wonder if you would be able to give us an hour or two this afternoon? Doctor Mathers has had to leave for some emergency or other and we are way behind on our exit examinations."

Phillip's mind wandered for a few seconds. He moved the receiver to the other ear in time to hear her saying, "How on earth we will have all seventy-five done and everything else that needs to be accomplished by next week—

when they are due to be shipped—is beyond me. So ... would it be a possibility, doctor?"

"Perhaps." Something amorphous—the embryo of an idea—hovered at the edge of his mind ... something to do with what the woman had just ... "I am sorry, what did you say?"

"About what, doctor?" She sounded irritated.

"Next week."

"I said the ship leaves for Montreal then."

Phillip struck his forehead with the heel of his free hand, trailing the sentence like a banner across his mind once ... twice. And then the inspiration hit him. Of course, the ledger entries ... the letter to Ontario. He had been so caught up in the plans for Edwin's kidnapping—and now this letter of Lydia's —Amelia Dunn's latest revelations had completely slipped his mind.

When it came to compiling a dossier of her employer's shady dealings, the young woman had proved relentless as a rat terrier. Her evidentiary pursuits both consumed and delighted her. Her most recent find had clearly been her piéce de resistance. Now, by God, he would take that information and make it the rabbit in his hat.

"We desperately need your help. May we count on it, doctor?"

"You may count on a great deal more," he murmured.

"Beg pardon?"

"I said I can be in your office in one hour. But before I perform any of your seventy-five exit examinations, you and I have other business to attend to. Count on giving me at least thirty minutes."

———

Phillip did not wait to be invited. From her seat behind the desk, Harriet Bell swivelled about and watched him stride to the sideboard behind her, where he nonchalantly removed the stopper from the decanter and poured himself a glass of sherry. Sipping on the wine, he relished the heat of it in his gullet. He had purposely not offered her a drink, wishing to throw her off balance. The wariness he saw in her eyes when he took a seat opposite her told him he had succeeded.

She removed her spectacles and massaged the indentations they had left on her sharp nose. "You said there was something you wished to discuss, Doctor?"

Phillip deliberated for some time over the positioning of his glass on the desktop, milking the silence for its unnerving effect. Finally he answered. "I understand Brackwood House has a *situation vacant*."

"I am sorry?" The woman put her spectacles back on and frowned over their tops.

"A staff position available," Phillip said, enunciating slowly, as if he were speaking to someone slow-witted.

She shifted uncomfortably in her seat. "I am afraid you are mistaken. I know of no such ---"

"Is it not a fact that Brackwood House—indeed any Home such as this—is legally obligated to have on its staff an Inspector of Child Immigrants?"

"Er ... erm." Her eyes avoided Phillip's. She passed her tongue over her lips. "I do not ---"

"Know?" He made a harrumphing sound. "Astonishing." He examined his fingernails—first one hand, then the other—and polished them against his jacket lapel as he said, casually, "Does the name *Doctor Smith* ring any bells?"

Her swift intake of breath betrayed her. "No, none at all." She pushed away from the desk and rose, turning her back to him, her sights clearly set on the sideboard and its decanter.

Once she had gulped down one sherry, poured herself a second and had returned to her chair, he leaned forward, elbows on the desk, his eyes locked on hers. "Doctor Smith," he said. "The chap in Ontario to whom you have been issuing cheques every fortnight for the past several years. The chap, as it turns out, who is a complete work of fiction. Brackwood's Sudbury has never even heard of him. As far as they are concerned, there has not been an Inspector since the year dot. How loud, pray tell, are your bells ringing now, Madam?"

Her face flamed. "How dare you? I er ... you cannot---"

"What is his title, now?" Phillip tapped his mouth with his index finger as if for inspiration. "Ah, yes, surprise, surprise. The entry in the ledger said *Inspector of Immigrant Children*."

Her face paled. "My ledger," she whispered. "How did you ---?"

"It was not difficult, let me assure you."

"Amelia Dunn." She clenched her jaw and balled up her fist. "That little bit ---"

"Now, now, Harriet"—Phillip leaned back in his seat—"you must not get yourself in a lather. There is a perfectly simple solution. The situation is vacant and I shall fill it."

"You?"

"You will pay me the generous stipend that our dear Doctor Smith has been receiving all these years; you will arrange passage for me on the vessel departing next week. And you will arrange for Mathers to take over for me here."

She stared at him, slack-mouthed.

"Oh, and one other thing"—he rose and stood looking down on her—"you will do nothing to jeopardize Amelia Dunn's job. Understood?"

Harriet Bell nodded in the affirmative.

Phillip pressed on. "And you will give her carte blanche as regards the running of your office. As we all know, your books are in the very sorriest of states. A great many mistakes appear to have been made. Miss Dunn will see to it that these are rectified and you will assist her in every way you can. Are we perfectly clear on all this?"

Dazed-looking, she scratched the crown of her head and a couple of strands of her hair came loose. "I did the best I could." Her voice took on a whining quality. "They paid me a pittance for what I did. No one could have done a better job than I did."

"Good God, woman"—Phillip slammed his hand down on the desktop and she jumped—"at what? Stealing, cheating, lying, Lord knows what else? It is over, Mrs. Bell ... you are over. Finished. And it is up to you how you bow out."

"Bow out?"

"Cooperate ... make full restitution to all those you have wronged, then once all the affairs of the Home are in proper order, quietly resign. Refuse to do so, put any obstacles in Miss Dunn's way, and we shall have no compunction about reporting your activities to the Board of Governors. And I believe we all know what their next step would be." He could tell from the expression on her face she read his meaning, that there was no necessity for him to say the word *police*. "So, what is it to be, then?"

"The former."

"Just so we are clear ... cooperation followed by quiet resignation?"

"Yes," she snapped.

"Very good. Now, Harriet, you will need your pen and a letterhead if you are to make my appointment official."

While she dipped her pen, wrote and blotted in tight-lipped fury, Phillip topped up his sherry glass and wandered the length of the room. A little over-indulgence—perhaps even a celebration—was surely in order.

A new position awaited him, a position whose responsibilities he intended to take very seriously. After all, this industry—and make no mistake, the business of Home children *was* an industry—was rife with abuse and he would do his utmost to root it out and, where possible, set things right. Of course his agenda was a selfish one. And of course, at this juncture, foremost in his mind was the lot of one particular Home child. But in the end—and whatever the outcome—he would make a promise here and now: However long or short a period of time he undertook the role of Inspector of Immigrant Children, he would give it his absolute all.

He paused in front of the fireplace, studying but not really seeing the portrait of the Home's founder, Thomas Brackwood, centred over the mantel. He rocked back on his heels. For certain, the new job meant abandoning his practice for a time, although he had no intention of making it a permanent affair; old Doctor Bulmer would undoubtedly be happy to come out of retirement and act as locum for Phillip in his home practice during his absence. For certain, too, it meant leaving Delphine to sort everything out at this end. But she was one of the most capable women he knew. If anyone could pull things together, she could.

Lord—his heart missed a beat—just days until Thursday, the twenty-sixth and his departure. About a fortnight's voyage, then Montreal. After that, Ontario and the Brackwood Distribution Centre. And after that, Saskatchewan ... Plenty ... and Lydia.

He traced the edge of his glass with his thumb, studying the remains of the amber liquid as if it had oracular powers. What was Delphine going to say, though, when he told her? That he was a fool? He shrugged. She might well be right. But it was a risk he was willing to take.

"Done."

Phillip blinked himself back to the present and turned on his heel, bringing Harriet Bell's sullen face into focus. "Completed as you instructed, doctor."

After careful perusal of the document, he inserted it in its envelope and slipped it into his inside pocket.

"Is that all?" Harriet Bell made as if to get up, clearly anxious to be on her way.

"Not quite. I have one last requirement of you. Another document, or should I say a correction to one, and a deucedly important correction at that."

## CHAPTER SIXTY-TWO
### September 1890
### Hadfield Hall, Sussex, England

The giant sycamores flanking the long curving drive that dissected the grounds of Hadfield Hall swayed in the afternoon breeze. Leaves fluttered to earth in a shower of ruby, brown and yellow, blanketing the gravel over which the hansom wheels bowled, and adding to the frustration of the rake-wielding gardener. He paused in his work, no doubt thankful for the break, and touched two fingers to his temple in a salute as they passed. Delphine raised a hand in acknowledgment.

With the handle of her parasol, she reached up and tapped on the window above and behind her, catching the driver's attention and signaling him to slow down. There were things she needed to say to Edwin before they reached the house.

Neatly-trimmed lawns stretched away to the low stone boundary walls on each side. Terraces that from the children's accounts had once been jungles of weeds and brambles and overgrown bushes had been tamed and trimmed and newly-planted. Topiary and statuary abounded. Here—harbinger of autumn— masses of mauve Michaelmas daisies danced alongside clusters of chrysanthemums in white and maroon and purple. There, the last of summer's yellow and pink roses still bloomed.

Delphine touched the boy's arm, indicating the vista with a tip of her head. "Quite a difference, I believe, from last time you saw it."

Perched on the edge of the seat, excitement in every line of his slight body, he nodded.

During the train journey they had discussed Annabel ... what he might expect, how—after six months—he might find her very much changed from the sister with whom he was familiar. With a maturity beyond his ten years, he had said, "But she already was changed, Miss Latham. Mrs. Chistlegate forced her to be different, just as she forced me to be different."

"You are quite right." Delphine had temporarily dropped the subject when she noticed the fatigue on the boy's face and remembered that he still was not quite up to snuff, physically. "I think a little rest would be in order for you, young man," she had said. "It has been an eventful day." After a moment of protestation, he had fallen asleep, leaning against her, eventually slipping down until his tousled head had come to rest in her lap.

At the sight of the sleeping child, her chest had constricted; something welled up in her, bringing her close to tears. Something tender, compassionate, but at the same time, fierce and protective. An elderly woman occupying the seat opposite had said, "Yer young 'un's plumb tuckered out, poor lamb." Delphine had nodded in agreement, not bothering to correct the assumption that Edwin was hers, allowing herself the fantasy of motherhood for a time.

Thinking about it, now, she castigated herself for her foolishness. Motherhood clearly was not in *her* cards. Aunthood perhaps, if brother dear were ever to settle down. Still—she studied Edwin's eager profile now—were she, by some miracle, to marry and have children, she would want a boy like this one. Had Stanley lived, their son might well have looked like Edwin, so similar were they in colouring and build.

The boy must have felt her eyes upon him, for he turned, bathing her with a smile of pure joy. "Almost time," he said.

Time, also, Delphine thought, to quickly fill him in, as had been her earlier intent. "Edwin, can you attend to me, please?

He fixed her with an intense look and she said, "You remember when Annabel ran away and you were so upset that you became rather poorly?"

"Yes," he said, his face solemn.

"Well, Annabel, too, has been poorly. While she was away, you see, and became lost, a couple of footpads set upon her and hurt her."

"Beat her, you mean?"

"Yes, rather badly, I am afraid." That much at least they knew. The rest, whatever it turned out to be, would not of course be for Edwin's ears.

Edwin anxiously picked at his nails. "Oh, I say ... poor sis."

"She has been doing her level best to forget all that nasty business. And in the process, appears to have forgotten a lot of other things. Such as who people are. Me, for instance. So, there is a possibility, she may not remember you."

"Oh, she will, Miss Latham, I know she will. I am her brother."

Faced with such confidence, Delphine did not have the heart to belabour the point, so she directed her attention—and his—to the house, which loomed ahead.

Built of local stone in a warm golden hue, its lines were Georgian—square and uncluttered, with an abundance of simple rectangular windows, and a dearth of the fanciful turrets, battlements and overblown ornamentation common to the ubiquitous Gothic architecture of the day. "A rather pleasant place, is it not?" she said.

Edwin half-rose, craning for a better view. "Looks different, Miss Latham. Oh, I know why. The ivy is gone. Used to be all over the front. I climbed up it once. I was ever so high. But Annabel saw me and made me get down."

"Thank goodness she did," Delphine said dryly. "Otherwise you might not have been here to tell the tale."

"I cannot wait to see her." He was already on his feet and poised to leap out as the cab slowed to a crawl; it had barely come to a halt before he had the door open.

Delphine stayed put, waiting for the driver to hand her down, but Edwin remembered his manners and beat the cabbie to it. Once she had settled up with the fellow, Edwin grabbed the small suitcase which held her overnight necessities and a few essentials for the boy, tucked his kite under the other arm and said, "Shall I ring the doorbell or shall we just walk in, Miss Latham and surprise her?"

But there was no need for discussion. At that moment, several feet from where they stood, the front door opened, revealing a tableau made up of Mrs. Hadfield, Mrs. Boot, Annabel and her dog, Dolly.

Mrs. Hadfield supported herself with her cane. Behind her, Mrs. Boot peered over her employer's shoulder. Annabel—straight-backed, taller than her great-aunt by a head, her hair pulled back into a knot at her nape making her look a good deal older than her fourteen years—stood next to the old lady. Dolly, restrained by a lead and quivering with excitement, sat at Annabel's feet.

Edwin set down the suitcase and kite. Despite his former panache, he now appeared dumbstruck. As did everyone else. No one spoke. No one moved. Elastic seconds passed.

Finally, movement. Mrs. Hadfield raised a hand in greeting at the same time Annabel dropped the dog's lead. Astonishingly, the animal sat respectfully by as if sensing the importance of the moment.

"Edwin?" Annabel covered her mouth for an instant with an incredulous hand and trance-like, began to slowly descend the steps, her dog keeping pace with her. "Is it really you?"

Turning, grinning up at Delphine, the boy said, "See ... I told you she would remember me." Then with arms spread wide, he ran to meet his sister, calling out, "Yes, it is me. It is Edwin, really it is."

Annabel drew him close, laughing and crying and saying his name over and over, touching his face and hair as if she still could not believe her eyes, while alongside, Dolly barked and wagged and bounced and pirouetted like a circus performer and Ernestine Hadfield and Mrs. Boot looked on with the same expression of ineffable relief Delphine felt.

The children continued to cling to each other for several moments. Annabel was first to extricate herself. "I cannot believe it is you," she said tearfully, holding her brother at arm's length. "You look so grown-up. I swear you have shot up six inches."

"I have shot up? You are a regular bean pole." Edwin gave her a playful nudge. "I bet you could not beat me now."

"At what?" Annabel scrubbed away her tears with the back of her hand.

"The race." Dolly had trotted over and inserted herself between them. She stood on her hind legs, pawing at Edwin. "Who is this little blighter?" he asked.

"My dog, Dolly."

"Yours? Oh I say, you have your very own dog?" He reached down to pet the animal. "So, you think you can?"

"What?"

"Beat me."

Annabel giggled. "Of course."

"I am talking about all the way around the boundary wall and back to the sundial, like we used to do."

"I know."

"When?"

"Not right now, of course. Great-Aunt Ernestine is waiting. Come on. And Mrs. Boot. They have been ever so kind to me, Edwin."

"Great-Aunt Ernestine has?"

"Absolutely. She is very different now."

"And Miss Latham has been ever so kind to me." He grasped Annabel's arm and coaxed her over to where Delphine was standing. "Do you remember Miss Latham?"

Not quite sure what to do, Delphine extended a hand and said, "Hello, Annabel."

Although there was a hint of chariness in her expression, the girl's handshake was firm.

"You two know each other," Edwin insisted.

Annabel tilted her head quizzically and after a moment's hesitation slowly said, "You came to dinner ... gave Dolly a piece of meat."

"But you knew her long before that," said Edwin, with a hint of impatience.

"Yes"—Annabel placed a forefinger against her bottom lip—"I have a feeling I might have ---"

"No matter, dear," Delphine said. "I am delighted to see you again." Perhaps Annabel would remember her, perhaps not. Perhaps Phillip's Doctor friend, Reggie Fardoe, would still be needed. Maybe the girl's wounds had healed, maybe not. Only time would tell. She touched the girl's shoulder with a tentative hand and then gave Edwin a gentle push. "Your great-aunt has been most patient, standing there all this time," she said. "Mrs. Boot, too. So, off you go, now, and say hello."

Smiling with satisfaction, she watched the children ascend the steps, hand-in-hand.

Just wait until Phillip heard about this.

———

Delphine knew she was being ridiculous, but she simply could not wait. Of course she could use the telephone, Mrs. Hadfield had said. But not the one in the hall. She had had a second instrument installed in the library; it was quiet there and Delphine would be undisturbed.

Phillip answered on the second ring. Without ado, Delphine launched into her story, rattling on like an excited school girl. Finally, she had to stop for breath.

"That is all capital, Delphie, absolutely capital," Phillip said. "Actually I was going to ring you. Had everything lined up to do so when you telephoned."

"Really? Oh, and did I tell you they are out in the grounds, now, having a race of all things?"

"Yes, you did, actually."

"I just cannot be ---"

"Delphine, will you just stop for a moment, please, and listen to me. Perhaps sit down when you do. I have something rather important to tell you."

———

Delphine was still sitting, staring at nothing, some ten minutes after their conversation had ended. Mercy, her head was spinning. Phillip off to Canada. Lydia about to be married. Phillip determined to stop it.

Great God—she had not realized it until now—this was not just a mission of mercy for him, an attempt to rescue a hapless person; it was a case of a man going to the aid of a woman for whom his feelings ran deep … truly deep.

Now it all made sense … his seeming obsession with the fate of these children. But had he lost his senses, that was the thing? And oh Lord—she cupped her chin in her hands and closed her eyes—was he setting himself up for heartbreak?

## CHAPTER SIXTY-THREE
### October 1890
### Liverpool England to District of Saskatchewan, Northwest Territories, Canada

Phillip stood on the deck of the steamship, *Ontario*, as it pulled away from the Liverpool docks on the morning of the tenth of October. Staring down into the seas' churning depths, he was seized by guilt. He had abandoned his dear sister, expecting her to take charge of everything while he went knighting off for weeks, months even. He had abandoned his patients—some at death's door —and left them to a locum, albeit an excellent one. He had exhibited the rashness of a callow youth. But Lord help him, he could not help himself. Lydia must be rescued.

Rough seas made the seven-day voyage a grueling one for his seventy charges. While he enjoyed the luxury of a private cabin and suffered not a moment's queasiness, the Home children were not so lucky. Crammed below decks in fetid, unventilated quarters whose only amenities were an abundance of slop buckets, they vomited en masse and he spent every waking hour ministering to the sorry souls.

But by the time they reached the Brackwood Distribution Centre at Sudbury, Ontario, three days after disembarking at Montreal, most of the children had recovered enough of their rambunctiousness to give pause to Robson Featherstone, the superintendent there.

A doughy little fellow with a look of perpetual worry on his face, he pronounced them all hooligans. "Get worse every time," he said. "The dredgings of the workhouse and the jails before they come to you, I should not doubt. And why in creation we need someone like you, doctor, to ensure the welfare of all the little monsters like these who have already been sent on their way, is quite beyond me. 'Tis the welfare of the unfortunate farmers with whom they are billeted we should be worried about."

Phillip did not believe that for a moment. Stories of abuse of Home children were legion. Inspecting all the youngsters placed by Brackwood's during the past several years and still serving out apprenticeships would be far too daunting a task, so during the fortnight he had agreed to stay at the Centre to help sort out the horrendous backlog, he planned on poring through their records and selecting about thirty children who were scattered across the country from Ontario to as far west as the Vancouver area. If he found any of them were being mistreated, he would immediately extricate them from their situations and arrange for them to be returned to Sudbury and then placed elsewhere.

For now, though, thoughts of only one Home child occupied his mind, and the prospect of seeing her in approximately three weeks made his heart beat like that of a youth about to receive his first kiss.

Lord help him. He hoped … he prayed … he had not come on a wild goose chase.

### CHAPTER SIXTY-FOUR
#### October 1890
#### Plenty, Distirct of Saskatchewan, Northwest Territories, Canada

At my desk behind the shop's counter at half past five on this Monday afternoon, the twenty-seventh of October, I tried to shut out the distractions. Concentrate, I told myself, pressing my fingertips to my temples in tiny circular motions and once again smoothing the ledger's page in readiness for my third attempt at adding a column of figures.

Since the proposal ... announcement—whatever one chose to call it— almost three months ago, I seemed to have lost my mental acuity. I steepled my hands beneath my chin and grimaced. So little time left, but I must not succumb to misery. As Mama always said: *Cheerful is as cheerful does.* So cheerful I would strive to be.

To this end I slammed the ledger shut and stood to observe the antics of my friend, Sally, and little William beyond the swinging gate that separated the behind-the-counter area from the shop.

Crimson-faced from exertion, Sally stood, arms wide, singing out, "Come to Auntie, my darlin' boy." Reminiscent of a wind-up toy, William staggered towards her across the floor's uneven boards, finally collapsing at her feet as if his spring had wound down. He uttered an indignant yowl which ceased as soon as Sally scooped him up and balanced him on her hip. "There ... there, chicken." She plunked him down on the counter-top and handed him a bunch of keys to play with, maintaining a watchful eye on him while she conversed with me. "Proper little caution, isn't 'e, though?"

"Indeed he is." I gave a half-hearted laugh. The baby's antics *were* hilarious, but the jangle of the keys' metal against wood set my nerves on edge.

Another half-hour and it would be time to close, thank the Lord. Mrs. Dykstra had taken the day off, and so the care of both the household and the baby had fallen to me ... with Sally's help, of course. While I had spent most of the day wrestling with the accounts, she had been re-stocking shelves and chasing after William. A stone-and-a-half of unbridled one-year-old energy and curiosity, he had just learned to walk.

Lately I had found myself too distracted to be as loving and attentive to him as I should have been and so resentful of the maternal role that had been thrust upon me, there were days when I wanted none of him. So Sally's besottedness with the baby had proved a Godsend.

"Finally got a smile out of you," Sally said. "Been lookin' ever so gloomy for weeks, 'aven't you, though?"

"Sorry. I have had a great deal on my mind." I slumped in my chair. So far, I had told no one of my predicament, although Johann Brecht had apparently let Mrs. Dykstra in on his plans, but with an admonition that for the present, the news was to go no further.

Tired of the keys now, William had begun to whimper. Sally picked him up and bussed him on the neck, making him giggle with delight. "Worryin' about the children, are you?"

"Yes, always. But it is not that." I debated whether or not to say anything, but before I knew it, had blurted, "I am to be wed, Sally."

"Wed?" Sally almost dropped the baby; his face crumpled and he started to bellow. Over the noise, she shouted, "But how...? Who? You haven't been courtin' or any ---"

"Give him to me." I rose, and held out my arms. "I shall go and put him in his cot for a while. He will be quite safe until I am finished here. I cannot imagine there being any more customers now. When I come back, I shall explain everything."

By the time I returned several minutes later, Sally had made tea. "Asleep almost as soon as his head touched the pillow," I said, taking the proffered cup and settling in my seat at the desk.

Sally clambered onto the high stool behind the counter, a-dither with curiosity. "Tell me quick, or I'll burst, won't I though?"

Fortifying myself with a couple of swallows of the sweet, hot brew, I said, "Hold your cup steady. You are in for a shock."

"Alright ... I am holdin' it tight, aren't I though?"

"The ceremony is supposedly set for the latter part of next month, or the first part of December, when the circuit pastor makes his six-monthly stop."

Keeping her eyes on me, Sally felt for the counter top and noisily set down her cup and saucer. "Your weddin'?" She clapped her hands to her cheeks. "Circuit pastor? Where are you gettin' ...? Thought you were Church of England ... Anglican, didn't I though? Which church is it goin' to ...? Next month or the month after you say?"

"Yes. At his church."

"Great jumping Jehosaphat. Whose church? Who are you gettin' married to?" She glanced down at her own round belly, then at mine. "Lord almighty, not got yourself into trouble 'ave you?"

"Ye Gods, Sally, of course not."

"Then what happened... an' who is the groom?"

"Mr. Brecht."

After several seconds of slack-mouthed muteness, Sally said, "Mr. Brecht? You? You an' Mr. Brecht? I 'ardly know what to say."

"No congratulations, *please*," I said caustically.

"Not exactly jumpin' an' dancin' about it, are you though?"

"I should say not. There is nothing wrong with the man, but I detest the idea."

"So, tell me why in creation you are goin' to do it, then?"

"This is why..."

Once I had told my tale, Sally sat quietly, alternately sipping her tea and staring off. In the end, she put her cup aside and said with a decisive dip of her chin, "The way I see it, could be the best thing that ever 'appened to you."

I opened my mouth to protest. But Sally forestalled me with a raised hand. "Look, hate to say this, don't I though—an' you know I 'ave never thought any less of you for it—but you *are* a Home girl an' ---"

"What, Sally? You think I should shout hip-hip-hurray?"

"No. But think about it. You will get little William, an' 'e's a proper treasure, isn't 'e, though? Mr. Brecht's a gentleman ... a catch really ... still 'as all 'is teeth an' hair. A bit serious, I s'ppose, but 'e's a pleasant fellow. An' 'e does 'ave pots of money, so if you played your cards right, 'e might let you go 'ome for a visit, maybe even take you. At least, that way, you would see the children, wouldn't you, though?"

"A visit is not what I want, Sally," I said in frustration. "I want to be with them permanently. I want to find a way to get them away from those dreadful Chistlegate people and make a home for us there ... in England, where I belong."

Sally acted as if she had not heard me. "Must think a lot of you, too," she carried on, "mustn't 'e, though? So, you should be able to get anything you want out of 'im."

"He does not even know me, Sally. He just wants a mother for William and clearly"—I closed my eyes for a second and gritted my teeth—"someone with whom to share his bed."

"Doesn't sound so bad, does it though? I mean if you 'ave to share some man's bed, better it be someone young an' strong an' nice-looking like Mr. Brecht."

"Better it be someone you choose for yourself, someone you like ... love," I said, my thoughts all at once turning to Phillip Latham. How my heart had quickened around him. How safe I had felt in his arms that long ago day on the ship. How often had I lain awake at night dreaming of his mouth on mine, his hands roving over my body? Lord ... I snapped to, touched my burning face and in that moment felt a surge of fury. Where were the promised letters from the children? From him? I could hardly count that cursory note I had received a fortnight or so ago, which had said absolutely nothing of consequence and had left me feeling thoroughly bereft.

"If I had money," Sally clambered down off her stool, "I would give it to you, wouldn't I though. But money or no money, Lydia, sounds as if with the indentureship 'an all, Mr. Brecht 'as the law on 'is side."

"So in your estimation, I am done for then?"

"Not if you look at it my way." Sally placed an arm about my shoulders. "All things considered, I would say you are downright lucky."

"Lucky?" I felt my throat tighten. How could Sally say such a thing?

"Yes." Sally straightened and stood over me, arms folded. "So why not make the best of it. Oh an' by the by"—she raised her forefinger as if she had just remembered something—"if you are needin' a bridesmaid, I would be honoured, wouldn't I though?"

Looking up at her, I said nothing. Whatever I had expected from Sally, it had not been this. It felt very much like betrayal.

## CHAPTER SIXTY-SIX
### *October 1890*
### *Plenty, District of Saskatchewan, Northwest Territories, Canada*

The chaos of my thoughts kept me tossing and turning for hours that Monday night. I considered how much my life had changed. Four years ago I had been an inexperienced girl, safe in the bosom of my none-too-perfect family. Then had come my father's cowardly death ... my separation from my dear ones, and after that hardship heaped upon hardship. But I needed no one to tell me I had grown from these experiences. Had I not, I would have been unable to contemplate life as it appeared to be playing out, now, and I might well have followed Papa's lead.

A homily of Mama's came to me about people's desires in life and how they were so often led towards them along vastly different paths than they ever could have imagined. Perhaps this current path of mine—anathematic as it might appear—was such a one. Perhaps—and oh dear God, how I hated to acknowledge it—Sally was right.

With these disconcerting thoughts I finally fell asleep. And my groggy mind was still churning when I headed downstairs to the kitchen the next morning.

At quarter to seven William was still upstairs asleep. I found Johann Brecht already stationed at the breakfast table. Mrs. Dykstra had left a pot of porridge simmering on the hob. But I had no stomach for it. Nor had I the energy for avoidance. This time I met my future husband's gaze unflinchingly.

Something about him had changed. Not the fact that he had shaved off his moustache—with him this was an on-again, off-again fashion—but something else. Something in the way he looked at me. An *I-know-something-you-do not-know* kind of look was the only way I could describe it, and whatever his secret, it made his eyes shine. He had lost his stiffness, too, his formality. And he smiled a great deal, not in his usual deprecatory manner, but in a bolder fashion which threw me off guard. "Good morning," he said, handing me a cup of tea. "Good Morning, Mr. Brecht," I answered.

"Johann ... remember?" He passed me the sugar bowl. "You look tired, Lydia."

"I am. And frozen to the marrow." I drew my shawl about my shoulders. The fire Mrs. Dykstra had lit earlier might just as well have not been burning for all the heat it gave out. I chased a remnant of a sugar lump around my cup more energetically than I had intended, splashing tea in my saucer. To my surprise, Johann shot up out of his chair—serviette in hand—and had my spill mopped up in a trice. Clearly some hidden meaning lay buried in this morning's scenario, but in my present state of fatigue, I just was not clever enough to exhume it.

Mrs. Dykstra's entrance into the kitchen, with William in her arms, spared me the need for further deliberation and also served to remind Johann Brecht of the hour and of his appointment across town at his warehouses. Tossing back his tea, he pushed away from the table. He took the baby from Mrs. Dykstra, deposited him in his high chair and planted a kiss on top of his blond curly head. Then he turned to me and said, "You will be in the shop this morning?"

I frowned. "This morning and this afternoon." Half-day closing fell on a Tuesday, but I would, as usual, be in the shop for the entire day.

"Good." He headed for the door. "Then I will look for you there."

At the sound of the back door closing, Mrs. Dykstra said, "Strange that Mr. Brecht is in such fine mood."

"Why do you say that?" I asked.

William banged on the high chair's tray with his fists and made an unintelligible sound easily recognizable as a demand for food. Mrs. Dykstra quickly sat beside him and began to spoon porridge into his open mouth. "I am surprised he is not upset with news about preacher. I do not know truth of it, but they are saying he have problem ---"

"Who have … I mean has problem, the preacher or Mr. Brecht?"

Mrs. Dykstra fed the baby more cereal. "Both have problem. You too have problem." She wiped William's messy mouth with a towel. "*Und* me. I have problem."

I felt myself bristle. "What on earth do you mean?"

"They say it will be spring before preacher able to come to Plenty. So you cannot wed Mr. Brecht until then. *Und* I must leave here soon for caring of my sick child." She droned on about the need for another woman to come and live under this roof with me.

"I understand," I said, rising and heading for the door, doing my best to keep a straight face. "Everything will work out, you will see. Now, if you will excuse me, I have a positive mountain of work waiting for me."

Once in the hall separating the house from the shop, I danced a jig and grinned so hard my face hurt. Silly really … I did not yet have my freedom, I still had not heard from my dear ones. But glory be, I had been given a half year's reprieve.

Redolent of cinnamon, nutmeg and coffee beans, of the beeswax polish I had applied to the counter-top the day before, of dried lavender and autumn's first harvest of rosy apples, the shop was as soothing as a mother's arms.

Humming to myself, I moved along its silent aisles lighting a lamp here, a lamp there, feeling my tension slip away. No mountain of work awaited me; only those jobs I chose to do before the store opened in two hours.

But work was my most effective defense. So, once the entire area was softly illuminated, I set about laying and lighting a fire in the stove, piling on logs until it burned fiercely. After that I dusted furniture, refilled the flour bins and the candy jars, topped up the coffee bean and tea canisters, and rearranged a pile of seed boxes according to size.

Next came the stock room. Its shelves were stacked with merchandise waiting to be checked and priced.

No sooner had I started on a carton of parasols that had arrived from San Francisco the previous afternoon, than I heard the jingle of the shop's doorbell. It had to be Sally; she was the only one other than myself and Mr. Brecht who possessed a key. Rapid footsteps followed and sure enough she came huffing into the stock room, her face pink from the cold. And before I had a chance to ask what she was doing turning up at such an ungodly hour, she said, "Just had to get here early, didn't I though?"

I answered with a lift of my shoulders.

"Before you say a word," Sally went on, doffing her wrap and bonnet and peeling off her gloves, "want you to know how sorry I am." She hung her garments on a nearby hook on the wall. "Got to thinkin' 'ow it must've looked, me carryin' on like I did. 'ave a mouth as big as my posterior, don't I though?"

I was tempted to agree and point out that friends knew when to guard their tongues. But instead, I continued unpacking the parasols, scrutinizing each for defects as I told my friend not to fret. "I know you were doing your best to help," I said. "And actually, you may have a point. About accepting things, I mean." I smoothed the lace edge on the parasol I held and then tested the opening mechanism. "I have not quite decided."

It was the truth. Maybe my destiny *was* to surrender. On the other hand, maybe when the dreaded nuptial moment was upon me months hence, all rationality would leave me and I would bolt.

"Anyway, I just received some rather good news from Mrs. Dykstra. Apparently I shall not be *sold into wedlock* for several months."

Sally raised a questioning eyebrow. "What in creation are you talkin' about?"

After I had filled her in she said, "Doesn't matter when they 'carry you off to the church kickin' an' screamin', I still want to be your bridesmaid, don't I though?"

"If Katerina's funeral is any indication—you surely remember how peculiar it was—I doubt very much that they have such things as bridesmaids.

Which—to be honest—suits me no end."

With a dip of my chin, I indicated the half dozen parasols I had cradled in my arms. "Here," I said, and Sally took them from me. "I shall bring the rest, along with the price tags I have already penned. I have a space cleared on the shelf over by the front window."

Sally preceded me into the store. "What did you mean about suitin' you no end?" she asked over her shoulder.

I waited until we had reached the shelf and relieved ourselves of the parasols before replying. Reaching into my apron pocket for the price tags and starting to attach one to each handle, I said, "I meant that when this parody of a marriage does take place, then the simpler the whole affair the better." I felt the sudden prick of tears. Oh the sadness of it all. No dreams fulfilled. No strong-yet-gentle man enfolding me, heartbeat matching mine.

"As I mentioned yesterday, 'e is very well set, is Mr. Brecht," Sally said. "An' all this"—she spread her arms wide—"will end up bein' yours. If nothin' else you could squirrel some money away, couldn't you, though? Smart with those books, you are."

I chewed on my thumb nail. Never mind being clever with the books. Maybe I could feed him a little arsenic in his tea. Despatch the fellow smartly and be done with it, then go waltzing off in my widow's weeds never to be heard from again. At least not in this Godforsaken place.

"Then you could send money to your doctor friend for Annabel and Edwin and once they get away from them people—they are bound to sooner or later—they could come and visit you here, couldn't they though?"

"My doctor friend, as you call him, seems to have lost interest." I sighed inwardly. Oh Phillip, what happened? You seemed to care. There seemed to be something between us ... something more than ... I pulled myself up sharply. More than what? Concern ... compassion? Causes are all the go nowadays. That is all you are to Phillip Latham ... a cause. Home children ... waifs and strays ... sorry creatures all, whatever name you give them. And none sorrier than you and your nonsensical dreams.

Sally's nudge brought me back. "Didn't you say 'is sister 'ad been poorly?"

"Yes, I did." I said grudgingly.

"Well, then ...?"

"Well then, nothing. I am sick of talking about it, really I am. And of thinking about it. Nothing I do or say is going to change anything. So come on then, Sally. It is high time you and I had a bit of fun." I grabbed her arm and propelled her along.

"What sort of fun?"

"Hats."

Sally regarded me as if she thought I were demented.

"In the stock room," I went on. "Katerina apparently ordered them from Montreal, months ago, and they finally came in the other day. The very latest thing, my dear, *très elegante*." I used a falsetto voice that made Sally sputter with laughter. "The chicest thing this side of Paris."

------

Oh Lord, a good dose of silliness worked wonders, I thought, scrubbing at my tears and clutching myself about the middle. Although painful to the ribs, this unrestrained, right-from-the-belly variety of laughter was as palliative as the first rains after a drought. "Oh, Sally, please"—I drew out the word—"take off that deuced thing. If I laugh anymore, I swear I shall pop."

The *deuced thing* referred to the black straw boater Sally had on. The last and most overdone of the two dozen creations we had been modeling for each other, it was much too big for her and completely covered her eyes. And, like an altar to a heathen god, its wide brim was mounded with every imaginable fruit, flower, furbelow and feather in a variety of shades of pink, and purple that clashed abominably with Sally's carrot-hued hair.

Extending her arms and feeling the air, Sally took tiny, shuffling steps and said in a voice similar to that of a trance medium, "Help ... help ... is there anybody there? Everything 'as gone dark, 'asn't it though?"

Stifling another burst of laughter, I slipped behind her, tapped her on the back, and said, "Here."

Sally almost vacated her boots and threw her hands in the air. "Great Jumpin' John Wesley." She slapped a hand to her chest. "Tryin' to do me in, aren't you, though?"

"No more than you were. I told you I was going to pop if you did not stop. Oh Lord, Sally, I cannot remember when I had this much fun." I dabbed at my wet cheeks with the sleeve of my frock. "But I suppose we had better gather our wits and tidy ourselves up, the hats, too ... better put them back in their boxes, and then ready ourselves for the morning onslaught."

Sally quickly replaced the boater in its nest of tissue paper and then patted her hair. "Reckon we do look a bit 'iggledy-piggledy."

"Thank the Lord we do not have to open this afternoon." I tilted my head, all at once fancying I heard the shop's bell followed by the closing of the door. "You did not forget to lock up after yourself, did you?" I asked.

Sally's, "No," and a second one, off-stage, came simultaneously. Johann Brecht appeared in the doorway, a ring of keys dangling from his forefinger. "Sally forgot nothing," he said. He stared at first one, then the other of us, taking in our state of dishevelment.

Sally clearly felt a need to explain. "Doin' a bit of inspectin', Mr. Brecht," she said, indicating the hats.

"I see. Do you have a minute?"

Sally touched herself on the chest. "Me?"

"*Ya,* you." He smiled slightly and fixed me with the same secretive look he had had at breakfast. "We will leave Lydia to finish whatever it was she was doing"—he gestured for Sally to accompany him—"while we have our little chat."

As Sally headed for the doorway, I caught her eye and returned her look of confusion.

"I will be back for you in a moment," Johann Brecht said over his shoulder to me.

"Now, Sally, let me tell you what I wanted to talk about. Your normal hours are ... " His voice and Sally's response drifted out of my hearing.

The hairs on the back of my neck rose; the tension I had managed to slough this past hour returned in full measure. What now? What in creation was the man up to now?

## CHAPTER SIXTY-SEVEN
### *October 1890*
### *Plenty, District of Saskatchewan, Northwest Territories, Canada*

At the conclusion of his discussion with Sally, Johann Brecht afforded me no opportunity for conversation with my friend. "Go, please, and change into your Sunday best frock, Lydia, and make sure you dress for cold. You put on gloves and muffler, your winter coat and bonnet. Buggy has cover, *ya,* but still there is ice in wind."

Confounded by this turn of events, I stood rooted until Johann Brecht gave me a gentle nudge. "We have not time to lose." He extracted his watch from his inside pocket. "You will meet me at back of store in twenty minutes if you please."

"And then what?" I could not resist asking.

"We go for ride ... long ride."

I saw no reason for dilly-dallying and was ready and waiting outside in ten minutes.

"Good," Johann Brecht said, boosting me up into the buggy's seat. "You are early bird. Now"—he handed me a blanket—"you wrap this about yourself. Keep wind off you."

Thank the Lord the vehicle had a canopy, I thought, doing as I was told, and surreptitiously edging away from Johann Brecht as he settled next to me on the seat and said, "You are comfortable, *ya*?"

I shrugged.

"Off we go then," he said, grinning like an excited school boy.

He urged the two horses on with a crack of his whip and the vehicle lurched forward and swiftly gathered speed. Soon we were racing along Main Street … faster …. faster, the animals' hooves thundering over the dry, rutted surface, the wheels churning up a dust wake which mushroomed out to the boardwalks. People who had paused to watch were forced to cover their faces with whatever they had at hand. One fellow raised a fist while others shook their puzzled heads, no doubt wondering why the almighty rush.

Why indeed, I thought. And what was our destination? "Where are we going, Mr. Brecht?" I shouted to make myself heard.

"Not Mr. Brecht … Johann," he called out. "It is business. You will see." With his right hand he held the reins; with his left, he bracketed my shoulder. "We must keep you safe. We cannot have you falling out." He pulled me hard against him, hip to hip, thigh to thigh. The more I tried to ease away from him, the stronger his grip became. In the end I gave up and went limp, apprehension and anger manifesting as a deep pressure behind my eyes that built to a steady throb.

I turned my head slightly and watched the outskirts of Plenty slip by. Soon we were bowling along an old buffalo trail, and the open prairie, scented with goldenrod and wild sage surrounded us. Crows and blackbirds, scavenging the autumn-brown stubble of the grain fields, perched like omens on barbed wire fences. Here and there, stands of white poplars, stripped of their leaves, bent in the wind. A hawk plummeted to earth and then swooped gracefully upward, climbing higher and higher in the indigo sky, its struggling victim—prairie dog or rabbit, I could not tell—grasped in its talons.

I felt very much like that hapless creature. Although I would not die— unless of course, the vehicle overturned, which was a distinct possibility the way it was careening along—I certainly had no chance of escape.

My blood beat against my skull, and I closed my eyes, my head swimming with the din of the hooves and the wheels and the wind and Johann Brecht's cries of encouragement to the racing animals. "Where are you taking me?" I shouted, my stomach twisting into a knot.

He shot me a sidelong glance, his eyes bright as chips of glass below the windswept tangle of his hair. "Wait and see, dear girl," he said.

Up, up we sped, twisting here, turning there, cresting rises, dropping, slowing, then speeding up again. All about us, now, the prairies were pocked with the charred remains of autumn's fires. The buggy swayed and jolted over the uneven terrain, jarring my bones, my teeth, making me want to scream, *OhGodohGodohGod* ... make him stop.

And suddenly, as if by magic, he did.

We had come to a halt outside the entrance to what appeared to be a farm. Pastureland stretched as far as the eye could see and on a knoll at the end of a rutted serpentine road dissecting the property, a house was visible.

"Scheidt Ranch," Johann Brecht said, urging the horses through the open double gates, but restraining them so that their pace was slow enough to finally allow conversation. "What are we doing here?" I asked.

He patted the back of my hand. "Nothing of worry to you, Lydia."

After several minutes the ranch house loomed ahead. A sprawling, two-storey log edifice, it sported a high gabled roof with attic windows and a long front verandah divided by a flight of steps which led up to a door surely stout enough to ward off a Red Indian attack.

Johann Brecht secured his horses' reins to a hitching post at the bottom of the steps, then handed me down from the buggy.

No sooner had he done so than the front door opened and a short, rotund man with a monk's fringe of white hair appeared on the threshold. I had seen the fellow before, but I could not remember where or when. Perhaps it had been in the store ... or at Katerina's funeral. "Herr Brecht," he said as if he had been expecting him, *"Wie geht es Ihnen, Dir?"*

"Fine, Heinrich, fine." Johann Brecht took my arm and we ascended the steps.

"Come in ... come in," the man said, and we entered a high-ceilinged hall whose walls were mounted with a horrifying assortment of moose, bear and wolf heads.

Mesmerized by the sight, I backed up slightly and bumped into Johann Brecht. He steadied me and then nudged me forward. "Miss Lydia Fullerton ... Mr. Heinrich Scheidt."

I mumbled a reluctant, "How-do-you-do."

*"Ach,"* the fat man peered at me, spread his arms in an expansive gesture and said what sounded like, *"Das Mädchen. Schön, Herr Brecht ... Schön."*

"She is indeed."

"We go into study, *ya*?" Mr. Scheidt signaled for us to follow him down a wide hallway. He stopped at the second door on the right. "Here are we."

The smell of dust, old leather and burnt wood hit me as we entered the long, gas-lit rectangular room. On one wall there were three windows draped in dark green velvet. On the opposite wall was a massive, Germanic-looking book case of black wood with an excess of ugly carving. Its shelves contained a haphazard assortment of shabby, leather-bound tomes. A dark oak partners' desk with a chair on each side occupied one end of the room. At the other end —where we stood—two upholstered wingbacked chairs flanked a fireplace in which the dying embers of a log fire glowed.

Johann Brecht conducted me to one of the chairs. "You sit and warm yourself while Mr. Scheidt and I conduct our business."

I took off my bonnet and gloves and held out my hands to the heat. To my annoyance, the men were speaking in German. I listened with half an ear, understanding only the odd preposition but recognizing the authoritativeness in Johann Brecht's voice, as well as something that smacked of subservience in the other fellow's.

I observed the fat man reach into a drawer and extract a book or ledger of some type. Once he had set it on the desktop, they resumed their discourse, still in German. Perhaps he was a business crony who owed Johann Brecht money and they were discussing some kind of payment arrangement. That would certainly account for the ledger and his manner. I fidgeted in my seat. For some untold reason their prattling unnerved me. Ye gods, were they ever going to stop?

The answer came, right then, in the sudden dwindling into silence of their conversation. And all at once they shifted their attention to me. "You will come here please, Lydia," Johann Brecht said.

When I reached the desk, he bade me stand beside him. I was at a loss as to the reason, for he did not pursue his conversation with me but nodded to the Scheidt fellow as if to indicate a resumption of their discourse.

The fat man picked up the book I had seen him retrieve from the desk drawer earlier. He opened the leather-bound volume, cleared his throat several times and began to read in German. Whatever he was saying made no sense to me since I could understand only an *und* here, a *das* there. Maybe it was a religious treatise of some kind, over which the two would later—perish the thought—pontificate. In any event, he droned on and on, his voice deep, soporific, and soon my mind drifted, and the world around me ceased to exist.

*I was a child in the park with Mama, helping her push a perambulator whose parasol shaded baby Annabel from the heat. Ducks waddled along beside us and Annabel was crowing with delight. The sun bejeweled the rippling surface of the lake on which the boats bobbed about, their handkerchief-sized sails billowing in the breeze. I was happy. Safe. I would never leave Mama.*

"We go now." The voice slapped me back to the present. And when Johann Brecht's face swam into focus, and I felt his arm about my waist, my apprehension returned.

*"Auf Wiedersehen,"* Mr. Scheidt called after us as we descended the front steps.

"I take it your business"—I could have said, *your peculiar business*, but thought better of it—"is finished, Mr. Brecht," I said.

"Yes, Lydia." He beamed and seemed to puff himself up. "It is ... most certainly." He grabbed my hand. "Come, dear girl. Now it is time for our—how do we call it? Our ... treat, I think."

In a state of weary irritation, I allowed myself to be bundled into the buggy. And in no time at all we were off again, and hurtling along another rutted trail. If my memory served me correctly we were going in the general direction of Blackstone. But that would take several more hours ... and then we would have the journey back. And Ye Gods, by that time, it would be dark.

Johann Brecht had me jammed against him, as before, and I took great satisfaction in driving my elbow into his side as I yelled over the racket, "This is getting very tiresome. For pity's sake tell me where we are going."

His wild laugh made my scalp crawl. "Somewhere special, *liebling* ... very special. You will soon see."

The sun was just dropping below the horizon by the time we reached our next destination -- a small, simple-looking cabin constructed of rough-hewn logs, with two windows flanking the door and a high-pitched shingle roof with a central brick chimney.

Slowing to a trot before the front porch, we continued on a few feet further to the lean-two stable adjoining the house. There, Johann Brecht, tethered the horses then fed and watered them, seemingly oblivious of me. I sat, shivering and chafing my arms, more from apprehension, than from the chill in the air.

"I will unhitch them later," he said, back at my side and giving me his full attention, now. He leaned in and squeezed my shoulder. "Come, *liebchen*. We must get you inside where it is warmer I think, and while we can still see."

But I hunched down in my seat, my feet planted on the vehicle's floor. What in creation was this place, and why had he brought me here? All this dashing about was ludicrous. My nerves were in shreds and my body had to be black and blue from the punishment it had taken. I exhaled a furious breath between my teeth. I had no intention of budging. I would insist that he take me home, now.

"Hurry up, Lydia." Johann Brecht made an impatient gesture with his hand.

"No, thank you," I said. "I shall wait right here while you do whatever *mysterious*"—I curled my lip around the word—"things you have come to do here and then I should like to go home."

I glanced away and in that instant his arms snaked out, and before I knew what was happening he had grasped me about the waist and hauled me out of the buggy. No sooner had he let my feet touch the ground, than he swept me up again and held me hard against his chest, my face squashed against the rough tweed of his jacket.

Too stunned to react, I lay inert, my heart thrumping, while he carried me as easily as if I had been baby William, across the yard, up the cabin steps and onto the porch. The door must have been unlocked, I realized, for there was no fumbling with a key, just the noise of the latch being lifted. I felt him shoulder his way in, and once on the threshold, he paused to catch his breath and adjust his grip on me, giving me a chance to turn my head slightly.

The cabin, I saw, consisted of one room only, which smelled slightly of mildew and of wood ashes. To the left, a kitchen area ... dishes on a wall-hung shelf and small deal table with two chairs. On the wall opposite the door, a rock fireplace, with a fire already laid in the grate and a rainbow-hued rag rug in front of it. To the right, a three-drawer chest; atop it a blue-and-white jug and bowl and at its foot, a slop bucket. Forward of the chest and close to where Johann Brecht stood, a double-sized bed, spread with a brightly-colored quilt in the log-cabin pattern, and a ladder-back chair next to it. One or two framed prints on walls varnished to a high sheen.

Like a stage setting. Charming all of it. Inviting.

Terrifying.

Panic propelled me out of my inertia and I struggled to be free of Johann Brecht. Laughing, he staggered a few steps, then said, "Down we go," and dropped me like a sack of grain onto the bed.

Despite the softness of the feathers beneath me, the impact winded me, and I lay gasping for air as Johann Brecht turned away and went to the fireplace. While he was searching for matches in the painted tin holder mounted on the rock face below the mantel, I scrambled to a sitting position, then scooted to the edge of the bed.

"What is this place?" I asked, trying to keep the hysteria from my voice. "Why have you brought me here?"

He wheeled about, smiling. "What is this place, you ask. This is honeymoon cottage, *liebchen*. We are here for wedding night."

## CHAPTER SIXTY-EIGHT
### *October 1890*
### *Proximity of Blackstone, District of Saskatchewan,*
### *Northwest Territories, Canada*

Dumbfounded, I stared at Johann Brecht's back as he knelt before the hearth applying a match to the kindling in the fireplace and blowing on it to coax it into a blaze. Wedding night? Had the man lost his wits?

He crossed to the bed. "Come, *liebchen*, take off your coat and bonnet and make yourself comfortable."

I was still too stupefied to move and so he loosened the ribbon tie at my throat and removed my bonnet. I regained my senses when he started on my coat buttons. I pushed away his hand and in a voice I hoped was steady, and with as much dignity as I could muster said, "If you desire my comfort, sir, you will take me back to Plenty."

"Oh I will, dear Lydia, I will."

Relief flooded through me and I closed my eyes and silently thanked the God whose existence I had so often doubted. This was all a misunderstanding. A joke perhaps ... an unkind one for certain, but nevertheless ...

"But not tonight."

I snapped open my eyes and stared up into his face. "Beg pardon ... what did you ---?"

"We return tomorrow." His eyes dwelled in mine and my heart beat like the wings of a frantic bird against my rib cage. "I will take you away later, dear one, for a fortnight, a month. For proper honeymoon."

I heard the labouring of my own breath like bellows, loud and rhythmic. "But we are not married. How can it possibly be---?"

"We have been husband and wife for"—he extracted his watch from his inside pocket and, with a flourish, flipped open its cover—"one hour and twenty minutes I think."

"Husband and wife? You and I?" I heard in my own voice the shrewish manifestation of my panic. "Married? You are insane. You said we would be wed when the circuit pastor came to the Tabernacle. The end of next month ... or maybe December, you said."

"There was problem." He leaned down and stroked my cheek with the back of his hand. I was too numb to shrink from him. "Pastor was not able to come to Plenty until spring," he continued. "And I did not wish to wait that long ... I have waited too long already. So, I take you to another pastor."

"Another pastor? What in creation do you mean? All we have done today is visit your friend ... acquaintance ... whatever he is, at that ranch."

"Friend, acquaintance and pastor. You were present when he read us our vows, when we were ---?"

"Vows? You cannot possibly mean the jibberish that man was spouting was a wedding service?"

"*Ya,* it was wedding alright."

"But I had no part in it. I did not say a single word."

"It is way of our church, Lydia. *Ach*"—he tapped himself on the forehead with the heel of his hand—"in all excitement I almost forget." He reached into his trousers pocket, fumbled around for a moment and extracted a small object I was unable to see. Then he grabbed my left hand and I felt a ring slipped onto my third finger. "Now, we are official, *ya?*"

Incredulous, mute, I raised my hand and stared at the gleaming gold circle. *Trapped ... duped ... done for.*

"I must go and see to horses now," Johann Brecht said. "You undress and get under covers and wait for me, *liebchen.*"

Moments later, I lay fully-clothed beneath the quilt watching shadows dance across the walls. The fire spat and crackled. The wind whispered against the cabin windows, and in the distance coyotes wailed like grieving widows.

Had I been with a husband I loved, this could have been a place of bliss. As it was, it would be a place of loss ... of self, of hopes, of dreams. I turned on my side, covered my head with the quilt and brought my knees up to my chest, as if invisibility could save me.

Eventually I heard the door open and close, then the scrape of a match as he lit a lamp. "I hope you are ready for me, my sweet little wife?" he said, approaching the bed. When he threw back the covers and discovered my disobedience, he merely chuckled. "No matter *liebchen*, I shall have pleasure of undressing you myself."

I lay limp as a cloth-bodied doll as he began to do so. With the removal of each garment his breathing quickened and became harsher. Once he had stripped me naked his gleaming eyes lit on my breasts. He cupped them, kneaded and caressed them, described a slow deliberate circle around each nipple until it became erect. Then he ran his hands over my belly and stroked the vee of hair between my legs, moistening his parted lips with his tongue, whispering, "My beautiful Lydia ... my wife, *ach* I have waited so long ... too long"—he rolled away suddenly and sprang to his feet alongside the bed. "I cannot wait any longer, *liebling.*"

Death-cold and trembling, now, I watched him struggle free of his clothes. And when his member sprang fully erect from between his legs I stared at its size, its length, and shook my head in abject horror.

And then he was on top of me, his hot flesh burning mine, his hand insinuating itself between my thighs, prying me open like a reluctant mollusk, his voice low and pleading against my ear as I began to writhe and kick, "Do not fight me, Lydia. I will be gentle."

A searing spear at my centre.

Cleaving me.

Thrusting … thrusting.

His voice high and triumphant, now, calling out my name.

## CHAPTER SIXTY-NINE
### *October 1890*
### *Plenty, District of Saskatchewan, Northwest Territories, Canada*

I had little consciousness of our return journey the next day. I do know our pace was steady this time and that Johann Brecht addressed an occasional remark to me to which I must have responded, and that he placed a solicitous hand on my arm from time to time. Other than that I knew we left the cabin at first light and reached home at dusk.

By then my torpor had turned to cold, hard rage. And when he went to hand me down from the buggy, I shrugged him off so violently he almost lost his balance. "What you did to me was criminal," I said as he righted himself. "And you will not do it again, do you hear me?"

He smiled and I fumed. "*Ach*, Lydia, sweet Lydia, such fire," he said, infuriating me further by grasping my arm and steering me to the back door. "Come."

He did not release his grip on me until we were at the bottom of the stairs. "Your friend, Sally, stays here with baby," he said in a whisper. "We do not want to wake them. So we talk tomorrow. You go to your room and I go to mine, *ya*?"

He waited for my enthusiastic nodding to cease and then planted a kiss on my cheek. "Good night dear wife. Sleep well."

———

The next morning as I prepared to leave my room and head downstairs I found a note had been slipped under my bedroom door.

*I have news for you. We have need for discussion. You please come down to breakfast at eight o'clock. I will send Sally into store early with baby. Your husband, Johann.*

What now? Was I to be given a thorough dressing down? Not that it concerned me. What did concern me, however, was my physical helplessness … my inability to fend off his attentions. *You will not do it again, indeed.* No wonder he had been amused. He was a tall, solidly-built male. And look at me. I extended my arms, regarding my delicate wrists and small hands. In truth I was a puny woman, just as my great-aunt had observed. My wits were my only defense. How could I use them to my advantage, though, that was the thing?

But as it turned out I had no immediate need for my wits … at least as regards Johann Brecht. When I joined him for breakfast he told me that yesterday's post—which he had gone through the previous night—contained a letter reminding him about a series of meetings he had scheduled with various wholesalers in Winnipeg and Regina. "I am sorry I must abandon you so soon, but business cannot be put off."

"And how long will you be absent?" I asked, nonchalantly stirring my tea.

"Three weeks, I am sad to say."

"Three weeks … why that is ---" *Wonderful,* I thought, biting my lip to stop myself from grinning.

"Terrible, *liebling,* I know. But it will give you time for arranging household. You must hire woman … maybe nursemaid, too, I do not know these things. And you must outfit yourself … buy frocks … shoes … hats." He extracted a wallet from his inside pocket and took out a wad of bills. Peeling off several, he slid them across the table to me. "You take and use for whatever you are needing."

My heart lurched. Casually, I pocketed the money. Ye gods and little fishes … five hundred dollars. Sufficient to finance my escape. I could hitch a ride with someone going to Blackstone and then take the train to … to somewhere … and along the way I could find a job to tide me over until spring, and after that, book passage back to …

"I know what your thoughts are."

I returned to earth with a start at the sound of his voice. "You cannot run away, Lydia. You are indentured servant, remember? And you are my wife." His eyes were kind, his voice gentle. "We will have good life together, Lydia. You will learn fondness for me. And I will cherish you."

With that, he rose and bent over me, kissing me softly on the forehead, leaving me to sit and stew.

### CHAPTER SEVENTY
*October/November 1890*
*Plenty, District of Saskatchewan,*
*Northwest Territories, Canada*

"Everybody knows, don't they though?" Sally asked later, when I joined her behind the counter and opened my ledger. Customers were milling about, but none was within earshot. Astonishingly, William was sound asleep in the large, deep drawer which served as a substitute for his cradle when he was in the shop.

"Knows what?"

"That you and Mr. Brecht are married."

"How is that possible?" I asked sharply.

"Dunno. But they do, don't they though? Mr. Brecht must have told somebody an' that somebody must have told somebody else an' so on an'---"

"Yes, yes, of course. I understand, Sally."

"Mind you, I was first to know, wasn't I though? Mr. Brecht told me before you left that 'e was takin' you to the preacher." She made a sad face. "No bridesmaidin' for me after all. Anyway, you must tell me all about it." She winked and smiled knowingly. "The weddin' night an' all."

"Perhaps some day, Sally. But not now."

Undeterred, Sally went on with, "'ow does it feel to be a married woman?"

"I have no idea," I said dryly.

Sally tutted. "What should I call you now?"

"What you have always called me. Lydia, of course."

------

I had rarely known business to be so brisk as it was that first week after Johann's departure. I soon realized I—the Home girl who had nabbed Mr. Brecht—was the attraction. With only the occasional man in tow, the women came in droves, some mildly curious, others downright rude, eyeing me as if I were a zoological rarity and going out of their way to call me *Mrs. Brecht* in such a way that it sounded vaguely insulting.

On the Friday of the first week in November, a woman of a different bent asked to see me. Tall and regal-looking, with gray hair in a soft bun at her nape and dark eyes, she introduced herself as Effie White. She was the childless widow of a rancher, she said, a friend of an acquaintance of Mrs. Dykstra's and she had heard there might be a position open for a housekeeper or nursemaid.

Leaving Sally in charge, I bade the woman follow me into the living quarters, sat her down at the kitchen table with a cup of tea, interviewed her for half an hour and hired her. "Are you able to start immediately?" I asked.

"Certainly. I will need a few minutes to go my lodgings and retrieve my things."

"Come into the shop when you return and I will introduce you to your charge, baby William, and my friend and assistant, Sally Porter."

A few moments later, back in the shop, I caught sight of Sally bustling about among the pots and pans and cheerfully answering the questions of three customers. What a brick she was and how she brightened my days. I closed my eyes momentarily and smiled. Not that today—with cause for celebration on two fronts—required much more brightening.

First, Effie White's fortuitous arrival on the scene.

Second—six days early—had come the unexpected visit this morning from my *country cousin*. How I had welcomed the telltale cramps and later the trickle of blood from between my legs. This time Providence had surely saved me. From now on, though, Anna TwoBears, the Assiniboine woman, who had helped Katerina, would be my saviour.

I had managed a private word with her, two days ago, when she made her once-monthly stop at the shop with her assortment of herbs the customers swore by for their various ills.

Yesterday, the woman had returned and choosing a moment when there was no one else within earshot, pressed into my hand a paper-wrapped packet. "You make tea—two teaspoons in cup—after you lie with your man," had been her whispered instructions.

Thank the Lord I would have no need for tea-making of this sort for another fortnight. An involuntary shiver ran through me at the thought of what I had to look forward to.

"Cold are you, dearie?"

It took a few seconds for me to reorient myself to my surroundings and bring Agnes Palmer's concerned face into focus. She was a pleasant woman— a favourite of mine—and one of our best customers. "Cold? No ... I am fine," I stammered. "Someone walking over my grave is all."

"I have decided, finally. Reckon it is to be the ottoman. One-and-three-quarter yards the pattern says. Oh ... and there is the silk, too, for the lining and the lace trim. And I will have some of that navy-blue flannel as well. Reckon a skirt would be nice in that."

Once I had hauled the heavy bolts of fabric over to the cutting table and regained my breath, I suddenly thought about my new housekeeper and said, "Would you mind awfully if I asked Sally to take care of you while I go and have a quick word with Mrs. White? She is rather new at taking care of the baby and I want to make sure everything ---"

"Is humming along nicely. 'course I wouldn't, dearie. Off you pop."

I spoke briefly to Sally, then headed for the kitchen, where Effie White appeared to be managing admirably. She had spread the deal table with newspapers and was polishing the brass candlesticks and ornaments from the mantel, while William delightedly beat on a saucepan with a spoon.

I laughed and covered my ears against the din while the woman distracted the baby enough to spirit the spoon away. "I am glad you are here, Mrs. Brecht. I was wondering if it would be alright with you if I took the baby for a walk. It is a little on the chilly side, but it is a fine day and you have that lovely perambulator and I shall make sure he is well bundled up."

"Of course, go right ahead," I said. "The brasses can certainly wait."

After I had seen them off, I poured myself a cup of tea from the half-empty pot on the hob. And I sat back in my chair feeling rather pleased with myself.

I had on one of my four new outfits -- a fashionable costume in light brown figured cashmere purchased from Johann's store with Johann's money. I ran my hand over the soft material of my sleeve. Sally was absolutely right. There were, indeed, benefits attached to my new position. And I would do as she advised -- squirrel away as much as possible from my wages, wages I had taken it upon myself to triple starting last week. After all, my duties had increased a good deal more than three-fold. If asked to justify my actions— and I doubted I would be—I was quite ready to defend my stance.

Granted, the door to my freedom had been slammed shut. But some day the chance to re-open it would come.

I felt tears spill from my eyes. Some day I would see my darlings again. *And* Philip Latham. There would be no seeing Annabel and Edwin without seeing him.

But what could he possibily be to me, now? A figure from my past is all … a player on the stage of my dashed dreams.

### CHAPTER SEVENTY-ONE
#### *November 1890*
#### *Blackstone, District of Saskatchewan,*
#### *Northwest Territories, Canada*

Phillip felt as if he had been traveling forever when he stepped off the train at Blackstone the afternoon of Thursday, the sixth of November. In actuality, his time in transit—including the week aboard the steamship, overnight stays in Montreal, Ottawa, and a fortnight at the Distribution Centre at Sudbury, as well as transportation via an assortment of horse-drawn vehicles and two trains—had been twenty-seven days.

The station master had already told him Blackstone had no such thing as cab service and that his best bet would be to head for the general store two streets over. People from the outlying areas wishing to stock up on supplies always congregated there. Phillip should have no problem, the chap said, finding someone with whom to hitch a ride to Plenty. Oh and by the way, if he wanted a right fine place to stay while he was in town, The Queen's Hotel had opened its doors just a fortnight earlier.

Phillip set down his bags on the platform and arched his aching back then repeatedly stepped from one foot to the other so as to encourage the resumption of blood flow through his limbs. Not for him first-class train travel, he had decided at the outset, with the luxury of upholstered seats, his own compartment, a comfortable bunk and washbasin, and meals in the dining car. Altruism—surely misplaced, he thought now—had prompted him to travel second-class as the immigrants did ... simply, cheaply, purchasing food at each stop and then cooking it in the communal cooking room, seeing to his toilette in the communal washroom, using the same slatted wooden seat for sitting and sleeping.

Gingerly he rotated his stiff shoulders. Then he drew into his lungs air that was crisp and pungent with the odours of wood smoke and manure, as well as the soapy steam rising from a Chinese laundry opposite.

He adjusted his silk cravat and ran a hand over his chin. Lord, it was rough enough to sand a board. But better a rough chin than a cut throat. Which is what he might well have ended up with had he not abandoned his attempts to shave in the communal wash room with its dearth of hot water, as well as the lurching and swaying of the train which had had him staggering about like a pub patron on payday.

And 'struth, how aromatic he must smell after all these bathless days. He glanced down at himself and grimaced. His charcoal worsted suit looked as if he had slept in it -- he had. His waistcoat was missing a button and his starched collar and cuffs had wilted and were no longer white, but grey. Only his shiny black boots had, for some untold reason, survived the journey unscathed. No matter—he massaged a kink out of the back of his neck—taking his measure of the place and deciding that here no one would give his appearance a second look anyway.

What occurred to him first about the town was how hastily thrown together everything seemed to be. Clusters of tar-papered buildings—clearly occupied but unfinished—leaned upon each other; scattered among them were one or two sturdily-constructed homes, a laundry, a saloon and a building with a sign identifying it as a warehouse.

What struck him next was the horrendous noise made by the clattering of wheels and the drumming of hooves over the wide road onto which the station house backed. Spanned by cedar planks laid over its dried mud surface, it teemed with all manner of carts and wagons drawn by smelly, snuffling oxen and whinnying horses. There were individual riders, too, on horses and ponies and burros. Real cowboys, unkempt enough to be fresh off the range. Fake cowboys … remittance men, crisp and clean as Colonials and wearing spurs as large as dinner plates. Indians of the civilized variety, sans war paint. Well-dressed citizens alongside dreadfully-ill-dressed prospector sorts with beards down to their knees. Pedestrians clearly bent on flirting with danger, darted in and out of the traffic. And every so often, from the saloon the caterwauling of off-key songsters accompanied by equally off-key piano music could be heard over the general din.

Phillip scratched his head. A circus if ever there was one, and vastly different from Montreal's elegant eighteenth-century French architecture and meandering electric-lit streets, and from Sudbury's tree-lined avenues and wood-framed mansions. Circus or not, though—he picked up his bags—it was time for him to join the fray.

Finding the store was easy, hitching a ride no challenge at all, if he were willing to wait until four days hence. Of all the customers milling about, only one—Jacob Merkel, a cheerful fellow with a thick European accent—had plans to head for Plenty. "You come to livery stables—ask anybody … they tell you way—nine o'clock sharp Monday morning and I ferry you to Plenty," he said, slapping Phillip on the back as if they were old friends, then striding off before Phillip had a chance to confirm the arrangement.

"Are there rooms to be had at your new hotel?" Phillip asked the shopkeeper.

"Reckon there's plenty," he said. "But yer'll be a sight better off over at Ma Malone's across the street"—he waved a vague hand—"two doors along from the laundry. 'tis cheap an' clean, so they say." He looked Phillip up and down. "Reckon yer can get yerself a bath there, if yer've a mind, and Ma puts on a right fine spread."

Two hours later, after a long soak in gregarious Ma Malone's tin tub, followed by a sampling of *her right fine spread* and an earful of her homegrown philosophy, Phillip dragged himself upstairs to his room.

He climbed between the covers and settled back on the pillow. No sooner had he done so than an image of Lydia Fullerton as he last remembered her manifested itself. Soft pink lips … blue eyes filled with hope ... tendrils of russet hair framing her sweet, trusting face. He felt a smile tug at the corners of his mouth. "Not long now, my dearest one," he whispered, his eyelids all at once heavy. "Soon all your troubles will be over."

## CHAPTER SEVENTY-TWO
### *November 1890*
### *Plenty, District of Saskatchewan,*
### *Northwest Territories, Canada*

Knowing that I enjoyed an hour's quiet during mid-day closing, Mrs. White took William for a walk about that time almost every day, weather permitting. And on this Monday, the tenth of November, the kitchen was mercifully quiet when I entered.

I boiled the kettle, made myself a cup of tea and sat down at the table.

No sooner had I done so, than I realized how hungry I was. I would make a couple of cheese sandwiches for myself and Sally, I decided, getting up.

Her name had barely crossed my mind when she materialized.

"Ye gods, are you a Welsh witch? I said, laughing. I just thought about you and here you are."

"Wish I was a witch. Then I could cast a spell on some fella, couldn't I, though, an' 'ave 'im fall in love with me? Speakin' of fellas ... there's one waitin' in the shop for you."

"Did you not tell him we are closed for lunch?"

"Well, yes, I did, didn't I though, but 'e asked for you. Gave me this envelope for you." She made a puzzled face. "Nothin' on it ... no address I mean."

She was absolutely right. A blank envelope ... no address ... no stamps. I went to the sideboard drawer for the letter opener.

"Who is this fellow?" I asked, slitting open the envelope.

"Dunno. Nice-lookin', though. Tall, really dark 'air, sort of fallin' over one eye. English I'd swear ... bit of a north country sound to 'is voice."

I extracted two sheets and unfolded them. Letters. The words swam before my eyes. I felt for my chair and sat. I blinked ... stared at the signatures. Annabel ... Edwin. I shook my head dumbly, disbelievingly. Letters from the children. But how in creation ...?

"Called you by your name—Lydia Fullerton—didn't 'e though?"

I could hardly speak for the thump of my heart. "His name, Sally ... did he give you his name?"

"No, but 'e's waitin' in the hall, isn't 'e though? Said I should pave the way. Didn't want it to be too much of a shock for you. Shall I fetch 'im now?"

"Yes ... send him through." I clutched the edge of the table and held on for dear life, my eyes glued to the doorway.

## CHAPTER SEVENTY-THREE
### November 1890
### Plenty, District of Saskatchewan,
### Northwest Territories, Canada

After a moment's hesitation Philip entered the kitchen. His heart racing, he took a few tentative steps towards Lydia, then stopped to take her in.

His dear, dear love, her face a perfect pale oval, delicate wings of brows in the same dark copper as her hair arching over eyes as blue as a summer sea. "What a beautiful woman you are, Lydia." He watched her eyes widen. "Yes … I said woman, not child. I know your true age … have known it for a long time now. And I love that woman … I love you, Lydia." There … he had said it, despite his resolve to take things slowly … to make sure she felt the same way and that his instincts about her had been right.

But hold on. He blinked and frowned, looked sharply at her. Deuce it all … that was not love he saw on her face. She was glaring at him with unalloyed fury in her eyes.

He held up his hands as if to ward her off. "Lydia, dearest, I know this is a great deal to absorb … my coming here unannounced like this. But when you hear ---"

"Why?" She said the word with such ferocity she choked on it.

He waited a few seconds for her to recover. "Why what, dear girl?" He felt awkward standing over her, so he grabbed a chair from the table, set it down a couple of feet from her and sat opposite her.

"Why did you come here, *now*. First you desert me ---"

"Desert you?"

"Yes." Her eyes glistened with unshed tears. "You do not write ... I hear nothing from the children—they could be dead for all I know—and then you turn up here without so much as a by your leave and say you love me."

"I know it must be an awful shock"—he sat forward, elbows on his knees —"and I am terribly sorry I had to do it this way. But there was no time, you see. It all happened so fast … the opportunity to come here, the decision to speak of my feelings for you. Incidentally, the children are fine, finer, in fact, than they have been in a very long time."

"Really … truly?" A tear spilled down her cheek; she brushed it away with the back of her hand. "Both are well?"

"Absolutely." Now was not the time to talk about Annabel's misadventure and its lingering effects. "You will see when you read their letters. It is all rather complicated, but they are no longer with the Chistlegates."

"Where are they, then?"

"With your great-aunt."

"Great-Aunt Ernestine?" Lydia's mouth dropped open. "But I do not understand. How ---?"

"You will, I promise, once I explain everything. But at present it is you I want to talk about, Lydia."

"What about me?"

"I have come to take you back with me"—he scooted his chair closer—"to England, to your family. As I told you, I love you, Lydia."

A couple more tears rolled down her cheeks; she ignored them. "You have come to take me back with you? You love me?" she repeated in an incredulous tone.

"Yes, my dearest girl." He fished his handkerchief out of his inside pocket and leaned forward, blotting her tears with it. Her initial reaction had been a little odd, but once the news had truly sunk in she was bound to be beside herself with joy … with excitement. "You have absolutely nothing to fear anymore," he told her. "I have in my possession signed papers that will give you your freedom."

"I do not understand. How is that possible?"

He laughed. "Because I am a worker of miracles. No … seriously, Lydia, you are officially freed of your indentureship. The details of how it came about can wait."

She shrugged. "Much good it will do me now."

"Lydia, dearest, it will do you an enormous amount of good. Now, you cannot be forced into that farce of a marriage you spoke of in your letter, nor can you be made to stay on here. You can return to England and spend the rest of your life with me."

He felt a rush of anxiety. Lord, look at her now. Such tragedy in her eyes, tears spilling down her cheeks. He tried to take her hands, but in a puzzling gesture she drew them back and folded her arms across her middle. "You are free, Lydia, do you not understand me?"

"Free?" She laughed a humourless sound, her cheeks flushing pink. "I am more in prison now than I have ever been, *Mr. Phillip-Late-To-The-Rescue-Latham.*"

He ran a finger under his collar. He literally was growing hot under it. Damn it, he had crossed an ocean, a Continent … the prairies. He was sore all over and bone tired; he had bared his soul and this was all the thanks he received. He raised a staying hand and got to his feet. "I am afraid you have me at a disadvantage, Lydia. I have no idea what you are talking about."

"This." She thrust her left hand up and under his nose and pointed to the plain gold band on the third finger. "Would you like to hear about my wonderful wedding?"

## CHAPTER SEVENTY-FOUR
### *November 1890*
### *Plenty, District of Saskatchewan,*
### *Northwest Territories, Canada*

Phillip's face paled as I told him everything. I needed the catharsis and in a perverse way I wanted to punish him for failing me … for telling me that he loved me now, when it was too late. And although, of course, I spared him the intimate details of my *honeymoon* in the cabin, I made it clear that I was married in every sense of the word. My only hope, now, as regards Annabel and Edwin was to persuade Johann Brecht to fund a trip to Canada for the pair, I told Phillip. And that could be years away.

Partway into my story he rose and started to pace. I wanted desperately to go to him, to feel his arms around me, as I had that day on the ship. I had seen the way he looked at me then. And now I had heard him say the words I longed to hear. But oh God, it was too late for us. There was nothing for it, but to send him on his way and be done with it. "So there you have it," I finally said with a brittle laugh, "the whole sorry saga."

Phillip stopped in his tracks. "That is as asinine a thing as I have ever heard," he said.

"Asinine?" I found myself repeating the word. It certainly was not the reaction I had expected from him. I had envisioned him quietly, politely, taking his leave of me, wishing me well, telling me the lines of communication between the children and myself were open, now, and that he was no longer needed as a conduit. What else could he do? What else could he say? After all, I belonged to another man.

"You cannot possibly have been wed in a ceremony where you did not utter a single word and understood nothing of what the pastor said," he went on.

"But I was."

"Where is this husband of yours, this Brecht fellow?"

"Away in Winnipeg. Gone for three weeks."

I studied the cleft in his chin ... imagined him saying, *Come with me now. This minute. Let me love you ... cherish you.*

Lord, I felt myself flush. My imagination would not change a thing.

"Good." Phillip paused by my chair, a determined look on his face.

I fiddled with the candlesticks Mrs. White had been cleaning. "Good?"

"Yes. It will give us time."

"For what?"

"For the million things I have to tell you. About the children, for one. About what I am going to be doing while I am over here, aside from my business with you, I mean. And for me to look into things. Something smells rotten in Denmark—or should I Blackstone ... or wherever it was you were married—and I intend to get to the bottom of it."

He suddenly knelt before me and captured my hands in his and my heart beat so fast I could hardly breathe. "Rest assured, dear girl, I did not come all these thousands of miles for nought. And I have no intention of abandoning you, now."

## CHAPTER SEVENTY-FIVE
### *November 1890*
### *Plenty, District of Saskatchewan,*
### *Northwest Territories, Canada*

That evening Phillip stopped in to see Lydia again with the news that the next morning he was heading to the headquarters of *The Tabernacle of New Life* in Regina. "I have spoken to several of the townspeople here and have received sufficient input to enable me to find the place when I arrive there," he told her.

"But what good will that do you?" Lydia asked, inviting him to sit at the table and partake of the cup of tea she had just poured.

"They will have records of all the marriages performed throughout the territory, as well as the names of those ministers or pastors performing them. I shall take the train from Blackstone tomorrow morning and seek out the bishop ... head man ... whoever the deuce he is."

"Can you not go directly to the Scheidt Ranch? I can no doubt obtain directions for you from Mrs. Dykstra, a church member of my acquaintance."

"Better to go directly to the horse's mouth, in my opinion. Find out from the hierarchy about this supposed minister fellow and then take it from there."

—

Philip retrieved his bag from the overhead rack and peered out of the window as the train drew into Regina station at a little after two the following afternoon.

Eight years earlier in the summer of 1882, southern Saskatchewan's scrubby settlement of Pile O' Bones had been designated a Canadian Pacific Railway Centre. Almost immediately, the Canadian government opted to move the Northwest Mounted Police headquarters to the settlement and it was re-christened Regina in honour of Queen Victoria.

Her Majesty would surely cringe, Phillip thought, were she to experience the town first-hand. Capital of the Northwest Territories or not, there was nothing remotely regal about it. Another thrown-together place, another Blackstone, but larger, dirtier, smellier and noisier, its only redeeming virtue the ubiquitous presence of the *Mounties* whose scarlet tunics and prancing horses added interest to an otherwise dreary landscape.

When he exited the station, Phillip asked one of these *Mounties* for directions to the closest livery stable, as well as to the *Tabernacle's* headquarters. A brisk five-minute walk took him to the livery. Another five minutes and he was aboard a rented buckboard, wondering if this expedition might turn out to be a complete waste of time.

He shivered against the wind's ice-tinged bite and pulled up his coat collar. Ten minutes at a fast clip and he arrived at his destination. Had he not noticed the painted sign below the roof peak identifying it as *Tabernacle of The New Life Regina*, he would have concluded that the white-wood-framed building was a barn. Except perhaps for the imposing pair of front doors with a wide flight of steps leading up to them, there was nothing church-like about the place. Which should not have surprised him, given what he had already heard about this peculiar sect.

He clambered down and secured the reins to a hitching post at the foot of the steps. If this church was anything like St. Bartholomew's, at home, it would be unlocked. He was about to try the door latch when the sound of hoof beats from behind, stopped him in his tracks, and he turned around in time to see an ancient, skeletal-looking fellow coaxing a horse to a halt below. "*Guten Tag,* sir," the man called out in a feeble voice. "Can you help me, please?"

"Of course." Phillip descended the steps in a flash. Lord, but the chap looked as if he was about to topple off his horse. Before he had a chance to, Phillip handed him down.

"*Danken. Mein* stick if you please." With a tip of his head, he indicated a cane tucked in the saddle bag. Phillip retrieved it, handed it to the chap and then hitched the horse's reins to a post alongside the buckboard.

"So"—the old fellow repositioned his spectacles on his nose—"you look for someone ... *ya?*"

After identifying himself, Phillip said, "Yes. I need to speak to the head—or circuit—pastor, I suppose. Would that be you, sir?"

"*Nein,* not me. I am record-keeper, not pastor. And *ze* pastor, I am afraid, is not here." He grabbed Phillip's arm. "If you will please help me up *ze* steps —*ze* cold make me stiff as corpse—we will talk inside."

As they entered the building, the man indicated an open door off to the right. "My office," he said.

Positioned against one wall alongside a fireplace in which a log fire had been laid was a desk piled with books and papers, and a chair; on the opposite wall was a bookcase containing an assortment of dusty-looking volumes, and against the third wall stood a small, cluttered oak table with two chairs.

The fellow—who said his name was Emmanuel Poetek—gestured for Phillip to sit at the table while he struck a match and lit the fire. Once it had caught, he joined Phillip. "You keep on coat, otherwise you freeze." He swept aside a pile of papers. "Now, young man, where were we?"

After several minutes of questioning Mr. Poetek, Phillip was able to ascertain that no pastor had been anywhere near Blackstone or Plenty since the previous year.

"*Ze* territory is huge ... bigger than your country, *Herr* doctor," Mr. Poeteck said. "Sometimes pastor must make hard decision. If six babies to be baptized in Saskatoon area and one bride waits in Blackstone, he choose the babies. *Und ze* bride must wait until next time he passes through. Babies die. *Und* to bring *zem* into God's Kingdom at ze earliest possible time is much more important *zan* to join *ze* man and woman in matrimony. You understand?"

Phillip nodded. "And when a marriage is performed, do you always keep a record of it?"

"*Ach,* yes. Everything goes into *ze* register."

"So the details are sent to you from all over?"

"Is right. It has been my sacred trust to enter *zis* information since we first establish Tabernacle in *zis* country fifteen years ago, to keep *ze* book up-to-date," Mr. Poetek went on proudly, "*und* to preserve *ze* history of our congregation."

"Would it be possible for me to look through your register, Mr. Poetek?"

"You help self. On *ze* desk ... *zat* large black leather volume."

Five couples appeared to have been married at various locations unfamiliar to Phillip, during the past six months. And ten baptisms had been performed. That there was no mention, however, of Lydia Fullerton or Johann Brecht, nor of Pastor Heinrich Scheidt—the chap Lydia had said married them —was no surprise.

"You do not happen to know a fellow called Heinrich Scheidt, do you, Mr. Poetek?"

"We have Sheidts somewhere." The old man momentarily touched his bony forefinger to his mouth. "I have heard *ze* name. *Ze* book over there on the desk ... *ze* maroon one."

Phillip raised an inquiring brow.

"In it are names and addresses of all members and for *ze* men, their occupations. If you will be so kind ..."

Phillip handed him the weighty volume.

"We look in *ze* esses." He moved his finger slowly down the page. "Aha ... here we have it. Scheidt ... Heinrich. Bison Creek ... is about fifteen miles from Plenty. Occupation ... pig farmer."

Phillip felt himself blanche. "You are certain?"

"*Ya.* I have bought very good pork from *ze* man."

"So he would never act as a pastor?"

"*Nein.* Never. Pastor is pastor. Pig farmer is pig farmer."

Phillip rested his elbows on the table and propped his chin in his hands, the shock of it all sinking in.

Whatever he had thought to discover today, nothing had prepared him for this.

### CHAPTER SEVENTY-SIX
### *November 1890*
### *Plenty, District of Saskatchewan,*
### *Northwest Territories, Canada*

Phillip would come by at eight o'clock to continue our discussion, he had said when he stopped by the store on his return from Regina this afternoon. And so at half-past-seven on this Friday night, after Mrs. White had settled William down for the night and retired to her quarters, I changed into one of my new frocks -- a fashionable confection of down-soft merino in a deep apricot shade, with leg-o-mutton sleeves and a high ecru lace collar, which I knew flattered my figure and was the perfect foil for my coloring.

To do justice to the gown, I would, of course, need an equally elegant coiffure. I sat at my dressing table and fiddled about with my hair for a time, arranging it first this way and then that, and finally opting for a chignon which I secured with a trio of tortoiseshell combs. I studied my reflection. A touch too severe, I decided, freeing a few tendrils about my face. Better ... much better.

I was pinching color into my cheeks when reality hit. My hands fell to my lap and I nodded dumbly. Silly fool, primping and preening like a debutante preparing for a coming-out ball. What good would it do me? Phillip's talk of not abandoning me was poppycock, for certain. Whatever happened, it would not change the fact that I was married to another man. Phillip had his life to live ... a life that could never include me now.

My gaze dropped to my ring finger. A wave of ineffable sadness swept over me and the tears I had kept dammed for days now, spilled down my cheeks. I rocked, arms folded over my ribs as if to quell a physical pain and mashed my fists against my mouth in an effort to stave off the sobs. Oh God ... oh God. Through a blur of tears I stared at the pale oval of my face reflected in the mirror. A wave of white hot fury all at once surged through me, so intense it made me tremble. Damn Johann Brecht. Damn him to Hell and back again. I pummeled my thighs with my fists. Damn him ... damn him ... damn him.

## CHAPTER SEVENTY-SEVEN
### *November 1890*
### *Plenty, District of Saskatchewan,*
### *Northwest Territories, Canada*

When Lydia ushered Phillip into the parluor, he saw how pale and drawn she looked, her eyes pink-rimmed, as if she had been crying. And he felt an uncomfortable tension in the air. All the more reason not to beat about the bush with the news of his discovery. Of course, she would be as shocked to the core as he had been, and horrified, too, at this out-and-out trickery. But in the end, once she had considered all the ramifications, she would surely be as elated as he was, now.

At her request, he uncorked the bottle of sherry on the sideboard. While he poured them each a glass she said, "My husband would have a fit, of course. The evils of drink ... that sort of thing. Although such evils do not prevent him from carrying a plentiful stock." She lifted the glass Phillip handed her and added with a wry smile, and in a flippant tone, "A toast to plentiful stock."

Oil lamps suffused the room in golden light and a fire snapped and crackled in the grate behind a wire mesh guard. Lydia motioned him to an overstuffed chair off to one side of the fireplace and opposite the one in which she sat. Bracketing the hearth was a brass fender, and within its confines a set of implements that included a poker almost identical to the one Lydia had wielded so comically that first day he had seen her in Mrs. Bell's study. How could he forget that moment? He eyed her over the top of his glass as he sipped. She had stolen his heart then and she still held it in the palm of her hand. How exquisite she was. Such fineness of form ... the tender line of her long neck ... the curve of her breasts. A woman in every way.

So very different from Beatrice. She had been a spare, serious young woman whose father had been a prominent surgeon teaching at McGill. In truth it had been a marriage of affectionate convenience. He stopped, castigating himself for his thoughts … for the comparison. Uncalled for, surely. Besides, this was neither the time nor the place for such musings.

He and Lydia began to speak simultaneously. Each stopped, waiting for the other to continue. They set down their glasses on the tables next to their respective chairs. After a couple of false starts, Lydia laughingly covered her mouth with her hands, a clear indication to him that he should take the floor. "Very well," he laughed, too. "Actually, I do have something rather important to tell you."

Lydia picked up her knitting. Her small hands flew, the needles *clickety-clacking* in the silence. "Do not for a moment think I am not listening; I find it rather calming and I am well able to listen and knit at the same time," she said.

Such a picture of domesticity. Such a feeling of companionability. Phillip felt his lips curve in a smile. How dear she was, her brow furrowed in concentration as she worked. So little time spent together, yet he felt as if he had always known her. She and Delphine would get on famously, he was certain. They were the same kind of strong-yet-gentle women.

Lydia must have felt his eyes upon her; she stopped knitting and looked up, one quizzical eyebrow raised, and said, "Something rather important, I believe you said."

"Of course." He cleared his throat. "Sorry." In her presence, his thoughts had a way of soaring off like migrating birds. He shifted position in the chair, crossed and re-crossed his legs. "About your marriage, Lydia."

"Yes." She dropped her ball of pale blue yarn and leaned over to retrieve it from the carpet. "I understand you were married once, Phillip?" she said as she unfurled..

It seemed an odd thing for her to say when the focus was on her situation. Had she read his mind moments before? In any event, she had asked the question and at some time or other he would have needed to broach the topic. "Yes, I was," he said, "several years ago. Her name was Beatrice. Unfortunately, she died in childbirth."

"I am so sorry. I should not have asked."

"No matter. Now, if you do not mind. Let us return to the subject under discussion. Your marriage. Remember I said I was going to look into it … that I thought it all rather peculiar and ---"

"Yes." She laid her work in her lap and fixed him with a wide, inquiring stare.

"Well, I did look into it while I was in Regina. And I do not quite know how to tell you this, Lydia, except to just come right out and say it: You were never married." He wanted to add, "Marvellous, eh?" but he held himself back, waiting to see her reaction.

She inhaled sharply. "Never married?"

"It was as I suspected ... that wedding of yours was a sham."

She fiddled with the lace at her throat. "I do not understand."

"You will, Lydia, once I tell you what I discovered today."

It took only a few minutes for his narrative. Throughout it, she listened intently, her face impassive, although her eyes swirled with unreadable emotions and her hands plucked at the stuff of her skirt.

When he had finished, he felt as an actor must feel delivering a play's last line on opening night and waiting for the audience's approbation or censure.

Finally Lydia broke the long silence with a bitter-sounding, "If I were a man I would kill him."

Philip rose and went to her side. He bent over and cupped her elbows, urging her to her feet. "It is not in your nature, dear girl."

"He has ruined me."

She stood before him, awkward, unsure, and he tipped her chin, making avoidance of his gaze impossible. "It was not your fault. Remember that."

"Fault or not, I am damaged goods, am I not?"

"You ... damaged? Never. You are good and dear and perfect, and absolutely blameless in all this." He could not help himself; he trailed a finger across her soft, pink mouth, and he heard her draw in a tremulous breath.

For one heart-stopping moment he thought about kissing her, but instead, he took her by the shoulders and sat her down again and in her expression he fancied he saw a mixture of relief and disappointment."

"Another sherry?" he asked.

"Yes, please. I am already a fallen woman. Why not add a little inebriation to my sins?"

She took the proffered glass from him and swallowed its contents without stopping for breath. She gasped, hit herself on the breastbone, clearly feeling the wine's burning course down her oesaphgaus. She coughed a couple of times and then looked up at him, her eyes filled with what looked like fury.

"Are you all right?" he asked, his hand on her arm.

"A pig and a pig farmer," she said vehemently.

"Pardon?"

"Johann Brecht and that Scheidt fellow ... they should wallow in the trough together." She held out her empty glass. "More, s'il vous plait."

"You are sure?"

"Positively."

"Sip this one, though, alright?" Phillip punctuated his request with a squeeze of her shoulder. "We have things to discuss ... serious things."

"Very well."

"I know this has all come as a horrific shock to you, Lydia." He stood before the fireplace, rocking on his heels. "And you really have not had a chance to absorb everything yet ... to realize what it means to you."

"That I have been had—if you will pardon the pun—in more ways than one?"

"Lydia." He said her name in a tone of gentle chastisement. "You really are free now. Truly free. And there is nothing to stop you coming with me, as I originally planned."

"Free?" Lydia rolled her eyes. "Do you think for one moment this will make any difference? Johann Brecht is not going to let me go."

"Oh I think he is, Lydia, once I have had a nice little chat with him. If I have to, I will hang *Mr.-Most-Upstanding-Citizen-Brecht's* dirty long johns from every clothes line in Plenty."

"Blackmail?" Lydia smiled almost mischievously. "Why Mr. Latham, you would stoop to that?"

"I would stoop to anything to get you away from this place and home where you belong. I love you, dearest Lydia. I will not see further harm come to you."

Her eyes widened and she did not seem able to pull her gaze away from his.

"We could just leave. No confrontation. No blackmail." He brushed his hair back off his forehead. "Pack your bags and be done with it. You could travel with me to Vancouver and on to Montreal—we would have to make several stops on the way, of course—and then we could take the boat home to England together."

"But ---"

"All on the up and up. Quite respectable. Separate quarters, of course. Obviously, I have no expectations." He wondered if his ears had turned red with the lie.

"It is impossible. I cannot leave just like that. I have William to think about ... and my dear friend, Sally. I need sufficient time with both of them. And another thing ... I will not take your charity."

"What charity?"

"My means are very limited, as you well know, and whatever the cost of this journey home, I must insist that once we are in England and I am suitably employed, I be allowed to pay you back."

"Can we not discuss this later?"

"No. Your word now, please."

He raised his hands in a gesture of surrender. "Very well, you have it."

"And I must fight my own battle, Phillip. If there is to be a confrontation with Johann Brecht, then I shall be the one to do the confronting."

"You are sure?"

"Absolutely. I must face my own demons, Phillip, or in this case, demon." She rose. "I should like you to go to Vancouver and see to the business you said you have to take care of there, and then return here and collect me. By then I will hopefully have all my affairs in order."

He would delay his departure until Monday or Tuesday, they decided. That way they could spend time together over the weekend. "I am anxious to hear about your work and I am dying to hear all about Annabel and Edwin, of course," Lydia said. "You must tell me absolutely everything."

"I will," Phillip said. "There have been a few ups and downs that you should know about. Now ... back to this decision of yours regarding Brecht. You are quite certain it really is what you want to do?"

"I am. I have never been more certain of anything."

## CHAPTER SEVENTY-EIGHT
### *November 1890*
### *Plenty, District of Saskatchewan,*
### *Northwest Territories, Canada*

In the parlour, and occupying the same chair in which I had sat during Phillip's visit a fortnight earlier, I knitted furiously, pausing every so often to mark the progress of the hands of the marble and ebony clock on the mantel.

I was still in a daze. I had yet to tell Phillip that I loved him. Or had I told him ... and forgotten it? There were so many things buzzing around in my head, I felt as if it might burst.

Knit one, purl one, knit one, purl one, my needles flew. I glanced up, saw that it was half-past six. Johann's telegram had told me he would be home tonight about seven o'clock. He had even added to the communication the words, "No dinner".

Oh he would have an appetite, all right, and one that had not been slaked in three weeks. Had the circumstances been different, had I been the weak woman of last month, I might have been terrified. As it was, I almost relished the reunion. I dropped a stitch, captured it with an annoyed click of my tongue against my teeth, and surveyed my progress.

The diminutive pale blue sleeve was part of a cardigan for the baby. I had finished the back, the two fronts and the first sleeve; this second one was about two-thirds done. I swallowed hard. Sally—bless her heart—had agreed to complete the garment.

And Sally—bless her heart—had taken William tonight, rather than leaving him here in the care of Mrs. White, whom I had persuaded to go and stay overnight with her sister-in-law. Better this way. If things became heated —as well they might—the baby would be spared … as would Effie White.

Tears welled in my eyes at the thought that this evening's *tucking in* of William had been the last, that very soon his dear, sweet face would be a memory. Katerina—rest her soul—would understand, though. However fond I had grown of that little boy, Annabel's and Edwin's needs must take priority, now.

Oh Lord—I let my work drop to my lap—poor, darling Annabel. Phillip had told me the whole story … or at least what he knew of it. He had been reluctant to, but I had sensed that he was holding something back and had wrested the details from him. Perhaps it was better this way, he had said; at least I would be prepared for any peculiarities in my sister's behavior. From all accounts, Annabel might go for weeks acting in a perfectly normal manner, and then a day would come when she retreated to her room and would speak to no one but her dog. Oh dear Lord, to think of the horrors that sweet child had had to endure; to think of what must be festering inside her.

I took up my knitting again. *In-over-through-off … in-over-through-off.* Healing would come eventually, Phillip had said, if not through the support and love of her family, then with the help of one of his professional associates. Let it come from me, I thought. Oh Lord, let it come from me, for in helping heal Annabel I would surely heal myself.

I paused in my work again. So many losses. So many hurdles. Paths twisting this way, then that. Endings. Beginnings. Partings. "Providence is always teaching us," Mama used to say. William … sweet baby William … in my life for little more than a year. Where was the lesson here?

Perhaps it was as simple as loving while you could… giving all you could give … letting go when you knew it was right to do so.

I sniffed and dabbed my moist cheeks with the back of my hand, thinking that I would miss William far more than he would miss me. Which was natural. I had been so much less of a presence in his life these past few months. First there had been Mrs. Dykstra, now Effie White. Not to mention Sally, who had been more mother to the tot than anyone, and had assured me that if she had anything at all to do with it—and she would make sure she did, wouldn't she, though—her darling little chicken would never want for love.

Sally would do whatever else she could to help, too, she had said, for wasn't this situation with Phillip Latham the most exciting, romantic thing she had ever heard of?

Not wishing to leave behind a trail of chaos when I departed, I had felt compelled to regale Sally with the whole sorry tale of the sham of my marriage and the crimes perpetrated against me ... and crimes they were, without a doubt. My trunk and two suitcases were packed and in the safe-keeping of Sally's father, who had also been made privy to the story and would happily drive Phillip and me to Blackstone tomorrow morning. My coat was draped over the back of my chair, I had already changed from slippers to boots and my handbag was on the floor beneath the side table.

The clock struck the quarter-hour. I jumped, awakening the butterflies in my stomach. Several deep breaths later, the frenzied flapping ceased. Fifteen more minutes and he would be here ... perhaps longer, if he was delayed. God grant that he was not. I covered my face with my hands. I just wanted everything over with.

By now, Phillip would be ensconced, once more, at Plenty's new hotel—*The Victoria*—which had opened the previous month. During the daylight hours, the rooftop and chimneys of the three-storey building four streets over were visible from the nursery. Room ten, second floor, was his, Phillip had told me when he stopped by the shop mid-afternoon to advise me of his return from Vancouver.

Sally had taken over for me, and Phillip and I had spent an hour together sitting cosily by the kitchen fire, drinking tea. Phillip had been upset about a couple of Home children he had inspected on a farm in the Fraser Valley, east of Vancouver. Girls, nine and seven, they were malnourished and showed clear signs of abuse.

"We English—as you well know, Lydia—do dreadful things to our children," he had said. "I had to load those two little girls onto the train with labels around their necks, like a couple of sacks of wheat, and send them back to Sudbury, counting on the good graces of their fellow passengers to see that no further harm befell them. And of course, you know, once they are back there, they will be shipped out again, and perhaps end up in the same kind of nightmarish situation."

"It is abominable," I had said. "But at least you are doing something about it, Phillip."

He had looked defeated. "Not nearly enough, though. It has really been brought home to me, observing the children like this. At Brackwoods, I somehow did not have a clear picture. But visiting the farms and seeing children treated no better than animals and knowing about your situation and Annabel's and Edwin's, has given me an entirely new perspective."

I stared into the fire and smiled to myself, thinking about how he had gone on to tell me about his dream to start his own orphanage, but an orphanage where children would be nurtured by a loving and caring staff until they were grown. Suitable property would have to be purchased and good people recruited, he had said. He had mentioned his sister, Delphine, as a possibility. And I had mentioned myself, reminding him of my desire to obtain gainful employment on my return to England.

Like Phillip, I had a room booked at *The Victoria* for tonight. The plan was for me to meet him in the lobby at nine. Although, of course, we were not leaving Plenty until tomorrow, I positively could not spend another night under the same roof as Johann Brecht.

I took up my knitting again; it had the calming effect I needed. So many plans … so much to think about. I was to travel with Phillip across the country for the next few months—all on the up and up, as he put it—helping him with his visits to the Home children. And when spring came we would return to England.

Astonishing to think that I had spent so little time with Phillip—an hour here, an hour there during these past weeks—that I really knew little about him, and yet I was quite prepared to go with him … not exactly to the ends of the earth, but across a continent. And whether or not I had told him, the simple fact was … I loved him. Like my *penny dreadful* heroines, I thought, smiling and nodding to myself, I had loved him since the first moment I saw him. And miracle of miracles, he had come halfway across the world to tell me he loved me.

A glowing coal fell onto the hearth behind the fire guard, jerking me out of my reverie. I got up and shoveled the ember back onto the fire and swept up the ashes. Just then the clock struck seven. A moment later, I heard the sound of the door and, "*I am home, liebling.*"

### CHAPTER SEVENTY-NINE
#### *November 1890*
#### *Plenty, District of Saskatchewan,*
#### *Northwest Territories, Canada*

My heart hammered at my temples. My throat went dry. I backed away from the fireplace, felt blindly for the chair then sat ramrod straight, my eyes riveted on the doorway. Courage Lydia, courage. No turning back, now.

"Good evening, Johann," I said, as he entered. He had already removed his topcoat and was unbuttoning his waistcoat and loosening his collar and tie as he entered.

"Good evening, dear Lydia."

I had steeled myself for an embrace, but he let me be, dropping into the chair opposite. He leaned back and stretched out his long legs, his pale eyes sliding over me from the top of my head to my feet. "You are well?"

"Yes, thank you." I needed to tell him right away about William, before he decided to go and look in on him. "Sally Porter has taken the baby for the night," I said, uncertain what his reaction would be.

He ran a hand through his hair. "How very thoughtful of you *liebchen*," he said with a slow smile and a nod of approval, "then we will not be disturbed." He crooked his forefinger and patted his lap. "Come and sit here."

I could not have gone to him if I had wanted to. For all my earlier panache, fear had me in its thrall. But the paralysis lasted only a moment. And when he patted his lap again and said, "I have missed you, wife. Three weeks is a long time," fury freed me and I sprang from my seat, and stood, hands on my hips, chin tipped in defiance. "Wife?" I spat the word at him, "I am not your wife, as you well know."

Clearly stunned, he sat bolt upright in his chair.

"You deceived me …you took advantage of me … you raped me. You are a criminal. I could have the mounted police arrest you for what you have done." Of its own accord, my voice climbed the scale, gathered speed. "You and your pig farmer friend. I know all about your little scheme. Wedding, indeed. Drivel all of it. We were never married. That Scheidt fellow is no more a pastor than I am, as you well know. You lied and connived. You had to have me three weeks ago, whatever the cost to me. You took me. Used me. Well … never again, do you hear me?"

"*Ya*," he nodded slowly, as if reflecting on what I had said, and then with surprising diffidence, lifted his shoulders and added, "So ... I do not know how, but you have found me out. And you are right, I am, as you say, *verachtlich*. I am sorry, Lydia. I gave into my baser nature and for that I am ashamed. But what is done is done, *liebling*, and we can make everything right now. We can make the marriage official ... legal, if you wish."

"I do not wish." I turned away from him and reached for my coat. "I am leaving," I said, rounding on him.

"Leaving?" He threw back his head and roared with laughter. "And where is it you are going, sweet girl? On *The Grand Tour*?"

"Back to England, of course." I put on my coat.

"Aaaa---aaah." He stretched out the word as if it were a revelation. "And how is it you will get there ... on your magic carpet?"

"By train and ship." I wanted to add *idiot* but controlled myself.

"And what will you use for money?"

"That is my affair." I turned away again, ready to retrieve my handbag. But I got no further.

So swiftly, so smoothly did he move that he had me clamped against him, feet off the floor, arms dangling, before I knew what was happening. "Do not leave me, *liebling*. Please … please. Everything I have is yours. We can bring your brother and sister here. You can have anything you want."

Moving my head to one side so as to avoid the shower of his spittle, I managed to gasp, "But I do not want anything of yours. I do not want you. All I want is …"

Suddenly dropping me like a sack of grain, he stepped away from me. "You dream, *liebchen*."

"Yes I dream." My heart was still thudding in my throat. "And I leave." I fumbled with my coat buttons.

"No, I will not have it." He gave me a little push which was enough to catch me off balance and I staggered back, sitting with a jolt in the armchair I had vacated moments before.

Johann Brecht fell to his knees and corralled me with his arms. "You belong to me, Lydia. Four more years, remember?"

"Not true," I shrank from him against the chair back, "I do not belong to you. I am free, now. Legally free. I have the paper from Brackwoods to prove it."

"Paper, what paper?"

"My handbag … on the floor …there."

Once he had the certificate, he spread it out on my lap, and after he had perused it for a few seconds said sharply, "How did you come by this?"

I did not answer. He did not need to know.

"Is rubbish, anyway. And you know what we do with rubbish, *liebchen*?" With a look of triumph on his face, he screwed up the document. "We burn it."

If he had expected histrionics from me when he tossed it into the fire, he was disappointed. I calmly watched the flames devour the paper. Phillip had told me he had had a solicitor friend in England make a copy, just in case. "It does not matter," I said. "Nothing you do matters. I know I am free." I strove to keep my voice even. "And I *am* going to leave." He still had me fenced in. "Now." I pushed on his arms with all my might.

He did not budge.

"Let me up."

"Ah, Lydia, my Lydia"—his hands went to my shoulders and he pulled me to him and began kissing my ears, my neck, my throat, "I will not let you leave. Not now … not ever."

"No … no." I whipped my head back and forth to avoid his lips. "Stop."

"Stop? We have only just begun, *liebling*." His hands snaked up under my skirt and he yanked at my drawers, dragging them down over my hips, and then he tried to part my thighs. But I used all my strength to hold my legs together and I pummeled him on the back with my handbag. His head snapped up and he looked at me, wild-eyed. "It is no use," he said, scrambling to his feet, sloughing his waistcoat and shirt, tossing them aside, bending to unlace his boots and kicking them off and then starting on his trouser buttons. "I need you"—the rasp of his breathing seemed to fill the room—"I must have you, Lydia. It has been so long."

Oh God. Not again. Not now. I tried desperately to hitch up my drawers. What to say? What to do? My frantic eyes scanned the room and came to rest on the hearth ... on the fireplace implements.

"You will not have me," I shrieked, lunging for the poker. When I came upright, my weapon in hand, he laughed softly, almost delightedly.

"You will not have me, do you hear?"

He was advancing on me now and I squeezed my eyes shut and swung at him with all my strength.

As solid brass met flesh and bone, my eyes flashed open.

Blood on his shirt front like a red ink spill. On his face a look of frozen indignation twisting into agony. A howl like that of the damned.

He staggered, pitched forward, sank to his knees, as I grabbed my handbag and fled.

Along the hall ...

Through the back door ...

Out into the night.

Oh, Lord help me, I had killed him.

## CHAPTER EIGHTY
### *November 1890*
### *Plenty, District of Saskatchewan,*
### *Northwest Territories, Canada*

Had the desk clerk come rapping on the door with a complaint from the occupants of the room below, it would not have surprised Phillip. Unable to distract himself with the provincial prose in the *Plenty Chronicle*, he had been pacing the floor like an expectant father for the past couple of hours.

He stopped at the window and drew out his pocket watch. Quarter past seven. His stomach rumbled, reminding him he had gone without dinner. No matter. At a time like this eating was the last thing to do.

Feeling claustrophobic, he had left the curtains open. A blanket of clouds had snuffed out the stars and the sky was black as octopus ink. Granted, here and there were lamplit windows, but without a lantern, Lydia was bound to have difficulty later, finding her way.

Damn it—he paced again—he should never have agreed to her plan. He should have insisted on being with her when she confronted Brecht. No, the man had never actually been violent, she had said. And no, she was not afraid of him. Perhaps she should be. God in Heaven, she was such a slip of a woman, while Brecht—according to a comment Sally Porter had made—was big as a lumberjack.

Phillip halted by the bed and sat on it. He would try reading again. He plumped the pillows, lay back and took up the newspaper. He had read only one sentence when a loud knock sounded on the door and he shot to a sitting position, his heart hammering. The desk clerk no doubt, come to chastise him for his heavy footfalls.

"Who is it?" His voice wavered with the shock of the interruption.

"Lydia."

He froze for a couple of seconds, then scrambled up. What in Hades ...?

When he flung the door open, she stumbled into the room, like an eavesdropper caught in the act, eyes wide and terrified in her flushed face.

"Lydia, what is ---?"

Before he had a chance to finish the question, she threw herself into his arms. "I ran"—she gasped for breath—"as fast as I could ... I could not see very well, it was so dark. We must leave now. Immediately." She clung to him, shaking. "Oh God, Phillip, oh God I have killed him."

"You have what?" He grabbed her by the shoulders and held her away from him.

"Johann ... he ... he ... I ---"

"Calm down, now." She let herself be led like a sleepwalker to the bed. He sat her down on its edge, quickly pulled up a chair in front of her, and captured her hands in his. "Now, take a deep breath—good ... and another—and tell me exactly what happened."

The words tumbled from her mouth like a snow-swollen stream. Partway through her story, he rose and donned his topcoat. And when her words trickled away to nothing, he said, "I must see to him. We cannot just leave him. You understand?"

She nodded dumbly, her face pale as moonlight, now.

"Can you tell me if there are any first-aid supplies in your quarters," he asked, "bandages, unguents and the like?"

"From Katerina's illness ... top of the stairs ... on a shelf in the wardrobe ... white tin box."

"You stay put. I will return as soon as possible."

She was coherent suddenly. "Let me come with you. Whatever the outcome, I am responsible. And I can at least try to help."

Not if there were a dead body, was Phillip's first thought. But if Brecht were alive, Lydia was right; her help could possibly mean the difference between life and death for the brute. "Very well," he said.

Instantly she was on her feet.

Moments later, they were out on the street, running as if their lives depended on it.

———

As soon as they entered the hallway, Phillip caught the sound of a faint moan. Thank God. The fellow must still be alive, unless of course, that was a death rattle he heard.

"The tin you mentioned, Lydia. Get it, please. Clean rags, too, and a bowl of hot water. He is in the parlour, right?"

She nodded. "I have to see first, if he is ---"

"No." Phillip raised a staying hand. "Let me."

"Mr. Brecht," he called out, not knowing if he was wasting his breath, "I am a doctor. I am here to help you."

"*Gott* be praised," came the faint answer.

Lydia froze and whispered, "He is alive."

"The supplies"—Phillip touched her on the arm—hurry please."

Bare to the waist, Johann Brecht was lying on a sofa in front of the fireplace. Phillip's physician's eyes took swift inventory as he looked down on the fellow. Folded shirt pressed against his middle -- blood-stained, but not a great deal of blood. Waxen face, but no near-death pallor. Eyes pain-filled but not glazed. Profuse sweating; breathing a bit on the harsh side. If Phillip had to hazard a guess from Lydia's description of how she had wielded the poker, he would have to say broken ribs. He would have to say, too, that thankfully her view of her own strength was grossly exaggerated, as was her perception of the amount of blood involved.

"May I?" He knelt beside Brecht and gently removed the folded shirt. The wound to the flesh was superficial, the bleeding already staunched.

"Who are you?"

"Latham ... Doctor Phillip Latham."

"Where ...? How did you ...?"

"Lydia," Phillip said evenly, his deft fingers probing for confirmation of his earlier hypothesis, and causing Brecht to suck in a loud breath through clenched teeth.

"My wife. But how do ---?"

"It is as I thought," Phillip cut in, "you have a couple of broken ribs."

"Is that all?" Lydia had just entered the parlour. "Thank God. I thought I had ---"

"All?" At the sight of her, Brecht tried to rear up, but fell back, gasping.

"You almost killed me, Lydia."

"*Tut, tut,* old chap, I should stay still if I were you," Phillip said, as Lydia advanced into the room, a bowl of steaming water in hand, and an assortment of rags and bandages tucked under one arm.

She glared down at Brecht, her mouth curled in contempt, "I have a jolly good mind to pour this over your head."

"Lydia"—Phillip cocked a warning eyebrow at her—"the sooner we get this over with, the sooner we can be on our way." He had best keep her occupied before she did something else she might regret. "Do you think you could find a clean shirt, a blanket and pillow."

Wordlessly, she passed him the water bowl, rags and bandages and casting a murderous glance at Johann Brecht, turned on her heel and left.

Ten minutes passed before she returned. "Trouble finding everything?" Phillip asked.

"No. Something I had to do," she said pleasantly, dropping the shirt, blanket and pillow on the sofa by Brecht's feet. But when she sat in one of the two overstuffed chairs flanking the fireplace, her eyes narrowed to slivers of blue ice and her lips compressed into a thin line.

Johann Brecht's suspicious gaze darted back and forth from Lydia to Phillip several times and finally came to rest on Phillip. "Who are you to her?" He let out a cry of pain as he tried to raise himself up again.

Dipping a rag in water, Phillip swabbed the wound none-too-gently. "Superficial ... no need for stitches. Who am I?"—he paused and met Brecht's dark stare—"a doctor, as I told you. And"—he pressed firmly—"as I also told you, you need to stay still. If I do not get you bound up just the right way, one of those ribs of yours could puncture your lung, and I am afraid that would be the end of you."

"You know my wife?" Brecht asked warily.

"No." Phillip selected a wide bandage from those Lydia had handed him and began winding it around Brecht's mid-section, signaling him to sit forward each time he encircled him. "A rather difficult proposition, I should say, since she has been dead for ...?" He raised a questioning eyebrow at Lydia.

"The end of May."

"Six months." Phillip secured the bandage end with a couple of safety pins. "Now, the shirt. Good. Pillow behind your head. Blanket. Right. All set." He got to his feet.

Brow furrowed, Brecht said, "I did not mean Katerina, before, when I asked you if you knew my wife. I meant that one." He jerked his head in Lydia's direction.

"Ah"—Phillip gave a knowing nod and went and sat on the arm of Lydia's chair—"this one you say." He touched her on the shoulder.

"*Ya,*" Brecht snapped, moving around uncomfortably.

"But she is not your wife ... never was ... never will be. We all know that, do we not?"

Brecht's face turned crimson, whether from fury, guilt or his ineffectual attempt to sit up, was uncertain.

"Nor is she your servant," Phillip went on. "Lydia is a free woman, bound to no one, as she has already told you."

"But I ask again, what are you to her?"

"That is our business."

Clearly Lydia could keep quiet no longer. She moved to the edge of her seat. "I will tell you what he is to me," she said. "Everything you are not. He is kind, gentle, strong ... a man I can count on. An honest man, a ---"

"Have you had her, too, *Herr* doctor?" Johann Brecht barked, "I have had her as a husband has a wife. *Ach,* but she is sweet. And she was pure."

Lydia turned crimson. Her "Be quiet," and Phillip's were simultaneous. He shot to his feet. Two long strides and he had his hand clapped over Johann Brecht's mouth. A pulse throbbed at Phillip's temple and a tide of furious colour rose up his neck. "One more word, damn you," he said, "and I swear I will break every other rib in your body."

Lydia got up and stood over Brecht, now, shaking. "I abhorred every second of it, do you hear me? All I thought about was getting away from you. All I ever ---"

"Do not waste your breath on him," Phillip said quietly, removing his hand from the man's mouth. "Let us leave him to it."

"But you cannot leave me like this. I will need help," he looked from one to the other of them with frantic eyes. "Can you not fetch somebody to stay with me?"

"What do you think, Lydia?" Phillip asked.

"I think he is quite the most pathetic creature I have ever met." She made a show of dusting off her coat sleeve. "And I think we should leave him to his own devices." With that, she left the room for a moment and returned with an envelope in her hand; she dropped it in Johann Brecht's lap.

"What is this you give me?" he asked.

"Something for you to chew on after I have left," Lydia tossed off as she and Phillip made for the door.

Once they were outside, Phillip said, "What was it you gave him?"

"Just a little *billet-doux.*"

"May I ask what about?"

"My reputation. One word sullying my name, I said, and a letter held in a friend's safekeeping, would go to the editor of *The Plenty Chronicle* detailing his—Johann's Brecht's—nefarious activities."

"You have written such a letter?"

"No. But he will never know it, will he? Call me foolish ... petty. But I want him to stew, Phillip. I want to feel I have some power. I have felt powerless for far too long."

"You are not foolish, Lydia, nor petty. I understand. And I hope you understand that we cannot leave him like that."

"I know," Lydia said with resignation, exhaling a long sigh. "Patient care is paramount, even if the patient is a positive brute. Lord"—she dug her fingers into his arm—"there is no possibility of his coming after us, is there?"

The moon slipped from behind its cloud cover for a moment and he glimpsed her worried face. "Not a chance. I would say he is going to be laid up for quite some time. What to do about him now, that is the thing."

"The Porters," Lydia said. "Come on, then." She tucked an arm through Phillip's and urged him along with her. "They live across the street ... down a couple of blocks. Since they already know all the sordid details, anyway, shall we see if one of them would be willing to spend the night?"

Mr. Porter volunteered. Sally would take over first thing in the morning, the pair agreed, while he ferried Lydia and Phillip to the station at Blackstone, as arranged. And Sally would sort things out with Mrs. White and Johann Brecht regarding William's ongoing care.

"Ye Gods and little fishes, what a day this has been," Lydia said, later, when Phillip delivered her to her hotel room—Number Nine, next-door to his. In the lamplit hallway, she slumped with her back against the wall and smiled up at him. "I believe I am tired."

He stroked her cheek. "Ye Gods and little fishes, as you would say, what a day tomorrow is going to be."

"Yes," she said, fighting back tears. "And all the other tomorrows." She stepped aside momentarily and sloughed her coat while he unlocked the door for her, and then she entered, threw her coat on a nearby chair, and turned back to face him. "Now, thank the Lord, I can keep my promise."

He gave her a quizzical look.

"To my dear Mama. Hold the family together, she said. And thanks to you, I am going to be able to do that. Edwin, Annabel and Lydia"—she choked over the names—"three against the world again."

He fished his handkerchief out of his inside pocket and blotted a tear from her cheek. "Four, Lydia. Three Fullertons and one Latham."

He suddenly could not help himself; he stepped inside the room and pulled her to him in a fierce embrace. Still holding her, he backed up against the door and used his body to close it. He felt her surrender, her breasts and hips hard against him, her small hands on his back drawing him even closer. He explored the delicate knobs of her spine, the firm roundness of her small buttocks, her hips, the fine bones of her shoulders. Oh God, how small, how insubstantial she felt. He must protect her, care for her. He touched her tiny ears, loosened the pins from her hair and ran a hand through the shining mass of it. Her rosy lips parted, her breathing quickened and she moved against him in a slow, sinuous way. When the time came she should be made love to with tenderness, with gentleness. He drew in a ragged breath. He was hard, rock hard, so hard it hurt. He was filled with passion for her, not tenderness. He was on fire. How he longed to take her right here, throw her across the bed, lift up her skirts, part her thighs and ...

Oh God. He went very still, suddenly, appalled at himself. He was no better than that German bastard. Lydia was not some strumpet, she was the woman he loved, the woman he wanted to spend the rest of his life with.

*So ...?* That deuced inner voice of his, and with only one deuced prompt this time. What was he supposed to make of it, for God's sake? He hitched his shoulders and no sooner had he done so, than the answer came. And gently extricating himself from Lydia, he threw back his head and laughed.

Lydia stepped away from him, a look of annoyance on her face. "You find me amusing?" she asked.

He gazed down at her. He had not cried since he was a boy, but now he felt the prick of tears in his eyes. "Never, my dearest darling. I find you adorable."

She beamed. "You do?"

"But I will find you even more adorable if you agree with me."

"About what."

"About this." He dropped to one knee, clasped her hands and said, "Lydia Fullerton, I love you, will you marry me? As soon as possible ... before we leave on our trek?"

"Yes ... oh yes"—she placed her hands over her heart—"of course I will, dearest Phillip. But not in Plenty ... for obvious reasons. And I am not certain whether or not I have told you this yet, but I love you, too."

Philip got up off his knees.

"Blackstone would do," she went on. "But not an Anglican Church; that would require the reading of the banns. Methodist ... Presbyterian, perhaps or some other denomin ..."

Phillip grabbed her by the shoulders and stopped her with a long, hard kiss. When he released her, she said breathlessly, "I will marry you on one condition."

"And that is?"

"That I not be made to wait for you a minute longer. I have waited too long already. I do not wish to be alone tonight, Phillip." She reached up and placed her tiny hand on his chest. "I have need of your love, your comfort … your strength."

He half-laughed, half-groaned. He kissed her throat, started to unbutton her bodice, his own shirt. "I have all the love, the comfort, the strength you could possibly need my darling girl."

## CHAPTER EIGHTY-ONE
### June 1891
### Aboard S.S. Parisian, bound for Liverpool, England

The second week in June, 1891, coincidence had Phillip and I sailing to Liverpool on the *Parisian*, the same Allan Line steamship on which I had traveled to Quebec City over two years earlier.

During the seven-day voyage—our much belated honeymoon—Phillip and I made love every day… sometimes twice a day. Often, tenderness governed our love-making, our endearments whispered, our caresses silken. Sometimes we were gloriously, delightfully unrestrained, loud and raucous, reveling in our union and our discovery of each other. We truly were insatiable, leaving our cabin only at mealtimes and for an occasional turn around the deck.

An accommodating Methodist minister in Blackstone had married us seven months earlier. After that, Phillip's job had taken us the length and breadth of the Canadian territories and had demanded nearly all our energy. Most nights we fell into bed too exhausted to do anything but kiss each other goodnight then sleep the sleep of the dead.

I had seen enough lice-ridden, beaten, over-worked Home children to last me a lifetime. I had bound wounds, wiped away tears and snot, held bony little sobbing creatures in my arms, helped Phillip pack at least a dozen children off to Sudbury for re-placement. I had been warmed by their gratitude, profoundly touched by their love for me, a stranger whom they would never see again. But the work had saved me. Without it, I do not think I could have borne those endless months of waiting until the ice melted and the port of Quebec City was once again open and we could go home.

⸺

When we finally disembarked at Liverpool's Albert Dock just after noon on Thursday, the eleventh day of June, I felt thoroughly disoriented. Our trunks were being sent on ahead to Hadfield Hall and so we had little baggage with which to contend.

The quay seemed to be rocking beneath my feet and I had to hang onto Phillip for dear life as we jostled our way through the teeming mass of seamen and touts and runners, of smelly urchins and bewildered foreigners. Ye gods, there was not a happy face among them. But I smiled at all and sundry. My heart sang, for at last I was on English soil and tomorrow—dear God, just one more day—I would be reunited with my dear Annabel and Edwin.

Delphine had planned on meeting us, but Phillip would not hear of it and had told her as much in one of the several telegrams they had exchanged. The journey was far too long and required an overnight stay and in his estimation, Liverpool was an iniquitous cesspool, and positively no place for a woman alone. Delphine had finally been persuaded to head south to Hadfield Hall and wait with the children for Phillip and Lydia's arrival.

Phillip had acquired the name of a guest house in a genteel section of the city. He hailed a hansom cab and gave the driver the address, and some fifteen minutes later we were rattling over the cobbles of a pleasant, sycamore-lined street. "Look at them," I shouted, beaming, nudging Phillip.

"Look at what?"

"The trees."

He glanced about, then sidelong at me. "What about them, Lydia?"

"They are sycamores. Look at their lovely big green leaves."

He reached over and touched my forehead. "Are you quite well, my darling?"

"They are English, Phillip … and they have leaves … and they give shade. And they are not those detestable, scrubby jack pines."

At that, Philip threw back his head and roared with laughter. "You really are the funniest, the dearest woman, Lydia Latham."

"Got beech an' elm an' oak an' ash," the driver called down from his high seat, as he brought the cab to a stop outside a three-storey villa. "All got leaves, they 'ave," he added, a moment later, as he handed me down.

"Splendid," I said, surprised at the keenness of his hearing. "That is simply marvelous news."

Phillip could barely contain himself as the fellow unloaded the bags and carried them up the path to the front door of the guest house. My husband managed a straight face while he paid the cabbie and asked him to return the next morning at nine, but once the hansom had pulled away from the pavement, a great gust of laughter exploded from him and he said in perfect imitation of the driver's Liverpudlian brogue, "All got leaves they 'ave." So loud was Phillip's outburst that it brought our landlady—whose name was

Mrs. Bagley, we had been told—out onto her front steps.

A stern-looking type, she stood gazing down her nose at us as we sheepishly approached, her arms folded across her middle. Her "'ow d'yer do, I trust yer will be comfortable 'ere, it bein' a quiet an' decent establishment," sounded more of a reproach than a welcome.

We thought it prudent to refrain from our usual amorous shenanigans while under Mrs. Bagley's respectable roof, so after a chaste night we boarded the hansom cab at nine the next morning and headed for Lime Street Station and the train to London. There we would stay one night before taking another train southeast to Burgess Hill.

I tingled with a mixture of excitement and apprehension. So near and yet still so far. Let Providence continue to shine on us, I prayed. Let our progress to Hadfield Hall be speedy and uneventful.

———

Thanks to Philip's telephone call to my great-aunt, Thomas Mason was waiting outside Burgess Hill Station with the phaeton when we arrived there at two o'clock on the afternoon of Saturday, the thirteenth of June.

He showed no surprise when I introduced Phillip to him as my husband, but the elderly fellow certainly did when I suddenly threw my arms around him, and almost bowled him over with my enthusiasm. "Mr. Mason," I said, steadying him and stepping back to have a good look at him, "gracious me, you are still working?"

"Am that, although expect the mistress'll be puttin' me out ter pasture when she gets one o' them new-fangled 'orseless carriages they're all' goin' on about these days."

"I doubt that, Mr. Mason. What about the Boots, are they both still here?"

"That they are. Soldierin' on the pair o' them."

"Splendid. I cannot wait to see them again and everyone else, too. Cook and Daisy and Prue. They are all absolute treasures," I said to Philip, and then to Mr. Mason, "They are still with you I take it?"

"Aye, that they are. A new one as well. Name's Bella. She's alright."

"Let my husband help you," I said, witnessing the fellow's struggles with our luggage.

I was dizzy with excitement a half-hour later as Thomas Mason drove through Hadfield Hall's imposing wrought iron gates, clearly left open in anticipation of our arrival.

"Gate' 'ouse 'as been done up since you was 'ere," Mr. Mason said, jerking his thumb to the right, indicating a charming sandstone cottage, with a hipped, banded slate roof and gabled second floor windows. I hardly recognized it. The last time I had seen it, it was derelict. Now, white lace curtains graced the windows, the door brasses gleamed, the privet hedge was neatly trimmed and the flowerbeds flanking the crazy-paved path bloomed with blue delphiniums, scarlet poppies and white daisies. The Boots lived in another tiny cottage behind the main house, so Great-Aunt Ernestine must have installed someone else here.

"Big 'ouse, too," Mr. Mason said nodding ahead, as we bowled along the curving drive.

"The grounds are astonishingly different," I said. "This was all beginning to look like a jungle when I was last here."

My heartbeat quickened and my stomach twisted into a knot. I clutched Phillip's hand. Dear God, what if the children did not recognize me? What if they did, but wanted nothing to do with me? Annabel especially. What if today was one of her *withdrawing-to-her-room* days? What if Phillip's sister detested me?

Were they as nervous as me, I wondered, anxious fingers pressed to my mouth now, as we drew close to the house. Were they watching through the window? Thomas Mason brought the phaeton to a stop before the front steps and Phillip was quick to help him down and unload our bags. "Do not worry, old chap," he said, "you go and do what you have to with the horses, we can make our own way."

Phillip signaled me to precede him up the steps. The hooves of the pair of horses kicked up a noisy spray of gravel, and made the ensuing quiet seem unearthly. Nothing moved. Not a bird. Not a leaf. The balmy air, too, had a hushed quality about it. "Surely they know we are coming," I said, uncertain why I was speaking in such a hushed tone.

"Of course they do, my dear. I telephoned. They must be in the back somewhere. Give a knock … a good loud one. My hands are full."

I took hold of the heavy lion's head brass knocker and banged it hard three times.

In a minute, the door creaked open, seemingly of its own accord.

The hairs at the back of my neck rose. No one there. I looked up at Phillip.

"Go on," he said in a low voice, dipping his head in confirmation.

I barely had a foot inside when there were peals of laughter and two figures leaped out from behind the door. "Surprise," they shrieked at the top of their lungs.

I clapped a hand to my throat. My heart felt as if it had flown out of my chest and dropped back into it. I stood transfixed, my jaw slack. Great God in Heaven … the children.

How was it possible? Stocky, untidy Annabel transformed into this willowy, fine-featured creature, far taller than I, with hair swept smoothly up into a knot at her crown and eyes that spoke volumes. Joy, yes. But anguish, too, heavily-veiled but visible to a sister who knew her as well as she knew herself.

And Edwin—dear, frail little Edwin whose skinny shoulder blades had been like wings—all filled out now, and also taller than I, sturdy and straight as a hussar.

"Annabel ... Edwin." I spoke their names with wonderment.

"Yes." They both nodded. "It is us, Liddy," Edwin said, as if sharing a revelation.

"It is, it really is," I said, sobbing, and when I held my arms wide the pair stumbled into them.

The following moments disappeared in a confusion of hugging and crying and kissing and telling each other how much they had been missed, and vowing never to be parted again. Finally, we all stopped to gather our senses and I suddenly remembered Phillip. He stood off to one side, smiling, and I rushed over to him, grabbed his hand and pulled him towards the children. "Annabel ... Edwin," I said, "I should like you to meet my husband."

"A pleasure to see you again, children," Phillip said.

Edwin looked up, wide-eyed, as Phillip shook his hand. "I remember you. You are Doctor Latham."

"Indeed I am."

"How did you ... where did you ... ?" Annabel shook her head, looking from Phillip to me, then back at Phillip's proffered hand, which she finally took and allowed to be shaken.

"It is a long story," I said. "I will tell you all about it later."

At that moment, a middle-aged woman clad in a maid's uniform appeared. "This is Bella," Annabel said. "She will take your coats and show you to your room. Dinner is at seven and formal attire is not necessary."

Something about the self-assuredness with which my sister conducted herself made me catch my breath. When I had been forced to leave her she had been a jolly, carefree child. Now she seemed more adult than I.

"Thank you, Annabel," Phillip and I said simultaneously. "And thank you, Bella," I said.

Annabel tucked her arm through mine; Edwin hung on the other. Philip happily stood by. "You must meet Miss Latham," Annabel said, "she is lovely."

"I can certainly vouch for that," Phillip said.

"She is his sister, you remember?" I laughed. "And now, my sister-in-law."

"And you must meet Dolly," Edwin said. "She shares Annabel's room."

"My friend," Annabel said, "my very best friend. I tell her absolutely everything. But now that you are here, I ---"

"She is a dog," Edwin cut in, "a jolly nice little thing, actually, and heaps of fun."

"And of course," Annabel went on, "Great-Aunt Ernestine is most anxious to see you again."

"Really?" I said with a touch of acerbity.

As if to reassure me, Edwin said in his elder statesman's voice, "She is really not a bad old stick."

"She is resting at present and will be down shortly." Annabel unhooked her arm and touched my cheek as if to reassure herself that I was real. I covered her hand with my own, looked sidelong at her and said, softly, "I do so love you my dear sister, and I will always make certain you are safe ... always."

Annabel's lower lip trembled. She smiled bravely, tucked my arm through hers again and said. "Miss Latham is waiting in the drawing room."

Phillip had been hovering in the background, clearly not wishing to intrude on us. His enthusiastic, "Good show," startled me.

"She did not want to interfere with our reunion," Annabel continued. "She said we are to join her when we are ready."

"Let us do that, now, shall we?" I glanced from Annabel to Edwin to Phillip.

The children's answer was to grin at each other and then propel me along at breakneck speed, with Phillip loping along behind us. At least they had the good grace to slow down just before we reached the drawing room and give me time to collect herself.

"Mr. and Mrs. Phillip Latham," Edwin announced with great pomp and circumstance, entering ahead of us and standing to one side like a footman.

"Phillip ... Lydia." A tall, slender woman, dressed in a dove gray frock, rose from a chair by the window and swished across the flower-decorated carpet towards us. She and Phillip exchanged a quick embrace. "Thank God you are back safe and sound, dear brother," she said to him. Then she turned to me and said, "Delphine Latham ... so very pleased to finally meet you." She took my hands in hers, regarding me with warm hazel eyes uncannily like Phillip's, but wider, larger. "My brother has spoken of you so often, I feel as if I know you."

"And I, you," I said. "I have seldom heard a brother speak so highly of a sister."

Delphine laughed a musical laugh. "Except when the sister has something to say that the brother does not wish to hear."

"Never," said Phillip, grinning.

"I quite often speak highly of Annabel," Edwin piped up, and his sister gave him a gentle cuff on the arm.

"Come, dear"—Delphine indicated the nearby sofa to Lydia—"you, too, Annabel and Edwin. Sit there next to each other. And I shall sit here with my dear brother, where I can see all three of you and pour the tea. It is three lumps for Annabel, three for Edwin, one for Phillip and one for me. How many for you, Lydia, dear?"

"One please."

I could not help staring at Delphine while she poured, milked and sugared five cups of tea. She was so graceful and had such an air of serenity. "Here we are." She handed me my tea and then glanced up at the clock. "Almost half-past three. Your great-aunt will be down any minute now. You cannot imagine how excited she is at the prospect of seeing you."

*Indeed, I cannot,* I thought, remembering our last meeting.

Delphine must have detected something in my expression, for she added, "The old lady has a great many regrets and a great need to make up for lost time. I know it is none of my business, Lydia, but try not to judge her too harshly."

Judging my great-aunt with any measure of harshness turned out to be an impossibility. When the old lady entered the drawing room at a quarter-to-four, tearfully said my name, enfolded me in her bony embrace, and said, "Forgive me," my heart melted.

"Please do not cry, Great-Aunt." I helped her to her chair and then knelt beside it and took the old lady's twisted hands in mine. "Everything is fine. I am fine. And as I am sure you must know by now, I have married Doctor Latham. You remember the doctor, do you not?"

She fumbled with her lorgnette and scrutinized Phillip through it. "Oh the handsome doctor who came here … how many years ago was it? I cannot seem to remember. You married him." She chuckled. "Well good for you, my dear, you have done well for yourself."

"Not as well as I have done for *my*self," Phillip said, coming to stand by my chair and stroking my hair.

"It is all so wonderful." Ernestine Hadfield dabbed at her rheumy eyes with a little square of ecru lace, then looked at each of us in turn. "You are all so wonderful." She sniffed and laughed. "How very lucky I am to have you all here. How fortunate I am"—she tipped her silver head in my direction—"that no one holds any grudges." She cackled to herself. "A cause for celebration if ever there was one. Let us ring for Bella, shall we? Have her bring in the sherry."

Edwin leapt up and dashed for the bell pull. Once he had given it a couple of jerks, he said nonchalantly, "Shall I be allowed a glass?"

"Indeed you shall, young man," Great-Aunt Ernestine said.

The boy's eyes almost popped.

"Everybody shall. Bella must fetch the Boots, Thomas Mason, Cook, Daisy and Prue. And we must not forget Ledward, either. No doubt he is outside somewhere planting or pruning."

When everyone was finally gathered, the staff had finished fussing over me and congratulating me and Phillip, and the glasses were filled and raised, Ernestine Hadfield said, "To the Fullerton children and the Lathams ... my dear, dear family."

"To the Fullerton children and the Lathams," came the chorus.

"To us," Edwin and Annabel followed on gleefully.

"To we two sisters and our brother," I said, my heart so full, I could barely speak. "And to my darling husband, Phillip, and my sister-in-law, Delphine. And to Great-Aunt Ernestine, of course. And most of all to the memory of dear Mama ...

... and of a promise kept."

# *Epilogue*

## THE HIGH HOLLINGHAM HERALD

### 8th July 1891

### *"A Larger Than Expected Family"*

On Thursday last the second of July, Mrs. Ernestine Hadfield, one of the county's most illustrious benefactresses, vacated Hadfield Hall, her home for the past thirty years, for quarters of a sight more modest sort-- the gatehouse at her magnificent estate.

No ... the dear lady has thankfully not fallen upon difficult times, but has generously turned over her home to her great-niece, Mrs. Phillip Latham (née Lydia Fullerton) and her husband, Doctor Latham. Not only does the place have these new occupants—along with Mrs. Latham's young sister and brother and Miss Delphine Latham, the Doctor's sister—but it also has been renamed The Haven, which indeed it is certain to be to the orphans who are set to arrive there a week next Friday.

"Not an orphanage of the usual variety," Doctor Latham was quick to inform this reporter, "but a permanent home for the children where they will be treated with love and kindness and will be given the chance to flourish and grow to adulthood."

When asked what she thought of the idea, the charming Mrs. Latham—an orphan herself, from all accounts—laughed and said, "I had always hoped that I would marry some day and have a large family. But never in all my days could I have imagined I would have fifty-five children."

Fifty-five -- the number of orphans the couple will be taking in. A large family, indeed. But judging from the beaming faces of the Doctor and Mrs. Latham as well as those of Miss Latham and Mrs. Hadfield, a family which will bring a surfeit of joy and gratification to all involved.

Our commendations to The Lathams and Mrs. Hadfield. And our very best wishes to each and every occupant of Hadfield Hall for happiness and success in the years ahead.

*The End*

CPSIA information can be obtained at www.ICGtesting.com
Printed in the USA
BVOW080657071112

304874BV00001B/5/P